Nine Lives

By

Tom Barber

*****

Nine Lives
Copyright: Tom Barber
Published: 9th May 2012

The right of Tom Barber to be identified as author of
this Work has been asserted by he in accordance with
sections 77 and 78 of the Copyright, Designs and
Patents Act 1988.

This book is a work of fiction and, except in the case
of historical fact, any resemblance to actual persons,
living or dead, is purely coincidental.

The Sam Archer thriller series
by
Tom Barber

NINE LIVES

26 year old Sam Archer has just been selected to join a new counter-terrorist squad, the Armed Response Unit. And they have their first case. A team of suicide bombers are planning to attack London on New Year's Eve. The problem?

No one knows where any of them are.

THE GETAWAY

Archer is in New York City for a funeral. After the service, an old familiar face approaches him with a proposition. A team of bank robbers are tearing the city apart, robbing it for millions.

The FBI agent needs Archer to go undercover and try to stop them.

BLACKOUT

Three men have been killed in the UK and USA in one morning. The deaths take place thousands of miles apart, yet are connected by an event fifteen years ago. Before long, Archer and the ARU are drawn into the violent fray. And there's a problem.

One of their own men is on the extermination list.

SILENT NIGHT

A dead body is found in Central Park, a man who was killed by a deadly virus. Someone out there has more of the substance and is planning to use it. Archer must find where this virus came from and secure it before any more is released.

But he is already too late.

ONE WAY

On his way home, Archer saves a team of US Marshals and a child they are protecting from a violent ambush in the middle of the Upper West Side. The group are forced to take cover in a tenement block in Harlem, their ambushers locking them in and sealing off the only way in or out of the building.

And there are more killers on the way to finish the job.

RETURN FIRE

Four months after they first encountered one another, Sam Archer and Alice Vargas are both working in the NYPD Counter-Terrorism Bureau and also living together. But a week after Vargas leaves for a trip to Europe, Archer gets a knock on his front door.

Apparently Vargas has completely disappeared.

And it appears she's been abducted.

Also:

CONDITION BLACK (A novella)

In the year 2113, a US 101st Airborne soldier wakes up after crash landing on a moon somewhere in space. All but two of his squad are dead. He has no idea where he is, or who shot him down.

But he quickly learns that some nightmares don't stop when you wake up.

For my father, Anthony.

ONE

The hotel room was as dark as a cave.

Curtains drawn, the lights turned off, everything was as still and silent as a tomb. In the darkness, three red numbers and two red letters glowed like the end of a lit cigarette.

7:00 am.

The man in the bed hadn't set an alarm; he didn't need to. He'd already been awake for hours. Today was the biggest day of his life, the culmination of a year of planning and preparation. It had been close; the whole thing had almost fallen apart at the last minute. But he'd recovered and dealt with the problem; figured out a Plan B.

And if everything proceeded as planned, over a thousand people waking up this morning would be dead by the end of the day. Probably more.

Hopefully more.

But if it doesn't work? The man felt his stomach tighten, like an anaconda squeezing the life out of its prey. He didn't want to consider that outcome even for a moment. Lying motionless under the sheets, staring at the ceiling, he did his best to banish the doubts starting to whisper at the back of his mind.

There's nothing to worry about. Everything is in place. He'll be happy and proud. You'll get a hero's welcome when you return.

And the past will be forgotten.

Pushing aside the top sheet and rolling from the bed, the man moved to the curtains and opened them a fraction, peering outside.

It was a dark and cold 31st December morning in London. Three hundred yards away, the giant airfield of Heathrow Airport lay protected by a tall mesh fence, topped with swirling cylinders of razor-wire. On the airfield itself, planes were scattered intermittently around the tarmac, as small as toys from this distance, coloured amber from the lamp-posts that stood over them.

The man watched a plane glide along a runway and move smoothly into the sky. As the vessel left the tarmac, the wheels under the Boeing 757 retracted, pulled back inside and closed off in a compartment as the wings took over and did their job. The airplane moved with a grace that belied its immense weight and passenger load as it soared into the London sky.

Lost in thought, the man in the hotel room watched it go.

Sitting back on the bed, he picked up a holdall from the floor beside him and lifted it, resting the bag on his bare thighs. Opening the zip, he checked inside and saw everything was still there. He knew it would be, but he couldn't help double-checking; the act felt reassuring, which had been an elusive commodity these past few days.

Reaching inside, he pulled something out of the bag and turned the object, examining it. It was a faded yellow brick, about the length of a television remote but as thick as a good book. A letter and a number were printed on the side, in bold black lettering; beside it was typed a further description, in smaller font.

C4. Composition C. Plastic Explosive.

In his hand, the weapon was harmless enough. But if used properly, this one brick of plastic explosive could easily kill a hell of a lot of people. With the fourteen others in the bag, the resulting charge could demolish a skyscraper, wiping out everyone inside.

Holding the brick in his hand, the man looked up through the gap in the curtains as another plane swept off the runway and drifted into the sky.

Beside him, the red figures on the electronic clock ticked forward.

7:01 am.

Fifty eight minutes later it was still before 8 in the morning, but Director Tim Cobb, head of the Armed Response Unit, had a feeling that today was going to be the worst day of his life.

At thirty-nine years old, Cobb had pretty much seen it all. He'd joined the government fresh out of Cambridge seventeen years ago; a family friend had known he was about to graduate, and after pulling some strings had set Cobb up with a desk job at MI5. Since then, it had been more or less a linear path up the ranks and towards the top as he'd gained more and more responsibility. Along the way, Cobb had discovered that he possessed a knack for orchestration and leadership that set him apart from his peers; he was never destined to be the guy on the ground, but would be the figure in the ivory tower. If it was World War Two all over again, he'd be a General, marshalling troops and directing operations, not the Private in the fox-hole firing his weapon. Some men had a gift and Cobb's was to lead. Two months shy of his fortieth birthday, he had to admit that his life was pretty damn good. He had a doting wife and two fast-growing boys; he was healthy, experienced and at the peak of his career. He had everything a man could ask for.

Not to mention his own counter-terrorist unit.

Its creation had come about just a few months earlier. In the last few years, the London Metropolitan Police Service had been under considerable pressure; with stabbings and shootings becoming an almost daily occurrence in the city, the police had found themselves at a severe disadvantage when trying to maintain law and order on the streets.

However, the riots in the summer of 2011 had been the final straw. The whole world had watched for days as criminals and thugs ran amok, vandalising, stealing and burning cities all over the United Kingdom, causing chaos and widespread panic.

After the mobs had finally been quelled, the Prime

Minister decided he'd had enough; something needed to be done. He was aware that there were specialist response teams already in place serving as armed back-up for the Met Police, namely Armed Response Vehicles and the CO19 task force, but the PM had wanted a new squad to reinforce them. He'd looked at the American SWAT-team model and ordered the immediate formation of a new detail.

The Armed Response Unit.

The squad comprised an analyst and intelligence team and a task force, all of whom worked under the watchful eye of a Director of Operations. The PM wanted finesse and firepower, a professional team ready to be called into action at a moment's notice and to act decisively, ruthlessly and without hesitation. When word had spread about the formation of the detail towards the end of last year, Cobb had put his name in the hat to lead the outfit. He needn't have bothered; he was already at the top of the list.

After he'd been selected, Cobb was given the pick of the litter from MI5, MI6 and the Met to fill the rest of the spots on the new Unit. He'd gladly obliged, and had made some controversial choices. He'd assembled a five-man intelligence team that ran as smoothly and efficiently as a Formula One racing team in the pit; in their previous roles in the Met, most of these people had been spending their time pushing paper at stations around the city, becoming increasingly bored and frustrated, their talents not being fully utilised. But Cobb had an instinctive eye for potential; he'd plucked the five individuals from various stations with the PM's authorisation and given them a new home in his detail. So far, each one had more than justified his faith in them. He'd chosen well.

He'd also ruffled more than a few feathers by picking two guys in their mid-twenties for spots on the ten-man task force. *Doesn't matter how many years you've been a cop if you can't run up a flight of stairs* he'd said, as many older and more experienced officers were passed over in the selection process. Every man on the team was lean, fit and strong as well as intelligent, and they all possessed that indefinable extra quality that made them stand out. Cobb had the highest of standards for his Unit and he demanded that every person he chose meet them too.

The ARU had been together for close to a year but post-riots, it had been surprisingly smooth-sailing so far, almost as an irony. Apart from the odd weapon retrieval or tipped-off drug raid, the year had been generally uneventful.

From the seat behind his desk in his office at the Unit's North London headquarters, Cobb cursed inwardly.

I jinxed it, he thought.

The previous night, five days after Christmas with the kids in bed and his wife under his arm as they watched television, Cobb had sipped on a glass of Scottish single-malt and realised that all things considered, his life was the best it had ever been. He'd felt almost complacent as he went to bed.

Then his phone had rung at seven-thirty this morning.

Nothing had been revealed in the call, but that wasn't necessary. The man on the phone had said only four words. *Conference call. Eight o'clock.* But Cobb knew from the tone of the guy's voice that something was seriously wrong. He'd been out of his front door in ten minutes, fired up the engine to his car and headed into the city as quickly as he could. His recent increase in salary meant he'd been able to move his family to an upmarket home on the outskirts of Surrey. From his front door to the Unit's headquarters in North London normally took him thirty two minutes depending on traffic, but this morning he'd made it in twenty seven.

Sitting at his desk, he checked his watch. *7:59am*. The

Unit's HQ was the envy of other departments, but then again Cobb knew that was the way with every new government location. The building would stay high up on the pedestal until a new place cropped up, knocking it a rung down the ladder. It was a solid building, consisting of two floors. The lower level housed the holding and interrogation cells as well as the locker and kit rooms for the task force, where they changed their clothes and stowed their weapons. Upstairs, the floor was split into two sides. To the right was where the tech team operated, a clustered nucleus of computer screens and large monitors, all under the observant eye of Cobb from his office. The left side led to a rectangular Briefing Room, which the field team used as their base of operations and also as a place to wait when they were on call.

Despite the trepidation he was currently feeling, Cobb felt a brief moment of calm. He knew he was surrounded by professional and quality operatives, people proud of their job and determined to do it well. As a unit, the intelligence team was thorough and forensic, and the task force was efficient and dependable.

Cobb's smiled faded.

He had a gut feeling that today, they were going to need to be.

Without any cue, a large television screen in front of his desk suddenly came to life. One of the advantages of modern technology meant the days of conference meetings with everyone in the room were now an option, not a necessity. The monitor was attached to the wall across his office, the screen split into two sides. To the left was a man with short, buzz-cut grey hair and tired bloodshot eyes.

John Simmons. Although he knew his name, Cobb wasn't overly familiar with the guy, but he knew he was one of the bosses at GCHQ, the government's communications headquarters. Based across the country in Cheltenham, GCHQ monitored every phone-call and email made to or from the nation, scanning for any unlawful or terrorist activity. To Simmons' right in a separate shot were two other men. One of them was Pete Rogers, the Prime Minister's Chief of Staff. He was a good man, short and solid who bore a strong resemblance to Michael J Fox. Cobb had known him for over ten years, and they had been friends for just as long.

And beside Pete was the Prime Minister himself. Before the formation of the ARU, Cobb had only met him once when he was still at MI5, but his new position meant they now interacted on an almost weekly basis. Cobb liked him; he was a good man with good intentions, but like most heads of government, he was paying for the mistakes of the guy who'd held the post before him. He was three and a half years into his tenure, with elections coming up, and Cobb knew it was unlikely he'd be around for the next four.

Rogers opened the exchange, which brought Cobb's attention back to the room.

'Morning, Tim,' he said, his voice slightly tinny over the television.

Cobb nodded.

'Good morning, gentlemen.'

'This is Deputy Director Simmons, joining us from GCHQ,' said Rogers.

Cobb flicked his eyes to Simmons, on the left portion of the screen.

'Good morning.'

Simmons didn't return the courtesy, jumping straight into his report instead. *Probably can't wait to share the burden*, Cobb thought.

'I'll get straight to the point, Director,' he said, clearing his throat. 'For the past eight months, I've led an operation to take down a major terrorist cell operating here in the UK. Around twelve weeks ago, I was successful in getting one of my men into the group,

14

undercover. Working with him, we gathered a slew of information and evidence, enough to lock up each member of the cell for five to ten years at least.'

He paused.

'However, I ordered my team to hold back.'

'Why?' Cobb asked. He didn't like where this was going already.

'Because there was a potential case here to put each member of the cell away for twenty years,' Simmons replied, speaking quickly. 'I don't need to tell you that chances like that don't come around often.'

The ARU Director nodded, taking a sip from a mug of coffee on his desk that he'd poured earlier. It needed sugar.

'Go on.'

'The most recent reports from my man were concerning to say the least. He told me that the cell was planning a series of attacks. Across London. This weekend.'

'So let's move in right now and take them,' Cobb said, putting down his coffee. 'Why wait?'

On the right side of the screen, he saw Rogers bow his head.

'That was my intention,' Simmons continued. 'Everything was in place. We knew their day-to-day routines, habits, locations. I'd been in contact with Chief Superintendent Kessler, and he had his CO19 task force on call, ready and waiting. We were all set to move in and detain the whole cell this morning'.

A *but* hung in the hair. Cobb glanced across the screen to Rogers and the PM. They were both silent, looking grave. Cobb sighed.

'Let me guess. They've disappeared.'

Simmons rubbed his blotchy face and nodded, looking tired and beleaguered.

'I lost contact with my man in the group forty-eight hours ago. I thought he'd have resurfaced by now, but he hasn't. And twenty four hours ago, the entire cell just vanished. They dumped all of our surveillance. They've gone silent; completely off radar. None of them are using phones or computers, so relocating them is proving to be a bitch.'

Cobb didn't reply. He was thinking about the situation.

New Year's Eve.

Nine terrorists on the loose across the city.

And no idea where any of them were.

He pinched his brow. 'Jesus Christ. You've really dropped us in it this time, John. Seriously.'

Simmons didn't respond. Inside Cobb's office, a second television was mounted beside the first monitor and its blank, dark screen suddenly switched to a slide.

Nine faces appeared, each one either a mug-shot or a front-on surveillance capture. They were all dishevelled, untidy men, save for the man on the far right. Each photograph had a number above it in capitals too, from *One* to *Nine*.

'My team's doing everything humanly possible to try to find them,' continued Simmons, as Cobb scanned the photographs. 'But I need your help, Director. We're up against the clock. This lot could strike at any moment. Together, we need to find them and either take them in, or take them out.'

'Could they have travelled abroad, John?' the Prime Minister asked, speaking for the first time. Dressed in an immaculate suit and softly-spoken, he was the epitome of calm, especially compared to Simmons on the screen beside him.

Simmons shook his head. 'Border authorities have been thoroughly briefed, sir. If any of them tried to use their passport or a fake, they'd get flagged in the system instantly. That is, if they even made it inside the airport in the first place. Security teams are in place at the three majors, and at the ports. But so far, nothing. Which means they're all still here'

16

'Of course they're still here,' Cobb snapped, irritated. 'It's New Year's Eve for Christ's sake. There're going to be thousands of people all over the city today and tonight. They've got a laundry list of potential targets. Why the hell would they leave?'

He suddenly stopped, realising he hadn't asked a crucial question.

'What kind of attack were they planning, John?'

Simmons paused.

Cobb saw him lick his lips.

'Suicide bombing.'

'Jesus Christ. This just gets better and better.'

'Home-made explosives, packed into a vest with nails and ball-bearings,' Simmons continued. 'Each charge could potentially kill a hundred people depending on the surroundings.'

The Prime Minister leaned forward, his face becoming larger on the screen.

'Before you lost touch with your man, did he mention any specific or intended targets, John?'

'Even if he had, they'll probably have changed them, sir,' Cobb interjected. 'Clearly they know that we're onto them.'

'I'm afraid not, sir,' Simmons said, answering the PM. 'My agent said that information was being kept until the last minute by one of the men.'

'Which one?' asked Rogers.

'Number Nine on the slide.'

Cobb flicked his gaze to the man's photo. He was the only guy who wasn't unkempt and definitely stood out as the leader. The man was handsome, especially compared to the shabby appearances of the men in the other photos beside him. He had dark-features, Middle Eastern maybe, but cold, dark eyes.

Cobb stared at his photo as Simmons spoke.

'His name is Dominick Farha. We don't have much on

his background. Our files suggest that he's related to the leader of some drug cartel in the Middle East, but that's irrelevant right now. What's important is that he's the one who commands the cell. He'll be deciding the targets. We need to find this guy first; he takes full priority.'

There was a pause. Simmons stared straight into the camera.

'Director Cobb, I spoke with the Prime Minister before we began this call. We want you and your team to track down Number Nine, the leader; Dominick Farha. And we need you to do it as soon as possible.'

Cobb glanced at the Prime Minister for his approval, who saw the movement and nodded.

'You have my complete backing, Director. Use whatever force you deem necessary. That's authorised. But for God's sake, do it before it's too late.'

Cobb nodded. 'Yes, sir.'

The next moment, the screen went black. The call had been ended.

Which meant it was time to go to work.

At that moment four thousand miles away, another man was having the worst day of his life.

Or, more accurately, the last day.

He'd just woken up in a strange place. He opened his eyes, blinking, confused.

Where the hell am I?

He was lying on the floor, staring up at a white ceiling. Through a roof-light, he could see clouds in the clear blue sky above him. *I must have nodded off*, he thought. As he gathered his senses, he realised there was a bizarre feeling coming from underneath him. The ground felt as if it was moving, rocking side to side, almost like a baby's crib, which was making him feel nauseous.

Wiping sleep from his eyes, the man went to stand up.

He couldn't.

Looking down, the man saw that his feet had been looped through the holes of a concrete cinder block.

And the gaps in the rectangle had been filled with cement.

It was packed tight against his ankles and lower calves. He tried to wiggle his toes, but they were jammed solid, the cement pressed around his feet, locking seventy pounds of unmovable weight to the end of his legs.

Panicking, he reached over to try and loosen his feet, but suddenly realised he was being watched and turned.

A vastly overweight man in a beige suit was standing to one side of him, grinning from ear to ear. Short and obese, he had a sun-burnt bald head and small dark eyes like a shark. Behind him were two other men. They were enormous, each of them six-foot-five and easily over two hundred and fifty pounds.

The man on the floor looked over at them for a brief moment, then remembered where he'd been before he fell asleep.

And who these men were.

Fear immediately washed over him, drenching his body.

'Having a nightmare?' asked the fat man, grinning as he saw the moment of recognition on his captive's face. The smile pushed the fat on his face around the collar of his shirt so it bunched and spilled over the starched fabric with nowhere else to go.

He suddenly turned to the two big men and nodded.

They moved forward, grabbing the terrified man under each armpit and hauled him to his feet, lifting him effortlessly into the air in the same motion. It was a brutal display of strength. They walked through a door, carrying the man with the concrete on his ankles outside, who suddenly realised what the rocking was.

They were on a yacht.

Around them, there was nothing but clear blue water as far as the eye could see. No other boats or ships, no sign of a coastline. High above, the Middle Eastern sun pounded the water below, giving off a blinding glare as it caught the ripples from the surface of the sea.

Either side of him, the two giants didn't stop, carrying the captive to the edge of the yacht's white deck.

Towards the water.

Suddenly realising what was coming, the doomed man started thrashing desperately, trying to force his way free from the vice-like grip. It was hopeless. The cement block had dried solid, plus he had over five hundred pounds of muscle gripping him tight.

As he started pleading, begging and screaming, he heard the fat man laughing behind him.

'So long, you piece of shit,' he said. 'Don't forget to hold your breath.'

The man begged, one last desperate plea for mercy, like a child.

Then the two enforcers threw him into the sea.

The moment he hit the water, the weight around his feet pulled the man down like a bungee cord in recoil. He entered with a splash and suddenly vanished under the surface, cutting him off mid-scream.

And then it was silent. Peaceful. The only sounds in the air were the water lapping against the side of the yacht and the call of a seagull somewhere in the distance.

Across the deck, the overweight man in the beige suit smiled to himself as he pictured the victim screaming silently below, plummeting toward the ocean bed and his watery grave.

As his two enforcers turned to look at him, he shot his cuff, checking the time on a golden Rolex.

'Back to the bay,' he ordered one of the men. 'I've got a plane to catch.'

TWO

The layout of the Briefing Room at the ARU's headquarters was simple. It was about the size of a rectangular school classroom. As you walked in, to your left was a table pushed against the wall. On its desktop an aluminium coffee machine took pride of place, surrounded on either side by a big box of tea bags, stacks of polystyrene cups and some packets of biscuits dumped on the countertop.

The other end of the room was set up as a briefing space, with two rows of chairs placed in front of a screen. However, this morning so far only three of the seats had occupants; they were the officers who'd been the first to arrive after receiving the call from Director Cobb. Behind them, the rest of the team was starting to trickle in through the door one by one, quickly joining the three already seated.

By the drinks stand, a good-looking young blond officer poured himself a cup of tea as he stifled a yawn. His name was Sam Archer and he was the youngest member of the task force. He and the other officers had been given the week off for Christmas on the condition that they stayed on call and were always contactable the entire time. Archer's phone had rung at 8:15 am and he'd made it up here in twenty minutes. Unlike some of the older men, he didn't mind the constant commitment and unpredictability of the hours. After all, it was what he'd signed up for.

At twenty-six years old, Archer was still pretty inexperienced in counter-terrorist police work compared to most of the other guys in the ARU. When he'd told his colleagues at his old station at Hammersmith and Fulham earlier in the year that he was applying for the ARU, most of them had laughed in his face. *Good luck with that one*, they'd said.

They weren't laughing now. Archer had crushed the fitness and marksmanship tests, adept with both pistol and sub-machine gun, and despite his age, he'd already put in over six years on the street. It had got to the point where the brass weren't considering the reasons why the young officer couldn't join the Unit, it was *why not*. Whenever he was asked in the interviews if he thought his age would be a problem, he gave the same response every time. *If you're good enough, you're old enough.*

And he believed it. His whole life, the only thing he'd ever wanted to be was a police officer. His father was a Sergeant in the NYPD and although they hadn't seen each other in over ten years, Archer had grown up idolising him. For anyone who knew the boy, it came as no surprise that the man had ended up with his own badge and gun twenty years later. Being selected for the ARU a few months back had been a huge step for him; Archer came to work every day ready and raring to go, the voices in his head reminding him how inexperienced he was.

He was desperate to get out there and prove himself, but he knew that would only come with time.

As he drank from his tea and was about to move forward to join the others, he paused and smiled when he saw his best friend Chalky enter the room. The squad had been given the week off, but Chalk liked to burn the candle at both ends; while Archer liked a beer, he was typically in the sack before 1am, but Chalky figured that being asleep before four equalled a pointless existence. And when he went out drinking, he didn't exactly hold back.

'Jesus Christ, you look dreadful,' Archer said, as his friend approached. 'Where the hell did you end up last night?'

Chalky grunted a response as he arrived by the drinks stand. Grabbing a polystyrene cup, he poured himself a thick coffee; black, three sugars. He paused for a moment, thinking, then added a fourth. Archer winced.

His full name was Danny White, but as long he could remember everyone had called him Chalky. He'd once said that the only people who called him by his proper name were his mum when she was pissed off with him and Sergeant McGuire, their commanding officer. Archer had met him eight years ago on the first day of basic when they both signed up to join the police. He was four years shy of thirty, like Archer, and was of similar physical stature, both of them six feet tall and solidly built at a hundred and eighty-five pounds.

However, that was where the similarities ended. Archer's blond hair and blue eyes were a stark contrast to Chalky's dark, almost Mediterranean complexion, an irony given his nickname. After training, they'd been processed to the same division in the Met, and had decided to apply to the ARU together. Archer didn't have much family left, but he quietly considered Chalky to be the brother he'd never had.

'You left too early last night, blondie,' Chalky said, rubbing his temples. 'For a change.'

As Archer went to answer, an officer in his mid-thirties entered the Briefing Room, following three others. His name was Deakins, a barrel-chested, outspoken veteran, and he immediately noticed Chalky's condition.

'What's the matter, Chalk, too many cocktails?' he called.

The hungover officer flipped him the finger as the other guys in the room laughed. They knew Chalky's habit of putting the same amount of energy into his nightlife as he did into his career. Most of them had done the same thing a few years ago when they were his age. However, he got away with it due to his ability in the field. It didn't matter if he'd had one drink or twenty the night before, if a call came in, they all knew that Chalky would be standing there right beside them, ready to go.

As two more officers entered, a short, stocky man walked in behind them and the room instantly quietened. His name was Sergeant McGuire Cobb's second-in-command and head of the task force, though every guy on the team just knew him as Mac. Almost thirty years of frontline combat and policing experience had left Mac as a consummate professional and a man not afraid of sharing his opinions with his superiors as frankly as he did with his peers and subordinates.

He didn't talk much about the past, but Archer knew Mac had done three tours in the Gulf, and had seen action in Bosnia and Iraq again after 9/11. He'd joined the police after he left the army in 2005, and had risen fast due to his obvious skills and leadership abilities. He had a quick temper but one thing was for sure, whatever he may have lacked in charm, he more than made up for with loyalty. Everyone who operated with the Unit knew better than to mess with his men.

'Morning lads,' he growled, a voice battered by years of onslaught from cigarettes. *Like Al Pacino would sound if he was English and Cockney,* Archer thought, as he moved forward to sit in an empty chair.

Mac stood in front of the men and went to continue, but then noticed Chalky's condition by the coffee stand.

'Jesus Christ Chalk, what time did you get home last night?' he asked.

'I didn't, Sarge,' Chalky said, sipping his coffee and taking a seat beside Archer.

Mac had left the door open and the last person to enter the room was a slim, attractive young woman with dark hair and glasses; she walked in briskly and closed the door behind her. Her name was Nikki; in a world where everyone knew each other by either their last name or a nickname, she was the exception and not just because she was female. She'd earned that respect. At only twenty eight, she was already the lead analyst within the intelligence team stationed next door. Cobb had plucked her from behind a desk at Hammersmith and Fulham, and he'd struck gold. Forensically attentive and consistent, she served as the eyes and ears for the task force when they were out in the field.

Along with Archer and Chalky, Nikki epitomised the new generation of police, fast-tracked and blending in well with those more experienced. It was something the Prime Minister had apparently demanded for the detail. He wanted it to be a unit that would be around for the future, long after he was gone. Archer knew Cobb had pissed off a lot of people by picking the three of them for the squad and the trio were all desperate to justify their selection.

Nikki took her place beside Mac, dark-haired, delicate and petite beside his stolid frame. Including Mac, all ten officers were now gathered in the room. Each man was dressed in off-duty clothes, jeans and sweaters thick enough to protect against the chilly air outside blowing in from the North. There were also a few yawns being stifled; if the call hadn't come in half an hour ago, most of them would still have been in bed.

'Morning lads,' Mac repeated. 'Sorry about interrupting your leave, but this one's come straight from the top. Listen up.'

Beside him, Nikki clicked on a laptop.

An image appeared on a white screen in front of the group. Nine photographs, each one accompanied by a name and a number printed above in bold lettering.

'Take a good look boys,' said Mac. 'These handsome fellas are our new best friends. All nine of them are planning to bring in the New Year with their very own firework displays, but are planning to use some very different things that go *boom*. Like home-made explosives, nails and bits of glass.'

He paused, letting each man in the room observe the mug-shots projected on the wall.

'GCHQ had eyes on this lot, but apparently they got

wise and scarpered into the city. Now they want us to clean up and bring these ugly bastards in before they go and do something stupid.'

Chalky pointed at the wall, at Number Nine. 'The bloke on the right looks different from the others, Mac. Sharper.'

Mac smiled. 'Well today's your lucky day, Officer White. Each unit has been assigned a different target and he just so happens to be ours. Maybe when he's in custody, you can interrogate him over a candlelit dinner.'

Everyone laughed.

'Who is he, Sarge?' Archer asked, staring at the guy's photo. 'Chalky's right. He doesn't seem to fit in with the rest.'

Nikki answered him, reading from a page in her hand.

'His name is Dominick Farha,' she said. 'There's not much about him on file. It looks as if he may be linked with a drug cartel in the Middle East.'

'He's also the leader of this lot,' added Mac. 'The most recent surveillance says he's been staying at a flat in Knightsbridge, so that's our first stop. Our day doesn't end until all nine of these boys are in custody. Understand?'

The men nodded. Deakins raised his hand.

'Use of deadly force?' he asked.

'Use discretion,' Mac replied, candidly.

A sandy haired officer, Fox, interjected.

'Can you elaborate on that?'

'Well, let me put it this way,' said Mac. 'If we kick in the door, and he's sat there in his underwear eating corn flakes, then there's no need to use your weapon. But if you walk in and he's got a bomb strapped to his chest, then you make an intelligent decision.'

He paused.

'And make sure I'm standing behind you when you make it.'

The room laughed.

'Any more questions?' Mac asked.

There were none.

'Alright, lads. Get your kit. Chalky, drink some water. I want you all outside in ten.'

He turned and strode out of the room. Director Cobb was outside waiting for him, and together they walked to Cobb's office to talk alone. Nikki moved to the door to return to her desk in the tech area; before she left, she dumped a stack of papers on a table by the doorway.

'Take one of these before you go,' she told the team from the doorway. 'Photocopies of the slide. All nine guys.'

As she departed, the remaining officers in the room rose, draining their drinks and heading towards the door, tossing the empty cups into a rubbish bin beside it. Archer remained where he was sitting, staring intently at the screen. Beside him, Chalky groaned, rubbing his temples.

'Can't believe this. It's derby day, Arsenal-Spurs, and I'm stuck here doing this shit,' he grumbled.

Archer didn't reply. Turning, Chalky saw his friend's eyes were fixated on the projection.

'Arch? What are you looking at?'

Archer frowned, then turned.

'Nothing. Number Three looks familiar, that's all.'

Finishing his cup of tea, Archer rose, patting his friend on the shoulder.

'Drink up Chalk. Its game day,' he said with a grin.

Turning, the young blond officer walked to the door and grabbed a photocopy, moving out of sight as he headed downstairs to get changed into his gear.

Now alone in the Briefing Room, Chalky rolled his eyes.

Finishing his coffee, he climbed to his feet with a groan and followed him.

THREE

Twenty miles across London, a series of jars and bottles stood on a brick wall in the middle of an empty park. They were stacked in a line, like a makeshift shooting gallery.

Suddenly, one of the bottles exploded. A gunshot echoed around the field and a flock of birds on the grass across the park reacted to the noise of the gunshot, flapping their wings frantically and lifting off from the ground, flying away from the threat of danger.

Twenty yards from the row of glass vessels, a thirteen year old boy stood still as he held the pistol that had fired the bullet. His brown eyes were wide with shock and excitement, having just experienced the sheer power and accuracy of a real handgun for the first time.

He stood motionless, savouring the moment.

Then his dark features broke into a broad smile and he lowered the stolen pistol, turning it to one side and examining it in his hands.

It was a nine-millimetre Beretta 92, the famous Italian pistol. Holding both a fifteen-round magazine and a reputation as one of the most accurate handguns on the planet, the weapon was a firm favourite for law enforcement and military forces around the world, particularly in the United States. It was also just a bit too big for a thirteen year old's grip. After all, the pistol was designed to be held by a soldier in combat or by a policeman on the street, not by a thirteen year old boy in his local park.

Behind the young man, two of his friends were staring at the gun, wide-eyed and clearly impressed after that first shot. Turning, the teenager carefully passed the pistol over to one of them, who stepped forward and took it in his hands. Raising the weapon, he aimed at an empty *Coca-Cola* bottle on the far right of the targets,

28

lining up the fore-sight on the centre of the glass. He suddenly remembered something he'd seen in a war movie about snipers and started taking deep breaths as he tried to slow his breathing. It seemed to work. The fore-sight stopped dancing around and settled on the Coke bottle, straight and still.

But he was too tense, anticipating the weapon's response when it fired. He snatched at the trigger and the weapon boomed, pushing him back from the recoil. A plume of dust burst from the brick wall behind the glass targets as it took the bullet but the bottle remained intact. He'd missed.

As his friends laughed, the boy fired twice more in quick frustrated succession. The second shot hit the bottle, scoring a hit and restoring some pride, and the glass vessel shattered, disintegrating into a thousand fragments and sprinkling to the ground like fairy dust.

As the pair of gunshots echoed around the empty park, the boy turned to his friend, wide-eyed and excited.

'Where the hell did you get this?' he asked.

'My brother,' the kid replied.

'Saqib? What's he doing with a handgun?'

The dark-haired boy just shrugged.

He didn't want to think about it.

His older brother wasn't the kind of guy to carry around something like this. Only just turned twenty-three, Saqib had been as straight as an arrow growing up, never in trouble and never causing any. But then the riots of last summer had happened and the boy had watched his brother change. On the second night of the anarchy, their father had been killed, stamped to death on the street by a violent group who'd separated from the mob. His father hadn't done anything to provoke them, he'd just been trying to get past quietly as he made his way home from work. The group knocked him to the ground and kicked his skull in, causing deep cerebral fractures and a resulting brain haemorrhage.

He'd died on the street before anyone could even get him to a hospital.

Despite his age, the teenage boy had come to terms with his father's passing. True, he felt angry and bitter at what had happened, how unjust and unfair it all was. Not a day went past that he didn't wish that he'd been there, that he could have at least tried to do something to stop the gang beating his dad.

But despite his age, he already knew there was nothing he could do to change what had happened. His father had just been in the wrong place at the wrong time. And any lasting feelings of rage he might have felt at the cruelty of it all were swept away with concern for his mother who'd suddenly found herself a widow. Needless to say, she had taken the unexpected death of her husband hard.

As had his brother, Saqib.

Since that fateful night last August, Saqib had become a different man. It was almost as if the incident had planted a seed of hate inside him, and day by day that seed was growing, sprouting weeds that twisted and wrapped their tendrils through all his veins and arteries. His younger brother watched as he drifted away from all his old friends. He started drinking and doing hard drugs; he often wouldn't come home at night, and his mother would stay up until dawn, worried sick that she was going to lose another member of her family.

And he was spending a lot of time with a new group. There was one of them in particular whom the boy didn't like, a guy who called himself Dominick. He'd appeared on the scene a few months ago seemingly out of nowhere, and Saqib seemed to be hanging out with him a lot lately.

The youngster would never admit it to anyone, but there was something about the stranger that terrified him. He had a look in his eye that was unsettling, a gleam that contradicted all the smart suits and polished shoes that he wore..

One word came to mind, a word the teenager had picked up from his English class at school.

Psychotic.

Saqib had called his brother last night, asking him to bring round a takeaway for him and his friends. For some reason, he claimed none of them could leave the house, so the kid had to go and get it for them. That was all bullshit; they were just being lazy. Nevertheless, the boy had reluctantly headed out and picked up a couple of pizzas, taking them over to an address Saqib gave him over the phone.

On the way, he found himself praying that Dominick wouldn't be there.

He'd been in luck. There were only three people inside the house, his brother and two guys whose names he didn't know. Whoever owned the place had given up cleaning and maintenance a long time ago. The place was a complete dump. It was dirty and dank, and there was some strange thumping noise coming from the bathroom upstairs. Saqib had grabbed the pizzas without thanks or payment and told him to get the hell out. Pissed off and feeling used, the boy had walked through the hallway to the door, alone.

As he turned the handle he'd suddenly spotted a handgun resting on a table by the entrance.

Like a kid in a sweet shop, he couldn't resist. Fuelled by his feelings of being used the boy had grabbed the weapon, tucking it into the folds of his coat and then left. *Thank you guys*, he'd thought as he rushed off down the street, the pistol hidden inside his jacket. He couldn't wait to show his friends.

Another gunshot brought him back to the present, as the second boy fired at the glass targets again. He checked his watch. *8:55 am*. He had to be at work in the shop for his Mum before 9:30am which meant he also had to take the gun back, something he was dreading. But much as he didn't want to, he didn't have a choice.

31

'Bad news. I need to go,' he told his friends. He turned to the third boy, who was yet to fire the weapon. 'Want to try before I leave? I need to take it with me.'

The third teenager nodded eagerly.

Taking the weapon from the second boy, he aimed at an empty jar, closing one eye like he'd seen Clint Eastwood do in all his movies.

He pulled the trigger and the jar exploded.

Four thousand miles away the overweight man from the yacht was about to break the habit of a lifetime for the second time that day.

People called him Henry, but that wasn't his real name. He'd adopted it at the age of thirteen after watching the gangster movie *Goodfellas*. To this day, he could still remember the first time he saw the film and the tremendous effect it'd had on him. As an impressionable young boy looking for an identity, it had changed his life. He'd started wearing the suits and tracksuits the actor Ray Liotta wore in the movie. His voice suddenly developed a New York twang. And he started calling himself *Henry* after the lead guy in the movie, Henry Hill.

A number of older boys around him had seen this as opportunity for humour. With a short attention span, Henry the boy had never sat through to the end of the movie so he hadn't discovered that the character Henry Hill ended up being a rat for the FBI. They'd made cheap jokes, mocking him, deriding his stupidity; to his frustration, Henry knew he was too young to retaliate. Some of his tormentors were nineteen or twenty, far bigger and stronger than him.

But he'd been patient and he'd waited, never forgetting who'd ridiculed and teased him.

And when he was sixteen and been given a job as a *halcone* for a Riyadh cartel, he'd asked his new friends for some help on a private matter.

They'd gladly agreed.

To this day, his favourite method of killing someone was lifted straight from the Mafia stories that came out of New York. He had the person held down and sedated, and when they were unconscious their feet were passed through the holes of a cinder block, the gaps then filled with quick drying cement and locking their ankles tight.

He liked to be there when they woke up, watching that first moment of confusion and vulnerability as they wondered where they were. He would wait until the moment they realised their feet were lodged in over seventy pounds of cemented concrete.

By then, they were already being carried towards the water.

He'd often wondered what went through someone's mind as they went beneath the surface, dropping like a stone. Death was certain. They'd know they had less than a minute to live. *Did they fight to the end? Did they pray? Try to hold their breath?* He smiled. If he could, he would watch every single one of them land on the seabed. He'd seen it once, when he'd ordered an associate who'd betrayed him thrown into an aquarium. The guy had tried everything. Pulling his feet free. Scrabbling at the window, his eyes as wide as dinner plates, his screaming muffled through the water. Henry had watched from the other side of the glass, an inch from the doomed guy's face, grinning at him. *I should have brought popcorn*, he thought.

He'd killed his first man when he was sixteen. The guy had been one of his chief tormentors as a boy, endlessly mocking the overweight thirteen year old's new Mafia persona. Seven more of them had followed, one by one, their feet dried into concrete and thrown in the sea, screaming like scared little girls.

Funnily enough, since then no one had made any jokes anymore.

And the name had stuck.

Twenty two years later, Henry had achieved his position as head of the cartel by being cautious. He had a rule never to attend deals personally, letting those beneath him do it instead. He didn't fancy opening a car packed with millions of dollars worth of cocaine and suddenly find an entire police precinct descending on him out of nowhere. If his men got caught, they either went down without a word or shot their way out. They knew better than to talk to the police.

If they did, everyone they had ever loved would be killed.

His was a business built on two things; respect and fear. But in recent weeks, he'd been getting restless and wary. He could feel eyes on him. He knew the American Drug Enforcement Agency were sniffing about, like stray dogs looking for scraps of food. He'd received a tip off last night about a man who'd recently moved into a house near his compound, in the centre of Riyadh. He'd sent his two enforcers to investigate and they'd struck gold. Inside the house, the two knuckleheads had found a shitload of surveillance equipment, cameras, listening devices, bugs and a DEA agent himself. The guy had somehow wire-tapped all the phones inside the main house, recording and photographing Henry's every move. Once the two giants had restrained the man, the drug lord had ordered him anaesthetised then carried to his yacht.

He smiled. Drowning the DEA agent earlier that morning had been welcome refreshment. For a brief moment, he felt his mood lift as he thought of the American right now at the bottom of the sea. But his presence confirmed Henry's concern that the DEA were getting close. Way too close.

Needing to get out of Riyadh and clear his head, several hours ago Henry had set up a quick meeting in Juarez, the first time in a very long time that he'd be face-to-face for a deal. It was an opportunity to make some good money, over four million US dollars, in exchange for 500 keyed bricks. The powder was second rate at best but they wouldn't know that until Henry was back in the air. It had been sitting in his aircraft hangar for months; now seemed as good a time as any to get rid of it.

Right now, he was standing on the tarmac of his own private airfield. In front of him, the two meatheads unloaded the bricks of cocaine from a 4x4 Escalade, carrying it up a set of unfolded stairs and loading it onto Henry's private jet. It was broad daylight, just past midday in Riyadh, and they were standing in the sunshine in the middle of the runway but Henry didn't give a damn if anyone was watching. The local police knew the consequences if they tried to make a move on him. Their own families would pay the price.

He'd been standing watching when one of his men approached, informing him of the latest situation in London. The man's name was Faris, Henry's right-hand man, his *lugarteniente* as the Mexicans called it. He was efficient and reliable with a different level of intelligence from the two muscle-bound assholes loading the coke into the plane. He proved it by what he said next. He'd proposed an idea which Henry had considered then agreed to it on the spot without hesitation. It was a good plan, full of initiative and it turned out that Faris had been proactive; he'd already set everything up.

An Albanian cartel based in Paris would meet them at a runway outside the city later that night. They'd agreed to an asking price of six million US dollars for the coke which was two better than Juarez. And Faris had also contacted Dominick, Henry's imbecilic excuse of a nephew. They would retrieve the boy tonight from the UK before the British police could get hold of him.

Apparently, he was eager to see his uncle face-to-face and finally explain himself after what he'd done.

Standing in the sunshine by the jet, Henry grinned. Not only would he finally get rid of this crappy batch of coke for one and half times the original asking price, he would also have his idiot nephew brought before him, begging for his life. Business and pleasure, his two favourite things, killing two birds with one stone. *Literally*, he thought with a smile.

So right there and then, he'd broken a lifetime of routine for the second time that morning and cancelled his trip to Juarez, opting to go to Paris instead. He knew he'd be pissing off a lot of guys in Mexico. These weren't appointments that you just missed, but Henry knew how much power he wielded and figured he could ride the wave.

Standing by the plane, he watched as his two enforcers loaded the last few bricks of cocaine into the jet. Once they'd stowed the powder the two giants reappeared, plodding down the steps and standing on the runway, awaiting further instruction.

Ignoring them, the drug lord walked forward and grabbed the rail, clambering up the stairs himself. It took him ten seconds; after all, he was carrying over three hundred pounds of fatty adipose and bulk. Eventually he made it inside and collapsed in a seat that had been specially widened to accommodate him, sweating and breathing hard from the exertion.

The two enforcers followed, taking their own seats. It was pleasantly cool, the air conditioning blasting out of the fans, cold, crisp and refreshing. Wiping sweat from his sunburnt scalp, Henry looked at the two giants sitting across the aisle as Faris secured the door.

They were morons, both of them, more biceps than brain cells, but necessary muscle, considering the enemies Henry had. He'd been planning to get rid of them for a while; he liked to cycle his security, needing to keep them sharp and on their toes, eager to please and scared to fail. He'd noticed recently that these two were getting way too comfortable. And like the shitty coke, today seemed a good as time as any to ditch them. He decided there and then that neither of them would make it back from Paris.

He glanced over at Faris who was finishing locking the hatch, his back turned. Truth be told, the man had proven to be a surprisingly worthy investment. Henry had taken him on just over a year ago from a recommendation after his predecessor had been shot and killed by a rival cartel. It had been a wise decision; Faris was good at his job and the business's profits had increased impressively with him on board.

But he asked too many questions and he was too intelligent for his own good. Henry knew there would come a day where Faris would challenge his position. It was inevitable, like two animals in the wild, the old leader and the young buck fighting for the right to head the pack. But he was ready for it. He'd waste the two meatheads in Paris then save Faris as a treat for when they arrived back in Riyadh.

He smiled to himself, feeling that tickle of excitement in his gut whenever murder was an imminent prospect, and heard a whining noise as the engine of the jet started to fully warm up.

The plane edged forwards to its starting position on the end of the runway, the long tarmac path stretching out ahead of them.

Faris walked into the cabin and took a seat opposite Henry. He noticed a broad smile on the drug lord's face.

'We'll be in Paris in five hours,' he said, watching his boss.

Without a response, Henry ignored him and closed his eyes.

Thinking of cement shoes.

FOUR

It was somewhat ironic that Dominick Farha had chosen
to rent an apartment in the Knightsbridge area of
London. In modern times, Knightsbridge was renowned
as being a pretty trendy and upmarket place to live, a
great location, adjacent to the always beautiful Hyde
Park and with Harrods, one of the world's most well-
known stores right there on its doorstep.

But what a lot of people didn't know was its dark and
somewhat sinister history. In the eighteenth and
nineteenth centuries the place was infamous as being a
haunt for highwaymen and thieves, who lay in wait in
the shadows to target those travelling westward out of
London. In recent years, it had also seen its fair share of
terrorism and crime. The Iranian Embassy siege of 1980
took place in the area, when six armed gunmen took
twenty six hostages in a stand-off that lasted for six days
until the SAS showed up. It had also been the victim of
an IRA car bomb, detonated in the neighbourhood in
1983 and a legendary bank heist around the same time,
when thieves had made off with over sixty million
pounds.

The address the ARU officers had been given by
GCHQ was an apartment on the third floor of a building
overlooking the park. The task force had moved through
the lavish lobby, two of them staying downstairs to
guard the exits while the rest had swiftly moved up the
stairs in their riot gear.

Opening the stairwell door, they crept down the third
floor corridor, coming to a halt outside apartment 3F. *F
for Farha*, Archer thought as he stood in line and waited.
Beside him one of the other officers, a man called
Mason, crept forward, a shotgun in his hands. It was

Benelli M3, loaded with a special breaching round, designed to take locks off doors.

The team collectively took a breath as he aimed the weapon at the door-handle.

He pulled the trigger.

There was a loud blast, and the lock on the front door exploded, splintering and disintegrating as it took the force of the shotgun shell.

Deakins, the point man, slammed the door forward and the officers piled into the apartment.

The policemen moved smoothly in a well-practised drill, dispersing by the door and quickly sweeping the apartment room-by-room. Each man was dressed in navy-blue overalls, the trousers tucked into black combat boots. Above a Glock 17 pistol clipped to their right thigh, a Kevlar tactical vest was zipped up tight around their torso holding spare magazines, tools, plastic hand-cuffs and a mobile phone. All of them save for Mason carried a Heckler and Koch MP5 sub-machine gun. Accurate and reliable, each weapon had a thirty-round magazine slotted into its base, two more tucked into slots on their tac vest, ninety rounds in total. If the policemen needed more than that then they were in serious trouble, but then again, they always had the firepower of Mason's shotgun to call upon if such a situation arose.

The officers checked every inch of the apartment; it was a large flat, with a spacious living area connected to two separate bedrooms and a bathroom. The place was finely decorated, expensively furnished and immaculately clean. The walls were painted a pale lilac, with a soft cream carpet.

Judging by the interior, one thing was for sure; Dominick Farha had a lot of money at his disposal.

But he wasn't here. As they completed their search and with no sign of the suspect, the officers re-grouped in the living room. Mac joined them, looking around with a grimace.

The place was empty.

He cursed.

'Shit. Anything?' he asked.

Archer appeared from the main bedroom and shook his head.

'Looks like he's packed his bags.'

Mac turned his attention to a brown-haired officer who'd appeared beside Archer in the doorway. His name was Porter, Mac's right hand man; the task force had only been together less than a year, but it was generally accepted that Porter would take over command whenever Mac retired. Professional, considerate and in his mid-thirties, Porter was known for two things. He never swore, and he never complained.

'Port, get on the horn to Cobb. Let him know,' said Mac.

Porter nodded. 'Yes, Sarge.'

Turning, he disappeared out of sight as the rest of the team convened in the living room.

'This doesn't change anything, lads,' Mac said. 'Find me something we can use. We still need to get this guy.'

The officers nodded and separated, preparing to tear the apartment apart to find any clue on Farha's whereabouts.

In a semi-detached house not too far away, an elderly lady was just beginning her morning routine. Since the sudden death of her husband the year before, she had taken great comfort in knowing roughly what was going to happen each and every day. *Wake up. Run a hot bath. Get dressed. Feed Tigger. Make a cup of tea. Read the*

41

newspaper delivered to the porch. Routine, routine, routine. What was mundane to the younger generation served as a loyal and reassuring friend to the old lady, unwavering and reliable.

Having just added the right amount of milk to a mug of tea poured to the perfect level, she shuffled through to her living room and took her place in a comfy armchair by the window. Placing the mug carefully on a coaster on the small table beside her, she leaned back with a sigh and looked outside.

It was a bright but chilly December morning. Frost from the previous night had clamped itself to the edges and corners of the window pane, leaving tiny white whorls and swirling patterns like intricate calligraphy. As she gazed outside, she noticed that the red rosebushes in the front garden hadn't been pruned properly in the autumn. She frowned, she'd have to do that when the weather warmed up in the spring.

But she also noticed something else.

Something odd.

Across the street, a young teenage boy was pacing down the pavement in a hurry. He was so focused on getting somewhere, the lad didn't seem to have noticed that the back of his coat had ridden up, catching on something jammed into the back of his waistband.

Frowning again, the lady looked closer then gasped.

Even from this distance, she could see what the object was.

The youngster stopped outside a house across the street, and her suspicions were confirmed. Walking up and knocking on the front door, he reached behind him and pulled the black shape from his belt.

It was a gun.

She knew her duty. Forgetting her cup of tea, she pushed herself up from the armchair and moved to the other side of the window. Scooping up the receiver to a telephone sitting on the table, she dialled three numbers

42

and waited.

The call connected as a voice arrived on the other end, asking a question through the receiver held to the woman's ear.

'Police, please,' the elderly lady answered.

In contrast to the lady's home, the interior of the house across the street couldn't have been more different.

It was dimly lit, the air reeking of stale cigarette smoke. With the curtains drawn, the lights low, three men sat at a kitchen table, playing cards. Two of them were smoking cigarettes while the other munched on some breakfast cereal from a bowl. Several small bags of cocaine were scattered carelessly on the kitchen table amongst the cereal and cards, joined by a nine-millimetre pistol. The gun had been dumped on the table so that the barrel was currently aimed at one of the men's chest, the safety catch on the weapon off. None of them seemed to have noticed.

The pistol was a Beretta. There was another one somewhere in the house, but they couldn't find it. A third gun was leaning against the wall, within reach of one of the two men playing cards. It was a Remington 870 shotgun, twelve-gauge, a fearsomely powerful weapon. Some firearms had to be aimed carefully to have the desired effect, but the Remington wasn't one of them. All a man had to do was aim at the central mass and pull the trigger. Whoever was unfortunate enough to be standing in front of it would be getting stuck back together with glue.

As the men sat there in silence, there was suddenly a knock on the door.

The trio froze and looked at each other; they weren't expecting a guest.

The knocking continued.

The guy sitting closest to the shotgun lowered his cards, rising from his chair and taking the weapon from the wall. The other two men separated, one of them grabbed the pistol using an armchair as a screen, as the third man moved to the door. He crept up to it, and peered through the spy-hole, then relaxed instantly and turned to his two companions.

'It's your brother,' he said to one of them.

As they put down the weapons, the man by the door opened it and turned without a greeting, walking back to the table and returning to his cereal.

The man who'd snatched up the pistol frowned, as his younger brother appeared from the hallway.

'What the hell are you doing here?' he asked.

The boy didn't respond, staring at the cocaine on the table.

'*Hey*!' Saqib shouted, grabbing his brother's attention. 'I asked you what you're doing here?'

The boy looked at him nervously.

'I borrowed something. I thought I should bring it back,' he said.

He pulled out the missing Beretta from behind his back, placing it carefully on the armchair.

The moment Saqib saw it, his eyes blazed with anger.

'*You little shit! Come here!*' he shouted, lunging at him, trying to grab his coat.

The boy had been expecting that reaction and already had a head-start. Before Saqib could grab him, he was almost out of the front door. He sprinted outside and ran off down the street, running to the corner and then fleeing out of sight.

Standing in the doorway, his brother squinted as his eyes adjusted to their first taste of the morning light.

Across the street, he noticed an old lady standing in her front room, a phone to her ear, watching him. *Nosy bitch*, he thought.

He glared at her for a moment, then turned on his heel and slammed the door shut, locking it behind him.

FIVE

Over in Knightsbridge at Farha's apartment, reinforcements had arrived. Cobb had been in touch with the CID, the Criminal Investigation Department, and they'd sent over a team of detectives who were more than accustomed to searching places like this for clues. Around them, the ARU officers were also still hard at work, examining everything they could find, searching every drawer, every shelf, every inch of the flat. They needed a lead and no one was leaving until they got one.

Archer was sitting at a desk in the main living room with a view overlooking Hyde Park. He'd found a stack of papers tucked in the top drawer that he was currently rifling through. There were bank statements from a well-financed account with a fake name, receipts from hardware stores. There was even one from *NEXT*, a woman's retail store, for a dress. That one seemed a bit bizarre.

Across the room, Mac appeared in the doorway, finishing a conversation with a detective from the CID. He saw Archer behind the desk and approached him.

'Anything, Arch?' he asked.

Archer shook his head. 'Nothing we can use. Just some old receipts. I guess it counts as evidence, but it's not telling us where the hell this guy is.'

Mac nodded as Chalky appeared from one of the bedrooms, overhearing the conversation.

'Maybe he's coming back?' he suggested.

Across the room, Fox shook his head as he examined the contents of a cupboard.

'No bags, Chalk. No clothes to speak of. There's nothing here. He's gone.'

Mac shook his head, cursing with frustration. Fox was right; they were too late to the party. As Mac went to continue, Porter suddenly reappeared in the doorway and interrupted him.

'Mac, I just spoke with Nikki. The Met want us to check out a weapon sighting in the area.'

Mac snorted, shaking his head.

'No way. We just got here. Tell them to put someone else on it. We're busy.'

'I tried. They said all the other suitable teams are in the south and east, conducting raids. We're the only unit in the area. It's our call.'

Mac sighed with frustration. Since the Firearms Act was passed, whenever a live weapon was reported in the city it was the responsibility of an armed police unit to go and retrieve it.

He checked his watch.

'Shit. Alright. Chalky, Arch, Port, we're going,' he ordered. 'Let's take care of it and get back here quick as we can.'

He turned to Deakins, who had just entered the room.

'Deaks, take over 'til I get back.'

Deakins nodded; he was used to this. For operational ease, the task force had been split into two teams. Mac was the head of First Team, which was himself, Archer, Chalky and Porter. Deakins was in charge of the other five guys in Team Two, and therefore was the unofficial second-in-command of the squad.

Mac moved swiftly to the door, Chalky right behind him and both followed Porter outside into the corridor, heading downstairs to the car. Rising from behind the desk Archer went after them, taking one last look at the expensive apartment behind him as he left and picturing the suspect's face in his head.

Dominick Farha.

The leader of the cell.

'Where the hell are you?' he muttered as he left the apartment.

47

He was just over ten miles away. In a hotel beside Heathrow Airport, the handsome dark-featured terrorist cell leader stepped outside Room 418, freshly showered and dressed.

As he clicked the door shut, he glanced either side of him, looking down the corridor which was empty. He knew he was being paranoid, but this close to freedom he couldn't afford to make any stupid mistakes. Caution was his best friend right now.

And after the last few days, he couldn't handle anything else going wrong.

As soon as he'd realised the group had been compromised earlier in the week, the first thought in his mind had been to flee the country. In any other situation he would have done exactly that. But however tempting the idea was, he'd quickly dismissed it. To stand before Henry with no kind of recompense after what he did would be like signing his own death warrant. He was already in some drastically deep shit, and to screw this whole operation up after all this planning and preparation would be like drying the concrete to his feet himself.

So, with sudden escape not an option, he'd been forced to consider the alternative. With every instinct prompting him to leave, he'd calmed himself down. He'd contacted the cell by using two of them as couriers and yesterday, had ordered the whole gang to meet at an empty warehouse on an industrial estate near the airport. Face to face meetings like this were extremely risky and dangerous at this stage, but they didn't have a choice. If they used phone or email, Farha knew the government's security would be onto them in an instant.

Addressing the group, Dominick had emphasised the fact the security services and police knew of their plans meant nothing. He'd deliberately kept the list of targets a secret and had never intended to reveal them until the very last minute, just in case of a problem like this. And he'd been damn relieved he had. It was far too late to change the plans now.

He'd finally revealed the targets, each member informed of their particular role which they'd all agreed to without hesitation.

Saying goodbye, the members of the cell had turned their backs and departed, going their separate ways, knowing they would never see each other again.

Farha had stayed at the warehouse, watching everyone leave. He'd arranged a couple of safe-houses for some of them and told the rest not to go home, but he knew that he would be the one the police would be concentrating on. Which gave him a dilemma. There was no way he could ever return to his apartment in Knightsbridge. A guy from a counter-terrorist task force would be there to open it for him.

But similarly, he couldn't move around the city. There was too much risk of being recognised and captured out on the street. He'd wracked his brains, searching for the answer as to where the hell he could hide out until his escape on Saturday night.

And then it had come to him, like a light-bulb going off in his brain.

A hotel by the airport.

It was organised mayhem in those places. There was an endless rotation of different faces and names in the building, so many people coming and going that he could disappear into the crowd as another anonymous guest. So he'd selected a hotel and used a fake name to check in, holing up in the room where he'd been for the past twenty four hours, out of sight. Right now was the first time he'd risked stepping out of the room since he'd arrived; he was pleasantly surprised at how calm and confident he felt. There was no-one about. No-one had a clue where he was.

And he'd be out of the country before the clock struck midnight.

Pushing a pair of sunglasses up over his nose, he started to walk down the quiet corridor towards the elevators. Dressed in a smart suit, he looked like a typical businessman staying at the hotel, his hectic lifestyle momentarily slowed until he hopped on a flight to New York or maybe the Far East.

Indeed, there was only one thing about Dominick Farha's polished appearance which looked slightly out of place that morning.

A large black holdall, slung over his shoulder.

'Alright, here's a bet. Ten quid says it's a water pistol,' offered Chalky, watching the street flash past his window in the back of the car.

The four policemen were inside a black 4x4 Ford moving quickly through the streets, speeding towards the location where the weapon was sighted. Porter was behind the wheel, Mac beside him in the front passenger seat, with the two younger officers sat behind them.

Archer turned to his friend. 'Deal.'

He offered his hand, to seal the terms. Chalky shook it.

'Who called it in, Port?' he asked.

'Old lady across the street. Said she saw a kid take a handgun into a house,' said Porter, swerving to avoid a car parked just too far into the road.

Chalky grinned at Archer. 'Told you. Might as well pay me now, Arch. At least it'll make this little journey worthwhile.'

'You making a point, Officer White?' Mac growled from the front seat, as he inspected the MP5 resting on his lap.

'Just that we're meant to be a special unit, Sarge,' he responded. 'Armed response, counter-terrorism, that sort of thing. But here we are, going to pick up a Super Soaker from some twelve year old kid who made the heinous mistake of carrying it down the street.'

'Have you considered that it might be a real gun?'

Archer asked.

'How many kids are walking around carrying real handguns in London, Arch?' his friend countered.

'OK, so let me ask you something Chalky,' said Mac. 'Why did you apply to join this unit? It seems to me that you're starting to complain about doing anything that actually involves police work.'

Chalky sensed his sergeant's irritation and backtracked. He knew better than to provoke him. 'Oh, I love the work, Sarge. I'm just saying it wouldn't hurt to have a bit of excitement once in a while.'

As he spoke, Porter turned to the right and pulled the vehicle into a gap on the kerb, applying the handbrake and turning off the engine. They were parked on a residential road, rows of semi-detached houses facing each other all the way down the street. They could see a few people walking down the pavements on either side, but the place was pretty quiet.

'We're here,' Porter said. 'Number 33, up ahead to the right.'

All four men looked where he'd indicated and saw the front door in question.

The curtains to the windows in the front room were all drawn, which was a mixed blessing. Whoever was inside wouldn't see them coming, but equally they couldn't get any idea who or what was inside.

Mac turned to his three officers, ready to go.

'Check your weapons. Arch, you're primary. Chalk, secondary.'

Archer nodded, appreciating the responsibility. *Primary* meant he'd be the first man through the door. Each man checked his weapon and went to open the doors.

'Oh, and Chalk?' Mac added.

The younger man paused, his hand on the door handle.

'Be careful what you wish for.'

Inside the house, the three men hadn't moved from the table, smoking their cigarettes and still playing cards.

But suddenly, there was another hard pounding on the door.

Three stiff knocks.

But this time it wasn't Saqib's brother.

'POLICE! OPEN UP!'

For a split second, the three men sat there frozen, staring at each other, wide-eyed with fear and shock.

How the hell did they find us? their faces said.

Then they bolted into action.

One of them grabbed the two bags of cocaine, throwing them under the couch in a frenzy as the other two rushed to grab the weapons scattered around the room.

They were trapped, with no way out.

But they weren't going down without a fight.

Outside the front door, the four officers could hear the sudden commotion inside the house.

Without hesitation, Archer stepped back and kicked the front door as hard as he could, but it wouldn't budge.

He tried twice more quickly. Nothing.

He put everything he had behind the fourth, and threw his body weight behind it.

This time, it worked and the door splintered open.

Pushing it all the way back, he moved into the house, followed by his three team-mates, shouting as he held his MP5 to his shoulder, tight in the aim.

'Police! Nobody move!'

Sweeping through the front hallway, he turned right, arriving in the doorway of the living room. The place was dark and dirty, like a seedy den.

But in the shadows in that split second, he saw three men standing there.

One of them was holding a pistol. This one wasn't a toy.

Immediately, Archer could tell it was the real deal.

But things got a hell of a lot worse.

He saw a second man across the room holding another weapon.

A pump action twelve-gauge shotgun.

The guy had it in the shoulder.

And it was aimed at Archer's head.

SIX

As a kid, Archer had always been bad at football, or *soccer* as his Dad used to call it. For the life of him, he could never kick the damn ball properly. Other boys his age had taken to the game with ease, able to seamlessly perform elaborate tricks and passes while Archer struggled to master the most basic of skills. But during one game at school, when he was about ten, he'd discovered that there was one thing he excelled at. Goal-keeping.

He'd been stuck in the goal-mouth by a coach during a school practice, probably to keep him out of the way of the more talented kids. But then during the game, the other team suddenly couldn't score. They'd thrown everything at him, but he stopped the ball every time. *He's got hands like buckets*, his coach had enthused upon seeing the boy's hidden talent. But even then as a kid, grateful as he was, Archer knew his gloves weren't the key to his success between the posts.

It was his reaction speed.

On this occasion, that same rapidity was going to save his life. Before the gunman had time to pull the trigger, Archer was already diving behind the far wall for cover.

'Shotgun!' he screamed, to his three fellow officers.

They all threw themselves back in the hall as the guy fired the weapon. There was a deafening explosion; white plaster and dust burst from the wall behind where Archer had been standing as it took the full brunt of the shell.

On the floor, his ears ringing, the young policeman looked up and saw one of the other two suspects fleeing frantically up the stairs ahead of him. Scrambling to his feet, Archer pursued the other man, chasing him down.

The wall shielded him from the guy with the shotgun, so he was momentarily safe.

The other officers had fallen back into the hallway, taking cover from the force of the blast. Chalky was the man immediately behind Archer, next in line. Seeing his friend run after the other suspect, Chalky took the initiative and moved into the living room, his MP5 up, as the man with the shotgun racked the pump. The weapon gave a loud double-crunch, as another shell was slotted into the firing chamber.

'Drop the weapon!' Chalky bellowed as he moved forward, the sight of his MP5 aimed on the guy's chest.

Suddenly he stumbled, tripping on an overturned chair-leg in the dim light, and fell, momentarily losing his grip on his weapon. He clattered onto the floor, landing just in front of the guy.

From the ground, he looked up.

And the wrong end of the shotgun met his gaze, an inch from his face.

It was so close, he found himself staring inside the barrel.

Behind it, he could see the man's face, eyes wide, hopped up from cocaine.

And the guy pulled the trigger.

Click.

The gun misfired.

A split-second later, the man holding the shotgun was thrown back, two rounds from Mac's MP5 slamming

55

into his chest. His finger twitched on the trigger as he fell and the shotgun erupted once more, white plaster exploding from the ceiling as it took the round. He was dead before his back hit the floor.

The other man, seeing his friend's demise, threw his Beretta to the floor in panic, holding his hands high above him and screaming in some foreign language. Mac moved forward to arrest him, never taking the front-sight of his weapon off the guy's chest. If he tried something cute, he'd be dead in an instant.

Across the room, Chalky leaned back against the wall, his eyes wide with shock. Porter dropped to one knee beside him, grabbing his shoulders, looking into his eyes.

Chalky stared back at him, confused. Porter's voice was muffled.

He was up close, holding him by the shoulders, looking into his eyes.

He was shouting, asking him something, but Chalky couldn't hear what he was saying. He stared back at him, his chest heaving as he sucked in air, looking at Porter's mouth as it moved as if he was watching a silent film.

On the upper floor, Archer was just finishing hand-cuffing the third man's hands behind his back. The guy was shouting and swearing, but the young officer ignored him, keeping his knee on the guy's back and pinning him to the ground as he used a set of plasti-cuffs from his tac vest.

Zipping them tight, Archer rose, lifting his MP5 back to his shoulder. Behind him, the man writhed and jerked around as he tried to free his hands, but it was hopeless; Archer had cuffed his ankles too, trussing the guy up like a Christmas turkey. He wasn't going anywhere.

Looking around him, Archer saw that there were only two doors on the second floor but both of them were shut.

He crept forward to the first, just as a shout came from downstairs.

'Clear!'

Arriving outside the first door, Archer took a deep breath. Closed rooms were a nightmare to breach. Someone could be standing just the other side with a shotgun aimed at the wood, waiting for the moment they heard movement in the corridor or when they sensed someone touch the handle.

There could even be a group of them in there for all he knew, each one pointing a gun at the door.

Taking a deep breath, he kicked it open and ducked swiftly inside.

It was a spare bedroom, and thankfully, it was empty. No one was there. The room contained just a solitary bed, no sheets or duvet.

But there were a number of things resting on the mattress.

Archer looked closer, and felt his breath catch.

Four large transparent bags had been dumped on the bed. Each one was about the size of a black rubbish bag, and each contained different items.

He looked closer and saw ball bearings and marbles.

Nails.

White powder.

And some kind of clear liquid that looked like bleach.

Beside the bags, three backpacks lay on the bed, along with a spool of wire.

57

Archer's mouth went dry as two words came into his mind.

Suicide bomb.

Staring at the bags on the bed for a moment longer, he then raced back into the corridor.

'*Mac!*'

Wasting no time, Archer moved to the second closed door across the level as Mac appeared below and started moving up the stairs. Same routine again; enter and pray there was no one the other side. Taking another breath, he raised his MP5 and kicked the soft wooden frame, as hard as he could.

The door flew open.

The moment Archer looked inside, he almost vomited.

The room was covered with blood. It was as if someone had got buckets of the stuff and thrown it all over the walls like an art project. A dead body was hanging limp, hand-cuffed to the shower rail, like an animal in an abattoir. The guy was naked. Pieces of him lay all over the tiled floor, the white walls red and spattered with his blood.

Archer covered his mouth as Mac appeared alongside him from the stairs. The older man's eyes widened and he paused, standing beside Archer; he'd seen some pretty awful things in his time, but this was up there with the very worst.

Beside him, the younger man coughed, the sweet smell of dried blood filling the air.

'What the hell did we just find?' Archer asked.

Mac stared at the dead body, hanging like a slaughtered pig from the rail.

'I don't know, Arch,' he said quietly. 'I don't know.'

SEVEN

Back-up arrived quickly. Within thirty minutes, the inside of the house was jammed tight like there was a party inside, except all the revellers were detectives from the CID and Forensics. The two surviving suspects had already been escorted to police cars outside and taken back to the ARU's headquarters for questioning.

Inside the living room, Archer finished up a conversation with a detective who'd asked him to talk his way through their entry. After shaking hands with the man, the ARU officer turned and moved to the front door.

He needed some air.

Outside on the street, it was just as busy. There were numerous police vehicles and white vans parked in the road, many of them parked at an angle across the street. It didn't matter; nothing was getting through. Yellow police tape had been pulled up behind them, wrapped around lamp-posts, blocking off the street and holding back the gathering crowd of curious residents and passers-by.

To his left, Archer could see that some news vans had arrived; they'd got here quickly, just as they always seemed to do. Looking up, he saw a helicopter was also circling overhead. He didn't know if it was a police chopper or one of theirs.

Amongst the mass of vehicles and people gathered in the street, Archer saw Mac talking with a blonde woman in white overalls from Forensics. The sergeant noticed Archer watching them, and waved the younger man over.

'This is Sam Archer, one of my men,' Mac told the lady as Archer joined them. 'He was the one who found the bags and the dead body.'

The woman ripped off her latex gloves one by one, and offered her hand.

'Kim Collins. Forensics.'

Archer shook it. Mac was holding a piece of paper in his hand, the photographs of the nine suspects. Lifting it so Collins and Archer could see, he pointed to three of the mug-shots one-by-one.

'All three of these boys were on the list. Numbers 2, 3 and 7. See.'

Archer looked closer. Number Seven was the guy they arrested downstairs, Two the man that Mac had killed. Number Three was the one that Archer had cuffed on the upper floor. The same guy whose photo he'd found himself staring at in the Briefing Room earlier.

He looks so familiar, Archer thought, staring at the black and white photo.

Where the hell have I seen him before?

Keeping his questions to himself for now, he turned to Mac. 'Did we take someone else's assignment?'

Mac shook his head. 'I spoke with Cobb. This place wasn't on the list to be raided.'

'Talk about luck,' added Collins, wiping her brow with the back of her un-gloved hand.

Archer looked over at her, her white uniform, and the horrific memory of the bathroom covered in blood flooded back into his mind.

'Do we know anything about the body on the rail?' he asked.

'My team's in there right now, trying to figure it out. He's in a real mess though. But I examined the bathroom myself earlier, and found something.'

'What was that?' Mac asked.

'Aside from the victim's, there's only one other set of fingerprints in the blood. Whoever killed him didn't wear gloves. He either didn't expect to get caught or just didn't care if he does.'

She paused.

'Someone really went to work on him. They pulled out his fingernails, gouged out his eyes, cut off his genitalia, flayed his skin. I've seen some bad ones and this is up there with the worst.'

Mac turned to Archer.

'I want the whole squad back at the Unit pronto. Our priorities just changed.'

Collins tilted her head as something caught her attention. A member of her team was calling her.

'Excuse me gentlemen,' she said.

The two men nodded and she departed, pulling another set of gloves from her pocket as she returned to the house.

Watching her go, Archer turned to Mac. He went to speak, but he saw that the older man's eyes had narrowed, looking past him at something.

Archer twisted round to see what it was.

'Oh Jesus,' he muttered.

Thirty yards away, a member of the team was sat slumped on the back of a police van, his eyes wide and unfocused, staring ahead with shock.

Chalky.

There was a constant buzz of movement around him from other police officers and forensics, but he remained motionless, lost in thought. Archer sighed. The near-escape with the shotgun was written all over his friend's face.

'One way to cure a hangover,' Mac said quietly, watching him.

'So the gun just misfired? Did the guy reload?' Archer asked. He hadn't seen the incident, but Porter had filled him in on what happened.

Mac nodded. 'He racked a round. Shell in the chamber. You heard the other blasts, kid. That gun was working just fine.'

He looked closer at Chalky.

'Tell you what, he's got nine lives, that boy. Someone upstairs must love him. I thought he was done.'

Behind them, Porter stuck his head out of a wound-down window from inside their police car. He had a mobile phone in his hand.

'*Mac?*' he called. 'It's Director Cobb. He wants to speak to you.'

Mac nodded, turning to Archer.

'We need to get Chalk out of here, Arch. There are cameras everywhere. I don't want that look on his face reappearing on the midday news. Get him in the car and we'll go back to the Unit.'

Archer nodded. Mac moved over to Porter and took the phone from his hand to talk to Cobb.

Taking a deep breath, Archer walked towards his friend.

Chalky didn't seem to register his approach, still staring at the ground. Arriving in front of him, Archer stood still.

'Looks like you owe me a tenner,' he said, trying to lighten the mood.

Silence. Chalky didn't respond or show any sign that he'd heard him.

'Mac told me what happened. How are you feeling?'

Pause.

'How do you think I feel?' he replied quietly.

'You need to straighten up, Chalk. There're a load of cameras over there. The whole country will be watching this. We don't want you ending up on the six o'clock bulletin.'

For the first time, Chalky looked up at him. Archer hid his surprise. His friend looked as if he'd aged ten years in ten minutes. He looked physically and emotionally drained, all from a cocktail of shock, adrenaline and a bad hangover.

'It was an inch from my face, Arch,' he said. 'I could see inside the barrel. I shouldn't be here. I should be painted all over the wall in the house.'

'Well, you're not. You're still alive,' Archer said. Stepping forward, he put his palm under his friend's armpit, helping him up. 'C'mon mate, we're going back to the Unit. We'll get the kettle on and fix you up.'

It was weak at best, but Archer didn't know what else to say. It seemed to work however, as Chalky nodded, walking with no resistance alongside his friend towards the black Ford, away from any news-cameras searching for a scoop and the house that should have been his grave.

However, the two men were unaware that it was too late.

Someone was already photographing them.

From a vantage point across the street, a camera shutter clicked as a woman snapped a series of photographs, focusing tight on the two officers walking to the car. The shot was a close-up, the woman aiming the lens to make sure she caught their weapons, their features and most importantly, the badge on the right shoulder of their navy-blue uniform.

Satisfied, she lowered the camera. She had golden skin with long brown hair and a pair of emerald green eyes that completed her Middle Eastern beauty. Dressed in a dark work-suit with a white shirt, she looked as if she'd just stepped out of a conference or a business meeting, smart and official yet effortlessly beautiful.

She was on the second floor in a house across the street, leaning on a table that had been pushed up against the window to serve as a make-shift stand. Lifting the camera again, she tracked the lens back on the two young policemen as they arrived by a black 4x4. She pushed the button, snapping two more shots in quick succession. She thought for a moment, then took two more of the licence plates of the car.

Suddenly, a noise came from behind her. In the same instant, she snapped around, a pistol in her hand that she'd pulled from a holster on her hip, reacting with electrifying speed.

She waited, the gun aimed at the doorway, her aim as steady as a rock.

But it was nothing. Just the boiler turning on, or a mouse running around in the attic, the kind of subtle noises that houses always made.

Slowly, she lowered the pistol, flicking on the safety with her thumb and slotting it back in its holster on her dark suit trousers. Turning back to the desk, she clicked open the side of the camera and pulled out a memory card.

A small netbook was resting on the table beside her. She clicked the memory card into the side of the computer, and waited for it to load. As she did so, she found herself looking at a framed photograph beside the laptop. A young couple, smiling arm-in-arm on a beach.

A series of photographs started appearing on the screen as they uploaded to the computer. Snapshots. Two unkempt men, hands cuffed behind their backs, being pushed towards a police car. Shots of the policemen in the navy blue overalls, the men with the MP5 sub-machine guns. She'd got some good close-ups. One of the officers was a good-looking young guy with blond hair and blue eyes. The woman had found herself staring at him through the view-finder of the camera. He seemed almost too handsome to be a cop, more suited to a movie set or a billboard. He stood out, a real contrast to all the other dark-featured hard-faced men down there. The rest of the photographs uploaded and were all of this police task force. She wasn't interested in anybody else.

Reaching down, she pulled a phone from her pocket and pressed *Redial*, lifting it to her ear. The phone rang twice, then connected. There was a lot of noise in the background from the other end. She put her other finger to her free ear to close out any other sounds, listening closely.

'I've got some news,' she said.

'What?'

'The police found three of them. Two were arrested. I think one was killed.'

There was a pause.

'*Where?*'

'Some safe-house near Dominick's place. I had no idea they were here. I saw it on the news. I rushed over quick as I could and took up surveillance.'

A pause.

'*Was he there?*'

'No.'

There was another pause on the other end of the line. She took the opportunity to tap some keys on the keyboard with her free hand, forming an email.

'I'm sending over some photos,' she said. 'Most of them are of policemen from a unit I haven't seen before. I think these guys made the bust. They could be a real problem if they get to Dominick before we do.'

'*Or a solution,*' the voice said.

She frowned, as she hit *Send*.

She didn't see how that statement could work.

'*Listen,*' the voice continued. '*I've had an idea.*'

Inside the hotel restaurant and sitting by the window, Dominick Farha had just finished an egg and toast breakfast with a tall glass of orange juice. It had been surprisingly good and he'd enjoyed every bite.

Around him, the restaurant was busy with other guests taking seats and breaking their fast. Some were moving along a buffet across the room by the wall, loading up on yoghurts and muffins, while others waited at their table for a waitress to bring them a cooked meal. Farha was holding a newspaper in front of him, examining the headlines as he drank from a thick cup of coffee. He was still wearing his sunglasses, which made reading the paper a slight challenge, but it reduced the chances of being spotted or recognised by anyone looking for him.

As he read the articles and headlines in the broadsheet, one thing pleased him.

Neither he, nor any other members of the cell, were in any of the paper's reports.

He smiled.

After today, that was going to change.

To his left, he suddenly sensed a stirring in the room, one that pulled his attention from the newspaper. He saw a score of other diners sitting to his left watching something across the restaurant, momentarily ignoring the food on their plates. He lowered the broadsheet to see what was so interesting.

It was a television. An aerial view from a helicopter of a street that Farha instantly recognised. There was a banner headline that ran across the bottom of the screen, bold black text on a yellow background.

Breaking News: Armed man killed in London police raid. Explosive materials, weapons and dead body found in house.

He immediately felt his stomach clench, his pulse quickening.

How the hell did they find them?

He glanced around, left and right, slowly. *Have they found me?*

No one seemed to be paying any extra attention to him. They were all more interested in the report on the screen.

He took slow breaths, thinking hard as he lifted the broadsheet back up in front of him, covering his face.

Then he made a quick decision.

Lowering the newspaper and leaving it on the table, he grabbed the black holdall from under the table by his foot, rose and strode out of the restaurant. He was headed straight back to his hotel room and the television inside.

He needed to watch the news alone.

And think.

EIGHT

At the ARU's headquarters, the unexpected discovery of the three members of the terrorist cell had left Cobb both extremely relieved and extremely worried.

The safe-house they'd been holed up in wasn't on any of the databases or listed on the raid-sheet to be searched, which was more than concerning. Right now he had Nikki and her team working the three guys' mug-shots through every file they had. Mac had just called, saying he was on his way back and that he'd ordered the team from Farha's apartment to return. Two of the arrested suspects were already on their way here for questioning. The other was headed to the morgue.

As Nikki worked at her computer in the tech area, Cobb stood behind her in silence, desperately trying to think where the other six suspects could be. It was only by a stroke of ridiculous luck and a nosy old lady that they had stumbled upon these three. They couldn't rely on such good fortune again. Turning, he withdrew to his office, shutting the door behind him as his mind ran through every possible scenario.

Lost in thought, he sat back in the chair behind his desk. His office was a modern design in that the walls were made of clear transparent glass, which meant he could see what was happening outside without leaving his desk.

It also meant he saw the moment the newcomer arrived, escorted by the detective who manned the front desk downstairs.

The stranger was dressed in a dark suit, with a badge clipped to the breast pocket that said *Visitor* in bold red letters. He was wearing a blue shirt with a red tie, smart but simple, no bullshit. The guy looked like a typical corn-fed Southern boy in his mid-thirties, lean and tanned, blond hair bleached from years of sun combed smartly over green eyes. *Kind of like a younger Robert Redford* Cobb thought, as he watched the two men approach his door. *American. He has to be.* He noticed the newcomer paid no attention to the processes of the intelligence team behind him, which told Cobb that he'd seen it all before. *A government guy.*

Cobb rose from behind his desk as the detective escorting the man knocked on the glass door. He nodded, and the two men entered.

'Sorry to disturb you, sir, but this is Special Agent Crawford,' said the detective. 'He's with the DEA.'

Cobb hid a frown. The DEA was the United States Drugs Enforcement Administration, the agency tasked with leading the world-wide war on narcotics from the frontline. On any day regardless, Cobb would have been baffled as to why this man had walked into his office. The DEA battled cartels and dealers in South America and at their own borders, not in the UK. His presence here today was too coincidental and it filled Cobb with immediate unease. It had been a morning full of unpleasant surprises and he could do without any more.

Swallowing his sense of foreboding, Cobb nodded to the detective who turned and departed, leaving them alone.

The visitor stepped forward, offering his hand and introducing himself.

'Jason Crawford. As your man said, I'm a Special Agent with the DEA. Pleasure to meet you.'

Cobb shook the man's hand. 'Tim Cobb, Director of Operations.'

He waved a hand towards the busy intelligence team in the Operations area.

'I don't mean to be rude, Special Agent Crawford, but now really isn't a good time.'

Crawford turned to glance at the ops room. He looked back and nodded.

'I understand, Director. Believe me, I wouldn't be here if this wasn't crucially important. I only arrived from Paris twenty five minutes ago. I flew here just to speak with you personally.'

Cobb was confused and didn't hide it.

'About what?'

The American looked into his eyes.

'Dominick Farha,' he replied quietly.

*

'Excuse me for asking Director, but how familiar are you with the current associations between drugs and terrorism?'

Crawford spoke to Cobb's back as he stood across the room, making them both a cup of coffee from his machine by the far wall. Cobb turned.

'How do you take it?'

'Black, no sugar. Thank you.'

Cobb finished making the two drinks then turned and passed one to the DEA agent, who nodded in appreciation. Cobb took his fourth cup of the day and sat back behind his desk. He knew all about the links between the two trades, but he decided to keep his cards close to his chest.

He wanted to test Crawford out.

'To be honest, not very,' he lied, answering the man's original question. 'Here in the UK the two are mostly exclusive. Neither gets to a very high level without being stopped; we're an island after all. It's hard to smuggle drugs through our borders and it's even harder to plan a terrorist conspiracy without us knowing about it.'

He paused.

Well, almost, he thought, silently cursing at Simmons' carelessness.

Crawford nodded, taking a sip from his coffee.

'Allow me to explain. In the last few years, my agency's most recent intelligence reports have shown that over sixty per cent of modern terrorist organisations are in some way involved with drug-trafficking or narcotics. The United States has deduced that there are forty-three recognised foreign terrorist organisations in the world, FTOs, as we call them. Of the forty-three FTO groups, we know for sure that at least nineteen of them are heavily involved with the major drug cartels.'

Cobb sipped his drink, nodding. Crawford continued.

'Since 9/11, military organisations all over the world have stepped up their game in regards to the war on terrorism, as I'm sure you know. The police and the military soon realised that if you remove the terrorists' funding, you severely impact their ability to attack. Staggering amounts of terrorist money have been seized since, in many repeated and successful attempts to cripple the financial coffers of these FTOs. As a consequence, those groups who were affected suddenly found themselves broke. If they still wanted to pursue their ideology, they needed to find a new way to fund it and re-establish a constant cash supply.'

He paused, drinking his coffee.

'And for most of them, the answer lay with drugs.'

73

Cobb stayed silent.

'The two businesses go hand in hand,' Crawford continued. 'They're both built on government opposition, intimidation, the latest technology and obscene levels of violence. You remember the Madrid terror attacks a few years ago?'

Cobb nodded. He'd been at MI5 when the disaster had happened in 2004. A series of co-ordinated bombings had struck the Spanish city's subway system, killing a hundred and ninety-one people.

'Well that operation was almost totally funded by the sale of narcotics. One of the first to do so. Other FTOs saw how successful those attacks were and decided to jump on the bandwagon.'

Crawford paused again, looking at the coffee cup in his hand.

'As more and more of these groups have realised the potential profits that are out there, there's been an unpleasant consequence. The two criminal businesses have started to merge. Hybrid organisations are now emerging; one side drug cartel, the other side terrorism.'

Cobb nodded. 'Like the Taliban.'

'Exactly. When the two were more mutually exclusive, the DEA mostly kept to itself as we focused on the cartels. But after it became clear that these unions were starting to be forged, we began working much more closely with both our own agencies and others around the world. And it's been a great success so far. In the six years from 2005 to 2011, the DEA, in co-operation with other government teams around the world, has seized over seventeen billion dollars in drug money.'

He paused, letting that last sentence hang in the air.

'So, slowly but surely we're winning the war,' he said, draining the last of his coffee.

There was a pause.

'Well I'm very pleased to hear that,' Cobb said. 'But forgive me for asking, but I'm not quite seeing how this ties into my Unit, Agent Crawford.'

The American halted for a moment, fixing Cobb with a steady stare. Cobb realised that he'd been weighing him up too, from the moment he entered the room.

'Can I rest assured that what I am about to tell you stays here?' Crawford asked quietly.

Cobb nodded. 'Of course.'

'The reason I was in Paris was an operation. A six man detail, including myself. Our target is the head of one of the most powerful drug cartels in the Middle East, a man known as Henry. I arrived at De Gaulle from Riyadh last night with three of my men. We got an advance tip off that there was going to be some kind of deal taking place outside the city later on this evening and I'm happy to say we've hit the jackpot.'

'How so?'

'The boss is going to be there himself. I can't emphasise to you enough how rare that is. He's the head of his own cartel. Men as powerful as he is don't just turn up at trades and business deals. They let the people under them handle it.'

Cobb nodded, thinking.

'OK. But I'm still failing to see how his relates to my team?'

Crawford looked at him for a moment.

'Because Dominick Farha is Henry's nephew.'

75

NINE

'There are certain names tagged in the file for my team's operation,' Crawford continued, as Cobb listened closely. The information Crawford had just given him had immediately grabbed his attention. 'A red flag comes up whenever one of the names is searched in any databases we share with other agencies. That includes the CIA, NSA, FBI and foreign organisations we have close ties with. One of those groups is MI6, and this morning, Dominick Farha's name came up. Straight away, I contacted Chief of Staff Rogers at 10 Downing Street. He informed me of the operation underway, of these nine suspects, all potential suicide bombers, and all led by Dominick Farha.'

He looked at the coffee cup in his hand, preparing his approach.

'Simply put, I want to help, Director. During my team's operation, I have managed to accrue extensive knowledge of Farha and his family. I think I could be of great assistance to you and your detail.'

Cobb nodded, but stayed silent. He liked the suggestion, but he knew there was also an ulterior motive here.

Crawford hadn't come all this way just to help him out.

'But let me guess. If Farha somehow gets in contact with Henry in Paris, you want us to hold back until your operation is over,' Cobb replied, putting two and two together. 'If we move in, your cartel boss will realise he's compromised and will disappear. And you don't get him at the drug buy.'

Crawford nodded slowly.

'Correct.'

Cobb went to speak further but paused. He noticed the American's expression had changed. He seemed troubled. Cobb had sensed something wasn't right ever since Crawford had walked in, but he had known better than to ask.

After a brief silence, the blond DEA agent spoke again.

'One of my men went missing last night,' he said. 'I'd left him running surveillance from outside Henry's compound in Riyadh while four of us flew to Paris to get a head start on the scheduled drug buy. I tried contacting him from the plane and again when we touched down at De Gaulle, but there was no response.'

He paused.

'Before the operation, each member of my team had been chipped back in the US. It's a transponder, tiny, small enough to fit in a syringe. It means if one of our operatives goes dark or gets in trouble, we can always track them down.'

He licked his lips.

'We located him by satellite an hour ago.'

'Where?'

'At the bottom of the Red Sea.'

There was a long silence.

'A diving crew are out there right now trying to retrieve him,' continued Crawford. 'He was exactly where the satellite said he was. Henry's favourite method of killing someone is to knock them out and put their feet in quick drying cement. Then they get thrown overboard to drown. And that's exactly what happened to my agent.'

A pause. Crawford shook his head.

'His name was Faber. A good man, real solid. Two daughters and a wife back home. We'd been working together for over a year.'

'I'm sorry,' said Cobb quietly.

Crawford nodded, his tanned face hardening.

'Needless to say, I've had enough of this shit. It's time to take Henry and his organisation down. It's clear that our two cases are intertwined, so I wanted to come here in person and offer the DEA's services myself. I promise my agency will assist you wherever we can, Director Cobb.'

He paused as something else came into his mind.

'By the way, has anyone discussed a motive with you yet?'

'For the planned attacks?'

Crawford nodded. Cobb considered the question, then shook his head.

'No. I figured it was just fanaticism.'

Crawford shook his head.

'A year ago to the day, Dominick was actually high up in Henry's organisation,' he said. 'Their relationship wasn't always this fractured. Farha, as a trusted family member, had been sent to New York on a business run that we were tracking. He'd set up a meeting with a brother cartel based in Queens, providing them with samples of fresh, top-grade cocaine from Juarez. It was New Year's Eve and Dominick had been drinking in a bar all day. The meeting was scheduled for a room inside the Four Seasons hotel. It must have turned sour.'

'How so?'

'Dominick ended up killing the two guys and making off with the samples and cash they'd brought. All in all, about two hundred and fifty grand.'

Cobb didn't reply.

'Now this put him in some seriously deep shit. One of the guys he whacked was a lieutenant within the other organisation and those are men that you do not want to mess with. Once details of what had happened spread, the New York crew put the word out. Seven figures on Farha's head, dead or alive; and our wiretaps revealed Henry was even angrier with him than the other cartel was. His little stunt had permanently ended relations with the New York organisation, and consequently took away a huge source of business. Dominick fled to the UK the next morning, a year ago tomorrow, and he hasn't contacted his uncle since.'

'But where's the motive for planning these attacks?' Cobb asked.

'Henry harbours a deep hatred for the United Kingdom. His parents were killed during the Gulf War when a British missile hit their home.'

Suddenly, it all fell into place in Cobb's mind.

He leaned back in his chair and nodded.

'Dominick thinks these attacks will make up for what happened in New York and please his uncle enough to let him back into his organisation. And keep him alive and protected.'

Crawford nodded. 'And his screw-up at the Four Seasons will stay there.'

Cobb frowned. 'Pretty extreme for a family argument.'

'Oh, to reasonable men like you and me, absolutely. But remember the kind of people we are dealing with here, Director. Right now, there are cartel hit-men scouring the world searching for Dominick and they have a long reach. With the protection of his uncle and his men, Dominick could survive. Without it, it's only a matter of time before someone finds him. And he'd be better off killing himself than if the New York gang ever took him alive. They'd make his death last weeks.'

With that, Crawford fell silent; he'd finished his report and showed his hand. The rest was up to Cobb.

The Englishman thought hard, assessing the situation, the scenario and his options.

Finally, he nodded. 'OK, I'm in. Let's do it.'

Crawford grinned.

'Fantastic. Let's take them all down, Director. Every single one of these assholes.'

The two men rose. Cobb walked around his desk and shook hands with the American, sealing the deal.

'There's one more thing,' added Crawford. 'One of my men is on his way here from Paris. He's a field agent, a good man. Used to be SEAL Team Six. I figured he could assist your ground team.'

He shrugged.

'It's either that, or he sits here with us. I couldn't leave him in Paris. He's a field agent, not surveillance.'

Cobb considered the proposition, then nodded.

'OK. He can attach to my task force as an observer. Tell him to come in whenever he lands. You can bring him up to speed.'

As Crawford nodded, Nikki approached the office and knocked on the transparent glass door to the office. Cobb beckoned her in.

'Sir?' she said, sticking her head through the gap in the doorway.

'Yes?'

'Sorry to interrupt, but I thought you should know. The two suspects have arrived. Frost is down there with them now. They're starting the interrogation.'

*

All the holding and interrogation cells in the ARU HQ were located on the lower level. The holding cells were simple rooms. Each one contained the basic facilities of a bed, wash-basin and toilet. The basin and toilet were made of aluminium instead of porcelain which prevented anyone locked inside from smashing them up and wielding a chunk of shattered porcelain as sharp as a razor. Lessons learnt from the past.

The interrogation cells were equally sparse. Each one was a rectangular shaped room, painted bone-white, with no furnishings save for a solitary table with a chair placed either side. There was no voice-recording equipment resting on the table like in the good old days; the room had been hooked up with several microphones, so every exchange was recorded from the outside instead. It was a useful inclusion, meaning the detective conducting the interrogation could concentrate solely on working the suspect. Indeed, the room looked like any other save for one thing; a long sheet of mirrored glass had replaced the left side wall. It meant people outside the room could look in, but no one could see out.

On this occasion, a young man was slumped in one of the chairs inside the cell, his tousled dark hair hanging over his face as he stared at the ground. His hands were still cuffed behind him; no-one had bothered to take them off, or alternatively no-one cared to.

He can't be older than twenty five, Cobb thought as he watched the young man through the glass in the small dark observation room next door. He was standing side by side with Crawford and Mac, having just made the necessary introductions. Cobb had updated Mac on the situation, informing him that the DEA and ARU would now be working together on the operation, and that an American field agent called Rivers would attach to the task force whenever he arrived.

Through the glass, the grey-haired detective who'd shown Crawford to Cobb's office was sitting in the chair across the table from the suspect. His name was Frost. Cobb had pulled him from the CID at what had proved to be an unwittingly perfect time for the man. Frost was the wrong side of fifty and had just gone through a messy divorce, so the offer of a new position in a new department was a welcome change of scene and just the late fresh start that his career needed. All his years of experience and excellent track record were the main reasons why Cobb had asked him to join the detail; he'd been with the CID for almost twenty years. Frost had a knack of extracting information and was a pro at conducting interrogations like these. As he watched the detective working on the suspect, Cobb reminded himself never to play a game of poker with the guy.

'So what was the target?' Frost asked quietly, more as an ice-breaker than anything else.

The young man ignored him.

'We know all about you. And your friends. We knew your every move. You were going to attack today, weren't you?'

The suspect kept his head down.

Said nothing.

Frost leaned forward on the desk, keeping his manner civil.

'You're in some deep trouble and I want to help you. But I can't do anything if you don't start cooperating. Do you understand that?'

Nothing. No response. The guy's matted hair hung over his face, like a curtain drawn across a stage. He didn't even twitch, as if he was made of stone.

This was going to take a while.

Outside the room, Cobb, Mac and Crawford continued to watch the scene in front of them, as silent as the suspect. The door from the corridor behind them opened, and Porter and Archer entered with a blonde woman in her late-thirties. Both the officers were still in their tactical gear, but their Glock 17 and MP5 sub-machine guns had been stowed in the gun-cage down the corridor. The woman was smartly dressed in a grey suit and trouser combo over a white shirt, professional yet feminine. Her name was Jill Sawyer, a lawyer attached to the detail.

'Good afternoon, gentlemen,' she said, as Porter closed the door gently behind them.

Cobb turned.

'How's the case, Jill?' he asked.

'Gift-wrapped. He's done for,' she said, nodding through the glass to the suspect in the chair. 'Two handguns, a twelve-gauge shotgun, a couple of bags of cocaine and enough raw materials for a bomb that could take out a football stadium. Oh, and a dead body in the bathroom. He's looking at twenty years, and possibly life. Depends if the judge is having a bad day.'

Archer and Porter were standing beside Mac, watching the interrogation inside the glass as they listened to Sawyer's summary.

Mac turned to Porter, speaking quietly.

'Is the other suspect talking?'

Porter shook his head.

'Looks like he doesn't speak a word of English. Deakins and Fox are in there with him next door, trying to get something out of him.'

Mac swore.

'I also spoke to Nikki outside,' Porter continued. 'She just received a call from a lady named Kim Collins from Forensics. Apparently she wanted to pass on a message to you.'

'Concerning?'

'The guy on the shower rail. She said his fingerprints came back from the lab. Apparently, he's a government agent. Or *was*. He'd been undercover in the cell.'

Mac took this in, then looked past Porter to Archer, who was watching Frost try to engage the suspect through the glass.

'How's Chalky?' he asked.

Engrossed in the interrogation next door, Archer gave him a quick look and shrugged.

I don't know, his face said.

Through the glass, Frost told the suspect that he was going to get some coffee. He rose, and walked to the exit, pulling it open and entering the observation room. He closed the door behind him; it was sound-proof so there was no risk of being overheard.

'I'm going to grab a cup of coffee, sir' he told Cobb. 'Give him some time to think.'

'Did you get any kind of read on him?' Cobb asked.

'No. Not yet.'

There was a pause. Frost nodded and moved to the door that led to the corridor.

'I know this man,' a voice suddenly said.

Although it had been said quietly, everyone in the room heard it and turned.

Archer was staring intently at the suspect. He was the one who'd spoken.

'What was that?' Cobb asked.

The younger man turned to him.

'I know this man, sir. I've seen him before.'

'What? Where?'

'I don't know. But I've definitely encountered him in the past. Ever since I saw his photo this morning, I've been trying to figure it out. It's been bothering me all day.'

'You're sure?'

'Positive.'

There was a long pause.

'Go in,' Cobb said.

Archer turned to him, unsure.

'Sir?'

'Go in. Talk to him. Maybe you'll recall where you know him, or how. Maybe he'll remember you.'

Archer saw Frost rolling his eyes by the door, the grey-haired veteran dismissive of the younger man.

'You're wasting your time,' he declared. 'The guy won't say a word. Not yet. Give him a couple of hours to sweat, then maybe he'll talk.'

Ignoring him, Archer turned to Mac for reassurance. His was the only opinion in the room aside from Cobb's and Porter's that he really cared about.

The older man looked at him and nodded.

'You heard the man. Do it, Archer.'

TEN

The suspect didn't look up as Archer entered the room.

The young officer closed the door quietly then took a seat in the empty chair Frost had vacated. On the desk in front of him, he saw that the photocopy detailing the nine suspects had been laid in an open folder. Archer didn't need to look at it for reference.

He already knew this guy was Number Three.

There was a moment's silence.

'How are you doing?' Archer asked. *Idiot*, he thought to himself instantly. *How do you think he's doing?* He paused and mentally cut himself some momentary slack. He'd never done this before and the atmosphere in the room was tense. He felt uncomfortable too, especially since he knew his bosses were watching him through the glass, Frost obviously dismissing him as just some rookie kid, wet behind the ears and fresh from the farm.

'You want some tea? Coffee?' he asked.

For the first time, Number Three flicked his eyes up, looking across the table at Archer through his hair.

Archer saw a moment of confusion, then a glimmer of recognition in the other man's eyes.

'I know you,' the terrorist said, in a raspy voice, his eyes narrowing. 'Your name's Sam Archer.'

'How the hell did you know that?' Archer asked, baffled.

The guy seemed as if he was about to speak, but stopped himself, and didn't respond.

Archer asked him again. 'How the hell did you know that?'

Neither man had glanced away. They continued to stare each other down, like two boxers across the ring before the bell, or rivals in a poker game.

Archer looked at him, silent, waiting.

Then finally, the suspect replied.

'Holloway Under-Sixteens. First team. You played in goal.'

And in that moment, everything fell into place in Archer's brain like a jigsaw, as if someone had just shaken the box and all the pieces suddenly fell into position forming a picture in his memory.

Holy shit.

We went to school together.

'That's what it was,' Archer said. 'I knew I recognised you. You were a few years behind me. Your name's Patel.'

The guy gave a slight nod, but said nothing more. There was a pause, and the nostalgia in the room quickly faded. Two old acquaintances who now had nothing more to say to each other. Nothing in common, save a brief part of their history. Two men sitting only a foot away from each other, but worlds apart in their morals and beliefs.

'So what the hell are you doing here?' Archer asked. 'How did you get mixed up in all this?'

The terrorist lifted his gaze and glared back at him.

Didn't respond.

'C'mon, talk to me,' Archer said. 'What are you hoping to achieve?'

Silence.

'People change. We're not kids at school anymore,' Patel replied, quietly.

'Yeah. Guys like us became doctors, or teachers. We're all getting married. Having children. None of us are plotting bombings, becoming terrorists, making home-made explosives.'

Patel didn't respond..

'You killed a man too. You butchered him like a pig.'

Patel shook his head, but still said nothing.

'So you didn't kill him?' Archer asked.

Silence.

'Look, this is your chance to tell the truth. You know what we found in that house. Bomb materials, coke, guns. Add them up and that's some serious jail time. But if you get convicted for a murder charge that severe, you'll be going away for life, no question.'

Archer's old schoolmate looked up.

'It wasn't me,' he said. 'I didn't do it.'

'Well who did?'

'He brought him in. Told us to stay where we were downstairs or we'd be joining the rat on the rail.'

'Who's *he*? The guy you say did it?'

The terrorist shook his head, looking straight up at the police officer.

'You don't have a clue, do you?' he said. 'You've no idea what's coming. It's going to be a long night for you, Archer.'

A silence fell. Archer stared at the hostile young man sat across the table. He hadn't seen him in a few years, but the teenager he remembered had been charismatic and friendly.

He looked at the man opposite him and could hardly believe it was the same guy.

'Why are you doing this?' Archer asked, quietly.

Across the table, the terrorist looked back at him, expressionless.

'*Why?*'

'Yeah. Why? I know you. You were a good kid.'

Number Three shook his head; his eyes dropped to the floor.

'You got a girlfriend, Archer? A brother? Sister?'

'Why do you ask?'

'You remember the riots?'

'Of course.'

'On the second night, a group of them ran into my dad on the street. He was on his way home from work. Minding his own business, causing no trouble. They killed him. Beat him to death. Stamped and kicked his skull in.'

He paused.

'A witness said they were laughing as they did it. They even mugged him when he was unconscious. These were all local guys. Born and bred in the area.'

Silence.

'Together, do you know how long they got? Six years. For manslaughter. They killed my father and four of them get six years in a joint sentence.'

Turning his head, he suddenly hawked and spat on the floor, clearing the bile from his throat.

'Now what if that was someone *you* cared about?' he asked Archer.

'I'm sorry,' Archer replied quietly. Patel didn't react. 'But you think hurting more people is going to help?'

Looking up, Number Three fixed the policeman's gaze.

He had a strange look in his eyes, almost feral.

'Look around you, Archer,' he said. 'Open your eyes. This is a war. You're part of it, whether you like it or not.'

'Bullshit. I don't buy that. Wars have soldiers. Heroes. You're a terrorist. A coward.'

The suspect glared across the table at him.

'But you think you're one of the good guys, don't you?' Archer followed. 'So does that make me the bad guy?'

A pause.

'It's like any war, Archer,' Patel replied. 'It depends which side of the table you're on.'

Silence.

'Dominick Farha. Where is he?'

'I don't know.'

'No idea?'

'No clue. And I don't want to know where he is either.'

'Why?'

'Because he scares the shit out of me.'

Patel paused for a long moment.

'I thought we were cool, but that guy, he's got a screw loose. He's nuts, bipolar or something. The guy in the bathroom, he did that. That was all him.'

The thought of the man seemed to produce a strange reaction in Patel. Archer saw the angry glare in his eyes momentarily subside, like a wave pulling back from the shore. He looked up at the blond police officer, his old acquaintance.

'Look, we go back a long way, so I'm going to warn you. Let him go, Archer. Seriously. He's connected to the kind of people that you've only ever seen in nightmares.'

He paused.

'You keep chasing him, and he'll kill you and everyone around you. You'll never see it coming. Not with the guys he's associated with.'

Silence. Archer held his gaze.

'Let him go,' Patel finished.

A silence fell, but the terrorist's warning hung in the air. Archer could tell Patel was done talking.

'Thanks for the advice,' Archer said. 'But I'll take my chances.'

Without a word, Archer rose and moved to the door. But as he grabbed the handle, he suddenly remembered one last question, the most obvious one of all.

He turned back to the man at the desk.

'Just tell me one more thing.'

Number Three looked up at him from his chair.

'What was your target?' Archer asked.

There was a long pause.

'Paddington.'

Archer blinked.

'Tonight?'

The guy nodded. '6pm. Rush hour.'

Archer glanced at his watch.

That would have been fifteen minutes from now.

Shaking his head, he twisted the door handle and walked out of the cell.

Seventeen miles away, Dominick Farha was perched anxiously on the edge of the bed in his hotel room. The sun hadn't yet dipped over the horizon but he'd pulled the curtains shut regardless. The television on the cabinet in front of him was still showing footage of the house raid from earlier in the day. There hadn't been any further updates to the story, but to Farha, each minute that had passed since he'd first seen the report had felt as long as an hour.

Three of the team had been compromised. *Had to be expected,* he realised, especially considering who the three recruits were. They weren't high value, just dumb cannon fodder, which was exactly why none of them had been given priority targets. They were set to hit King's Cross, Paddington and Euston stations at 6 pm, just a quarter of an hour from now. Collateral damage, at best, serving as a distraction so the other members of the cell could pursue the more important targets amidst all the chaos and panic. It was a shame that they'd never even made it to the stations, but then again, the rest of the cell could surely make up for the losses if they kept their shit together and did their jobs properly.

As he watched the repeated footage on the screen showing the exterior of the house and all the police gathered on the street, he felt his mood lift for a moment.

He realised the cops would have found the rat in the bathroom. Dominick and his uncle shared a lot of differences, but one thing they both had in common was their shared hatred of government officials, especially informants. Dominick had taken out all of his frustrations and anger from the past year on the guy, a man he'd trusted. His mouth duct-taped, his hands cuffed, the guy had bucked and thrashed like an unbroken stallion as Farha went to work on him. Especially when the knife started approaching his groin.

Chuckling, he rose and moved to the window. Hooking his finger behind the curtain, he peered outside through the gap. He felt his brief good mood fade. The unexpected raid had left him feeling agitated and paranoid again.

The wait was agonising. He couldn't afford to leave the room and take any stupid risks like going out in public, yet here he felt like a sitting duck. His mind started playing out scenarios; he'd seen on the report that two of the suspects had been taken into custody for questioning.

Right now, there could be a task force in the lobby, making their way up to him, tipped off by one of the clowns from the house.

The first he'd know about it would be when they blasted open the door and either shot or arrested him.

Taking a deep breath, he forced his heart-rate to slow, willing himself to calm down and relax.

No one knew he was here. He was within mere hours of escape, of salvation, of protection.

Besides, I can't leave yet, he remembered.

I'm expecting a guest.

The moment the thought crossed his mind, there was a knock on the door, right on cue. Dominick didn't panic. He already knew who it was. He checked his watch; *5:45 pm. Right on time*, which boded well for future events planned for that evening.

He moved to the door, but checked himself and peered through the spy-hole first. *No stupid risks.*

He saw who was outside, and relaxed, twisting the handle and pulling it open.

A woman was standing there. She was young, maybe nineteen or twenty, with long dark hair and big, innocent brown eyes the colour of mahogany. They lit up when she saw Dominick and she smiled widely, delighted to see him.

Smiling back and taking her hand, he drew her into the room; before shutting the door, he stuck his head out into the corridor, checking left and right, just to make sure she hadn't been followed.

No stupid risks.

It was empty. No one was there.

He allowed himself a brief smile, then closed the door quickly.

He and the girl had business to attend to.

At the moment that Dominick Farha shut the hotel room door, a whistle blew in a stadium across the city and the Premier League derby game between Arsenal and Tottenham Hotspur was underway.

It was the 5:45pm kick-off, right on schedule, the match taking place on Arsenal's home patch, the Emirates Stadium. Despite the chilly December air, the atmosphere inside the ground was electric; there were

60,361 seats in the stands and not a single one was empty. The supporters packed into the ground were split almost exactly down the middle, half white, half red, half Tottenham, half Arsenal. The fans cheered and roared like two Celtic tribes standing opposite each other before battle as the ball started moving around on the pitch. The rivalry between the two teams was as old as the game itself.

But there was one man who wasn't paying attention to the game.

He was staring straight ahead, his eyes fixed and unmoving, as if he was in a trance.

He was in the middle of the Clock End, the South Stand, behind the Tottenham goal, and stood out as the only fan in sight not wearing an Arsenal shirt or scarf.

Despite the winter air, beads of sweat trickled down his brow as if he was in a sauna, like raindrops sliding down a window pane.

His hands jammed in his pockets, the guy stood so still he didn't even blink.

It was as if he was made of stone.

On the field, Arsenal began to build an attack from the back. They were a team renowned for the intricacy and technical mastery of their passing and attacking play, and this sequence was no different. With great skill, the players cut and weaved, tapping passes then dashing forward to elude the Tottenham defence. Slowly, they were making their way down the pitch.

Towards the man in the coat.

The Arsenal fans around him had started raising the volume of their cheering and chanting, as the attack started to show promise.

60,360 sets of eyes watching one ball.

At that moment, the man in the coat started to mutter something.

Something memorised.

A creed.

A prayer.

He pulled one of his hands free from his pocket.

He was holding a switch.

It was connected to a black wire that ran into his coat.

On the pitch, one of the midfield players hit a perfect through-ball. Arsenal's striker ran onto the pass. All alone, he bore down on the Tottenham goal-mouth with only the keeper to beat. Feinting a shot, he dodged past him. The open goal was to his left. All he needed to do was tuck it into the net.

He kicked the ball, as the crowd gasped, holding their breath like the split-second before a crescendo.

The man in the coat did the same.

He closed his eyes.

He pressed the button.

ELEVEN

Inside his office at 10 Downing Street, the Prime Minister was also standing still, staring straight ahead. He was in front of his desk, leaning back against the polished wood, deep in thought.

This whole thing with the suicide bombing cell was a nightmare situation and the circumstances leading up to the current police operation were consuming his every thought. Although three of the suspects had been located during the day, there were still six of them out there, and now the sun had gone down.

One thing was for sure; it was going to be one hell of a long night.

He glanced at the clock hanging on the wall to his right, an expensive Swiss model, Roman numerals mounted on an ivory white backing all surrounded by highly-polished gold plated metal.

The slender black dials were pointing at *5:47pm*.

Just over six hours till midnight and the New Year.

The Prime Minister shook his head. *What a way to close this one out.*

It had been a rough twelve months for him and his cabinet. Elections were due to start in April, with opposition leaders already campaigning around the country for the right to take over the helm. The proud man leaning against the desk sighed. He was desperate to continue, to make a difference. In his head, he thought he might have a chance of being re-elected for another four years, but in his heart he knew it was unlikely to happen. And if anything went wrong tonight, it would be the final nail in the coffin of his tenure.

He closed his eyes, trying to think. The room was silent, save for one constant, quiet relentless noise, the Swiss clock on the wall.

It ticked away mercilessly like a metronome.

Or a bomb.

The PM had seen the breaking news reporting a raid in North London earlier in the day, just around lunchtime. He'd spoken to Director Cobb, who'd confirmed that two of the nine suspects had been arrested and one of them killed. Thankfully however, none of the police officers were hurt; that was the most important thing, and the good news. The bad news was that the house hadn't been on any list, or even on anyone's radar. If it hadn't been for sheer blind luck and an inquisitive, public-spirited old lady, they never would have known the three suspects were there.

Every other raid conducted across the city by the other counter-terrorist and police teams had been unsuccessful. Every single one. Which meant six other members of the cell were still out there. And no one seemed to have any idea where any of them were.

There was a knock at the door. He opened his eyes.

'Come in.'

The door opened, and a woman in her mid-thirties stepped inside. She was cradling a stack of folders in the crook of her arm, a warm smile on her face as she saw her husband. For a brief moment, the Prime Minister felt his mood lift. It was his wife, Jennifer. She closed the door behind her and moved towards him.

'Pete gave me these to pass on to you,' she said, placing the stack of folders on the desk beside the PM. 'Reports from today.'

He didn't respond; she noticed him looking over at the clock.

'Everything alright?' she asked.

He nodded and forced a smile, but it was half-hearted and unconvincing. She moved across in front of him, up close, reaching up to adjust his tie.

'Look at the state of you,' she chided. Pausing, she read her husband's mind. 'They won't succeed, sweetheart. Our best men are out there right now, searching for them. And I hate to say it, but something like this was bound to happen at some point. It's the way things are now. You know who we are. Our standing in the world. We'll always have enemies.'

He sighed, shaking his head.

'Do we even know who this enemy is?' he asked her. 'Pete told me earlier that six of these men were born and bred right here in the UK. How is that possible? Are we doing something wrong? What happened along the way that they would even consider doing something like this?'

'You can't sit here and ponder their motives. You'll drive yourself insane.'

He nodded; he knew she was right. But he couldn't shake his malaise. It almost felt as if all the errors and mistakes he'd made in the last three years were culminating tonight, like some gargantuan trial or test he had to pass.

He bowed his head and sighed.

'The people who've held this office before me led this country through its darkest times,' he said quietly. 'Endless conflicts. Two World Wars. The Falklands. The Gulf. Afghanistan. They knew who the opposition was.

The soldiers knew where to stand their ground and fight the enemy. Mostly.'

He paused.

'But how do we fight these men? Where? Out there, on our streets? And what do I tell the country? That we're at war with ourselves?'

He shook his head.

'And how on earth do we stop an enemy who actually wants to die?'

The last sentence stayed in the air. But rather than withdrawing, Jenny pierced his gaze, her soft demeanour hardening.

'By granting his wish,' she said, quietly.

Silence.

Suddenly, there was a hurried knock at the door; in almost the same instant, it was pushed open. It was Rogers. He looked pale, an expression on his normally amiable face that the PM hadn't seen before. His wife saw it too.

'Goodness, Pete, you look dreadful. Whatever is the matter?' she asked.

The Prime Minister stayed silent.

He knew something terrible had just happened.

Inside Room 418 of the Heathrow Marriott Hotel, Dominick Farha was standing by the window again, pushing back the curtain an inch with his fore-finger and scanning outside.

On the bed behind him, his new companion was hard at work. The young woman had a white dress made of thick cotton laid across her lap. Beside her, the holdall containing the vast quantity of bricks of C4 explosive rested against a pillow.

She lifted a brick from the bag and slid it into a compartment sewn into the gown. It was a perfect fit, snug and secure. Beside it, five other bricks had already been tucked into the glove-like pockets. She raised the dress in front of her, testing the weight, lifting the garment up and down.

She smiled.

'It worked. It holds.'

Farha turned. 'Good. Keep going.'

He saw her smile up at him.

'You look beautiful,' he added, as an afterthought.

That had the desired effect and she returned to her work with renewed passion, desperate to please him. Dominick watched her, keeping his thoughts to himself.

He'd met her a few months ago in a book shop in the city. He'd been trying to find a manual on home-made explosives and had found one under *Science*, written by a guy named Stoffel. The girl had been standing a few feet away from him in the same aisle. He'd sensed she was checking him out and he decided on a whim to strike up a conversation with her. The conversation progressed to coffee, and soon they were meeting up repeatedly during the next few weeks.

At the time Dominick had been in the midst of identifying and persuading willing recruits play an active part in his suicide bombing plan, but was finding the long drawn-out process frustrating and tedious. Convincing them wasn't the hard part; he'd always possessed a certain amount of charisma, able to turn on the charm whenever he needed, and could almost always get people to do what he wanted. Finding a sufficient number of the bombers was the issue.

During that scouting phase he'd been playing along with the girl and feigning interest, more as a way of alleviating the crushing boredom than anything else. She'd fallen for him hard which was irritating, making him feel like a rock with a limpet attached.

But then he'd had an idea.

He got her drunk one night, then after they slept together, he brought up the real reason why he was in the UK. He'd watched her response closely; if she reacted badly, he had a pillow ready to suffocate her. But she'd been interested. He'd adlibbed his way through the next part, and was amazed how well it worked. He outlined a plan, and she agreed to it the next day, without a query. He realised she was so infatuated, she'd do anything he wanted. All he had to do was tell her he loved her every now and then, and she was like putty in his hands.

Looking down, he saw her continuing her work.

He couldn't remember her name.

But suddenly, he remembered something else. He checked his watch.

'Oh shit.'

Moving from the window, he grabbed the remote control from the bed and flicked on the television. Seeing as he'd been watching it earlier, the first channel that came up was the news.

However, they were no longer showing footage from the house raid.

The shot was now inside the studio, two concerned-looking newsreaders staring grimly into the camera, their mouths moving in silence on the muted TV as they talked to the nation.

A new bulletin was running across the bottom of the screen.

Breaking News: Explosion at Emirates Stadium, hundreds feared dead.

Farha froze.

He felt a shiver of excitement.

He did it.

Holy shit, he did it.

He'd been worried that the guy would never make it inside the stadium, that he'd get stopped at the entrance. But he'd made it.

Turning to the young woman whose name he couldn't remember, Farha grinned.

'It's begun.'

Across the city, another man was watching that same news report.

He was standing outside a bar in a shopping centre in Angel, North London. Ahead of him, the pub was quickly filling up, partygoers and revellers, all of them having a good time and getting an early start in to the New Year celebrations.

The man however, was all alone, with no friends around him.

Taking a sip of the soft drink he'd just ordered, he paid no attention to the festivities inside the pub. He was only interested in the series of televisions mounted behind the bar, thirty feet away.

A news report had just flashed onto the screen. The volume was off, so most of the people inside hadn't noticed it yet, but gradually they each started to pause mid-conversation, attention turning to the television monitors.

The man glanced at his watch.

5:50pm.

Give it ten minutes, then leave.

Glancing down, he checked something else. Two black holdalls were resting by his feet. Each one was packed full and weighing close to forty pounds, zipped up tight and seemingly innocuous.

In ten minutes, the man would finish his drink and get the hell out of there.

The bags, however, were staying behind.

TWELVE

Across town, the entrance doors to the ARU burst open as if there was a hurricane blowing through the building and officers from the task force sprinted out into the car park, racing towards the three Unit vehicles parked across the tarmac.

Archer and Porter were running side-by-side, zipping up their tactical vests while cradling two MP5 sub-machine guns. Ahead of them, Mac was already standing by one of the black Fords.

'*Let's go! Let's go! Move it!*' he shouted.

Archer and Porter arrived at the car. The blond officer yanked open the rear door and climbed into the back seat as Porter jumped in behind the wheel.

'Where the hell is Chalky?' Mac shouted, to no one in particular.

The two men didn't need to respond. The Unit sergeant had already spotted him.

'*Chalky!*' he bellowed across the parking lot. 'Pull your finger out!'

The dark-haired officer was lagging behind, just now passing out of the entrance. Mac's words shifted him into another gear, however, and he sprinted forward, jumping into the back seat beside Archer.

The car was already moving as he pulled the door shut, and the wheels squealed as they bit down into the concrete; the vehicle shot forward, moving out of the car park and speeding off down the road towards the stadium.

The other two cars followed close behind in hot pursuit.

A single vehicle passed them by the turn to the car park, quietly pulling into the parking lot. It was a small dark-blue BMW, immaculately clean, fresh from some rental company. The car moved to an empty space with VISITOR printed on the tarmac in white letters. The driver applied the handbrake and killed the engine, then stepped out and shut the door behind him.

He was a strongly built man in his early thirties, stern dark features with a tanned face. Not wasting any time, he walked swiftly across the tarmac to the entrance, pulling open the door.

Inside, a detective was sitting behind the front desk. By the time he looked up, the newcomer had already pulled ID from his pocket which he flipped open.

'Special Agent Rivers, DEA,' the dark-haired newcomer said. 'Director Cobb's expecting me.'

Across the Channel, the private jet carrying Henry and his three men was just coming in to land, the plane gliding down towards a deserted airfield outside Paris. There was a jolt as the wheels hit the tarmac and the jet rolled forward, eventually slowing and coming to a halt.

They'd arrived.

From his seat, Henry glanced out of the window to his left. In the distance, he could see the golden lights of Paris, the unmistakeable outline of the Eiffel Tower, but flicking his dark eyes down he turned his attention to the airfield immediately outside the window. It was completely empty, save for a black Escalade waiting for them on the edge of the tarmac, parked a sufficient distance from the jet so there was no risk of a collision.

Grunting, Henry hauled himself out of his seat and moved to the exit. The pilot had pressed a mechanism to open the door and release the stairs, and they unfolded slowly to the runway. From this vantage point, he narrowed his eyes and took another look around the airfield.

It was deserted and quiet, surrounded by forestry and hedge growth. A good choice for future events planned that evening.

Once again, Faris had done well.

He gripped the rail as he lumbered down the stairs, followed by his two enforcers. Behind them, Faris was staying on the jet. Once they were gone, the plane would be re-routed to London to collect Dominick. Henry and the two meatheads moved across the tarmac, arriving at the car and climbing inside. There was a driver behind the wheel, a man who worked for a trusted associate and he'd already fired the engine.

Without a word the man took off the handbrake, and they headed through the exit gates and onto the road towards Paris.

As they gathered speed, Henry felt his phone vibrate in his pocket, his private line.

Taking it from his pocket, he pressed *Answer.*

'You're not going to believe this,' the voice on the other end said. *'A bomb just went off at a football stadium in London.'*

Henry paused. He felt his mood darken.

'How many dead?' he asked.

'No more than two hundred.'

Henry's free hand clenched with anger, the knuckles on the chubby fingers turning white.

Just when he thought his nephew couldn't get any more stupid, he had completely outdone himself.

'Which stadium?' he asked quietly.

'*The Emirates. Arsenal's joint. Looks like it was a suicide attack.*'

Despite his rage, Henry breathed a small sigh of relief. Not everything was lost. But his idiot nephew had just complicated things tenfold.

'*We've got problems*,' said the voice, echoing the concerns in Henry's mind. Their operation would have been relatively straightforward and simple before. Now it was going to get considerably harder, and all thanks to the inanity of his nephew. *If it even takes place*, Henry thought. The complications that had just been layered to their plans were a potential nightmare.

'Wait and see how it plays out,' he told the person on the other end. 'And get back to me.'

The call cut out and Henry returned the phone to his pocket, feeling his mood blacken as dark as the night outside the car.

He sat in silence as the car moved down the road towards Paris.

Once again, Dominick had screwed up.

And that meant someone was going to die tonight.

On the lower level of the Armed Response Unit's headquarters, Frost was sitting in the interrogation room again, trying to sweat some more information out of Number Three. He'd been next door with Cobb and the American DEA agent when news broke on the explosion at the stadium. As the task force had rushed out of the door to get over there as quickly as possible, Cobb had sent Frost straight back inside to the suspect. He wanted answers and he was going to get them.

Frost watched the suspect closely. The guy's stance in the chair had changed since they'd last been in this position. He'd sat back, no longer looking at the ground, but his eyes were still half-open, staring at the desktop through the matted hair that hung lankly over his forehead. Frost had been shocked when the young officer from the task force had got the terrorist to open up; in truth, it had unsettled him. Cobb had brought him in specifically for the brunt of the interrogation tasks; that was his job. He was expected to deliver, and didn't want to become surplus to requirements around here. It was time to earn his pay-check.

'This whole situation just escalated,' Frost said. 'One of your friends just blew himself up at the Emirates during the game. He's killed over a hundred people, probably more. Which means this just went from a criminal conspiracy to an actual terrorist attack. And that makes *you* the proud property of Her Majesty's Government.'

He let his words sink in. The young man in front of him didn't seem to react, but Frost saw him shuffle into his seat slightly.

Push him.

Don't give him room to breathe.

'Right now, you're a done deal. Twenty years, minimum. That takes you past your fortieth birthday. And that's assuming the judge is in a good mood- you could even get life if he's not. And don't go looking for sympathy anywhere. People in this country may have their differences, but the one thing we all hate is terrorism. It's been that way for hundreds of years. Why

111

do you think people burn a Guy Fawkes effigy every year?'

The suspect shifted in his seat again.

Frost could see he was sweating, and kept up the heat.

'Don't be fooled. This isn't like the movies where you serve two years of your sentence and get off for *good behaviour,* or whatever they call it in Hollywood. You're going to serve every minute of those twenty. I'll make sure you do. But if you start talking, I can help you. I'm one of the only people left who can. And luckily for you, I'm one of the few people left who's actually going to bother.'

There was a pause. He observed the terrorist closely.

He had him.

Frost didn't speak further.

Just waited for the inevitable.

'I don't know anything,' Number Three finally muttered.

Frost took the opening, pressing him. 'You need to give me something, kid. Anything. What do you know about Dominick Farha?'

The suspect flicked a glance up at Frost and started to shiver slightly, as sweat streamed down his brow.

'Not much. We met through a friend. That guy. Number Eight,' he said, nodding to the page on the desk.

He couldn't point. His hands were still cuffed behind his back.

Frost looked down at Number Eight's photograph. 'How long ago was this?'

'About six months.'

The guy paused. Frost saw him fighting back tears; he was starting to fold. This kid was in way too far over his head, and by the looks of things the reality of the situation was just starting to sink in. The tough guy who'd been sitting in his chair an hour ago was gone.

'Dominick was good to me,' he continued, his voice trembling. 'No one cared about my dad. He listened, set me straight. Told me who the real enemy was.'

'So the next logical step was strapping a bomb to your chest,' Frost said. 'Let me guess, that was his idea?'

The suspect didn't respond.

'So would he be joining you in this venture?' Frost asked.

The guy nodded slowly. 'That's what he said.'

'OK, so where is he?'

Silence.

'You know officers raided his apartment earlier. He wasn't there. It looks like he might have left the country.'

He looked across the table at the suspect, who was fighting his emotions. The hard-faced, hostile young man brought into the cell a few hours ago had vanished, replaced by a scared, confused kid. He didn't know anything they could use.

Frost could see that clearly now.

Taking a deep breath, the grey-haired detective rose, stretching his arms over his head. He closed the folder on the desk in front of him.

'You know, I think you're telling the truth. You don't know anything useful. From my point of view, it seems as though you were so angry and hell-bent on revenge for what happened to your dad that you never stopped and thought clearly for a moment. And Farha played you like a piano. And now you're in here, and he's out there, probably on a beach sipping a cocktail somewhere. But then again, I think you're starting to figure that out yourself.'

He paused.

'And by the way, what do you think your dad would make of all this?'

Silence.

Frost closed his folder and picked it up. Walking to the door, he stopped by the wall and turned.

'Happy New Year, kid. I hope it was worth it.'

Twisting the handle, he walked out.

His head bowed, the would-be terrorist clenched his jaw as tears streamed silently down his face. All the anger and blinding rage that had soaked his body for the past sixteen months had washed away in an instant, replaced instead by fear and perspective. Suddenly, he could see everything clearly. All his defences crumbled, like a sand-castle in the tide.

And he wept.

Upstairs, Rivers had been shown in by the guy on the front desk. The man had been notified by Cobb that he was expecting the American, so the desk detective had led him upstairs then left him alone. The American had been forced to leave his sidearm at the front desk though. No weapons of any kind were allowed on the first floor.

The DEA agent had taken up a spot to the side of the ops room, well out of the way. He'd caught on the car radio on the way over here that there'd been an explosion at a soccer ground across the city.

The scene in front of him confirmed it.

Analysts were rushing everywhere, talking into phones and typing away on computers as they tried to pull up surveillance from outside the venue. Crawford had mentioned that the detail had a ground team, but they didn't seem to be around. Rivers guessed they were in the black cars that he'd passed on the way into the parking lot.

Just as the fellow DEA agent's name entered his head, Rivers saw him appear from the stairs to his right. He was with a tall beleaguered-looking man who Rivers took to be Cobb, the leader of the Unit.

Crawford saw his man and approached swiftly. Behind him, a phone rang in Cobb's pocket, and he took it out, answering the call and striding to his office, closing the door. Crawford extended his hand and Rivers shook it. It was only twenty four hours since they'd last seen each other, but a familiar face in strange surroundings was always welcome.

'Bad timing, huh?' Rivers said.

Crawford nodded. 'You can say that again. A terrorist just blew up a soccer ground.'

'I heard. Casualties?'

'Not known for sure so far. But over a hundred at least.'

'Shit. Any further threats?'

Crawford looked at him as if he was a fool. Then he realised Rivers had come straight here from De Gaulle. *He's got no idea what's going on.* All he'd been concerned with today was closing out their operation on Henry, staying in contact with Agents Flynn and Brody to catch the drug buy at the airfield.

Crawford nodded slowly, then led the fellow DEA agent into the empty Briefing Room.

'I'll update you on the situation. Take a seat.'

He walked over to the noticeboards on the right side of the room as Rivers sat in one of the empty chairs. The photographs of the nine men were still pinned to the wall.

The newcomer took a seat, looking at the mug-shots stuck to the board.

'Get comfortable,' said Crawford. 'This is going to take a while.'

THIRTEEN

The black ARU Ford carrying Porter, Mac, Archer and Chalky weaved in and out of traffic as it sped towards the stadium. They were getting close. Outside the window, hordes of fans were streaming along the pavement, fleeing the scene. They all looked traumatised, children crying, adults beside them wide-eyed with shock and fear as they raced away from the stadium.

Behind the wheel Porter skilfully manoeuvred through the streets, the flashing front and rear fender lights on the vehicle helping him forge a path through the traffic. The three officers beside him were each adjusting a throat microphone that they would use to communicate on the ground. With a small mic strapped around the neck, an earpiece tucked into their ear, they could talk to each other by pushing a pressel switch clipped to the front of the tactical vest.

Swerving to avoid two Tottenham fans running across the road, Porter listened to an earpiece in his ear. Instead of his throat mic, he had a hands-free connected to his mobile phone.

He turned to the men beside him.

'Nikki found him on the cameras outside the entrance gates,' he said. 'It was Number Five.'

Mac hit the dashboard in front of him violently. *'Shit!'*

'Estimated dead?' Archer asked, as he finished adjusting the strap on his mic.

Porter turned a hard left, listening as Nikki spoke into his ear from the other end of the call.

'A hundred and fifty. Same again wounded.'

Archer stared at him.

The London Underground and bus bombings of 2005 had killed just over fifty people. That was a horrific disaster, one that would go down in history as one of the darkest days in the nation's history.

The casualties here were three times that.

Outside, the streets and pavements were getting clogged with more and more fans fleeing the football ground. They were getting close.

As he finished fixing his gear, Archer suddenly noticed that Chalky was unusually quiet. He hadn't said a word the entire trip.

Turning, he saw that his friend looked pale. And he noticed something else.

'Hey.'

Chalky looked at him.

Archer pointed to the MP5 sub-machine gun resting on his friend's lap.

'You left the safety off,' Archer told him.

Chalky glanced down. His friend was right. The weapon was set to *Fire*, a round in the chamber as it lay on his lap.

The angle it was resting meant the barrel was aimed straight at Archer's ribcage.

If it had gone off, he'd have been killed instantly.

'Oh. Thanks,' Chalky muttered, correcting his mistake and clicking on the safety catch.

Archer gave him a look, swallowing down his anger as Porter stopped the car and pulled on the handbrake.

Without a word, the four police officers stepped out of the Ford.

And the quiet of the car was instantly replaced by a cacophony of sirens, screaming and shouting.

They each slammed their doors and came to stand in a line, facing the car park. The four of them were momentarily rooted to the spot as they surveyed the scene before them for the first time.

'*Jesus,*' Archer muttered.

It was complete pandemonium.

Outside the big stadium there were fans everywhere, fleeing like ants from a nest as they streamed from every exit. Ambulances were scattered all over the car park, their paramedics working frantically amongst the wounded, a number that was growing by the minute. Those able to walk helped carry those who couldn't as they staggered towards safety; the scene resembled something out of a war movie.

Archer could see many of them were wearing Arsenal and Tottenham shirts singed and spattered with blood.

And above it all, a chorus of screaming and shouting filled the cold air, making the hairs on his neck stand up.

Behind the four officers the other two cars from the Unit pulled up to an abrupt halt beside the other parked Ford. The doors opened and the remaining six officers ran over, led by Deakins and Fox. Each man was fully-equipped with both the throat mic and MP5 sub-machine gun; they gathered in a semi-circle around Mac, waiting for instructions.

He turned to face them

'*Listen up!*' he ordered. He turned to Fox. 'Foxy, take Spitz and Mace. Go and check the other stands. Look everywhere. Rubbish bins, dressing rooms, offices, toilets, I don't care. This could only be half the job.'

Fox nodded, without a word.

He turned and ran towards the stadium with Spitz and Mason beside him, dodging those rushing in the opposite direction.

Mac turned to the remaining six men before him.

'The rest of you, stay out here,' he ordered. 'Move through the crowd. Help the medics and the other coppers. Gather the wounded, try to maintain calm and keep your eyes open for anything suspicious. Stay on the radio and stay mobile. *Move!*'

The men nodded and turned instantly, dispersing swiftly into the traumatised crowd.

Across the stadium car park, the young doctor called Hannah Gibbs was working flat out. When she'd seen her name down for the New Year's Eve shift three days ago at St Mary's Hospital, she knew she was in for a long night. Most people who celebrated the New Year were just out to have a good time; they had some drinks, had some fun and partied away until the early hours. But then again wherever there's alcohol, trouble soon follows, and the shift was renowned as an especially hectic and busy one with all the drunken injured stumbling in.

Two years shy of thirty, Gibbs had finished her degree in medicine at Nottingham University some four years ago, then moved south and taken up a post at St Mary's. Although she'd been there for less than four years, she thought she'd seen pretty much everything. Gunshot wounds. Stabbings.

But as she pushed the wheeled stretcher and looked at the crowd around her, she realised this was beyond anything she could have ever imagined.

She was in the middle of the car park, trying to make her way through the mass of wounded and emergency services who were using the tarmac as a sort of makeshift triage. She was attempting to push a gurney holding a female Arsenal fan she'd been treating who'd been close to the blast.

The woman was in a bad way; she'd been standing just ahead of the explosion, about seventy feet away with her back turned. It was a miracle that she was still alive. Her Arsenal shirt was torn, singed and covered with blood, her back riddled with nails and chippings of glass, some of it lodged in her vertebrae and spine. She was in such a critical condition that every second counted. A moment's delay, or hesitation, and she'd die in the ambulance or on the operating table. The clock was ticking, and Gibbs had to get her out of here immediately if she had any chance of making it.

Looking ahead, she saw an ambulance with its rear doors open, a slot available. Gibbs rushed forward as fast as she could, praying that someone wouldn't get there first and steal the spot. She made it. A paramedic was inside the vehicle, clearing space, he'd seen her coming.

Gibbs had already hooked the injured woman's vein up to an IV which she passed up to him carefully.

'This one?' he asked, hurriedly, looking at the injured woman lying on the gurney.

'Severe head and back trauma,' said Gibbs.' Multiple injuries. Nails, shards of glass in her neck and spine. She needs to get to theatre asap.'

He nodded as another man appeared from the side of the ambulance. The driver. He ran to the other end of the bed and together, the two men lifted it and pushed it into the ambulance, locking it in place.

The woman lying on the gurney didn't make a sound; Gibbs saw she'd passed out.

The driver slammed one of the doors, he reached for the other one, but Gibbs suddenly spotted something and grabbed his arm.

'Wait!' she told him. '*Hey!*'

She called to four wounded fans, who were slumped together on the kerb ten feet from the ambulance. They turned to look at her in unison, like four owls in a tree, dazed and wide-eyed with shock. Gibbs waved her arm frantically, beckoning them to come forward.

Climbing up and helping each other, they shuffled over.

'Get in,' Gibbs ordered, helping them one by one up into the back of the vehicle. When that was done, she turned back to the driver. 'We need to get as many of them out of here as fast as we can.'

The driver nodded and ran to the front door, climbing in behind the wheel. In the back, it was a tight squeeze, the group including the other paramedic gathered around the injured woman on the bed, but they'd all made it inside. Gibbs decided to jump in as well; she wanted to try and keep the woman alive until they could get her to hospital.

As she took a seat and reached forward to shut the door, she saw a news reporter hurrying into position on the tarmac close by. Amidst all the wounded and blood-stained medical help, she looked absurdly neat and polished, like a model who'd just stepped off the runway. The engine roared into life as the driver fired the ignition, jerking Gibbs back to the present.

She pulled the door shut.

With the siren blaring, the ambulance pulled out of the car park and sped off towards the hospital.

Outside the bar in the shopping centre in Angel, it was also time to leave.

The man standing beside the two black bags was still watching the screens inside. The volume was muted, so he couldn't hear the report, but he didn't need to. *A picture tells a thousand words.* The screen was showing all the wounded outside the stadium, smoke billowing from the South stand, people outside screaming and crying. It looked as if the whole place was packed with ambulance teams, paramedics and the injured.

Showtime.

Placing his glass down on a nearby table, he turned and walked away from the bar quickly.

No one was standing near him, so nobody noticed his departure.

Every person inside the pub was staring at the televisions, some covering their mouths with horror, all of them rooted to the spot as they watched the horrifying scenes unfold. The stadium was only a few miles from the bar; if they stepped outside they could probably hear the screaming in the distance.

Behind them all, outside the entrance, the two thickly packed holdalls rested against each other on the ground.

As he walked towards the exit, the man glanced back at the bags and smiled to himself.

Nobody would notice they were there.

Not yet.

FOURTEEN

Across the Channel, the Parisian café that Henry was using to kill time was located on Rue De Chevilly. Two miles from the city centre, it was convenient enough to allow easy access to the heart of Paris, yet was far enough out to give a sense of distance and escape from the hustle and bustle of the city.

The interior was warm and welcoming. Small tables and chairs were placed around the room, seemingly random yet adhering to some sort of pattern. A number of them were in use, patrons enjoying drinks and talking in quiet tones. In one corner, a number of people had gathered to watch two older men play a game of chess, the whole group engrossed.

Across the room, Henry leaned his considerable bulk back into his chair as he watched a television mounted on the wall in the café. Someone had switched the channel to *BBC World* and it was showing footage from outside the Emirates stadium.

Over a hundred feared dead, the banner headline was telling him.

Henry snorted. It was a shitty result. He knew from memory that the Emirates had over 60,000 seats inside. The ratio was one out of every six hundred killed. Only a hundred of them dead. A drop in the ocean. Pitiful. He wondered if Dominick was watching the report, wherever he was. He was probably pleased, figuring it was a good outcome, that it would buy him some credit whenever they next met. Instead of being sedated and waking up as he was being thrown into the Seine, he probably thought he'd be welcomed back into the fold with open arms, the prodigal son returned. Everything would be forgiven. Henry felt his mood darken at the thought of the boy.

He was in for a surprise.

His actions in New York had ended relations with a brother cartel which had been a major and profitable partner in recent years. Henry had worked tirelessly to set that one up. Not only had the boy cost his business a shitload of money, but one of the guys the moron whacked in the hotel was a *lugarteniente,* a lieutenant, one of the highest guys in the other group's organisation. No wonder the boy was desperate to get back in his uncle's good graces.

A waitress approached him, looking nervous. She was petite and slim like so many Europeans and held a pad and pencil in her slender hands, ready to take his order.

Before she had a chance to speak, he told her what he wanted.

'Coffee, three pastries. I'm hungry.'

He wasn't sure if she understood him, but he didn't care. He had a feeling she'd end up giving him what he wanted. People always did. Turning, he saw her cast anxious looks at the two giant men sitting fifteen feet away; they had their backs to her, watching the door. Henry saw her weighing up whether to approach them, but decided against it and hurried back behind the counter to fetch Henry's order.

Clever girl, he thought.

Tilting his wrist, Henry checked the time on his Rolex. He had a few hours to wait. Faris had gone with the jet and the pilot to London to fetch Dominick, the coke still inside the cabin. The business deal with the Albanians based here wasn't set to happen until after midnight, Paris time, and he was only twenty minutes from the airfield so it wouldn't take long to return. All he had to do now was sit back and wait for his cocaine to return and for his nephew to be brought into the café, served up like a sacrificial lamb.

The waitress reappeared carefully carrying a tray. She was quick, impressively so. She arrived at the table and laid down a full cup of coffee with a pot of milk and sugar, which were then joined by a plate holding three Danish pastries.

She stood up nervously, seeing if he was happy. Ignoring her, the feared drug lord grabbed one of the pastries and pushed it into his mouth, chomping down.

It was delicious, fresh from the bakery, and the frosting smeared over his lips as he munched down on the treat.

After watching him for a moment, the waitress turned and scurried away.

In London at that moment, the accident and emergency ward of St Mary's Hospital was in meltdown. Gurneys and the wounded were rolling in as if they were coming off a factory line. The most seriously injured were being seen to immediately, the rest tended to as soon as any staff became available. It was relentless work, as the injured just kept coming and coming.

By reception, the unfortunate Chief of Surgery for the evening, a grey-haired man in his fifties called Jeff Mays was desperately trying to direct operations and maintain some semblance of order.

Hannah Gibbs suddenly appeared, pushing her way through the double-doors. She still carried the IV hooked up to the injured woman on the bed, who remained unconscious and motionless on the frame. A group of medics rushed over. One of them picked up a medical

126

pad resting on the bed which Hannah had filled out on the brief journey over.

'She's critical,' Gibbs told him.

He nodded, rapidly reading the sheet, then followed the bed as it was wheeled away out of sight.

Gibbs paused for a split second, breathing hard. She turned, preparing to find another ambulance and head back to the scene. But as she went to walk back towards the entrance, she heard someone calling her name. Turning, she saw it was Chief Mays standing by the reception desk. He was beckoning her over.

She moved towards him, dodging a wounded Tottenham fan who was being helped into the ward.

'Have you seen Beth or Will?' Mays asked as she arrived by the counter, referring to two of her fellow medics who were on rotation for the evening's shift.

Gibbs thought for a moment, then shook her head.

'I checked in at 5.30. The next thing I knew, I was in an ambulance heading to the stadium.'

She thought for a moment.

'Come to think of it, I didn't see either one of them over there.'

'Well I'm not surprised. Neither one showed up for work. I'm not happy, Hannah.'

He looked at her like she knew something he didn't.

'Well, I haven't seen them in a couple of days,' she replied. 'I thought they had time off.'

'They haven't. And wherever they are they have an ambulance. I've been trying to call them but they won't pick up and answer.'

He shook his head.

'I don't know what they're playing at but I need every available pair of hands.'

Grabbing a pad from the desk, he passed it to Gibbs. It was a contact sheet, a list of phone numbers for everyone on shift tonight printed on the paper.

'Keep trying. Find out where they are,' he ordered. 'Tell them I don't even care that they're late, I just need them both here soon as possible.'

Hannah looked out the entrance and at the sheer volume of wounded in the room around her. She needed to get back to the stadium, not waste time doing errands like this.

'But Chief-,' she said.

But he was already walking away. Gibbs cursed under her breath, and snatching the phone she started dialling a number.

Despite her frustration at being made to perform this mundane task, she was also surprised. She'd known the other two medics for four years.

And neither of them ever missed work.

Inside a dark vehicle across the city, a fluorescent light flashed on and off like a firefly.

It was a mobile phone. The small dark shape rang quietly, muffled and dimmed from inside a white piece of pocket fabric.

It belonged to a woman lying in the back of the vehicle.

She was lifeless, her body limp and sprawled in a heap, like a puppet with the strings cut. Another dead body had been dumped on top of her, a young man staring with lifeless eyes at the rear doors of the vehicle.

Both of them were surrounded by a pool of congealed blood which had clotted and thickened, sticking them to the floor of the vehicle. The bruising around the young woman's neck showed that she'd been strangled. The man had put up more of a fight, so his throat had been cut.

The phone continued to ring quietly, flashing on and off.

But no one was ever going to pick up.

Fifty yards away, the man from the shopping centre checked the traffic as he strode across Upper Street towards the vehicle. Cupping his hands together, he blew hot air into his palms. It was cold, too cold. Dodging the traffic that passed down the road in front of him, he approached the vehicle parked on the kerb.

An ambulance.

Checking to make sure no-one had followed or was watching him, the man moved around the side of the stolen white vehicle. Pulling a set of keys from his pocket, he opened the door and climbed inside, slamming it shut behind him.

A sudden noise from the back of the vehicle startled him. He snapped his head round but realised it was just the dead bitch's mobile phone. He relaxed; the damn thing had made him jump.

Ignoring the constant, quiet ringing, he grabbed a set of overalls from the front passenger seat beside him. They were light green medical scrubs; he'd planned to use what the guy in the back had been wearing, but he'd had to cut his throat and the prick had bled all over the white paramedic outfit as he died. He'd been forced to improvise but after raiding the ambulance he'd struck gold.

Pulling off his shirt, he started to change into the uniform quickly.

Over his shoulder, the phone continued to ring.

Back inside the shopping centre, a bartender had moved out from behind the bar with a cloth. If his boss asked, he was wiping down tables, but in reality he was using the opportunity to gain a moment's respite from the mass of customers at the bar, leaving a colleague to handle the orders. There had been a brief lull when reports of an explosion at the Emirates had flashed onto the screens, but business was now back in full swing and it was exhausting work, constant shouted orders, people vying for his attention.

As he moved from table to table, giving each one a cursory wipe, the barman zigzagged his way towards the exit. Picking up an empty glass from an outside table, he noticed something against the wall.

Two black bags, sitting alone and unattended.

He frowned, then looked around.

There were sets of chairs and tables out there, but no one was using them. It was too cold.

He shrugged. Someone must have left the bags by accident. They'd realise soon and would be back any minute to collect them, no doubt worrying that they'd have been stolen.

The barman decided to move the two holdalls behind the bar for safe-keeping and until whoever owned them returned. He walked over and dropped to one knee in front of them. They were both bulky, packed full, and curiosity got the better of him.

Holding the rag and glass in his right hand, he reached forward with his left and pulled the zip of one of the bags open.

Tilting his head, he looked inside.

An instant later, he gasped, snapping upright and dropping the glass.

It hit the ground and shattered into a hundred fragments.

FIFTEEN

Outside the Emirates, most of the ARU task force
officers were scattered amongst the crowd. They were
helping the wounded and paramedics, organising the
mass of people and most importantly, keeping an eye out
for any further threats. The day had been wildly
unpredictable so far and there were still five terrorists out
there somewhere.

Across the tarmac, Fox quickly appeared from the
bowels of the stadium, Spitz and Mason jogging beside
him. The sandy-haired officer pushed the pressel button
on his vest as the three of them approached.

'We checked the stadium, Mac,' he said, his voice
coming up over the ear piece in each officer's ear. 'There
was nothing else. Place is clear, far as we can tell.'

'*Roger that,*' came Mac's voice. '*Move into the crowd
and do what you can to help out*'.

As the three men dispersed, Porter's voice came up
over the radio.

'*Mac, we've got another problem.*'

'*What?*'

'*I just spoke with Nikki. An emergency call just came
into the Met. Two bags, left outside a bar in Angel.*'

Helping a wounded man into an ambulance amongst the
crowd, Archer heard this and turned.

He spotted Porter, standing by their police car. His
face was tense.

132

'They sure it's a threat, Port?' Archer asked, pushing the button on his vest as he looked at Porter.

He saw the other officer nod.

'*A guy opened one of the bags,*' Porter's voice replied. '*Said it was packed with what sounds like C4 explosive.*'

The radio went silent. From their positions all over the car park, each man froze as this registered.

'*The clock's ticking, Mac,*' Porter added. '*We need to get over there now.*'

Mac's voice responded instantly, his tone changed.

'*Right, First team, we're going. Archer, Chalky get over to the car. Deakins, take over 'til we get back.*'

The three officers ran from their various positions towards Porter, who'd already jumped into the front seat and was firing the engine.

Back at St Mary's Hannah Gibbs put the phone back onto the cradle slowly.

She was confused.

Every paramedic she knew made it a point of honour to always be contactable, no matter what the situation was. It didn't matter if they were on duty or off, they were always near a phone. She didn't want to jump to conclusions, but for some reason Gibbs felt an uneasy feeling seeping into the pit of her stomach.

Something wasn't right.

She considered what could have happened. There was the possibility that the two of them were secretly an item; right now they could be holed up in a hotel room somewhere, the ambulance parked outside, the television off, no idea of the situation at the stadium. But as soon as she considered the idea, Gibbs frowned.

That was tenuous at best, and highly unlikely. Even if they were together, neither would be that unprofessional. In her head, the cautious part of her mind was going off like a fire alarm.

Something felt off.

Standing at the desk, she made a quick decision. *Better safe than sorry*. Picking up the phone again, she dialled three buttons. The call connected.

'Police please,' she asked.

There was a wait as the operator transferred her. Then another voice appeared on the other end of the line.

'Good evening. What is your emergency?' the guy asked, from the Metropolitan Police call centre.

'I'd like to report two people and an ambulance missing.'

*

Not long after, the black Ford carrying the four ARU officers screeched to a halt on Parkfield Street outside the N1 shopping centre. Mac and his three men piled out of the car, slamming the doors and running to the entrance.

Around them, people were being evacuated by security but Archer knew they weren't getting out fast enough as he raced towards the mall. The building was an open design, two levels, but with a courtyard serving as the central hub and no glass windows or any doors at the entrance. You could walk straight in. Even from here the four newly-arrived officers could see scores of people still inside, eighty of them at least, spread out over the two tiers.

Many of them seemed in no rush to leave.

To compound the problem, the evacuees were gathering in a crowd not fifty yards from the entrance to the courtyard. A handful of security guards were keeping them what they thought was a safe distance away, but they had naively underestimated the blast radius and power of true plastic explosive. Archer knew that if the bags inside were really full of C4, then without cover, all of these people would die or be critically wounded if the bomb went off.

Inside the centre, a guard directing operations saw the four armed policemen arrive and rushed over, obviously relieved to see them. Archer saw three stripes on his shoulder, denoting his rank.

'John Pierce, Head of Security,' the man said as he arrived, out of breath.

Mac didn't introduce himself. He didn't have time.

'Where are the bags, John?' he asked quickly, as the five of them moved forward into the galleria together.

Pierce pointed up and to his right.

'On the Second Tier, outside the bar. Barman said he found them all alone, no one around, like they'd been left behind accidentally. Checked inside, saw a load of explosive and some wires.'

Mac nodded, looking at the upper level.

'Bomb disposal?'

'I contacted them. They said they'd be here in fifteen minutes.'

'Do you have CCTV installed?'

Pierce nodded. 'The monitor room is this way.'

He raised his hand and indicated to a corridor to their left on the lower level.

Mac turned to Porter, who was already moving forward.

'On it, Sarge,' he said, rushing off towards the room with Pierce alongside him.

In the left corner of the Lower Tier was a winding concrete stairwell, leading up to the Second Level. Now just the three of them, Mac, Archer and Chalky moved quickly towards it, taking the stairs two at a time and dodging past people still coming down in the opposite direction.

Navigating their way up, the three men reached the Upper Tier and started to fan out, each of their weapons tucked into the shoulder and aimed as they scanned the level.

It was mostly clear. The odd person was still rushing for the stairs, but the whole tier was pretty much empty, most of the remaining people downstairs on the lower level. But it was eerie as hell.

In front of them was the dark foyer of a cinema.

Archer could see boxes of popcorn and drinks that had been suddenly dropped, scattered on the floor with their contents strewn everywhere, telling the story of how quickly people inside the building had fled.

The three officers separated as they quickly checked the rest of the level, moving fast and silently as they searched for any other threats as yet undiscovered.

But the rest of the floor was clear.

After a few moments, they re-joined at the middle intersection of the level.

Together, the three of them looked over at the bar.

They could see the two black bags. They were leaning side by side against each other, seemingly harmless. To an onlooker, they looked just like luggage that someone sitting outside had carelessly left behind.

Staring at the holdalls, Archer felt a brief moment of relief. Thank God the barman had checked inside. If he hadn't, the centre would still have been packed with people and the contents of those bags would never have been discovered.

Not until it was too late.

He shot his cuff, checking the time on his watch. It had just gone 6:08pm.

He looked around the level.

There was no sign of the EOD, the bomb squad, yet.

'What do we do, Mac?' he asked.

The older man was staring at the bags, his face grim.

'We wait.'

A hundred yards from the shopping centre, the man who'd ditched the bags hadn't yet noticed the evacuation taking place across the street.

He was the other side from the main crowd, on Upper Street, so he was oblivious to the noise and commotion and also the arrival of the four ARU officers.

Now dressed in the lime-green paramedic's scrubs, he'd climbed into the back of the ambulance. Completely ignoring the two bodies dumped there, he was kneeling before a package of bricks stacked neatly in a square. Wires ran from the stack, connecting into a mobile phone that was placed on top of the pile. In all, there must have been thirty bricks of plastic explosive underneath.

The man allowed himself a smile. In the past, he'd always had to use home-made plastique mixed in his bathroom basin and bath-tub. The stuff was so volatile that he could never fully relax when he was in close proximity to it. But Dominick Farha's bank account had allowed for much greater quality in this operation.

And the boy had done good.

The C4 was a devastating weapon, ten times more potent than the home-made crap he'd been forced to use previously and a hundred times more stable. Combining explosive chemicals with a plastic binder to hold it together, the resulting putty was secure and durable, easy to both transport and mould. Once it was wired up, all the plastic explosive needed was a detonator. He'd hooked up a mobile phone to a small blasting cap which was conjoining all the wires. When he called the phone the resulting charge would pass into the cap, triggering a small explosion. That was all the C4 needed to do its job and follow suit.

The resulting chemical reaction of the nitrogen and carbon gases would expand at over twenty six thousand feet per second.

The shockwave would be catastrophic and the explosion instantaneous.

One minute, everything would be fine.

The next, everyone and everything unfortunate enough to be within the blast radius would be vaporised.

Taking up a set of pliers the man set to work. He had to finish cutting some last lengths of wire to connect the last two blocks of C4.

From the inside of the dark ambulance, he was completely unaware of the crowd of evacuees gathering this side of the shopping centre.

For now.

SIXTEEN

Inside the galleria, Mac and the two younger officers were trying to stay calm. They were still on the Upper Tier and there was still no sign of the bomb disposal team. Every second felt like a minute.

Sweating, Archer looked over at the bags.

None of them knew what exactly was inside, but they all knew they could explode in a heartbeat.

Archer checked his watch again anxiously, looking around.

'Shit. Where the hell are they, Mac?'

Beside him, Mac seemed calmer. But only just.

'They'll be here soon. Hang on. Ten minutes'.

'We might not have ten minutes,' Chalky muttered, looking at the bags.

'This is bad,' Archer said. 'If those bags go off, we're done for. They'll turn this place into a crater.'

Mac nodded. 'And kill everyone on the street outside,' he added. He paused. 'We hold, Arch. It's not our job to defuse it.'

The younger man nodded reluctantly.

Suddenly, a noise came from behind them and Archer and Mac spun round, their weapons aimed.

It was just an employee rushing out of the cinema.

He saw the police officers and the empty galleria around him and ran for the stairs, his eyes wide with fear.

Watching him go, Archer turned to ask Chalky something.

But he wasn't there.

Archer swivelled round, and caught sight of his friend.

He was walking towards the bags.

In the same instant, Mac saw him too and swore

'*Chalky!*' Archer shouted. 'Chalky! Get back here!'

Across the tier, Chalky ignored him. Mac and Archer split, taking up make-shift protection behind two concrete pillars; Mac leaned round, bellowing at Chalky.

'*Officer White, get back here! That's an order!*'

Chalky disregarded him, walking slowly and coolly towards the bar.

He was now only five feet from the two black holdalls.

On Upper Street, the man in the ambulance gently finished fixing one last wire to a remaining brick of explosive. He carefully connected the other end to the detonator and leaned back, inspecting his work.

It was ready.

Stepping over the two dead medics, he climbed back into the front seat, but as he did, something caught his attention to his left across the street.

He saw a crowd gathered outside the shopping centre, being held back by some security guards from the building. Staring at the throng, he cursed.

They found them already?

He was pissed. He figured the bags wouldn't have been noticed for at least another ten or twenty minutes, giving him plenty of time to get clear of the area.

Stepping out of the vehicle and slamming the door, he walked around the back of the ambulance for a better look. He'd left the package only fifteen or twenty minutes ago, but the place was already being evacuated. He'd planned to detonate the bags when he was on his way. He re-evaluated.

And decided to do it right now instead.

Behind the ambulance, he figured he'd be safe from the blast. Or if he wasn't, everyone else would get a second surprise on the street, when the explosive contents of the ambulance reacted to the shockwave. He wasn't planning on dying tonight, but he didn't really mind if he did, just as long as he took a hell of a lot of people with him.

He pulled a phone from the pocket of the medical scrubs.

And started dialling a number.

Inside the mall, Chalky stood over the two bags.

He could feel his heart racing, adrenaline pumping through his body. To his left, the pub had been completely deserted. Half-empty glasses of beer and wine were scattered on tables everywhere, chairs and bar-stools knocked to the floor. Above the bar, he saw a line of televisions showing muted footage from outside the stadium.

The place was silent and unnerving, like the building was holding its breath, as if something terrible was about to happen.

He knelt down in front of the bags. Across the Tier, Mac and Archer were shouting frantically at him, but to no effect; he'd tuned them both out.

They didn't have time. Chalky could sense it. He shouldn't have been here anyway. He should be dead, his head blown off in the house earlier in the day.

But for some reason, fate had spared him.

So he decided to make the most of it.

As he tucked his MP5 behind his back on its strap, he saw that the barman had left the first bag open.

Chalky reached forward to pull open the two sides.

Outside, the man by the ambulance was half-way through dialling the number. A pedestrian walking past saw the ambulance and the man standing there beside it, wearing his green medical scrubs.

'Oi mate, shouldn't you be up at the Emirates?' he offered.

The man holding the phone snapped his attention to the bystander, his eyes burning with hatred.

Startled, the other guy took the hint and averting his eyes quickly walked away, feeling the paramedic's gaze scorching into his back.

Inside the galleria, Chalky peered inside the first bag.

'Holy shit.'

It was packed with faded yellow bricks of C4.

Ten of them at least.

Reaching with his hand he felt inside the holdall, feeling carefully amongst the bars and wires. His fingers brushed the contents, but he couldn't seem to find a detonation device.

He turned his attention to the second bag.

Realising Chalky was just going to ignore both him and Mac, Archer ran to the edge of the tier facing Parkfield Street.

'Get them back!' he shouted to Pierce's team, pointing at the crowd which had swelled with curious onlookers.

There must have been close to a hundred people down there.

Across the tier, Chalky unzipped the second bag.

This one was also packed full of C4.

However, this time a phone was nestled on top of the bricks.

He could see that it was duct taped to a wire that separated and disappeared into the explosives. *The detonator*. He saw the display on the phone.

T-Mobile. Good signal.

Four bars.

He reached for the phone.

In trial runs, the man by the ambulance had seen the blast radius and sheer power of an explosion like this. Cover made all the difference. He knew the thickness of the ambulance should technically save his life.

One thing many people misunderstood about an explosion was what the most lethal aspect of it was. Most assumed it was the resulting fireball, like the ones they'd seen in the movies, but the terrorist holding the phone knew it was the shockwave. Whenever an incendiary device explodes, the chemical reaction releases an enormously powerful ball of energy. When that energy comes into contact with a person, it hits the inside of their body like a thousand small sledgehammers with knives taped to the end. All the blood vessels in their lungs rupture, and they drown in their own blood. In World War 2 the American soldiers had called it *shocklung*, an horrific, slow and agonising way to die. The terrorist holding the phone could see why Hollywood preferred the fireball.

However, he figured the ambulance was solid enough to protect him from the explosion and blast wave.

Moving behind the vehicle, he raised the phone, the number dialled in.

He took a deep breath.

And his finger moved to *Call*.

Inside, Chalky had the phone in his hands.

Outside, the terrorist smiled.

And he pressed the button.

'Boom,' he whispered.

Grabbing the wire at the same moment, Chalky squeezed his eyes shut and yanked the phone from the cord, as hard as he could.

He froze.

Nothing happened.

A split second later, a shrill ringtone echoed around the shopping centre.

It was coming from the phone; it purred and danced in his palm as it vibrated from an incoming call.

The young police officer looked at the caller ID.

Private Number, it said.

Without a thought, he pressed *Answer,* putting the phone to his ear.

Silence.

Whoever was on the other end wasn't expecting to talk.

Chalky heard a rustle, and someone breathing. Listening.

'Too late,' Chalky said.

He heard a sharp intake of breath.

Then whoever was on the other end hung up.

SEVENTEEN

With the threat passed Chalky sat back on his heels, panting as his body tried to suck oxygen back into his lungs to counteract all the adrenaline pumping through his veins. Without the phone attached, the explosives in the bags were safe. They no longer had a detonating charge.

He turned to Mac and Archer across the tier, both of whom had watched him yank the cord and heard the phone.

'We're good,' Chalky called.

Before either could reply, there was the sound of running feet nearby from the Parkfield Street side and three members of EOD, the bomb disposal unit, suddenly appeared. One of them was in a thick green blast suit and was pulling a helmet into place as he moved as fast as he could across the level. He saw Chalky sitting by the device and ran over awkwardly, as quickly as the bulky suit encasing his body would allow.

Arriving, he knelt beside the policeman in front of the bags and with a trained eye, examined the explosives and wires in the bags. There was a pause. However, after inspecting the detonator, he looked up and unclipped his helmet, turning to the other men and giving a thumbs up.

'We're good. It's safe,' he called.

Turning to Chalky, he offered his hand. The policeman shook it and rose, turning to walk away from the bar, the mobile phone still in his hand.

Across the level Archer was livid, and moved around the tier to meet him.

'What the hell was that?' he asked, furious. 'You trying to get us killed?'

Chalky tossed him the phone, ignoring his friend's anger.

'You're welcome,' he said.

Just as Archer prepared to take it further, Porter appeared behind them from the stairs.

'Mac!' he called, who turned. 'You need to come and see this!'

Mac nodded, and motioned to Archer and Chalky to follow him down. They moved to the stairs, Archer still glaring at the back of Chalky's head. He was pissed.

Porter quickly picked up the tension between the three men, then looked over at the relaxed bomb disposal team who were starting to pack away the C4 into a secure case.

'What did I miss?'

Downstairs, the building's security monitor room was just like any other. It was a basic set-up, a lone swivel chair and a series of small screens stacked on top of each other, each shot showing a different angle of the shopping mall.

Judging from the angle on two of the screens cameras were also mounted outside the building, one facing Parkfield Street and the other facing Upper Street. One of Pierce's security guards had been brought back into the building and was sitting in the chair, operating the system. Behind him, the four police officers and Pierce had gathered, crowding around him to get a good view of the monitors.

Porter reached forward and tapped a monitor, turning to Mac.

'Watch this.'

The guard pushed *Play*, as the group of men watched closely.

It was a view of the Upper Tier, looking down the level towards Parkfield Street. The bar was at the top left of the screen; people were flooding the tier, most of them strolling up and moving into the pub.

But a lone figure was standing outside, no one around him, having a drink.

And the two black bags were resting by his feet.

Taking a sip from his glass, the guy turned to look down the galleria.

His face was straight-on to the camera.

'Pause,' said Porter.

The guard hit the button.

'See?'

The men looked closer.

Lighting from the bar was illuminating the guy's face, but the shot was pretty grainy.

'Can you enhance it?' Mac asked the guard in the chair. The guy nodded and tapped some buttons. A white square suddenly appeared on the screen, framing the man's face. It rendered for a few seconds. Then the face reappeared in the box, much closer.

There was a moment's silence as each man peered closer. Mac unzipped a pocket on his tac vest, and pulled out a sheet of paper. The pictures of the nine terrorists.

He looked at the screen, then at the page, and tapped one of the photographs.

'Son of a bitch. Bull's-eye.'

The other men looked at the page. Beside Mac, Archer instantly saw who it was.

Number Eight.

'Keep running the tape,' said Porter.

The guard in the chair hit two buttons. The white square around the terrorist's head vanished, and the shot was back to normal size. He pressed *Play* and the tape continued to roll.

Number Eight continued to stand where he was, then seemed to cock his head to the side, staring into the bar.

Something inside had caught his attention.

The television screens, Archer thought.

After a spell, the guy put his glass down on a nearby table and checked his watch.

Turning, he started walking away, leaving the two bags behind.

'Stop,' said Archer.

The guard hit *Pause*.

'What time is that?'

The guard in the chair tapped the bottom right corner of the screen.

'Just before six. See?'

Archer looked closer. A small digital clock was tucked into the bottom corner of the shot, showing hours, minutes and seconds that constantly ticked over in white letters as it matched the action on screen. It read *5:59:04 pm*.

Archer nodded. 'Just after the explosion.'

Around him, the other men nodded.

The guard pushed *Play* again.

The group watched as the terrorist walked down the tier, the camera was positioned on the wall so that he moved straight towards and under it. He passed under the camera and disappeared out of sight.

'Shit,' said Mac. 'Where'd he go?'

'Hang on, sir,' said the guard, tapping another screen and pressing a button. 'Here.'

Right on cue, Number Eight reappeared under the camera, his back to the shot.

It was a view of Upper Street, the camera mounted high on the wall and facing the ground level, so the guy must have used the stairs to exit the galleria. They watched as he crossed the road. It was a dark December evening, which meant most of the other people walking by the shot were just black silhouettes, momentarily lit up by a shop's lights or a street lamp.

However, the shadowy figure they were watching ended up stopping on the kerb under a lamp-post.

Beside an ambulance.

They watched as he disappeared around the far side of the vehicle. After a moment, a figure appeared in the driver's seat.

'What the hell?' said Pierce. 'Is he a paramedic?'

The tape continued to play.

The shadow disappeared into the back of the vehicle, and nothing happened for a spell.

But after a while, the terrorist reappeared.

And he'd changed his clothes.

'Are those medical scrubs?' Archer asked, thinking out loud.

On the screen, the man pulled a phone from his pocket. A pedestrian walking past stopped beside him; they seemed to have a brief exchange, but then the other guy walked off. The man turned to his attention back to the phone in his hands, then disappeared around the far side of the ambulance.

Suddenly, Mac realised something and looked down at the clock in the corner of the screen.

It was just after 6:11 pm.

Ten minutes ago.

'Son of a bitch is outside!' Mac shouted as he grabbed his MP5 and ran for the door.

'Wait!' called Porter.

Mac turned, his hand on the door handle. The group watched on the screen as the figure reappeared in the driver's seat. The headlights suddenly turned on and pulling away from the kerb, he disappeared into the night.

As he left, a black van suddenly screeched into shot, zooming past him. *EOD* was printed on the side, the bomb disposal team.

'Shit,' cursed Mac, re-joining the group. 'Shit, shit, shit. We lost him. He was just outside.'

'Yeah, but we could never have known that,' said Archer.

Beside him, Porter was frowning, thinking hard.

'But where did he go?' he asked. 'And why in an ambulance? The hospital maybe?'

Archer suddenly had an idea.

He tapped the monitor, turning to the security guard.

'Can you rewind and get a read on those plates?' he asked.

The guy nodded. He pressed a button and the action started reversing, the ambulance reappearing and pulling back into the slot as people on the street walked backwards. The guard paused the shot perfectly, just as the vehicle was pulling out. Seeing as the camera shot was side-on, it was the only moment on the tape that the plates were visible.

Archer reached onto his tac vest, and pulled a mobile phone from a Velcro slot beside his left collarbone. Each man had one; it gave them fast and instant communication to Nikki's private line inside the ops room. He pushed *Redial*; the call rang twice, then connected.

'*Hello?*' came Nikki's voice.

'Nikki it's Archer. Can you do me a favour?'

'*Sure, Arch. Go ahead.*'

'I need you to check the Met's database and see if any ambulances have been reported missing in the past few days,' he said. He pushed a button, holding the phone up so the room could hear. 'You're on speaker-phone.'

There was a moment's pause. They could hear computer keys being tapped at the other end.

'*Funny you asked,*' Nikki said. '*A medic from St Mary's called the Met not twenty minutes ago. She said an ambulance and two of her friends hadn't shown up for work.*'

The men looked at each other.

'Did she give the plates?' Archer continued. There was another brief pause.

'*Yep. KV81 4MG.*'

Together, all six pairs of eyes checked the screen.

It was a perfect match.

'Right. Thanks,' Archer said, ending the call and putting the phone back in its sleeve on his uniform.

'There's our missing ambulance,' said Porter.

To his left, he noticed Archer was staring at the screen intently.

'What are you thinking?' Porter asked him.

Archer frowned.

'I'm thinking about the guys we picked up in the raid earlier. And the difference here. The stuff in the bags outside the bar, that's not ball-bearings and bleach. This guy wasn't playing cards and snorting coke when we found him.'

He tapped his finger on the ambulance on the screen.

'We're dealing with a whole new level of intelligence here.'

'And?' asked Pierce.

Archer looked at him.

'Let's be logical. Why didn't he strap the bomb to his chest? Why detonate remotely?'

The group thought for a moment.

'So he could walk away,' Mac said.

Porter nodded. 'And so he could do it again.'

Silence.

'Do you reckon there could be more C4 inside the vehicle?' Porter asked the room.

'Let's suppose for a moment that there is,' Archer said. 'If you were a bomber with an ambulance full of explosives, where would you go?'

'Somewhere with a crowd,' Pierce said, without hesitation.

Frustrated, Mac swore, confused and angry.

'Shit. OK, so where?' he asked.

And right then, the penny dropped.

All six of them realised at the same time.

Pierce went to confirm out loud where the guy was headed.

But before he could speak, the four ARU officers were already running for the door.

EIGHTEEN

Just over three miles away, Number Eight hit the
steering wheel of the ambulance in frustration. Traffic to
the Emirates was jammed tight both ways and he was
getting impatient.

Looking down, he saw a button by the radio console
that he'd switched off to avoid communication.

He pressed it, curious. All of a sudden, the siren on the
roof started blaring and wailing, startling him.

However, he watched as the other vehicles in front of
him suddenly parted like the Red Sea for Moses.

Behind the wheel, the terrorist took his chance and
accelerated through the new gap made for him.

He smiled.

He could ride like this all the way to the stadium car
park.

In a car twenty yards behind, a woman cursed as she saw
the ambulance speed off.

She was the one who'd been taking the surveillance
shots outside the raided house earlier in the day, the
photographs of the armed police officers and the
suspects. Ahead, the traffic light was staying red.

She took the opportunity to pull a phone from her
pocket, pushing *Redial*.

'It's me,' she said as someone answered. 'Good news.
I found one of them. I'm going to make an approach'.

'Well done. And good luck.'

'I'll be in touch,' she said, ending the call as the light changed to green.

Taking off the handbrake, she went as fast as she could in pursuit of the ambulance. She didn't need to see the vehicle anymore. She knew where it was headed.

She just prayed she'd make it in time.

Back at the stadium, the other ARU officers were finally starting to get a hold on the situation. Most of the critically wounded had been taken to hospital or were on their way there. The crowd had thinned and was relatively calmer, but hundreds of emergency workers, the less seriously injured and police were still streaming all over the place, and they weren't going anywhere for a while.

In the middle of the crowd, Fox spotted Deakins helping an injured woman into an ambulance. Tucking his sub-machine gun behind his arm, he jogged over, providing an extra pair of hands.

At that moment, the earpiece tucked inside his ear suddenly went off. It was Mac's voice. He sounded frantic.

'Deaks? Fox? Answer! Someone from Second Team answer!'

Closing the doors to the ambulance, Fox looked at Deakins, confused. The headsets covered a distance of seven miles, which is why each man had a mobile phone attached to his vest. They must have been within range, already on their way back from the shopping centre.

Fox pushed the pressel switch on his uniform, frowning.

'We're here, Mac,' he said.

'*We think Number Eight is on his way to you*!' Mac said. '*He's in a stolen ambulance, possibly containing explosives.*'

Deakins and Fox looked at each other.

Oh shit.

Around the car park, the other officers heard this exchange through their earpiece and all froze where they stood. Mac's voice continued.

'*All of you, look out for an ambulance with plates starting KV81. He could already be there. And get everyone the hell out of that car park as fast as you can.*'

Deakins looked around. He pressed the switch.

'Mac, there're ambulances everywhere here.'

'*Then get going! As I said, the plates begin KV81, I repeat KV81! We'll be there any minute.*'

And the radio went dead.

As Mac's transmission ended, the stolen vehicle turned into the car park for the stadium.

Number Eight had turned the siren off to avoid drawing any unnecessary attention to the vehicle and he felt a shiver of excitement as he entered the parking lot for the first time. He was worried it might have emptied slightly, but he could see scores of people still here. Close to two hundred, at least.

Moving forward slowly, he crept to a stop. He was still outside the crowd, twenty yards from the main mass of people, but it didn't matter. The blast would kill every single one of them, with change. He turned the engine off and stepped out, locking the door. Turning, the man started walking away from the crowd.

Behind him in the opposite direction, a male paramedic in his mid-twenties had spotted the new vehicle arrive, and with an injured man leaning on him for support he approached and tried the door. It was locked.

He saw the driver striding away, now fifty yards across the tarmac.

'Hey!' he called after him. *'Hey, you!'*

The guy didn't respond.

The paramedic watched in frustration as the guy seemed to pick up the pace, walking even faster away from him.

'Hey! I need some help over here!'

The guy didn't turn around or even acknowledge that he'd heard him.

Helping the wounded man to sit on the kerb, the paramedic looked around for assistance. He saw an armed policeman with his back turned, ten yards away, and approached him.

'Officer?'

'Not now, mate,' the guy said, without turning.

Undeterred, the young man tried again.

'Sorry to bother you. But there's a driver over there who just walked away from his ambulance. He must have heard me shouting. He locked it up and just left, but I need to get into that ambulance.'

For some reason, that got the policeman's immediate attention.

He snapped his head around to look at the medic.

'I've got a wounded man. I need to get him out of here' the medic continued.

The policeman ignored him.

'*Which man*?' he asked.

He turned and pointed.

Deakins saw a figure in green scrubs jogging away from the crowd towards the far side of the car park.

Oh shit.

Number Eight was already a good hundred yards from the ambulance.

He turned, looking over his shoulder, and saw an armed policeman start to sprint after him.

The terrorist started running too, racing ahead as he pulled the phone from his pocket and starting to dial the number as he fled. From this distance, the blast would kill him, but he was OK with that.

So be it, he thought, as he ducked behind a lorry. *I'll take them all with me.*

Behind the long vehicle, he allowed himself a moment of victory. There was no way the running cop could make it in time.

Smiling, his finger moved over to press *Call*.

'*Hey,*' a female voice suddenly said quietly from behind him.

Like all boxing trainers say, it's not the power punch, it's the punch you don't see that gets you.

And as the terrorist swung around instinctively, he met an elbow as it scythed through the air and smashed into his face, breaking his nose in an instant. The impact of the blow was completely unexpected and it hit him like a knock-out hook, putting him out cold before he could even hit the tarmac.

The guy ended up sprawled in a heap on the floor. His assailant, the woman from the car, saw the mobile phone resting in his hand and dropped to one knee to pick it up. Looking at the display on the phone, she saw that he'd already entered a sequence of numbers.

A split second later, an armed officer appeared from around the corner, an MP5 sub-machine gun tucked into his shoulder. She saw his uniform; he was a member of the team that had raided the house. *ARU. Armed Response Unit* her memory told her. The end of his weapon was aimed directly at her head, the front-sight moving up and down as he panted from the race to get here.

Before he had to ask, she slowly lowered the phone to the tarmac, maintaining constant eye contact with him. She saw him glance at the unconscious terrorist, blood leaking from the guy's nose, out cold on the ground, sprawled like he'd just drained a whole bottle of whiskey.

'Who the hell are you?' he asked, his weapon still aimed at her chin.

She moved her hand slowly to the jacket of her suit.

'May I?'

He nodded, panting, his finger tense on the trigger.

Slowly, she reached inside her jacket and pulled out an ID, flipping it open so he could see.

'Special Agent Shapira. I'm with Mossad,' she said.

Just as she pulled her badge, the black Ford carrying the four other ARU officers screeched into the car park to their right. Inside the car, the men could see their team-mates pushing the crowd back up ahead.

They also saw Deakins fifty yards away, standing beside a woman none of them recognised.

And between them a prone figure dressed in green medical scrubs.

Number Eight.

Porter pulled to a halt and all four of them jumped out. Deakins was now kneeling by the man on the ground, rummaging in the pocket of his scrubs. A mobile phone lay beside him, the rear cover off, the battery removed. As they ran over, Archer saw the guy was out cold; someone had blasted him in the nose and laid him out.

Deakins pulled out a set of car keys, tossing them to Chalky, and together the four newly-arrived officers ran towards the stolen ambulance, instantly recognising the plates.

Mac, Archer and Porter stopped fifteen yards away and Chalky moved forward alone, the keys in his hand.

'Careful, Chalk,' warned Mac.

To his left, the other ARU officers had pushed the remaining crowd back, all scared, confused and traumatised from the events earlier. Chalky slid the key into the lock of the vehicle carefully and twisted, it clicked and the mechanism shifted open.

He grabbed the handle and pulled open the door, followed by the other.

'Holy shit.'

There were close to thirty bricks of C4 sitting inside, all wired up to a mobile phone, same as in the shopping mall.

But also beside the stack of explosives were two bodies, a young woman and a guy, both dead, lying in a pool of dried blood. *The two missing medics*, Archer thought as he moved forward.

Nearby, members of the public and emergency workers who were close enough to see into the ambulance gasped in shock.

Mac turned to Porter, who was standing beside him.

'Tell EOD to get down here, Port,' he said.

He glanced at Chalky, who had walked back to join them.

'This time they can do it.'

NINETEEN

Across the city, Dominick Farha checked his watch from inside the bathroom of his hotel room.

It was time to go.

Looking in the mirror one last time, he adjusted his tie and smoothed back his dark hair. Satisfied, he opened the door moving back into the room and found the young woman standing there, waiting for him.

He looked down and examined her appearance.

She was wearing a voluminous green dress he'd bought her from some high-street store. The design was such that it completely concealed the second white dress hidden underneath which contained close to thirty five pounds of explosives, all packed over her stomach.

To an onlooker, she looked just like a young woman expecting her first child.

To him, she looked like his ticket out of here.

Satisfied, he gave her an approving nod and smile then looked around the room, checking for anything he didn't want to leave behind. There was nothing important, just a set of pliers and some clippings of wire. He felt a shiver of excitement.

This is it.

He turned to her. 'Ready?'

'Ready,' she replied. She was trying to hide it, but he could see that she was scared.

Moving to the door, Farha opened it and let the girl out of the room first. He switched off the light, and pulled the door shut behind him as he followed.

Outside in the corridor, he turned to her.

'Wait here for a moment,' he said. She nodded as he approached the room next door. He knocked twice. After a pause, a young man opened it. Dominick turned to the girl, holding up his hand. *Two minutes*, his fingers said. She nodded nervously and he stepped into the other hotel room, closing the door.

This room also had the curtains drawn and lights dimmed. The young man had been sitting on the bed watching the television. Farha suddenly realised the guy had shaved his head since he'd last seen him.

The other man noticed him looking.

'Don't want to get recognised,' he said in his American accent.

Dominick nodded. 'Good thinking. I just wanted to tell you we're leaving.'

'You sure he's going to welcome you back?' the other man said. 'You made a big mistake, Dom.'

'After today? He has to. I'll be a hero. He'll throw me a party,' Dominick replied. He said it confidently enough, but neither of them was sure he meant it. 'I just wanted to double-check everything with you before I go.'

The younger man nodded.

'American Airlines Flight 427' he recited. 'Non-stop from New York JFK. Lands Runway Six at 9:20 pm.'

Farha smiled. 'Good. I double-checked. It runs like clockwork. Just make sure you don't miss.'

The younger man grinned; reaching down, he tapped something resting behind the bed. A dark rectangular case.

'I won't.'

165

There was a brief pause; then the two men hugged each other. Dominick was surprised to feel sad that he was saying goodbye to the young man. He liked him; they went back a long way. When all the shit had hit the fan, he'd made a phone-call asking for the kid's help, expecting a rebuttal. However, he'd sweetened the deal, and consequently the guy had instantly said *yes*. Unlike some of the others, Dominick knew that this man would get his shit done tonight. He was reliable and loyal.

He hoped he'd make it out afterwards too.

'Good luck,' Farha told him, as they stood back. 'I'll see you across the water. Remember, the moment after you fire, get the hell out of here. Literally, the second after. The cops will be coming. Get outside and don't stop running.'

The young man nodded. 'Same to you. And watch your back, Dom. You know they're all still after you.'

Nodding, Farha turned.

Walking to the door, he pulled it open and departed.

Together again, Dominick and his female companion rode the lift down to the ground floor. After a few moments, it arrived with a *ding*.

Stepping out, the pair moved past other guests as they made their way into the lobby. As they walked across the marble floor and into the reception area, Dominick glanced to his right and saw a television mounted on the wall. The news. It was still covering the disaster at the stadium.

But there was a new headline, and it stopped him in his tracks.

Breaking News: Two further attacks at shopping centre and stadium foiled by police. Suspected bomber arrested.

Dominick froze, and cursed under his breath, long and hard.

He stood still, thinking as he stared at the screen.

How the hell did he fail? And twice?

He was one of my best guys!

He felt the woman beside him slide her hand into his which brought him back to the moment. Finally ripping his attention from the television, he gathered his composure and led his companion towards the exit.

Moving outside, he hailed a cab. As the taxi pulled up, he opened the door and helped the young woman inside, climbing in after her.

'Where to, mate?' asked the driver, loudly.

Dominick forced a smile.

'Heathrow. Terminal Five,' he replied.

TWENTY

'I don't believe this. Mossad had eyes on this lot as well?'

As he spoke, Cobb moved behind his desk and sat down in the chair. The task force had just returned, Fox and Porter taking the ambulance bomber through to the holding cells to be processed. Mac had stowed his weapon, then been called to Cobb's office. He was standing beside the DEA agent, Crawford and another dark-haired man he didn't recognise. He guessed he was their field agent who was going to attach to the task force. Mac liked the look of him already. He seemed solid and calm.

There was another person standing to the right of the room. Shapira, the Mossad agent. She had insisted on returning to the Unit's HQ with the ground team in order to speak with Director Cobb. Mac normally would have told her where to get off but given her assistance in taking down the bomber, he'd reluctantly said *yes*. He didn't know much about her agency, save that they were Israeli and specialised in covert operations taking place outside their borders.

'How long have you been on the group?' Cobb asked her.

'Around eight months,' she said.

Crawford turned to her.

'You're on British soil, in case you didn't notice. You normally take an interest in foreign terrorist plots?'

She gave him an icy look. 'Is that supposed to be ironic, Captain America? Terrorism is terrorism. It doesn't matter what country it's in. Dominick Farha is a priority target of ours.'

168

'And you didn't feel like sharing your intel?' Cobb asked.

'We knew of your operation to apprehend the cell, which is why we held back. We thought the British police could handle it and save us the trouble of getting involved.'

She paused.

'Clearly, we were wrong.'

Mac snapped his head round towards her, irritated.

'One more comment like that and I'll put you on the next plane back to Israel myself.'

Cobb pinched his brow, trying to think through all the confusion and different agendas.

'Well thank you for assisting my team. It's much appreciated,' he said cordially. 'But we can handle the rest of the operation ourselves.'

'Oh, I don't think so,' she said.

Cobb's expression hardened.

'I wasn't asking a question.'

Shapira jabbed a finger angrily towards Crawford and Rivers.

'So the DEA stay and Mossad doesn't? Should I get on the phone and tell that to my boss?' she threatened. 'After what I did for you at the stadium? And especially given what my agency has done for you in the past.'

Cobb knew where this was going. After the London transport bombings in the summer of 2005, MI5 and Mossad had started working together extensively. In fact, the Israeli group had been the first foreign agency to step forward and offer help in the counter-offensive.

Shapira was right. To discard her, especially after the help she'd given in the capture of the terrorist could cause a lot of problems.

And Cobb had more than enough of them tonight.

He shook his head. 'Fine. I don't have time to argue about this. Partner up with Agent Rivers here. You can join him and attach to the field team. And I mean *attach;* no rogue nonsense. You try anything off the straight and narrow, I'll join Sergeant McGuire in putting you on the next plane home. And I don't give a shit what you tell your boss. Are we clear?'

Mac saw her nod slowly, her eyes narrowed. Cobb rose from behind the desk and walked to the door.

'Gather the boys,' he told Mac, as he pulled the glass door open and moved into the Operations area.

Exiting the room, Mac walked over to the Briefing Room and stuck two fingers in his mouth, whistling. There was a rustling and the nine other task force members appeared, moving into Operations.

Cobb had taken up a position in the centre, standing in the middle of his tech team. He turned and addressed the room.

'Listen up,' he called.

A silence had already fallen. The intelligence group leaned away from their computers for the first time in hours.

'The shit just hit the fan people. We've had three attempted bombings in the past two hours. One of them succeeded. Over a hundred and fifty people are already dead. We can't change that. *But we can change what happens next,*' he emphasised, raising his voice. 'It's situations like these which is why this Unit was assembled. Five of the nine suspects are down. Four are

170

left. They're out there right now somewhere in the city. And we need to find them.'

He turned to the tech workers on his left.

'Nikki's team, I want you working closely with GCHQ. These guys must be using phones or email, I want them found and tracked. You'll be operating with me and Agent Crawford, from the DEA,' he said, pointing to the American.

He turned to the task force.

'Mac's team, you've already been acquainted with Agent Shapira here. She'll be joining you on the ground along with Agent Rivers, also joining us from the DEA. Great work so far tonight. Keep it up, lads.'

The men glanced over at the two new arrivals as Cobb turned back to the room. 'Questions?'

Silence.

'Then let's go to work.'

Heathrow's Terminal Five was the latest jewel in the crown for the city's well-known travel network. Opened in 2008, the building was foot-by-foot the largest free-standing structure in the United Kingdom, processing over thirty five million passengers a year. The Departures and Arrivals halls were stacked on top of each other on two separate floors, conjoining to form a giant hall thirteen thousand feet long and a hundred and thirty feet tall. It made a pleasant change from the usual beaten-up and tired airports people were used to passing through around the world. The interior of the building was immaculately clean and maintained, symbolising London's position at the cutting edge of world-wide travel and technology.

Outside the Terminal, a constant stream of vehicles were pulling up the ramp and stopping by a long kerb in front of the glass structure. Drivers stepped out, helping passengers unload their luggage which was then stacked on metal trollies. Taxi fares were paid and trollies were pushed forward as people made their way out of the cold night and towards the entrance to the giant hall.

As the large hand on the clock ticked to 8pm, one particular taxi came into view up the winding ramp. It moved into an empty bay and came to a halt by the kerb; the rear door opened and Dominick Farha stepped out.

The driver had climbed out to open the other rear passenger door, helping the obviously pregnant young woman out of the vehicle. She was unaccustomed to the unfamiliar weight weighing her down and stumbled as she got out of the taxi.

However, the driver steadied her and after Dominick paid the fare, the two of them moved towards the entrance of the Terminal.

As they walked, Dominick suddenly felt a jolt of concern. He spotted a couple of armed officers stationed near the doors to the entrance, each of them hard-faced and alert. Dominick could see them carefully watching each person as they entered the doors between them.

Ten feet from the white interior of the building, he felt one of the men staring at him. Staying calm, Dominick kept walking, holding a steady pace. Suddenly, the entrance to the building seemed a lot further away. Each step felt like ten, his heart pounding in his chest like a bass drum.

However, after a few moments he risked a glance and saw that the policeman was looking beyond them, his attention moved elsewhere.

Looking straight ahead and hiding his intense relief, Dominick led the young woman into the building.

Neither of them had been inside Terminal Five before and Farha noticed that the Departures floor felt as if someone had stacked huge concert halls side by side. There was a kind of muted echo that remained suspended in the air as the large building absorbed the sounds from the people inside and diluted them.

He saw long queues of people standing before desks, ready to check-in and get rid of their cumbersome luggage. Elsewhere, other travellers were standing before self-check-in machines, punching in numbers. Armed security had also been stationed in the building, incrementally positioned against the wall to the pair's right, their backs to the glass as they scanned the crowd, their hands resting on sub-machine guns slung across each of their torsos.

None of them, however, seemed to be looking at Dominick or his female companion.

Taking a breath, the leader of the terrorist cell glanced up. There was a black electronic board mounted on a pillar beside them. It was showing a list of pretty much every major city in the world in yellow text, alongside the plane number and departure time for each flight. He wasn't interested in the flights, though.

He was interested in the time.

Satisfied, he turned to his companion, talking quietly. 'Ready?'

She nodded.

'Tell me again, what time is your departure?'

'9pm,' she said quickly, her voice shaky.

She was nervous, which was only going to get worse.

Time to leave, Dominick thought as he looked down and smiled reassuringly at her.

'I have to go and get something from downstairs,' he told her. 'I need you to wait here.'

She looked up at him like a child, totally trusting.

'OK.'

'There's a lot of security,' he added quietly. 'I might be stopped and questioned.' He lowered his voice further, almost whispering. 'If I don't come back before nine, go on without me. Understand?'

She nodded.

'OK.'

It seemed they were the only letters she could muster.

However, the next moment she proved him wrong.

'I love you, Dominick.'

He winced at the use of his name. The hall was so quiet, every exchange was echoing, hanging in the air.

Clenching his jaw, he forced a smile.

'I love you, too,' he said quietly. 'Now, wait here. I'll be right back.'

He gave her a kiss on the cheek, then started walking towards the lifts to his right, a hundred yards away. He felt the young woman's gaze on his back.

Stupid bitch, he thought. He'd made it all this way, and she'd blurted his name out almost alongside the airport security guards.

Walking around the side of the lift, he moved forward and stepped into an empty cart. The whole system was made of transparent glass, so he could still see her standing there across the hall, watching him.

He tensed; for a moment, she seemed about to wave.

Don't do it bitch.

Don't draw attention.

However, she decided against it and smiled wanly at him instead.

He smiled back as the lift moved down slowly.

The moment he lost sight of her, the smile vanished.

A few moments later the lift arrived at the lower floor, Arrivals. The metal doors opened, and Dominick moved out swiftly. He looked around the hall as he walked across the polished floor and to his left, immediately saw what he was looking for.

A man was sitting in a chair against the wall thirty yards away, reading a newspaper. *Faris;* an ally of sorts, the man Dominick had contacted about setting up a meeting with his uncle. Dominick didn't know the guy well; he'd been taken on by Henry just before all the shit hit the fan in New York. If the situation was different, Farha would have been more cautious around him; he'd have had to be considering that he didn't know the guy and there was a seven-figure bounty against his name from the New York cartel. But he didn't have a choice. At this point, he was completely dependent on the man sat by the wall, so he approached him warily.

Faris sensed he was being watched and he looked up, his eyes locking onto Dominick's. The seated man was similar in height and build, but he had piercing green eyes that were currently impaling Farha like two spikes.

As he walked over, Dominick tried to gauge the seated man's mood and demeanour. He stood before him.

Without a word, Faris rose. Folding the newspaper and leaving it on the seat behind him, he walked towards the exit. He didn't ask Dominick to follow him.

He didn't need to.

Moving past the security stationed near the doors, the two men strode outside into the crisp English winter evening.

A black Mercedes with tinted windows was waiting by the kerb. Faris moved to the near rear door, and opened it and stood to one side, not looking at Dominick, seemingly bored. Farha took the hint, moving forward he climbed inside. The car was empty, save for the driver.

Faris sat in the seat beside him, pulling the door shut.

'Let's go,' he told the driver, the first words he'd spoken since they'd met.

The driver released the handbrake and the car moved away from the kerb, gathering speed and heading off into the London night.

TWENTY ONE

Inside his office at 10 Downing Street, the Prime Minister watched a television screen in silence. Beside him, his wife and Rogers stood equally silent as they observed the latest news updates from the chaotic events of the day.

Behind them, the curtains to the room were still open. The evening had arrived quickly; only darkness was now visible through the windows, the silver circular disk of the moon glowing in the sky.

The PM had received a call from Director Cobb a few minutes ago. He'd told him of the capture of Number Eight, which was good news. Apparently the ARU task force had been forced to defuse a bomb left at a shopping centre in Angel and then intercept a second device, which had been packed inside a stolen ambulance left outside the stadium.

Cobb said they'd appropriated an alarming amount of C4 plastic explosive. As he watched the news report, the Prime Minister licked his lips. The evening's events had already been horrific. If those two bombs had gone off, the casualties would have been catastrophic.

He pulled his attention back to the television. The female reporter was just about to deliver an update from outside the Emirates. Behind her, the PM could see countless emergency services still hard at work. They were going to be there all night.

'It has been a chaotic evening here, Fiona,' the lady said. *'We have just been informed of a recent shocking development. A second attack has been foiled in the last few minutes by police officers. We're told a man dressed as a paramedic parked a stolen ambulance in the midst*

*of the remaining crowd here, most of them walking
wounded and their supporters from the earlier attack. I
have been informed the vehicle contained enough
explosives to increase the death toll significantly.'*

Rogers glanced at the Prime Minister, the two men
exchanging a grim look.

*'Apparently, the suspect was planning to detonate the
device from a safe vantage point, by calling a mobile
phone attached to the explosives inside the ambulance. It
was only the swift intervention of the counter-terrorist
officers that prevented a further tragedy of unimaginable
consequences. And unbelievably, this is following eye-
witness reports of a third package left unattended in a
shopping centre in Angel, which officers were forced to
defuse. The suspect was detained and has been taken to
a police station for questioning. It is clear that these
attacks have been carefully planned and co-ordinated.
Let us just pray that there aren't more to follow this
evening. Back to you in the studio.'*

Rogers took the remote and muted the television as the
Prime Minister watched the shot cut back to the
newsreader in the newsroom.

'She's right,' Rogers said. 'It was co-ordinated to the
second. I think we've severely underestimated these
people.'

The Prime Minister didn't reply; his wife spoke
instead.

'So there are four of them left,' she said. 'Do we have
anything on them, Pete? Any leads?'

Rogers shook his head. 'Not much. The ambulance
bomber is our lifeline though. As Director Cobb said,
they took him alive. Right now he's our strongest bet.'

'Correct me if I'm wrong, but didn't Director Cobb
say the man was using C4 explosive?' the PM asked.

'Yes, sir.'

'For goodness sake, that's military stuff. Where the hell did they get this kind of equipment?'

There was a pause.

'Have you thought about cancelling the celebrations tonight, sir?' Rogers asked.

The Prime Minister nodded. 'I considered it, but I've decided not to. I'm not going to let terrorists dictate the way we live. We have good people out there; they'll track them down.'

There was a brief silence in the room.

'I've had an idea,' his wife suddenly said.

The two men looked at her.

'Why not release the photographs of the last four men to the press? It might drum up some leads.'

'Or cause a lot of problems,' the Prime Minister said. 'At the moment, the public think that this is probably it. They have no idea that there are four more of these lunatics out there.'

'The operation isn't a secret anymore, David,' she continued. 'We need to use every resource.'

Silence. The Prime Minister thought about it. He looked at Rogers.

'Pete, what do you think?'

He shrugged. 'I think we're running out of options, sir. These four could be anywhere. And if celebrations are still going ahead, there are going to be thousands of people all over the city in a couple of hours. We can't waste any more time.'

There was a pause.

Then the Prime Minister nodded.

'OK,' he said. 'Let's do it.'

Back at the ARU it was a case of waiting and staying ready for the task force. They all knew they had a long night ahead with four of the suspects still on the loose, which meant they could get a call at any moment. As the intelligence team worked away next door with Cobb and Agent Crawford, all the ground team could do was sit and wait.

Most of them were gathered in the Briefing Room, talking and drinking cups of coffee as they sat around by the noticeboards, making the most of a moment's rest. Someone had grabbed a marker pen and drawn a big X over five of the suspects' faces, leaving four to go. Number One, Four, Six and Nine.

Across the room, Archer was standing alone by the drinks stand, pouring himself a cup of tea. Someone entered to his left; he turned and saw it was Special Agent Rivers, the other DEA operative aside from Crawford. Archer wasn't sure why the American agency had joined this operation seeing as Cobb hadn't explained. Archer didn't know much about their operations and practices, but he had seen the late-night reports and documentaries on their gruesome and very much ongoing war with the drug cartels.

The American approached the stand, taking a cup and pouring himself some coffee. Archer offered his hand, introducing himself. 'Archer.'

The American shook it. 'Rivers.'

Archer studied the DEA agent as he drank his tea. He seemed calm and very contained, no unnecessary speech or movement; although he was barely talking, his demeanour shouted *ex-military*. Deciding to give him

180

space, Archer turned and walked to the window behind him, looking out at the frosty night.

In the car park he saw a figure sitting alone on a bench. He looked closer.

It was Chalky.

From this distance, Archer could see a cigarette burning out between his fingers as he stared straight ahead, lost in thought. Archer sipped his tea, his eyes not moving from his friend. He was concerned.

'I've seen that look before,' came a voice.

Rivers had walked up beside the blond officer, looking out at Chalky.

'Which branch of the military were you?' Archer asked, eager to change the subject.

'SEAL Team Six.'

'No shit? You were the guys who took down...'

He didn't need to say the name. The whole world knew about Seal Team Six's assault on Osama Bin Laden in Pakistan the year before. They'd stormed the compound by helicopter where he'd been hiding out in the middle of the night, shooting the world's most wanted man dead.

'My Dad's a cop in New York,' Archer continued. 'Apparently a load of people went down to Ground Zero. There were thousands of them. They had a party.'

Rivers didn't react, or respond.

'So were you there, that night?' Archer asked, interested.

Rivers nodded. 'I was there.'

The young policeman went to ask further questions, but he saw the expression on the American's face and held his tongue.

The other man seemed about to speak, but Agent Crawford suddenly appeared by the door motioning for his fellow agent to join him.

Rivers threw his coffee in the bin, the cup still three-quarters full, and turned to the door.

'What was it like?' Archer asked, before he left. 'The operation. Being there.'

Rivers paused.

'Disappointing,' he said.

Turning, he walked away.

Across London, the driver of the black Mercedes was doing a good job. The needle on the speedometer had been tucked just under eighty the entire journey and they were making good time.

In the back, there was no need for the passengers to talk in Arabic. The driver worked for Henry and knew what would happen if he opened his mouth to anyone about what he heard.

'It's been a while,' Dominick ventured.

Faris looked at him with disdain.

'Meeting inside the Terminal was one of the dumbest things you've ever suggested. Are you trying to get captured? There were cops everywhere.'

'I had to drop someone off,' Dominick replied, defensively.

'Who?'

'Just some bitch. No one important'

Silence. Faris shook his head and shot his cuff, checking the time.

'We'll be in the air within the hour. Your uncle's waiting for you in Paris.'

Dominick paled; he felt acid in his stomach.

'He came all this way?'

'Don't be flattered. He had business to attend to. You were just an added bonus.'

Faris suddenly opened the compartment separating their seat. Reaching inside, he pulled out a black pistol and drew back the top-slide, checking the chamber. Dominick saw the gleam of a bullet in the pipe, the weapon loaded.

Satisfied, Faris slotted it back into a holster on his hip. He'd had to leave the gun in the car before entering the Terminal, but pulling it out in front of Dominick had sent a message.

Now you're here, you stay.

'So what does he want?' Dominick asked, trying to hide his nervousness as Faris leaned back in his seat.

The green-eyed cartel lieutenant turned and smiled.

'What do you think?'

TWENTY TWO

Outside the Armed Response Unit's headquarters, Crawford led Rivers through the main exit and into the parking lot. He looked around to make sure they weren't being overheard. There was a young dark-haired officer across the car park sitting on the bench, but he was out of earshot and wasn't paying them any attention.

'Farha's getting on the jet,' he told Rivers. 'He'll be in Paris before eleven o'clock, French time.'

He pulled a pack of cigarettes from his pocket. Taking one out, he pulled a lighter and sparked it.

Rivers frowned. 'I thought you were trying to quit?'

Crawford looked at him. 'Pick your battles, right?'

Rivers answered his original statement. 'OK, this is good. So let's get in there and tell Cobb.'

Crawford shook his head, sucking the smoke deep into his lungs.

'I can't. Not yet.'

'What? Why the hell not?'

'Faber got killed because I got careless. I never should have put him that close to the compound. Now he's at the bottom of the ocean and all because I got too eager.'

'Yeah, but this just feels wrong. We can't withhold information from these people.'

'Look, I don't like it either. But Farha's not going anywhere. He'll be getting on the jet any moment. Flynn and Brody are waiting for him at the airfield. If we tell the Brits what we know they'll never let Farha get to

Paris. Henry'll get spooked, the jet will stay in the UK and the whole deal will be blown.'

He took another long pull on the smoke and looked at Rivers. They had developed a good working relationship over the past few months, but Crawford still called the shots. He was the one in charge of the operation.

'Listen, Ben. You joined this detail eleven months ago. But I've been working to take down this asshole for nearly two years. Tonight is the night I can do it. We get footage of the trade, that's all the closure we could ever need. This is a career-defining case for all of us; that includes you. Faber also got killed for it. So I want to go for the jugular, document this deal and then move in and take his ass down. Remember, we've got enough on this scumbag to not just put him away, but convict members of two other major cartels who operate with him, including the Albanians. That's millions and millions of dollars. Once we move in, the Brits can have Farha. He's basically in custody where he is already. Best case scenario, Henry kills him. Worst case, he leaves him alive and the Brits lock him up and throw away the key.'

Rivers frowned.

He could see Crawford's points, but his conscience was uneasy.

'Right now, I trust five people,' Crawford said, drawing on the Marlboro. 'You, me and our three other guys. This asshole runs one of the biggest drug cartels in the Middle East. He's linked with terrorism. He killed one of my men. And the evidence we have doesn't just implicate him, it takes down associates of his. This is a huge deal, a once-in-a-lifetime opportunity. Think about it.'

Rivers stared straight ahead.

Then he nodded slowly.

185

'OK. I agree. But you *need* to tell Cobb. We're in his house. If he finds out you're holding stuff from him, that could end any future co-operation we get from the Brits. He didn't have to include us in this; you know that. He could have put you on the next plane back to Paris after you arrived. He needs to be told.'

Crawford thought for a moment.

'OK. I'll talk to him.'

'About what?' came a voice.

They turned. Shapira had appeared from the entrance silently. She was standing ten feet behind them, her arms folded, her attractive eyes narrowed.

'Nothing. Just double-checking some facts,' said Crawford.

He nodded to Rivers, flicking away the cigarette, Crawford turned and together the two men moved back inside.

Shapira stayed where she was, her head turning as she watched them pass.

At the front desk to the Heathrow Marriott Hotel, the concierge tapped away at a computer as she finished checking in an elderly couple booked in for one night. Dressed in a smart red work suit and white shirt, she had a golden name-plate clipped to the pocket of her red jacket, *Sally* typed in neat lettering beside the hotel logo.

'Where are you off to in the morning?' she asked politely as she typed on the computer on the desk before her.

The lady looked at her husband and smiled.

'San Francisco.'

'How nice,' Sally said. 'I wish I was going with you.'

She passed over their room key, directing them towards the lifts. The man took the key, thanked her and picking up their luggage, the two of them shuffled off.

Watching them go, Sally picked up a small bottle of water sitting just under the desk before her and unscrewed the cap, sneaking a cold sip. Across the foyer, a television was mounted on the wall. It had only recently been installed; she didn't know whose idea it had been to put it there, but it was a gift from heaven for the employees who drew the short straw and worked nights. One thing was for sure, it made the shifts go a hell of a lot quicker.

Taking advantage of the momentary lull in guests, Sally watched the screen.

It was the news, still covering the attack on the stadium. A camera crew had got near the stand that took the blast. Seeing the footage of the damage shocked Sally; she'd caught glimpses of the reports all day and remembered that there'd been some kind of raid that had happened earlier in the afternoon too; maybe it was all connected. For once, Sally actually felt glad that she was holed up behind this desk for the evening. She didn't fancy being in a crowd around the city tonight. Not with all these attacks going on.

Just then, a family of four appeared through the entrance, dragging their luggage behind them as they approached the front desk. Sally put her bottle of water away, and prepared to check them in with her practiced smile. But just as they arrived in front of her, the television screen across the foyer suddenly changed. Out of the corner of her eye, she saw four names and faces appear. A headline ran beneath them.

Breaking: Four terrorist suspects remain at large. Considered extremely dangerous.

The family arrived at the desk, waiting for Sally to focus on them.

The man asked her a question, but she didn't hear what he said.

She was staring at one of the photographs.

'Oh my God,' she whispered.

At the ARU HQ, Archer was still standing by the window in the Briefing Room, the other guys sitting fifteen feet to his right and talking amongst themselves.

He appeared to be watching Chalky down in the car park, but his mind was elsewhere. Rivers' response to his question earlier had confused him. *Disappointing*, he'd said. When word had spread of the success of the Bin Laden operation last May, the SEAL guys had been hailed as heroes, not just in the US but around the world, but Rivers seemed almost despondent when he spoke of it. Archer was baffled.

As he stood alone and pondered, he noticed another figure across the car park. Shapira. She was holding a phone to her ear, talking, seemingly ignoring the cold. Archer knew a couple of the guys weren't happy about being saddled with two extra operatives that none of them knew, but he didn't mind. She'd prevented a potential catastrophe by knocking out the bomber before he could detonate the ambulance at the Emirates. Archer had no problem with her at all.

Behind the young officer, Mac walked into the room, drawing a paper cup from the stand and pouring himself a coffee.

'How you doing, Arch?' he asked, joining the younger man by the window.

'Better than him,' Archer replied, jerking his head towards Chalky.

Mac looked down into the car park at Chalky.

A silence followed.

'Can I ask you something?' Archer asked quietly.

Mac nodded.

'Have you ever had any close calls? Like, really close calls? The kind of thing that he went through today with the shotgun.'

Mac laughed, which caught the younger man off guard.

'Arch, if I told you about each one, we'd be standing here all night.'

He paused for a moment, thinking back.

'When I was in the army, we were sent out on a patrol through Helmand' he recounted. 'I was driving the Humvee. As we went through the town, a kid ran out into the road chasing a football. I braked. And realised it was a set-up. Some dicker with a handgun ran up across the street and fired it at my window. I was leaning forward, so it skimmed the back of my neck. Literally. I felt it touch the hairs. The poor bastard next to me wasn't so lucky. Smithy, his name was. Well it hit Smithy smack in the temple, just under his helmet.'

Archer stayed silent.

'And there's plenty more where that came from. Since I was sixteen, I've been either a soldier or a copper. Never been good at anything else. All that stuff, it's part of the work. I figured that out a long time ago. The sooner you accept that, the sooner you can do your job properly.'

Archer looked out through the glass at Chalky.

'I'm worried about him.'

'Of course you are,' the older man replied. 'He's your mate. He almost died today. He should have died today. And he knows it. First time that happens, it shakes you up. He'll get over it.'

'It's not just that,' Archer said, lowering his voice. 'I'm worried about his decision making. I'm afraid he's going to get someone killed.'

Mac sipped his coffee.

'How old are you, Arch?' he asked.

That damn question again.

The younger man looked into the distance through the window.

'Twenty six.'

'You're young,' said Mac. 'Youngest guy in the Unit.'

'I put my time in. I earned my spot'

'You don't need to tell me that. I was the one who selected you. Put you in my First Team with Chalky and Port. If I had a single doubt about you, I never would have picked you for my squad, believe me.'

He paused.

'But tell me, before today, have you ever been shot at?'

Silence.

'No,' Archer said quietly.

'Stabbed?'

Archer shook his head.

'Ever been near explosives in the field?'

Archer didn't need to respond; they both knew the answer.

Mac sipped his coffee and tapped his temple.

'That shit, it all messes with you up here,' he said. 'You come within an inch of death, let me tell you, your priorities shift in an instant. The world becomes a different place. Some lads can't handle it.'

He nodded at Chalky.

'And some get reckless. They take stupid risks. I saw lads in Iraq try to go out on patrol without a helmet, or just walk through IED land like they were out in the park. They got lucky once and figure that they can keep doing it.'

'I thought you'd have lynched him for what he did in the shopping centre,' Archer said. 'I was waiting for you to do it. He ignored your orders.'

Mac looked at him. 'You heard that phone ring, right?'

Archer nodded, slowly.

'You know what that would have done wired to the C4?'

Archer didn't respond.

'Because if it had been, you and I wouldn't be standing here right now, having this conversation, Arch. They'd be mopping us up with a bucket and sponge.'

He paused.

'He acted like an idiot. I'm not denying that. He put himself at risk, as well as you, me and everyone on the street. He ignored my orders. But he saved my life. And yours. He took a huge risk and somehow, it paid off. So

191

we move on and focus on the next one, and hope that everything falls our way again.'

Mac turned to him.

'All the training in the world can't prepare you for situations like that. You just make a decision and hope to God it's the right one.'

He drank from his coffee cup, thinking.

'My career's almost over. I know that; I'll be done soon. But you're a young guy, Arch. You've got all this ahead of you. I don't know where you're going to go, or what you're going to encounter. But take it from me, at some point, you're going to come face to face with death yourself. Could be tonight, tomorrow or ten years from now.'

He paused.

'Just don't blink first.'

Archer stayed silent, taking this in.

But as he did so there was a sudden movement at the doorway and Porter suddenly appeared, moving in from the Operations area.

'Mac, we've got a location on Farha!'

There was a split-second pause.

Then every guy in the room made for the door.

At that moment, the black Mercedes that was carrying Dominick Farha pulled into a dark airfield, somewhere in the south-west area of the city.

Looking out of the window, Dominick saw a sleek, familiar private jet parked on the end of the runway, facing the tarmac stretch, ready to go.

The car moved over the grass and came to a halt on the runway beside the plane. Faris nodded, and the pair of them stepped out.

As soon as they shut the doors, the car did a 180 and left, moving back onto the road and off into the night. The field was completely empty, save for the two men and the shadow of the pilot in the cockpit of the small plane.

It was time to get into the air.

The steps to the jet were unfolded; the two men walked up them briskly and boarded the aircraft. Inside the plane, Dominick was surprised. There were stacks and stacks of cocaine bricks piled neatly at the back, tightly bound and keyed, around four or five million dollars' worth. He stared at them as Faris withdrew the steps and pulled the door to the jet shut, locking it.

'Like I said, he had business to attend to,' said Faris, as he moved into the cabin, noticing Dominick looking at the cocaine. 'You were just the cherry on top.'

Dominick swallowed and turned, taking a seat in the cabin directly opposite Faris.

The engine to the jet started to whine, as they prepared for take-off. Dominick checked his watch.

8:20 pm.

Three hundred and sixty five days of waiting.

A whole calendar year.

Finally, he was getting out of here.

Inside the Departures hall of Terminal Five, the young dark-haired woman with the pregnant belly was patiently waiting, her eyes searching for any sign of Dominick. She couldn't see him anywhere.

For the briefest of moments, that nagging doubt whispered at the back of her mind again.

Maybe he won't come back.

But in the same instant, she scolded herself, wracked with guilt at entertaining such a thought.

Of course he'll come back. He's just been delayed.

Looking up, she checked the time on the electronic board.

8:20 pm.

Forty minutes to go.

As she continued to search for any sign of Dominick, she caught sight of a pregnant woman with her family sitting to her right by the wall. She was leaning back in her seat to take some of the weight off her back.

Their eyes met. The woman smiled in understanding.

We're in this together, the smile said.

The younger girl's stomach gripped.

She didn't smile back.

TWENTY THREE

At the ARU's headquarters, Cobb returned to the Operations area having just been downstairs watching his team set up an interrogation. Number Eight had been processed and placed in one of the rooms and Frost had just joined him, ready to go to work.

As Cobb re-entered the analyst team's area, he saw the task force wasn't in the Briefing Room. Just as he was going to ask where the hell they were, Nikki sensed his arrival and turned from her desk in front of him.

'Sir, great news; we got a lead on Farha's location.'

'What?' Cobb's eyes widened. 'Where?'

'A Marriott hotel, outside Heathrow. The concierge was watching the news and saw the photographs released by Downing Street. She said Farha had been a guest at the hotel; he's been there for a couple of days under a false name apparently. Our team are on their way. Agents Rivers and Shapira went with them.'

'Son of a bitch,' Cobb said. 'A hotel by the airport. No wonder we couldn't find him.'

'You think he's trying an escape? Or a hijack?'

Cobb shook his head.

'No. No chance. He wouldn't get through the security checkpoints.'

He thought for a moment.

'A hotel like that, it's busy as hell. Zero routine, structure, different faces and names every day. It's a good place to hide out. I'm guessing he thought he'd be invisible there.'

'Almost,' Nikki added.

Behind them, Crawford appeared from the corridor, having just come up the stairs. Cobb sensed they were being approached and turned.

He noticed the American looking into the empty Briefing Room, a somewhat rueful look on his face.

'Something wrong?' Cobb asked.

'I need to talk to you, Tim,' the DEA agent replied.

*

Across the city, a chorus of leather boots smacked on the marble floor of the lobby as the ARU task force rushed through the entrance to the Heathrow Marriott Hotel.

Startled bystanders stepped back as they saw the sudden arrival of the group of armed officers. Mac led the team to the front desk as the concierge stood waiting for them. She was a young girl, in her mid-twenties, blonde and pretty; her name-tag said *Sally*.

'You made the call?' Mac asked, arriving quickly by the desk.

'Yes, sir,' she said. She passed him a room key over the counter. 'Room 418. I haven't seen him leave. Our security are holding back as requested.'

Mac grabbed the plastic key-card and turned to his men quickly.

'Deakins, take Team Two. Cover the exits,' he ordered. The officer nodded and moved off with five of the men.

Mac turned to Archer, Porter and Chalky.

'You three, we're going upstairs.'

Without a moment's delay, the four men ran together to the stairwell.

Behind them in the lobby, Rivers and Shapira watched the team move; the two of them hadn't been included in the police sergeant's orders.

Shapira felt her irritation rise but noticed that the American beside her didn't seem to care. If anything, he looked kind of bored.

'You want to take a look around?' she asked him.

He looked at her for a moment.

Then he shrugged and nodded.

'Beats standing here.'

Upstairs, a husband and wife were strolling down the corridor of the 4th floor on their way to the lift. They were both dressed up smartly; the man had arranged dinner for them both downstairs, a prelude to their romantic week in Rome starting with their 10am flight from Terminal Five tomorrow morning.

However, they stopped in their tracks when four police officers suddenly erupted from the stairwell beside them, sub-machine guns tucked into each man's shoulder, their faces tense. The woman made to make a sound, but she instinctively covered her mouth as the lead police officer put a finger to his lips, looking at her as the other three moved past the pair.

The couple watched as the four policemen moved swiftly but cautiously down the corridor.

They came to a stop outside Room 418.

Closest to the door, Mac had a white key-card in his hand as Archer, Chalky and Porter took up a position behind him.

He eased it slowly and gently into the lock.

There was a soft click; a light on the metal panel that housed the lock flicked from *red* to *green*.

And in that same instant, Mac pushed down hard on the handle and the four officers stormed into the hotel room, tracing with their MP5s.

It was empty.

'*Are you kidding me?*' Cobb asked, incredulous, standing in his office with Crawford. 'You knew where he was and you withheld that information? My team are at the hotel right now, wasting their time!'

'Listen to me!' Crawford implored, as Cobb paced back and forth before him furiously. 'Just stop for a moment and listen.'

Cobb paused. He glared at the DEA agent angrily.

'Right now, the man is on his way to an airfield outside Paris. I have a team waiting there for him. His uncle will be there too.'

Cobb was losing patience. Crawford raised his voice a hair.

'C'mon man, think for a moment. Heads of cartels do not go face-to-face for drug buys; it's like a goddamned unicorn. My team are already in place; they'll witness the transaction then the moment it's done, we'll move in and apprehend them all. Dominick Farha isn't going anywhere.'

He paused.

'And we also agreed on this earlier. I warned you that the boy might get in touch with his uncle. You agreed to hold back.'

'That was then,' Cobb said. He pointed at the television in his office covering the attack at the Emirates. 'This is now.'

Crawford didn't reply. Cobb rubbed his face, frustrated; then sighing, he moved around his desk and sat down behind it, shaking his head.

'I've got terrorists and bombs all over the city on one side; I've got the biggest drug dealer in the Middle East on the other. And all in one night. Jesus Christ.'

Crawford nodded, staying quiet. He could see he'd got through to Cobb, but he could also understand the torment the Unit's boss was going through. He had his target and knew exactly where he was, but he couldn't make a move on him yet.

'I'll need to talk to the Prime Minister and contact my men,' Cobb continued. 'They're wasting their time at the hotel.'

'But at least we know where he is,' Crawford said, gently.

Cobb thought for a moment. Then he nodded.

'Yeah. We do.'

Behind the reception desk to the hotel, there was a door to a room that contained all the security monitors for cameras mounted in the building. The concierge was sitting in a chair in front of them, Fox leaning over her shoulder.

Despite the array of screens, the pair were watching one of them in particular.

'Stop,' Fox suddenly said.

Once she did so, he tapped the screen.

'There. Son of a bitch. There he is.'

As he spoke, Archer and Chalky appeared in the doorway behind him. Mac had already told the rest of the team that Farha wasn't in the hotel room, but Deakins and the other men were still blocking off the exits in case he was still inside the building.

'Look at this,' Fox said, seeing the two men arrive.

The pair moved over and peered closely at the screen.

It was a shot of the lobby. The time in the corner of the screen said *7:49 pm*, less than an hour ago. As the tape ran, all four pairs of eyes watched a man walking through the reception area towards the exit. He was dressed smartly, in an expensive-looking three piece suit.

As the guy walked past the camera, he suddenly stopped for a moment, looking at something on the wall.

'The television,' the concierge said. 'He's watching the news.'

The camera was mounted just above and to the right of the television monitor, so it gave a clear, front-on shot of the guy.

It was Dominick Farha, no mistake.

Standing beside Chalky Archer looked closer, examining Farha's appearance.

But there was another person walking with him. A young, pregnant dark-haired woman; she couldn't have been older than twenty.

'Who the hell is she?' asked Fox, as the concierge hit a button.

The tape continued. The frame just included the front entrance, so they watched the man and woman walk through the doors.

They saw Farha hail a taxi then open the door, helping his companion inside. He climbed in after her, pulling the door shut and the vehicle moved away.

'Shit,' said Fox. 'So where the hell did they go?'

Without a word, Archer grabbed a piece of paper and a pen resting on the desk and scribbled down the licence plate of the taxi cab. He left the room, grabbing the mobile phone from its sleeve on his tac vest. The other three were still fixated by the shot on the screen.

'Rewind and run it again,' requested Fox. 'There's got to be something here we can use'.

The concierge pressed a button, and the tape wound back, everything happening in reverse. The moment Farha and the girl disappeared out of the shot, she hit *Play*.

Once again, the pair walked into the shot from the lift.

They stopped momentarily as Farha turned his attention to the television screen.

'Wait.'

Fox and Chalky looked down.

The concierge was frowning.

'What is it?' asked Chalky.

She was peering hard at the screen, leaning forward. 'The way that girl was walking.'

'What about it?' asked Fox.

'Didn't seem right. Looked strange.'

'Of course it did,' Fox replied. 'She's pregnant.'

The receptionist thought for a moment.

'Actually, no. I don't think she is.'

Fox and Chalky stared at her, confused.

'What makes you say that?' Chalky asked.

The concierge rewound the tape and hit *Play* again. They watched the shot for the third time; however, on this occasion no one paid any attention to Farha, focusing on the girl.

'Look at that,' said the concierge, pointing at her as the tape ran. 'A pregnant woman doesn't walk like that. See how rigid she is?'

The men looked closer. She was right.

The girl looked like she was straining, struggling with the weight on her stomach.

It looked wrong somehow.

'Looks almost…robotic or something,' said Fox.

'Like she's weighed down,' the receptionist added.

'But with what?' Chalky asked.

Upstairs, Porter and Mac were rummaging through Farha's hotel room, searching desperately for any clues or evidence that could give them an idea where the hell he'd gone. So far, they'd found some clippings of wire, a small set of pliers, a needle and spool of thread.

Porter looked at Mac, then at the items they'd tossed on the bed. He felt uneasy.

Given the known interests of the man who'd been staying here, all these items were pointing to something pretty damn sinister.

'I don't like the look of this, boss,' Porter said.

Mac shook his head, looking at the pliers and clippings of wire.

'Neither do I.'

At that moment, the earpiece in each man's ear crackled. '*Mac, its Fox. I'm downstairs in the security room, looking at the CCTV. We found Farha. He left in a taxi about an hour ago.*'

'Where'd he go?'

'*Arch is checking on that. There was something else, Sarge. He had a woman with him. Young girl, looked like she was pregnant. Lady down here thinks otherwise. We reckon the bump might be concealing something.*'

Mac and Porter looked at each other, then at the surface of the bed.

The pliers.

The needle and thread.

The wire.

Just then, Archer's voice came up over the radio. '*Cab company said the driver dropped them off at Heathrow forty minutes ago. Terminal Five.*'

Mac and Porter stared at each other for half a second.

Then the two men ran for the door.

TWENTY FOUR

Upstairs in the hotel, Rivers and Shapira were walking the other floors. They knew it was highly unlikely that they were just going to bump into Farha, but it gave them something to do other than just stand and wait in the lobby.

They were on the top floor. Together, they'd moved all the way down from the far end to the lifts but hadn't encountered a soul.

Turning the corner, Rivers suddenly cannoned into someone. Stepping back, he looked at the guy. He was Middle Eastern, but that was where the similarities with Farha finished; this man had a shaved head and glasses.

'Sorry, man,' apologised Rivers.

The guy nodded and moved off down the corridor without a word.

Just then, a radio that Cobb had given Rivers crackled in his hand. It was the sergeant of the task force.

'All teams, lobby, now!'

Rivers and Shapira looked at each other, then ran for the stairs, bursting through the stairwell door.

As he raced down each flight, the American found himself thinking about the man he'd just bumped into on the top floor.

Goddamn, that guy looked familiar.

Inside Terminal Five, the girl in the green dress was starting to shake with fear.

Dominick hadn't returned and her back was in agony from the lethal weight sewn into the front of her dress. But that was nothing compared to the weight on her conscience. What had once seemed like such a romantic and committed gesture was now turning into a fully-fledged nightmare.

She suddenly felt very alone.

Everything inside her wanted to walk out of the building and run away.

Or curl up into a ball and just hope it would all disappear.

But her feet wouldn't move.

He'll come back, she told herself as she trembled, standing there in the Terminal with people all around her.

He has to.

Scared and alone, she looked up at the clock, trying not to cry.

8:54 pm.

Six minutes to go.

*

Four minutes later, the three black 4x4 Fords chewed up the airport ramp at breakneck speed and pulled to a halt as close as they could get outside Terminal Five, the tyres screeching as the rubber dug into the tarmac.

Travellers standing nearby were shocked by this sudden arrival and were even more taken back when ten armed officers piled out of the doors, each cradling a sub-machine gun.

Together, the ARU team sprinted for the entrance, Rivers and Shapira jumping out of the third car and following close behind. There was armed airport security stationed by the doors who'd seen this dramatic arrival. Fox ran ahead and started talking fast, explaining the situation to them.

The two men he spoke to listened intently, then together both sets of security swept into the Departures hall.

Inside the building, the young woman was shaking. Her whole body was icy cold, yet sweat was gathering on her forehead as if she had a fever.

She was a hundred yards inside the building, standing alongside a restaurant packed with customers.

She looked up at the neon sign above her.

Carluccio's, it said, in bright blue neon.

She dropped her gaze to all the people inside.

There must have been close to fifty of them at least, most of them smiling and having a good time, killing time before their flights.

Turning, she swallowed and checked the clock.

8:59 pm.

One minute.

By the entrance doors across the hall, Mac turned to Deakins.

'Take Team Two downstairs to Arrivals. Go!'

Without a word, six of the men ran to the lifts.

As Mac shifted his attention back to First Team, a man with a radio and three armed airport police ran over having seen the task force arrive from across the hall.

Mac moved forward to meet them. He recognised the man holding the radio; his name was Richards, Head of Security for Terminal Five. Mac knew that he would have been fully briefed of the situation with the nine suspects, given his role. Neither man bothered with greetings; they didn't have time.

'We've tracked the leader of the terrorist cell to this building,' Mac said. 'We think he's still here.'

It took a moment for this to register. *Oh shit*, Richards' face said.

Mac continued, not wasting a second.

'He's Number Nine on the list. Also, he's with a young woman. She appears pregnant, but we think the bump is concealing explosives of some kind. Tell your men.'

Richards nodded without a word, turning to a group of his gathered team of security.

Mac swivelled to see his own men had already moved off into the hall.

Searching for Dominick Farha and the woman in the green dress.

Her back turned, the girl was as yet unaware of the commotion by the doors and the arrival of the task force.

But suddenly, she heard the echo of boots running across the hall.

Turning, she saw a squad of armed policemen dispersing, obviously looking for something or someone.

Her blood ran cold.

They knew.

It was only a matter of time before one of them saw her.

She looked up at the clock.

9:00 pm.

It was her departure time.

Her hand moved to her pocket. Stammering, she started reciting something Dominick had told her to memorise. He'd assured her that they'd be saying it together, hand-in-hand, as they prepared to move on to the next life.

Standing alone, her lips moving almost imperceptibly, she whispered her way through the paragraph as she desperately tried not to throw up.

Fifty yards away Archer was by a check-in booth, frantically scanning the crowd.

He cursed. Nothing. He couldn't see either of them anywhere. Around him, people standing in queues for the check-in desks were clearly un-nerved by the sudden arrival and focused activity of the policemen around the giant hall.

Given the day's events, they were understandably on edge.

Archer looked down the left side of the building, all the way to the wall. *Shit*. They needed to evacuate the building immediately.

As the thought ran through his mind, he turned and looked the other way.

He saw the woman.

She had her hands hidden in the folds of her emerald-green dress.

· She was staring straight ahead, and her lips were moving as she muttered something to herself.

He started to run.

TWENTY FIVE

The young girl was almost all the way through the passage in her memory. Tears were brimming in her half-open eyes distorting her view, the hall swimming like crystal in front of her. A commotion to her right broke her concentration, stopping her just short of the closing prayer.

To her right, she saw a policeman racing towards her.

He was young, with blond hair and a kind, handsome face, but not at that moment. He pulled to a halt forty feet away, and lifted a machine-gun jammed into his shoulder, the other end pointed at her head, shouting at her.

'Police! Put your hands up!'

She looked straight at him, petrified.

Obeying, she lifted her trembling hands from the folds of her dress.

Around her, people started to run and scream in terror.

There was a switch in her hand, connected to a black wire that disappeared into the folds of her gown.

Seeing the wire and switch, Archer aimed his crosshairs on the girl's chin.

'Drop it!'

She stared at him helplessly, like a doe caught in the headlights.

She had big brown eyes, the colour of hazelnut; tears welled and spilled from them down her cheeks.

For a split second, Archer hesitated.

'*Look at me!*' he ordered. '*LOOK AT ME! You don't need to do this. You don't need to die here!*'

Her chin quivered.

'*Don't do this!*' he shouted again, aiming his foresight on her forehead.

She looked at him for one last time.

'He never came back,' she said, tears spilling from her eyes.

She closed them.

'*No!*' shouted Archer, clenching his finger on the trigger of the MP5.

But suddenly, there was a gunshot from another weapon.

The girl's head snapped back as she took a nine-millimetre bullet in the forehead.

People around the Terminal screamed as the gunshot echoed around the giant building. The bullet exited the back of her skull and slammed into the bar of the restaurant, shattering bottles from the impact, and the girl was dead before she hit the floor.

Blood and brains had spattered all over the pristine white linoleum floor behind her. Turning, Archer saw Mac, his weapon aimed rock-steady at the girl, the air filled with the smell of cordite from the gunshot.

Porter and Chalky ran forward as other officers stayed back, keeping any civilians from getting close. They needn't have bothered; the Terminal was almost completely empty by now.

Kneeling by the dead girl, Chalky eased the detonator from her hand as Porter checked for a pulse.

'She's dead,' he confirmed, stating the obvious.

As Archer caught his breath, Chalky pulled a knife from his tactical vest and made a small incision in the front of her gown.

He peered inside, and turned back to Mac immediately.

'We're going to need bomb disposal, Sarge. Again.'

Archer was still standing, motionless. From his position, he could see the girl's face beside Porter's knee. The bullet had taken her in the middle of the forehead. The front of her head and face was completely intact, save for the small dark hole ringed with maroon.

He saw her big brown eyes staring up at the ceiling.

A final tear fell from her right eye and slid down her cheek to the white floor.

The EOD arrived quickly and set to work dismantling the device as airport security kept every civilian outside the building, as far back as they could get them from the blast radius.

The ARU task force and police were also told to exit as the device was still unsecure, but the defusing was straight-forward; there were no trips, no collapsible circuits. The guy in the blast-suit turned to his team-mate standing across the hall and gave the thumbs up. The message was passed on, and the various ARU officers and airport police moved back into the building.

It was safe.

Archer had already walked back inside and was standing alone, thirty yards from the dead girl. He was watching the bomb team remove each brick of C4 from a white dress hidden under the green gown, stowing them carefully. Someone had laid a blanket over the woman's face

'You OK?' Fox asked as he joined him, the two men standing side by side.

Silence.

'I couldn't kill her, Fox,' Archer said quietly, staring at her body.

'Doesn't matter, mate. She's dead. No one got hurt.'

'Yeah. No thanks to me.' Archer cursed, shaking his head. 'Shit, I'm an idiot. I looked into her eyes. She was scared. Confused. No idea what she was doing. And it made me hesitate. And it almost got everyone killed.'

'But you were the one who spotted her. If you hadn't, we might all be dead now.'

Archer didn't respond.

'Maybe I don't belong here,' he said quietly.

The sandy-haired officer turned. 'What?'

'In this Unit. She was seconds from killing us all and I hesitated. I couldn't shoot her. What use is that? Suppose everyone was right, maybe I am too young for this.'

Fox shook his head.

'Before I joined this detail, I was in an armed response vehicle,' he said. 'Rode in that car for four years. We were arresting drug-dealers, confiscating weapons, real front-line stuff. I thought I'd seen everything, you know?'

He paused and jabbed a finger at the dead girl.

'But this isn't normal, Arch. None of what's happened today is. You can train all you want, but nothing prepares you to do something like that,' he said. 'You know why you hesitated?'

Archer looked at him.

'Because it meant something to you. As it should. Cobb, Mac, they tell you to take responsibility for every shot fired. But that also means for every life you take.'

The pair of them looked at the girl, and Fox shook his head.

'And that's the difference between people like us and people like them.'

'Tell you what, I owe you one, Mac,' said Richards as he watched the EOD team work. The two men were standing together in the middle of the Terminal, a distance from Archer and Fox. 'We had no bloody idea she was here. Or who the hell she was.'

An armed airport policeman was standing near the bomb team talking in lowered tones with the lead disposal guy. Turning, the officer approached Mac and Richards.

'How're we doing, Parsons?' asked Richards as the man got closer.

'Last of the explosives been stowed, sir. There's an ambulance outside. I'll tell them to come in and collect the body.'

'How's the crowd?'

'An old man fainted and some kids are going to have nightmares for a while. But other than that, everyone's ok.'

With that, Parsons turned and departed. On the way, he passed Porter who was moving swiftly towards Mac.

'Sarge?' he asked.

Mac turned. 'Yeah?'

'I need to talk to you for a moment. Alone.'

Mac took the hint and walked away from the airport security with Porter.

'I just spoke to Director Cobb about Dominick Farha,' Porter continued, in a lowered voice. 'He said that the DEA know where he is.'

Mac's eyes widened. 'So tell them to send the info. Let's go get him.'

'Cobb said we had to hold back.'

He paused.

'Apparently, Farha got out of the country on a private jet. He's on his way to Paris as we speak. There's a DEA team waiting to tail him when he gets there. Cobb said that there's a drug trade happening at the airfield where Farha will land; he'll be there, along with his uncle, some drug baron from the Middle East. Agent Crawford wants to get that on camera, then move in and take them both.'

Mac looked at him in disbelief as Rivers approached them.

'Did you know about this?' he asked the American, accusingly. 'We speed over to the hotel, all that effort, but you knew Farha wasn't there?'

'If we hadn't come down, we never would have found her,' he replied, pointing at the dead girl. 'And remember that Crawford has shared all that information with you. No one said he had to.'

Mac glared at him, then pulled the photocopy from the pocket of his tac vest.

'OK. He's your problem now,' he told Rivers with venom. 'If you lose him, you can find him. So let's move on to the other three.'

Rivers was standing close, but he'd stopped listening to the sergeant.

He was staring at the sheet of paper in his hand instead.

'What's wrong?' Porter asked, noticing the change on the man's face.

Then without a word, Rivers suddenly turned and sprinted for the exit.

TWENTY SIX

Back at the Heathrow Marriott, Number Six was confused. He was watching the news channel in his room, waiting for the first reports of an explosion at the airport, but nothing had happened.

Rising, he pulled back the curtain to see if there was smoke coming from the direction of the Terminal building.

But nothing.

The bitch better not have failed, he thought. She probably had. The girl was useless. He didn't know where Dom had picked her up, but she was sickeningly mawkish and sentimental towards him. To his credit, Dom had used that infatuation and manipulated it to achieve what he wanted. She was soft and weak and it was likely the airport police had intercepted her or she'd found some other way to screw things up.

But that doesn't change shit here, he thought.

Turning, he checked the clock on the desk by the bed.

9:15 pm.

Time to get to the roof.

He reached behind the far side of the bed and with a grunt from the effort, pulled up a long dark case, dumping it on the bed. It was about two feet in length, a worn military case that had probably been stacked under a tarpaulin in a desert somewhere for the past couple of years. He pulled a long black holdall from under the bed and started tucking the case into the bag. He didn't want any other hotel guests to see what was printed on the side, in thick black letters.

RPG-7.

Rocket Launcher.

He finished wrapping the bag around the case. Grabbing a thick coat, he pulled it on and zipped it up tight. It was cold outside, and the last thing he needed was any unnecessary shivering. He then picked up the strap for the bag and looped it over his shoulder. Turning, he moved to the door and double-checked that he had everything he needed. He could never come back here. He was travelling light, he had clothes on his back and money in his wallet to get a taxi and disappear.

Satisfied, he clicked off the light and departed.

Outside the room, he walked swiftly down the corridor. A couple coming the other way were blocking his path; the two of them saw the guy with the big bag wasn't going to stop, so the two of them had to press their backs flat against the wall to let him pass.

Ignoring them, he stared with focus at the stairwell by the lifts.

The only thing on his mind right now was getting to the roof.

'What the hell's going on?' Porter asked, behind the wheel of one of the squad cars.

He'd followed Rivers out of the Terminal to one of the ARU Fords as he'd run off, the American saying that they needed to get back to the Heathrow Marriott. Shapira had caught on fast and jumped in the back seat too, equally puzzled by the American's behaviour and unwilling to be left out.

'Number Six was at the hotel! I ran into him upstairs.'

Staring at him for a moment, Porter put his foot down and the car climbed past seventy as it roared past other traffic.

'What? Where? Are you sure it was him?'

'Positive. He'd shaved his head, so he looked different. But I saw his face, man. It's him. He was on the top floor.'

He thought for a moment, remembered something else.

'Oh shit.'

'What?'

'He was coming out from the stairwell when I bumped into him. He wasn't out of breath so he'd probably walked down, not up and we were on the top floor. So he must have been coming-'.

'From the roof,' finished Shapira.

Flooring the accelerator, Porter checked the rear-view mirror. He saw another black Ford weaving in and out of traffic, following close behind. He guessed some of the other lads were inside.

His suspicions were confirmed when the earpiece in his ear went off.

'Port? It's Fox. What the hell's going on?'

Port pushed the pressel on his uniform with one hand while keeping the other on the wheel.

'Rivers thinks he saw Number Six at the hotel earlier. Apparently the guy was walking down the stairwell, coming from the door to the roof.'

There was a pause.

'He's sure?'

Porter didn't reply. He turned a hard right, and the car raced down a side road towards the entrance to the

Heathrow Marriott, buses and slower moving cars flashing past the windows.

As soon as the car screeched to a halt outside the hotel, Rivers was already out and running through the entrance to the lobby.

It had been Dom's idea. The two of them were old friends; they'd met in a club in New York City a few years back. When Dom had been putting this plan together at the beginning of March, the young man's phone in Brooklyn had rung. Not much had been revealed, but he'd picked up on what Dom was asking of him and the reward that would come his way if he did it.

Without a moment's hesitation the guy had packed his bags, jumped on a plane, and headed to London.

Back in New York, his life was going nowhere and he knew it. He'd had some luck with a couple of low-level drug deals, but he was a small fish in a very big pond. He knew there was only so far he could go before the big sharks came swimming. When he made it to London, Dom had put him up in the flat he was renting. He'd told him about the ideas for the attacks, why he'd had to flee New York so abruptly after what happened at the Four Seasons, why it was imperative he laid low until he made things right with his family. How his uncle, Henry, hated the United Kingdom. The young man didn't know much about Dom's uncle save that he was a powerful and dangerous man who operated in the drug trade. Dom had told him that if he helped him, Henry would be so impressed that he'd probably employ him. He'd be rich. Protected. Living in the sun, far away from the Brooklyn back alleys and dark streets selling rocks and angel dust to crack-heads and junkies.

Dom had outlined his initial plan. It was solid but there was a problem; the young man wasn't prepared to go down the suicide bombing route. He wasn't a fanatic and certainly didn't intend to kill himself, not to mention that he also didn't have a clue what he was doing with explosives.

Dom had agreed with him that suicide bombing was moronic and that they would leave that to those who were stupid enough to do it.

He'd come up with this plan instead.

Take out a commercial jet.

The younger man liked the idea; although the targeted jet would be full of fellow Americans, he didn't give a shit. The only thing he had ever cared about was himself. Once he fired the launcher, he'd be out of the hotel in less than a minute. *Stay low, out of sight. Give it a couple of days, then get out of the country.* Dom had promised he'd be in touch. After that, hopefully, he could meet with Henry and talk about a role in his business.

He was already in position. He'd opened the door to the roof, closing it behind him and was now standing facing west. He was glad he'd worn the coat seeing how frosty the night was. He lowered the case to the ground and unzipped the bag, pushing the cloth back. Kneeling, he undid two clips and eased the lid open. It was an RPG, or Rocket-Propelled Grenade; the weapon was a Russian model, designed to take out tanks or low flying aircraft. Assembly of the weapon was simple. It was only two parts, the launcher and the rocket.

He pulled the launcher from the black inner casing and lifted it to his shoulder. The weight felt good; it had a pistol grip for firing which he curled his fingers around, looking down the sight. The weapon was sleek, in good condition and he'd used it before.

He knew it would be accurate.

Carefully, he reached into the case and slid out the second part. The warhead. An armour-penetrating grenade propelled by a rocket. He tipped his shoulder and slid the missile into the front of the weapon. It locked into place with a *click*. Dom had managed to get hold of some high-quality equipment for the group. C4, RPGs, Semtex plastic explosive, but unfortunately there was one disadvantage with the weapon resting on his shoulder; it wasn't a heat-seeker.

He'd have to hit first time, but then again, that wouldn't be a problem. In practice runs against selected targets out on the empty moors in the Welsh countryside the young man had proved extremely accurate with the launcher. Dom reassured him it was equally effective against aircraft, despite being designed to take out a slow-moving tank. He'd informed him about the success of the weapon in Somalia in the early Nineties. Apparently, rebels had used this weapon to take out two Black Hawk helicopters, which left the young man sufficiently impressed.

When he fired, the plane was going down.

A noise jerked him back to the present.

The jet was coming into view from the sky ahead.

It was three hundred yards away, descending from the dark ahead and to his left. The 9:20pm from New York, right on time.

Full capacity, over two hundred and fifty souls on board.

He shifted his hips, letting the launcher slide snugly into place against his shoulder. Then he slowly rose to

222

stand upright. He took long, deliberate breaths, trying to slow his heart rate.

Putting his eye to the sight, he lined up the plane. He'd have to aim ahead of its flight path, but the jet was moving smoothly and calculating its course was easy.

The rocket would get there in three seconds.

His finger fell back to rest on the trigger in the pistol-grip.

This is it.

Nice and slow.

Taking a breath, he started squeezing the trigger gently.

Suddenly there was a noise behind him and the entrance to the roof burst open.

He turned, with the weapon still against his shoulder and saw the guy he'd bumped into on the corridor earlier.

He now had a pistol in his hand, the woman he'd been with and some other cop beside him also carrying firearms. *Shit.* He saw all three of them momentarily freeze as they realised what he'd been about to do.

Then their weapons all came up, sighted on the terrorist's head.

Number Six stood motionless, not intimidated, aiming the rocket launcher at them from ten feet away.

'Drop it, asshole!' the American guy shouted.

'Put your guns down! If I fire, you all die!' Number Six screamed back.

None of them moved. It was a stand-off, except one of them had a rocket launcher.

223

The young guy sensed the plane was approaching the runway behind him in the airfield.

He could hear it, getting closer and closer.

And in that moment, he realised he was done. There was no way out. He would never allow himself to get taken to prison, so he had to make a choice.

Three of them, or nearly three hundred of them.

He decided.

He suddenly turned in one swift motion.

And the fearsome weapon swivelled towards the plane.

TWENTY SEVEN

After the terrorist attacks of 9/11, police around the
world had developed various methods and tactics when
confronting a suicidal terrorist. The UK had called theirs
Operation Kratos. Members of the British government
and police had visited Israel, Sri Lanka and Russia to
consult with their security forces. Unlike the West, those
nations had been accustomed to suicide bombings for
many years and as a consequence had devised systems of
attack that were beginning to be universally used around
the world.

There were common themes. They'd found in most
life or death situations any explosives a terrorist had
control of were extremely sensitive to motion; hence, the
conventional tactic of shooting the chest was likely to
cause a detonation via twitching or jerked reactions.

Another key discovery had been that suicide bombers,
if discovered prematurely by police, were more than
likely to continue their attack regardless. Which meant
stealth and covert tactics had to be in place to avoid them
realising they'd been identified until it was too late for a
terrorist to react.

For Rivers, Shapira and Porter, the second finding
wasn't relevant here. Clearly, the guy knew all about
their presence.

But the first was.

The key to prevent any twitch or movement on a
trigger or switch was to shoot the target through the
brain stem, thus instantly severing any motor neurone
activity.

And that's exactly what Shapira did.

As the terrorist turned towards the plane with the rocket launcher, she was the first to react. The Mossad agent fired her pistol twice, a lightning fast double-tap. Both shots took the guy in the lower portion of his neck, severing the stem. Blood and bone sprayed in the air, and he dropped like a stone.

But there was a problem.

They'd waited a millisecond too late.

Number Six's finger was already moving on the trigger to launch the weapon, fourteen pounds of grip pressure.

That was all it needed.

Smashing back the door to the roof, Deakins and Fox rushed into sight behind them as the terrorist went down; together, the five of them watched in horror as a cloud of light-blue smoke erupted from the rear of the weapon.

There was a loud *whoosh* as the rocket roared out of the tube and off into the air.

Headed straight towards the airplane.

The rocket chewed through the air towards its target, moving at frightening speed. The five people on the roof stood helplessly as it roared towards the Boeing 757.

It was going to be a direct hit.

The plane was about eighty feet off the runway; even if by some freak miracle the pilot saw the rocket, he'd have no time to do anything about it. He was flying a commercial airliner, not a helicopter.

It missed by a whisker. Literally, a hair.

The warhead thundered under the belly of the plane and zoomed off into the middle of the airfield, away from its intended target and any other planes in the vicinity. It ploughed on for another hundred and fifty yards, then self-detonated like a firework as the fuse inside reacted, exploding in the sky.

Back on the roof, everyone stood still for a moment, still stunned by the speed of what had just happened.

Then they all sagged with relief.

Taking a huge breath, Porter shook his head.

He was getting sick of this.

*

At that moment across the Channel, another plane was just about to land.

In the cool night air, two sets of wheels lowered from the undercarriage of the private jet. The pilot eased back on the throttle and the plane touched down lightly on the runway. It slowed and eventually came to a halt, turning and taxiing a short distance towards a waiting car.

From his seat inside, Dominick took a deep breath.

He'd made it.

Looking out of the window he saw a black Escalade waiting by the runway. Two large men were standing beside it. He didn't recognise either of them; it seemed Henry had changed his entire crew since they'd lost contact, but then again, the man went through his security detail like a wolf chewed through a carcass. God only knew how many of them he'd killed over the years. They were too big to drown, so Henry often just machine-gunned them when they were least expecting it.

Beyond the two men in the distance, Dominick could see the bright lights of Paris. French time was an hour ahead so it was fast approaching midnight. His eyes settled on the unmistakeable shape of the Eiffel Tower,

227

golden and no doubt dressed up with fireworks in preparation for the display that would bring in the New Year.

Back in the cabin, Faris was already on his feet, swinging on his suit jacket which he'd laid to one side during the flight to avoid any creases. The pilot had pressed the mechanism in the cockpit to open the exit door and the stairs to the jet unfurled slowly towards the tarmac.

Faris went to move down the aisle then turned and looked at Farha, his hand near the pistol on his hip.

He didn't say anything.

His face said it all.

Butterflies fluttering around in his stomach, Farha rose from his seat and moved to the door, stepping past Faris. He walked down the stairs quickly, Faris close behind him, and set foot on foreign soil for the first time in a year. It should have been a joyous occasion for him, finally out of the UK, but instead he felt sick with nerves and fear. He was trapped; from now on whatever happened to him was up to those around him. And he hadn't even spoken to Henry yet; he had no idea what his reception was likely to be.

As he tried to stay calm, Faris stepped past him and walked towards the black Escalade.

The two enforcers had seemed big from the plane, but up close they were enormous. Farha saw each man had a pistol tucked in a holster, poorly hidden under their jackets. The guns seemed as small as toys hanging under their ridiculously broad shoulders. He felt bile rise in his throat. A year ago, he'd commanded guys like this without a second thought.

Now, he felt completely helpless as he stood before them.

'So what's the deal?' Faris asked the two men. 'Where is he?'

'He's at a café in the city,' one of them said.

'He's waiting for you,' the other added, grinning wolfishly as he looked at Dominick. 'He said the Albanians aren't going to be here for another hour or so.'

Faris nodded. Without another word, the two giants turned and moved back to the car. One of them climbed into the driver's seat, the other in the passenger seat beside him.

Faris turned to Dominick. 'What the hell are you waiting for? Get in. I'm cold.'

He obeyed; walking over and opening the door, he climbed into the back. Faris got in beside him and once they'd both shut their doors, the big guy behind the wheel fired the engine and the car moved off towards the lights of Paris.

Inside the car, Farha glanced at his watch. *9:21 pm*, London time, which made it 10:21 pm here.

An hour and forty minutes till the New Year.

With every fibre of his being, he prayed that he'd be alive to see it.

Four hundred yards across the airfield in the shadows, two men watched the car depart.

They were bedded down deep in cover under some mesh netting, camouflage paint smeared across their faces as they lay prostrate, grim and silent. They'd chosen a good location with thick bushes and hedge-growth beside them, right on the edge of the airfield. To any onlooker, they were invisible. No one could ever know they were there.

One of them had his eye to the lens of a Nikon camera; he clicked the shutter, snapping photographs of the departing car and the licence plates.

Beside him, the other man pulled a phone from his pocket.

'Be careful,' the man with the camera whispered. *'The pilot.'*

His companion nodded. The pilot was still in the cockpit, facing in their direction three hundred yards down the runway. If the man in the shadows didn't cover the light on the phone, the man would see it.

Concealing it carefully with a black cloth, the man pressed *Redial* under the fabric and lifted it to his ear. The call rang three times and then connected.

'Brody. How are we doing?' Special Agent Crawford asked.

'Sir, we're in place. Farha just landed,' Brody whispered. *'It looks like they've taken him to see the main man but I think they'll all be coming back. Seems like the deal isn't going down yet. The plane is still here.'*

'It's OK,' came Crawford's voice. *'Special Agent Cruz is in place. Farha isn't going anywhere without us knowing about it.'*

'When are you due back, sir?' Brody whispered.

'Rivers and I have to stay here for a while longer. But stay on them. The moment the deal is done, call me. I've spoken to the Saudi Police and DEA back-up. They'll be ready and waiting for when the jet lands back in Riyadh.'

'Yes, sir,' Brody whispered.

The call ended.

Agent Brody returned the phone to his pocket and together, the two men lay in total silence in the darkness.

Waiting for the cartel drug lord and his nephew to return.

TWENTY EIGHT

On the ground floor of the Unit's headquarters, Cobb was momentarily alone. He was standing in the observation room to one of the interrogation cells; through the glass, Frost and Number Eight were sitting across from each other, like two players in a chess game. Crawford had been here until a minute ago too, but he'd stepped outside for a cigarette. They'd both just been updated by Nikki about what had happened at the airport and hotel. Porter had told Nikki that Shapira had shot one of the terrorists just before he fired a rocket launcher at a commercial jet coming in from New York.

A rocket launcher.

Cobb rubbed his eyes wearily. Today had been like one long bad dream. It was as if fate had saved all the bad luck and trouble from the year and packed it all into one day, stalking them like a nemesis.

And the night was still young. Two more of the terrorists were still out there somewhere. Three, considering the cuffs hadn't yet gone on Farha.

Despite the worry, Cobb realised he was enjoying being alone in the small dark room for the moment. It felt like the only quiet room in the building, a place for him to think and ponder.

But just as those thoughts came into his mind, the door behind him clicked open as Crawford walked in, closing it behind him gently. He was carrying two mugs of coffee.

'I just spoke to two of my men,' he said, passing one to Cobb. 'The jet's landed outside Paris. They've taken Farha into the city'.

Cobb gave him a look. Crawford read it.

232

'Don't worry. Three of my guys are in place. He's not going anywhere.'

'The guy is currently the most wanted terrorist in Europe. And we're just leaving him alone to drive around Paris and catch-up with his old crew,' Cobb said. 'One of his people just tried to take out a commercial jet. Another tried to blow herself and an entire Terminal up at Heathrow for Christ's sake.'

He sighed.

'What am I doing?'

Crawford nodded.

'I understand; I totally get it. But please, just wait a little longer. We're talking ninety minutes. The moment the buy is done, we can move in. I have almost an entire DEA division on standby in Riyadh, as well as the police force there. They'll be waiting for them the moment the jet returns. Anywhere Farha goes right now, we'll know about it. Don't worry, I have constant surveillance on him.'

Cobb nodded, reluctantly. A silence fell. With Farha under the DEA's supervision, Cobb and his team needed to focus on the remaining two terrorists still out there.

Together, their attention naturally shifted to the interrogation happening through the glass.

'So who was she? The girl?' Frost asked, inside the interrogation cell.

The bomber said nothing. Frost reached for a cup of coffee he'd brought down from upstairs and took a long sip. He also used the moment to examine the guy in front of him closely.

He was different from his two cohorts, the guys they'd picked up from the raid earlier in the day. Frost could see that straight away. This man was impassive and cold. The other suspect hadn't been able to look Frost in the eye, but this guy was holding the detective's gaze, a contemptuous smile on his lips.

And strangely, he still seemed relaxed, despite the apparent failures of the evening and his broken nose.

All in all, the guy looked smug, which was unnerving the detective.

It was a look that said *I know something you don't.*

This was a completely different scenario from the other with the previous suspect. The kid had started tough and ended the interrogation in pieces, but the guy sat before Frost right now seemed arrogant, looking at him with a smirk on his lips. His nose had been smashed, broken by the Mossad agent; someone had stuffed two pads of gauze up his nostrils but blood was seeping through, staining the white bandage red.

'Who was she?' he tried again. 'The girl from the airport.'

This time, the terrorist responded, which surprised him.

'I didn't know her,' he said, his raspy voice sounding nasal from the padding up his nose. 'Farha picked her up a couple of months back.'

'Were they together? An item?'

The man looked at him. 'Who gives a shit?'

'He must have had some hold on her to make her do what she did.'

The guy shrugged.

'He used her. She was stupid. A stupid bitch. Now she's dead. A stupid dead bitch.'

The terrorist paused. He looked at Frost, closely.

'But he got away, didn't he?'

'I'm asking the questions.'

'Must piss you off,' the man continued, with a grin. He sniffed, and some blood dropped from the gauze to the table. 'He was so close and you lost him.'

Frost allowed himself to feel a small moment of victory. *That's what you think, you smug prick.* The suspect had no idea that the DEA were currently tracking Farha's every move. Cobb had informed Frost of the situation before he'd started the interrogation so this time, it was the detective with the gleam in his eye. The terrorist noticed it.

Riding the momentum and enjoying the power shift, Frost tapped the photocopy in front of him.

'Forget about him. I want to know about these two,' he said, pointing to Number One and Four. 'Where are they?'

The guy shook his head, snorting as more blood spilled from the makeshift bandages stuffed up his nostrils.

'No way. I'm not saying shit until I get a lawyer.'

'That could take a while. Traffic's bad on New Year's Eve. Could take all night.'

Number Eight's smirk suddenly changed into a full-on grin.

Something Frost had just said had triggered it.

'What time is it?' he asked.

Frost ignored the question. Said nothing. He didn't want to respond and let the power swing back towards the suspect like a pendulum. You grant a request, then before you know it you end up granting the next one. Anyone the wrong side of this table needed to be reminded every second who was in charge, otherwise things could spiral out of control. Frost had seen it before. Give them an inch, they'll take a mile.

The suspect could sense Frost was trying to keep the upper hand and kept grinning like a Cheshire cat.

'C'mon, you can tell me the time. Nothing weak about that. I'm the one wearing the cuffs, remember.'

Frost looked at him. His jacket was off, the sleeves of his shirt rolled up; he glanced at his wrist.

'9:50pm.'

The suspect whistled, blood staining his upper lip as it leaked from his nose.

'You'd better get moving, old man. You haven't got time to play stupid games. And you'll be very interested in what I have to say, I guarantee. That's a promise.'

Frost held his gaze. He didn't know if this was a play, or the guy was telling the truth. He watched him carefully and felt his stomach tingle.

The guy knew something.

It was written all over his face.

Frost tried another approach, picking his words carefully. He had to, seeing as the whole exchange was recorded on tape.

'We could persuade you to talk. You never know. We can be very persuasive when we want to be.'

The suspect grinned. 'Go ahead. I'm getting bored, anyway. And I've got nothing but time.'

He paused.

'Something you're running out of.'

TWENTY NINE

Outside the room, Cobb and Crawford were watching closely as they both sipped on coffee from the two mugs. They saw Frost rise and move to the door. He entered the observation room and joined the other two men, closing it behind him.

'What do you think?' Cobb asked immediately. 'Has he got something?'

Frost looked at him, wiping his brow.

'I hate to say it, but yes, sir. I think he has. He wouldn't be that cocky without good reason.'

Cobb double-checked the time on his watch.

'Shit. We've got just over two hours until midnight. There're crowds gathering all over the city,' he said. 'Bombings, rocket-launchers, stolen ambulances. What the hell are this lot going to come up with next?'

Crawford was looking intently at the suspect through the glass, saying nothing.

Cobb noticed.

'What are you thinking?' he asked the American.

'I've encountered my fair share of guys like him since I joined the Agency,' he said as he watched Number Eight next door. 'Ninety-nine per cent of all the terrorists and extremists out there, they're too fanatical for their own good. Past all their ideology, dogma, whatever the hell they believe in, most of them struggle to think for themselves. Which is what makes them so easy to manipulate.'

Cobb nodded. 'Like the boy from the raid. Number Three.'

'Or the girl at the airport,' said Frost.

'Exactly,' continued Crawford. 'And remember guys, this man wasn't suicidal. He tried to detonate two separate devices remotely. Which tells us two very important things. One, he's intelligent.'

'And two?' asked Cobb.

'He wants to live. He's got no reason to lie; he's telling the truth. And he's the only lead you have right now. As you said, there are crowds gathering all over London, waiting for midnight. And the clock's ticking.'

Cobb looked through the glass at the suspect, who was looking at the table, a slight smile on his blood-stained lips.

Crawford was right.

Across the building, the task force had just returned from the airport and the hotel. Seeing as they had to be on call and couldn't afford to be pinned down to any one area, the CID and airport police had taken over the crime scenes. After stowing their weapons in the locker room, it was once again a case of sitting around and waiting, each man poised to spring into action at a moment's notice. One thing was for sure, the coffee machine in the Briefing Room was having the busiest day of its life.

After the team had met up at the hotel and headed back, those who needed to be were filled in by Porter, Deakins and Fox on what had happened on the rooftop. Any reservations the officers had about the newcomers, including Mac's, were forgotten. Rivers' speed of thought and Shapira's speed on the trigger had saved everyone on the jet from being killed. As he stood to one side in the Briefing Room, Rivers watched as the female Mossad agent shook hands with Sergeant McGuire by the door. The American felt especially indebted to her. He'd hesitated a split-second too long.

As a medical team and the CID arrived at the hotel to take over the crime-scene, Shapira had taken the DEA agent to one side and asked about the situation with Dominick Farha. She told him she'd invested a lot of time in his case, a case which would end only with his capture, and said that she could see something was going between the Americans and Cobb that she didn't know about.

Knowing he owed her, Rivers had updated her on the DEA's current involvement. Their surveillance positioned in place in Paris, tailing him, holding back until two of their agents caught the drug deal. He'd told her all of it willingly; he didn't just owe her one, he owed her more than two hundred and fifty, one for every soul on board the airplane that she saved. Shapira had been grateful; she'd thanked him, saying that Mossad wouldn't interfere but it was good to be kept in the loop.

Now that they were back, most of the guys on the task force were sitting across the room, either drinking coffee or just trying to rest. Rivers moved to the stand and took a cup. He didn't feel like it but he poured out some coffee regardless. His body was still in Riyadh time and he needed the caffeine.

As the cup filled with the brown liquid from the spigot, the American saw the young blond officer walk in, the one who'd been asking him about the op with Bin Laden. Archer, the guy was called. The policeman rubbed fatigue from his eyes and walked over, joining the DEA agent and making himself a cup after Rivers was done.

'Talk about deja-vu,' Archer said. 'And I don't even like coffee.'

Rivers smiled as Archer shrugged.

'I guess it's a day of firsts.'

There was a pause. The two men ended up standing side by side by the window, holding their coffee, waiting for each cup to cool.

'Good job with the guy at the hotel,' Archer continued. 'I don't know how the hell you figured that one out, but thank God you did.'

The American nodded without replying, staring out of the window. Shapira was across the car park, a phone to her ear.

She saw the two men watching her and raised her hand in a brief wave.

'Don't thank me, man. She was the one who tagged him,' said Rivers, lifting his hand in acknowledgement.

A pause.

'You said earlier you used to be a SEAL?' Archer asked.

Rivers nodded.

'When did you leave?'

'End of last year.'

'Why?' the police officer asked.

He shrugged. 'Wasn't the right place for me anymore. Lost my appetite for it. Once that goes, you're done. I was discharged but wanted to stay working for the government. They helped me out, saying I deserved some sun and transferred me to Crawford's detail in the DEA. Before I knew it, I was on the next flight to Riyadh.'

A pause.

'That operation. Bin Laden,' Archer started.

241

'Geronimo,' said Rivers.

The police officer paused, confused. 'Say again?'

'Geronimo. That was the codename for him.'

Archer smiled and nodded. 'Were you nervous? About who the target was?'

Rivers shook his head, sipping his coffee. 'Didn't have time to be. We'd rehearsed the actual assault for months. They rebuilt a scale replica of his compound in Pakistan at our training facility in Virginia, but we didn't know what it really was or who the real place belonged to. We must have drilled that assault over a hundred and fifty times. I was in the first squad, coming in from the roof. By the end of all that training, I think I knew that compound better than my own house in Portland.'

He sipped his coffee. Archer listened, in silence.

'They told us who the target was for the first time just before the mission. Literally an hour before. Guess they didn't want us getting nervous, or any shaky trigger fingers out there. Guys having nightmares weeks before it happened, freaking out, worrying if they were going to make a mistake. Shit like that.'

He paused, then sighed and continued.

'I'm not a hero, man. I had nothing to do with the end result. I never even made it inside the house.'

Silence. Archer didn't reply, watching the American

'We trained for days, weeks, months. A once in a lifetime opportunity to write ourselves into the history books. But our helicopter, the one I was in, the turbines got caught in a wind tunnel over the house. It screwed with the rotors and we crashed just outside the compound. One of the biggest military operations in American history, and I'm injured before I even get there. The crash knocked me out. When I woke up, I was being stretchered out and the operation had been successfully completed.'

He paused.

'I'm good friends with the guys who got inside, who found him. I'm one of the few people in the world who actually knows who each of them are. Those guys, man they've got some stories to tell their grandchildren.'

He drained his coffee, shaking his head.

'I just wish that I did too.'

Silence followed. Rivers stood for a moment, holding the empty polystyrene coffee cup in his hand. He then dropped it in the bin and walked out of the room.

Turning, Archer watched him go.

Disappointing, the American had said earlier, when Archer asked him how he felt about the raid.

Now he understood why.

'We've got a lawyer on her way,' Frost said.

He'd collected himself and was back inside the interrogation room, opposite Number Eight. This time he decided to stay standing. He felt it gave him a psychological edge and reinforced the hierarchy in the room.

Across the table, the arrested terrorist leaned back; it didn't look as if he was buying the act.

'She'd better hurry.'

'We've got a few minutes till she gets here. Why don't you start talking?' said Frost. 'Make it easier on yourself. Who knows, it could improve your standing with the judge.'

He knew it was pointless, even as he said it. He could see the smug look in the terrorist's eyes. The control in the room had shifted and they both knew it. Frost had all his chips on the table and the terrorist was holding the winning hand.

However, the man spoke, much to Frost's surprise.

'OK, I'll give you a teaser. Just a little one.'

Reaching across the table with his handcuffed hands, he tapped one of the nine mug-shots on the photocopy with his finger.

Number One.

'This guy's going to attack at midnight.'

'Where?' asked Frost.

The suspect laughed.

'No way. You're not getting off that easy. I want to cut a deal. Time off my sentence.'

Frost shook his head. 'Keep dreaming. That's never going to happen.'

'Then good luck finding him,' said the terrorist. 'Because I *guarantee* you, he's out there right now, getting ready. You'll never see him coming'.

His smile faded.

'And I'm losing patience. If I was you, I'd agree a deal with your boss while I'm still willing to talk. If I go quiet, every person who dies is on you.'

Frost didn't move. To leave now would mean following orders from the suspect, but to stay meant wasting valuable time. But he didn't have a choice; he had to talk to Cobb. Gritting his teeth, he turned and walked to the door. He heard a sound from the table behind him.

Glancing sideways he saw the terrorist smiling as he made a ticking noise, moving his finger from side to side, like a metronome.

Cobb and Crawford were still outside, and they were both losing patience. Cobb checked his watch as Frost joined them, shutting the door.

'It's past ten. Less than two hours to midnight. Shit,' Cobb said, frustrated. 'And we all agree he's telling the truth?'

The two men nodded.

'I can't ask the PM to cut time off his sentence,' Cobb said. 'He murdered two kids, the medics. If we did cut his time and the press got hold of it, they'd have a field day. And what the hell do we tell their families if they ever found out?'

'What if he served the time, but in a different prison?' Crawford suggested. 'Isolated, secluded, no threat from any other prisoners. He'd still be locked up. You'd have that.'

'After everything he's done?' said Frost.

'Behind bars,' Crawford continued, turning to him. 'If he's telling the truth, we could get a head-start on his friend. The guy wouldn't know you had the drop on him. Your team and Rivers could be right there, ready and waiting for him to show up. You take him down, maybe he knows where the final suspect is?'

Cobb swore, assessing his options. Inside the cell, he saw the prisoner leaning back in his chair, self-satisfied and complacent.

'I need to call the PM,' he said. Turning, he pulled his mobile phone from his pocket as he walked to the exit.

Now how the hell do I start this conversation, he thought.

THIRTY

In the small Parisian café on Rue De Chevilly, Henry had also just received unexpected news.

His phone had rung as he began his third cup of coffee and fourth pastry, waiting for Faris and the two lunkheads to deliver his nephew.

The moment he heard what the situation was, his appetite had vanished instantly.

He'd sat motionless for fifteen minutes since the call ended, considering his options and looking for a solution.

He'd found one.

The evening would still go ahead as planned; he hadn't come all this way to leave empty-handed. But there was now extra business to attend to. Something risky and dangerous. A job for someone who would probably never make it back.

A job for his nephew.

If it succeeded, the plan of action would buy him some time. He needed to get back to Riyadh as quickly as he could. But he wasn't leaving until he'd dumped the coke with the Albanians and got his hands on the cash.

Satisfied with the fast strategy he'd formulated, he glanced outside. The weather was cold. Pedestrians hurrying past outside were wrapped up in thick coats and scarves. Henry hadn't given the weather a thought before he'd left and had come from the sunny heat of Riyadh, completely unprepared. The shitty climate here had been pissing him off ever since they'd landed. He'd never been to France before and decided on the spot to never come back.

247

He checked his watch. The deal would go ahead in the next couple of hours, then he could get on the jet and get back to his world. Sitting there with the cold coffee, the bad weather outside and a headache, Henry now remembered every reason why he never attended deals or why he rarely left his own country. But through his irritation, he understood how this place could be a good business-ground for gangs like the Albanians. Looking around the café and on the street he saw that the French kept to themselves, getting on with their lives and minding their own business, which was ideal for guys like him.

Outside, movement on the street brought him back to the present. The moment he'd been waiting for.

A black Escalade pulled up outside and once it parked, the two meatheads and Faris stepped out.

And then, from the other side, Dominick appeared.

Even from this distance, Henry could see that his nephew looked like he was on the verge of throwing-up. The drug lord smiled.

The boy would never know that a mere phone-call made a few minutes ago had just saved his life.

The four men entered the café. As one of the giants pushed open the door carelessly, a bell hanging above it gave a *ding*; other people in the café glanced up then looked away as they saw the intimidating men enter.

The foursome walked in and stopped, ten feet from where Henry was sitting.

Ignoring Dominick for the moment who looked as if he was about to piss himself, Henry signalled one of the enforcers to approach. The guy lumbered over and bent down to listen.

In his ear, Henry told him of the new situation and what he was going to do.

The man nodded then straightened.

'Take your friend with you,' Henry added. The enforcer looked at him for a moment, wondering what he meant. Then his slow brain kicked into gear and he nodded again.

Turning, he signalled for his fellow giant to follow and the two of them strode out of the cafe, their shoulders so wide that both guys had trouble fitting through the tight doorway.

From his seat, Henry saw Faris frown, watching them go and he approached Henry's table.

'Where the hell are they going?' he asked.

Henry ignored him, fixing his gaze on Dominick instead.

He gestured to a stool that he'd pulled in front of his table, and he saw the younger man's eyes flick down nervously.

'Take a seat.'

The Prime Minister and his wife sat in silence in his office as Rogers ended the call on the speakerphone. Director Cobb had been on the other end. He'd just updated the PM on the current situation with the terrorist, the information he claimed to have and his demands.

Leaning back in the chair behind his desk, the Prime Minister thought hard. He looked at his wife and Rogers, who were both sitting in chairs opposite him.

'What do you think?' he asked.

Both of them looked uneasy. Rogers spoke first.

'I think it's our only option, sir. He's our solitary lead, and he damn well knows it.'

The Prime Minister turned to his wife. Although officially she would play no part in the formal decision-making, he valued his wife's opinion above all others.

'Jen?'

She shook her head. 'After what he did, we should grant him clemency? The whole thing just doesn't feel right.'

A brief silence fell.

'OK, let's take a step back,' said the Prime Minister quietly. 'Say I agree. He'll tell us where this attack will take place and we can move in ahead of time, ready and waiting for the other terrorist.'

He paused.

'Or I say no. And pray that he's lying.'

Roger and the PM's wife didn't respond. They didn't need to.

All three of them knew there was only one option.

'He'd still be behind bars, sir,' said Rogers. 'He can't hurt anyone else from in there.'

The Prime Minister made the decision.

'OK. Call Director Cobb back.'

Rogers nodded and pressed *Redial* on the phone. He jabbed a button for the speakerphone and the ringing from the receiver filled the room.

Cobb answered immediately. Rogers had told him they'd call back shortly.

'*Sir?*'

'Tell the man he can serve the time in seclusion,' said the Prime Minister. 'He has my word on that. But no time off. He does every minute of his sentence and not a minute less. That's my only offer. And he can take it or leave it.'

'*Yes, sir,*' Cobb said.

The call ended from Cobb's end, wasting no time.

Inside the PM's office three people sat in silence, each with their own thoughts.

Across the room, the clock on the wall ticked to 10:30 pm.

Ninety minutes until midnight.

In a dark house across the city, a man sat alone in a chair in the middle of a drab living room.

The curtains were drawn, the room still and silent. A roof light above him filled the room with an ethereal white glow, the moon bathing the inside of the house with its cold, pale light.

Sitting naked, the guy was hunched over, putting the finishing touches to a piece of clothing resting on his lap.

Tossing aside a set of pliers, he lifted the cloth to examine his work.

It was a vest. Black, thick, similar to a tactical vest that a police officer would wear. It had a number of compartments sewn into the black cloth and each one was packed full with either one of two things.

Steel nails.

Each one as long as a man's finger.

And Semtex plastic explosive.

Holding the vest in front of him, the man inspected his work. It looked good. The Semtex was a shade of bright orange, ludicrously colourful for such a dangerous weapon. It shared all the power and destructive capacity of C4, but Semtex was harder to trace and easier to mould. It could be shaped to follow any curvature or fit into a slot, and sniffer dogs never picked up on it.

The man nodded.

Where he was headed tonight, he figured there may be a few of them about.

Rising, he lifted the vest over his head and threaded his arms through the gaps so it settled on his bare shoulders. He adjusted it, bouncing gently on his heels to test the weight. It felt good. The vest had a V shape collar, the bulk of the weight carried around his torso and hips, but nevertheless it still looked slightly bulky.

He carefully started to push and shape the malleable plastic explosive, getting it to flatten and follow the curve of his torso.

As he did so he stared straight ahead, his eyes half-open.

He was starting to become focused.

Behind him, another man was staring too. He was lying in a pool of congealed blood, thick and coated to the floor. The man's throat hadn't just been cut; someone had sawn through it as if they were cutting a loaf of thick bread. Stripped naked and dumped on the floor, the body looked like a Roman statue in the white light of the moonlight. The way his head had lolled back meant the man wearing the vest was standing where the corpse's gaze had fallen.

The dead eyes stared accusingly at the terrorist across the room.

He finished adjusting the vest, the last jacket he would ever wear.

Satisfied, he moved across the room and grabbed a pair of trousers, pulling them on.

He was ready to go.

THIRTY ONE

It took them just under ten minutes to draft the contract.
Jill Sawyer, the bomber's somewhat reluctant defence
lawyer, had arrived and she oversaw the construction of
the document. Her trained eye ensured there were no
loopholes or room for manipulation, nor any points of
contention that would come back to haunt them later.

After it was completed they printed off a copy and
together, Frost and Sawyer moved back into the
interrogation cell. The suspect looked up as they entered.

'Well?'

'You win,' said Frost. 'The Prime Minister has agreed
to a deal.'

The guy smirked, pushing the gauze stuffed up his
nostrils further into his nose.

'Reduced sentence?'

'No,' said Sawyer.

The terrorist looked at her for the first time, his smile
fading.

'So what then? You'd better not be jerking me
around.'

She laid the contract on the table before him. 'You'll
do the time, but at a different facility. You'll be isolated,
minimal contact with other inmates.'

'That's it? A different prison?'

'Trust me, it'll be paradise compared to Belmarsh,'
said Frost. 'When word gets round inside as to who you
are, you're going to be a marked man wherever you go.'

He saw the suspect absorb this. Belmarsh Prison was located towards the south-east edge of London. It was known for two things amongst the criminal community; firstly, as the central detention centre for any terrorists captured and convicted in the UK. There were so many of them in there it was as if someone had called a town meeting. And secondly, Belmarsh was renowned for its inter-walls violence. Unlike some other prisons in the UK, the guards and wardens took a no-bullshit approach to the inmates. They were in charge and they let every con inside the walls know it. Every man doing time in there had to earn every minute of his sentence.

However, despite the notoriety of the prison, Frost saw the terrorist still weighing up his options. *C'mon you bastard, take it*, he thought. They were running out of time. This was their only option. If this deal was going to mean anything, they needed the information now.

'This is all official?' the terrorist asked, deliberating.

Sawyer nodded, pulling a pen from her jacket pocket, passing it to him.

'It is. I'm serving as a witness.'

Beside her, Frost was getting impatient.

'It's a one-time offer. Take it or leave it.'

Number Eight looked at him, enjoying the power.

For one tense moment Frost thought he was going to say *no*.

But after a long pause he leaned forward, slowly taking the pen from Sawyer's hand and signed the contract. Frost hid his relief. The moment the nib of the pen left the page, Sawyer took it back from him and the grey-haired detective beside her started pushing.

'Right, start talking. Where's he going to be?'

The bomber leaned back. 'Trafalgar Square. Midnight.'

'Whereabouts?' continued Frost, searching for further detail. 'It's a big place.'

'I don't know where exactly,' he replied. 'But he'll be there. Trust me.'

Outside the room, Cobb heard this and turned to Crawford.

'Time to go to work.'

Fifty yards from the runway in the shadows of the Parisian airfield, the two DEA agents hadn't moved. They were still tucked away in the darkness on surveillance, silent and invisible.

In the air, they could hear distant cheering. High up in the sky, premature fireworks had already started going off in the distance. However, neither man was celebrating yet. They had plenty of work left to do this night.

Earlier, they'd watched as the pilot moved from the cockpit of the jet down the steps to stand on the tarmac. He'd sparked a cigarette and stood there smoking, cradling something in his arms. The man on the left, Agent Brody, had looked closer with his binoculars. It was an HK CAWS automatic shotgun, a savage German weapon. It housed a ten shell magazine that clipped into its base. If a guy pulled the trigger, the chemical reaction and force of the blast would push the mechanism back as it fired, slotting another round into the chamber automatically. In an experienced pair of hands, someone could fire over two hundred shells a minute with it. Ridiculous firepower with gruesome results. Someone pointed that thing at you there was no point in fighting. Just get on your knees and beg.

And its presence in the pilot's hands confirmed something to the two agents.

The cargo they were interested in was definitely still inside the jet.

Suddenly, there was a rustling from behind them. Flynn and Brody snapped their heads around with a jolt, startled. They looked into the darkness, tense. Waiting. But it was nothing, a false alarm. Just an animal, out hunting for late-night prey. Nevertheless, neither man moved for a moment. They stared into the pitch black. Finally satisfied it was safe, the pair turned their attention back to the jet.

But then there was another sound behind them.

A crunch.

A foot stepping on a stick or branch.

They twisted round again.

Two men were standing there.

They were Henry's enforcers, the two giants.

They'd crept up out of nowhere and the two DEA agents were momentarily frozen with shock.

Each enforcer was holding something in his hands, a silenced AR 15 Carbine assault rifle. Each one had a magazine clipped to its base. Thirty rounds, set to fully automatic.

The two men stood over the two agents, who lay there helpless.

Then one grinned and raised his weapon.

'Boo.'

THIRTY TWO

Inside the Briefing Room at the ARU's HQ a crowd had gathered. The task force were sitting in chairs paying close attention as Cobb and Mac stood beside a large map of Trafalgar Square that had been pinned to the noticeboard.

Beside it to the right, Archer saw the copy of the nine suspects was still pinned to the board, a big black X over six of the faces. Agents Crawford and Rivers were standing behind the group, next to Agent Shapira. They were staying out of the way but listening intently.

'Right, for those that missed it, we've been working on the ambulance bomber downstairs,' Cobb said. 'And we got something. He's given us a golden piece of intel.'

He pointed to Number One's mug-shot.

'He's assured us that this man is planning an attack in Trafalgar Square at midnight. Which gives us just over one hour to prepare.'

'How reliable is the intelligence, sir?' Fox asked.

Cobb pursed his lips. 'Solid. We cut him a deal'

There was murmuring in the room, as the men heard this. Mac stepped in.

'*Hey! Hey!* Shut your mouths!' he ordered.

'Unfortunately, it was our only choice,' Cobb continued. 'Trust me, if there was any other option, I would have taken it in an instant. But he had the upper hand and the stakes are too high.'

He paused.

'Anyway, let's look at the positives. For the first time today we actually have a jump on one of these guys. I've already spoken to the Chief Superintendent in charge of policing the Square this evening. I updated him on the situation; his men know what the suspect is planning and what he looks like, and they're also expecting you all down there.'

'Why don't we just shut down the Square?' Deakins asked. 'Would save us a hell of a lot of problems.'

'The suspect has no idea that we know his plans,' Cobb replied. 'We have a head start on him. If we cleared the Square, he'll most likely never appear.'

'And probably attack somewhere else,' added Mac.

There was a brief silence as the men absorbed this. Serving the crowd up as bait. It didn't sit well with any of them.

'Excuse me for stating the obvious, sir, but that seems like a whole lot of risk doesn't it?' Fox said. 'What happens if we don't find him in time?'

'He's right,' said Deakins. 'We're using the public as a lure.'

'If anyone has a better idea, I'm all ears,' said Cobb. 'I wouldn't even consider such a plan if I had a viable alternative. And there's every chance the crowd won't be as big as usual after the explosion at the Emirates. There might only be a handful of people down there. But nevertheless, it's situations like this which is what you've all trained for. I'm putting my faith in you.'

Silence followed. In the lull, Mac stepped forward and pointed to a space on the map of the Square, towards the south-east corner.

'Team Two, you're going to split up. Deakins, I want you on surveillance in this building here. Take two

260

members of Second Team, and one of our newcomers,' he said, gesturing to Rivers and Shapira. 'You'll be up on the eighth floor. It's an office building, I spoke to security and they know you're coming.'

Deakins nodded, scribbling down notes as Mac looked at the officer beside him, Mason.

He pointed to a building on the west side of the Square.

'Mason, you're going to be here, with the rest of Second Team minus Fox. Same deal, it's an office complex. Fifth floor. You'll be facing the crowd, so I want you checking every single person.'

Mason nodded. Deakins raised his hand.

'Rifles, Sarge?' he asked.

Mac shook his head. 'Can't do it. Too risky. There might be a shitload of people down there and we don't want any of them catching a stray bullet. Binoculars and side-arms only. If you see a situation from up there, just call it in to the guys on the ground.'

He turned his attention to the other men.

'First Team, plus Foxy, we're going to be amongst the crowd in the Square in plain clothes.'

Taking his forefinger, he drew an imaginary circle around the centre of the map.

'Scan the people around you, but don't get sucked in. I need all of you to stay mobile. We'll be on radio, so work as a team and work fast. As I said, hopefully the crowd will be lighter than usual.'

Mac stepped to his left and pointed at Number One's photo.

'Take a good look at the mug-shot lads. We know what he looks like but he might be disguised or layered up from the cold. Search for signs. The crowd are going to be relaxed, smiling, enjoying themselves so see who stands out. They might be sweating, or jumpy; wearing excessive clothing. Look for any bags, or for anyone walking awkwardly like the girl at Heathrow. Muttering or mumbling, you know the routine. You see anything, don't hesitate for a second. Call it in and move fast. Every second is going to count down there.'

He turned to Cobb.

'Anything else, sir?'

Cobb shook his head. 'Just find him.'

Mac nodded and turned to the room. 'I want you outside in five minutes. Plain-clothes, side-arms and radios. Let's move.'

The team moved quickly towards the door.

Sitting on the left, Archer went to follow, but Porter grabbed him.

'Arch,' he said quietly but urgently.

The blond officer noticed he seemed uneasy and stepped to one side with him.

'What is it? You OK?'

Porter was looking around the room, worried.

'Where's Chalky?' he asked.

Archer paused.

He turned, searching left and right, and then went to the door, checking the corridor.

Porter was right.

Chalky wasn't there.

He'd missed the briefing.

Seeing as France was an hour ahead the clock had already struck midnight in Paris. The street outside the small cafe was lit up with bright flashes of blues, reds and greens as fireworks boomed into the sky from the city centre. There was a faint sound of cheering, muffled by the walls of the café as the gathered crowds celebrated the arrival of the New Year.

But Dominick Farha didn't know what to feel as he sat opposite his uncle at the table, who was currently awaiting a response. He was still alive, which was a cause for celebration, but the proposition that had just been outlined to him was crazy. Close to impossible. But he didn't have a choice; if he said no, he'd be at the bottom of the Seine before morning, either drowned or shot in the head. His self-preservation was taking over. He had to say *yes*.

He picked his next few words carefully.

'So if I do this, you and I are good?' he asked quietly. 'We forget New York?'

Henry smiled.

'You do this, and I'll forget New York ever happened.'

Across the table, Henry took the two questions as confirmation. He raised a pudgy hand, jabbing it towards the window of the café.

'There's a vehicle waiting for you outside. The driver belongs to an associate of mine. He'll take you to a helipad and from there, the pilot will take you where you need to go. He'll wait for you to do your task. If you are successful, he'll bring you straight back here to the airfield. You can board the jet and we'll leave for Riyadh. I'm willing to wait for you to return. But not for long.'

He paused.

Farha felt acid in his gut.

'When you get it done, take an ear. You won't have time for anything bigger. I want to see proof; and a trophy.'

Farha nodded, hiding his misery.

'Go,' said Henry. 'And don't fail me. If you do, rest assured I won't be this nice.'

Farha nodded again.

'Thank you, Uncle. I appreciate it,' he lied, rising and moving to the door.

Beside the entrance, Faris looked up at Henry from a newspaper, catching his eye. *Should I stop him?* his face said. Henry shook his head.

The bell dinged above the door and his nephew moved outside.

The drug lord watched him walk to the car, climb into the passenger seat and shut the door. Then the driver fired the engine and the vehicle pulled away from the kerb, moving off into the night.

Faris approached, having watched Dominick leave. He was confused.

'You let him go?' he asked.

Henry nodded. 'I sent him on an errand. Don't fret. We don't need to worry about him anymore; he's not coming back.'

He checked his watch again, just as the Escalade appeared on the street, pulling up outside. The two meatheads had returned right on time. As they stepped out of the car, Henry was relieved to see that they'd stowed the two assault rifles in the vehicle. He'd had a flash of concern that they'd walk into the café carrying them. For any other person that would be a ridiculous consideration, but these two really were that stupid.

'Time to go,' he told Faris, who nodded. Henry noticed he looked slightly on edge, which was unusual.

He suppressed a smile.

You'd be climbing up the walls if you knew what I have in store for you.

As they walked to the door Henry noticed the look on the barista's face, behind the counter. Henry hadn't paid, but knew she wouldn't dare confront him about it. He'd expected murder tonight; so far he'd been denied, his nephew's life saved by fate and circumstance, but he was going to get what he wanted, like a fat kid in a sweet store.

But the woman was sensible.

She looked down at the counter, avoiding eye contact and hiding her relief as the sinister, strange men left her café.

Archer found him downstairs in the men's toilets, alone. As soon as he walked in and caught sight of his friend, he knew that they were in some seriously deep shit.

As everyone kept reminding him, Archer was still a young guy, four years shy of thirty. But despite his youth and relative inexperience, he had already seen the way alcohol could affect someone's life. He'd witnessed it first hand with his parents. His father had never been violent because of it; he wasn't that kind of person. But it had got to the point where their marriage couldn't continue because of his drinking. His father had packed his bags when Sam was sixteen and flown back to New York.

He'd never come back.

As a consequence and like many kids who grew up in similar circumstances, Sam Archer the man was wary of alcohol. He was always the guy keeping Chalky in check when they were in a bar or pub.

This time however, he was too late.

There was a row of four washbasins on the left of the bathroom opposite four cubicles. Chalky was by the second closest to the wall. He looked exhausted and unsteady, still in his navy blue combat overalls and boots.

Archer saw a bottle of whisky resting against the porcelain basin.

Despite his friend's arrival, Chalky made no attempt to conceal it.

And almost half of it was gone.

'What the hell is that,' Archer asked, quietly.

Chalky didn't respond; instead, he reached for the bottle.

Archer moved forward swiftly and swiped it before his friend could grab it.

'What the hell is wrong with you?' Archer asked in disbelief, struggling to keep his voice down. 'Are you kidding me?'

He saw Chalky staring at the floor, avoiding eye contact, his eyes blurry, well on his way. Upturning the bottle, Archer poured the remaining contents down the plughole then threw the empty vessel into the rubbish bin beside him; it disappeared in an instant, hidden amongst the tissues and paper towels.

He turned back to his friend, cornering him.

'Are you a complete idiot? We're about to go out into a crowd of thousands of people looking for a suicide bomber and you're getting drunk?'

He searched his friend's face for an answer but Chalky still wouldn't make eye contact.

However, even with his head bowed, Archer could see there were tears there.

Sighing, he backed off, shaking his head.

'Jesus Christ, Chalk' he said. 'What the hell are you doing?'

'I shouldn't be here, Arch,' he replied.

He paused.

'I can't do this. I'm finished.'

Archer grabbed his friend by the shoulders, looking into his eyes. They were bloodshot and bleary from whisky and exhaustion. He should have died at least twice, even three times today. But Archer knew what the problem was.

The shotgun.

'Look Chalk, I don't know why it happened,' he said. 'Fate, luck, chance, whatever. Maybe you're meant to do something in the future, something important. I don't know. But if you truly want to quit, hand in your notice when this is over.'

He paused, lowering his voice.

'But you *can't* act like this. Not right now; you're better than this. There're people out there depending on you right now. Shit, I'm one of them. We all need you at your best. Not like this.'

There was a movement by the door.

Archer twisted around and saw it was Porter; he'd quietly entered the room. He was already dressed in jeans and a zipped up coat, ready to go, the holster and pistol clipped to his belt. He saw Chalky's condition and put two-and-two together.

'You alright, Chalk?' he asked, moving forward.

Archer released his friend and turned to the other officer as he approached.

'If Mac or Cobb see this, he's done for.'

Porter nodded, moving past him to Chalky.

'C'mon, drink some water, mate,' he said, helping him to the tap. 'It'll help.'

Chalky obliged without a word, bending down and twisting his head to slurp from the tap.

'Splash some on your face too,' Porter added, watching him, keeping his hand on his back as support.

As Chalky obeyed, Porter turned back to Archer.

'What do we do? We're leaving in two minutes. What on earth do we tell Mac?'

Archer thought for a long moment. Weighed the options.

'He has to come. Mac won't see him once we're in the crowd. Let's just keep him quiet in the car and he can sober up on the street. We'll brief him when we get down there, away from the others. You know what he's like; he'll dry up fast.'

Porter nodded in agreement.

'OK. You two better go and get changed. I'll cover for you with Mac, but hurry.'

Together, they turned to look at the dark-haired officer, who'd turned off the tap and was standing back upright, trying to blink his slightly glazed, blood-shot eyes into focus.

Archer grabbed his shoulders and his attention.

'Listen. You think long and hard before you make any decisions tonight. Understand?'

Chalky looked at him with surprising sudden clarity.

'He's a suicide bomber, Arch. If I think, I'm dead.'

THIRTY THREE

Ten minutes to midnight on New Year's Eve, Trafalgar Square was just about the busiest place in the entire country. Like Times Square in New York, it served as a centre of celebration as partygoers bid farewell to the old year and welcomed in the new, all under the bangs and lights of a mesmerising fireworks display.

When the clock struck midnight one thing was for sure.

This was the place to be in the city if you wanted to have a good time.

Unfortunately for the Armed Response Unit, that seemed to be the case tonight. Cobb had told them back at HQ that the Prime Minister was adamant that no celebrations be cancelled despite the bombing at the Emirates Stadium. Archer had celebrated here with a girlfriend two years previously and it was so packed you couldn't have jammed another person into the place.

Cobb's thoughts earlier were partially right. It seemed as though some people had decided to stay at home this year, the crowd thinner than usual which was a slight blessing. The officers needed to be able to move around, to react and chase down a suspect at a moment's notice and the lighter numbers meant they had room to manoeuvre. But there were still a lot of partygoers gathered in the Square.

Hundreds of them, at least.

Archer was positioned outside the main crowd, near a barrier to the south. He was standing just to the right of Nelson's column which loomed high above the throng, the best view in the Square. A hundred feet in front of him two large water fountains splashed away, the crowd jammed tight around them. Someone had hooked the fountains up with an LED lighting system and they glowed blue and red as water burst from the main funnels and showered into the porcelain bath surrounding them.

Up ahead, a stage had been set up on the north side of the Square, just in front of the National Gallery. Some flavour-of-the-month pop band was performing on stage as a crew behind them rushed around, double-checking the vast array of fireworks that would shoot into the sky at the top of the hour.

Archer had wrapped up warm. He was wearing a dark green coat lined with cream-coloured sheep's wool which concealed the Glock 17 pistol slotted into a holster on his right hip. The earpiece to his radio was tucked inside his ear so he could communicate with the other guys scattered across the Square. He held the pressel switch in his hand, both of them jammed in the pockets of his coat, with a mic clipped to the inner lapel; with his collar up he blended right in with the crowd.

He glanced around him. Everyone he could see was well-layered up with thick clothing to combat the chill. It meant any one of them could have been concealing something. Archer scanned every single person he could see for anything unusual. He'd read stories from the past of women and children being held down at gunpoint and having explosives attached to them, or women threatened with violence against their kids if they didn't comply. He'd heard from guys in the army that in Afghanistan, the Taliban would send women and children out to serve as spotters, knowing that the opposing side wouldn't fire on them. The enemy didn't play by the same rules.

If it was hot weather, anyone wrapped up in thick clothing would have stood out in a heartbeat. But right

271

now, everyone in front of Archer was potentially a suspect due to the bulkiness of their clothing. He felt his breath catch. Serving the crowd up as bait was a huge risk by Cobb. The team couldn't afford to fail.

Moving to his right, he scanned the crowd, searching for anyone who fit Number One's description. Most of the people watching the stage were wearing hats which was making it even harder. A true needle in a haystack.

Archer cursed under his breath.

Where the hell are you?

In his ear, he heard a voice crackle. *Mac.*

'Deakins, sound off.'

Archer glanced through the crowd, but he couldn't see Mac or the other officers. He shifted his gaze to a building flanking the Square to his right.

Somewhere on the eighth floor was Deakins with a surveillance team by the windows.

'Nothing, Mac. There're a shitload of people down there. We're searching as hard as we can.'

There was a pause.

'Chalky, get your finger out of your ear,' Deakins followed. *'You might as well have Policeman printed across your chest.'*

Archer shook his head, rolling his eyes as he heard this. Chalky had kept silent during the ride over, downing water and avoiding talking to Mac. Archer prayed he was sobering up fast, wherever he was in the Square.

Mac's voice continued. *'Mason, report.'*

'Nothing, Sarge. We're checking everyone, but so far, no sign.'

272

Fox's voice came up over the radio. His voice sounded as worried as Archer felt.

'Mac, I've got a bad feeling about this. We need to clear the area. This guy could be anywhere.'

Mac's voice responded. *'We wait. Cobb's orders. Stay calm, lads. He'll be here. Keep your eyes peeled.'*

Archer searched the crowd again. But everywhere he looked there were families, young kids, couples. No one matching the suspect. *Shit.*

He checked his watch.

11:54pm.

Six minutes until midnight.

And the guy wasn't anywhere to be seen.

'Where the hell are you?' Archer muttered.

Twenty miles to the south-east, an unmarked police car pulled up outside a block of tenement flats. The driver applied the handbrake and two police officers stepped out, shutting the doors behind them. Their names were Edgar and Wright, both of them Detective Inspectors and both dressed in plain-clothes. They were part of an undercover patrol that roamed the streets, able to intervene in any unlawful activity instantly without fear of being recognised before they made their approach.

Across the courtyard, they saw a woman standing outside the door of a flat on the ground floor. She was dressed in a pink dressing gown, wrapped up tight against the cold with the noise of a television blaring out from the flat behind her.

The two policemen approached her.

'You made the call?' Edgar asked quietly, pausing in front of her.

She nodded. According to dispatch, she'd contacted the police call-centre ten minutes ago. She'd been channel-hopping and seen four mug-shots of four wanted terrorists on the news.

And she was convinced that one of them was living next door.

Edgar and Wright were already in the area and took the call. Requesting back-up from Hammersmith and Fulham, they'd driven over here as fast as they could. Reinforcements would arrive any minute. Even though this woman would probably prove to have an over-active imagination, they had to follow-up every possible lead.

'Which flat is it?' asked Wright, quietly.

She pointed to her left, their right.

'There.'

The two men examined the exterior. They couldn't see anything from the windows.

The curtains were drawn, the lights turned off.

'Is he in there at the moment?' whispered Wright.

The woman shrugged.

'I'm not sure.'

The two policemen nodded; together, they crept forward to the door. Edgar slid his hand forward and checked the handle, twisting it gently. It was common practice for many suspects or criminals to leave their front doors unlocked, sometimes even already open.

This one however, was locked tight.

He glanced at the door itself. It was a cheap design, eaten away and softened by years of inclement weather and no maintenance. Edgar was a big guy, over six feet and built like he belonged in the front row of a rugby scrum.

He glanced at Wright, who read his mind and nodded.

Stepping back, Edgar dipped his shoulder and smashed his weight into the frame as hard as he could.

The lock splintered and the door gave way.

Pushing it all the way open, the two men moved into the apartment. In typical nosy-neighbour fashion, the woman in the pink gown peered round the doorframe to look inside. She couldn't help herself, her curiosity piqued.

However, she instantly wished she hadn't.

She gasped, a hand flashing to her mouth as she stifled a scream.

In front of her, Edgar and Wright had momentarily frozen, shocked by what they saw.

A naked body was dumped on the floor. It was a man. He was lying in a pool of sticky blood that had congealed around him. Edgar looked closer, horrified. Someone had gone to work on the guy's neck with a blade; it was a real mess.

As the two policemen stepped closer to the dead man, back up arrived behind them in the courtyard, three police cars with lights flashing pulling to a halt. Edgar knelt by the body while Wright disappeared to inspect the rest of the apartment, searching for the homeowner.

He reappeared after a few moments.

'He's not here,' he said.

Edgar didn't respond. He was staring at the corpse's face.

The man's dead eyes were gazing lifelessly across the room; the moonlight shining down from a roof light made him almost look as if he was made of marble.

'What? What is it?' Wright asked, noticing his partner's reaction.

Edgar looked up at him, confused.

'I think I know this guy.'

THIRTY FOUR

Inside Trafalgar Square, Archer checked his watch.

11:59pm.

Despite the intensive search, there was no sign of Number One anywhere.

On the stage across the Square an MC had taken the microphone and the crowd rippled and chattered with excitement, preparing for the countdown to bring in the New Year.

Behind them, Archer snapped his head back and forth, frantically searching while constantly moving to change his line of sight.

Nothing.

No-one.

'London, are you ready?' shouted the MC down the microphone.

Archer scanned the crowd frantically.

The terrorist was nowhere to be seen.

High above the Square in a building on the south-east corner, Deakins was standing by a window in a long dark rectangular conference room. Rivers, Spitz and another officer were also in the room, each man at a different window with binoculars in his hand.

They were searching their designated area as anxiously as the men on the ground. What had seemed like a dangerous plan an hour earlier now looked as if it was going to be catastrophic.

But suddenly, Deakins spotted something.

He tensed like a cat who'd seen its prey and took another hard look with his binoculars.

'Mac!' he said. 'Mac come in!'

Across the room, the three other men snapped their heads around to look at him, hearing the urgency in his voice.

'What is it?' came Mac's voice.

Deakins double-checked with his binoculars as he talked rapidly into the radio.

'South-west corner, near the trees. There's a guy matching the target,' he said, looking closer through the field glasses.

The three men beside him did the same.

'He's wearing a thick coat and backpack I repeat, south-west corner, guy matching the target wearing thick coat and backpack. *Someone get over there!'*

Across the Square, the MC on the microphone had started the countdown.

The crowd shouted with him, excited.

Twenty seconds till midnight.

Deakins kept his binoculars on the guy in the coat and backpack, watching helplessly from his vantage point.

The man had just entered the Square from the south.

He was moving towards the crowd.

Down below, Mac, Fox and Porter found themselves close together, one side of the fountain. They were fighting their way through to try to get to the edge of the crowd, which would give them a clear run around the Square to the south-west.

But the crowd was focused on the MC and getting through was a nightmare.

The mass of people had started chanting the countdown.

Fifteen seconds to go.

'Shit!' shouted Mac, pushing the switch to his radio. *'Someone get over there!'*

Across the Square, Archer was already running. He was the only one who could get there before the clock struck midnight.

'Ten!'

'Nine!'

Archer had pulled his pistol. He was thirty yards from the guy, bearing down on him as fast as he could.

He saw the man's face. Deakins was right.

It had to be him.

The man saw Archer coming and turned.

His hands were jammed tight in his pockets.

And he was muttering something to himself.

'Eight!'

'Seven!'

'Put your hands up!' Archer shouted at the guy as he came to a halt a few feet in front of him, his pistol on the guy's forehead.

The man looked at Archer, terrified, his eyes as wide as dinner-plates.

He lifted his hands from his pockets, trembling.

There was something in his palm.

'Six!'

'Five!'

'Don't move!' Archer ordered.

He kept his weapon trained on the guy's forehead, moving forward rapidly.

He grabbed the man's hand and looked at the black object.

It was a mobile phone.

He dropped it to the floor and grasped the zipper to the guy's coat.

'Four!'

'Three!'

He pulled it down.

'Two!'

He stared in horror.

'One!'

It was just the guy's sweater underneath.

No explosives.

There was nothing there.

'HAPPY NEW YEAR!' the crowd shouted.

Behind Archer, Mac, Fox and Porter had arrived, all three of their weapons drawn. Archer grabbed the suspect and spun him around, unzipping his backpack, peering inside.

It was full of books.

No explosives.

'Shit!' Archer shouted, turning to his three fellow officers. 'It's not him!'

Fireworks started to go off above them, a series of loud *bangs* and *booms*, each one lighting up the Square for a brief moment with its bright colours. The crowd *ooh'd* and *aah'd* with each explosion, watching the display above them in the sky. The guy in the coat was shaking. He still had his hands in the air and he was shivering with fear, unable to speak.

But suddenly, there were two thunderous explosions, behind the four policemen.

BOOMBOOM.

They came in quick succession and the sound was unmistakeable.

Two gunshots.

They all snapped around. A street police constable ten feet behind them had been thrown backwards, two bullets in his upper chest. Blood and bits of his torso and jacket were sprayed in the air as he fell back, his helmet striking the concrete with a loud smack.

Nearby, members of the crowd had heard the gunshots and turned. They saw the policeman on the ground and started to scream, backing off.

Amongst them, one man stood still.

Chalky.

He was twenty feet away and had his pistol up.

Aimed where the policeman had been standing.

'Chalky!' Mac screamed, in utter disbelief, confusion and rage.

Fox, Archer and Porter stood still, momentarily motionless, frozen with shock, staring at the shot cop. Other police constables nearby were already reacting, descending on Chalky. He lowered the pistol slowly as three street officers wrestled him to the ground, pushing his face to the concrete as they went to handcuff him.

'What the hell did you do?' Mac screamed, rushing towards him.

Archer ran to the policeman who had taken the two rounds.

The guy was flat on his back, not moving. Archer dropped to one knee beside him as two other police constables ran over to join him.

'Is he dead?' one of them asked, horrified.

Archer checked the guy's neck for a pulse; he couldn't feel one. He looked at his chest. The man was wearing a fluorescent yellow jacket, standard issue for a street officer of his rank.

It was spattered with blood, two maroon holes in the centre of his upper torso, seeping blood.

Archer ripped open the guy's coat, to check the wounds.

Then he froze.

Beside him, one of the two constables gasped.

The policeman was wearing a vest. It was shaped like a V, so the two bullets had hit his sternum, not the fabric.

But it was packed with nails and bright orange plastic explosive.

Archer looked down at the dead man's hand.

A switch lay there, resting in the open palm. It was hooked up to a black wire that ran into his coat.

Archer grabbed the man's police helmet and tore it off.

He saw his face.

He wasn't a policeman.

He was Number One.

THIRTY FIVE

The five members of Henry's crew had been waiting on the tarmac runway for just under ten minutes before they saw two cars approaching in the distance. The road was bumpy, and the headlights of the arriving vehicles bobbed up and down as they neared the airfield.

Each man, save for Henry, was armed. The pilot was still holding the HK CAWS shotgun, the two enforcers cradling AR 15 Carbines, fresh magazines slotted into each base. Faris had his pistol tucked in the holster on his hip, but he doubted he'd need it. The Albanians were a brother cartel, not an enemy, and the two organisations shared a good working relationship. The guns were there just to make sure everything ran smoothly. The amount of drugs and money about to be exchanged could make even the most honest man behave unpredictably.

Standing behind the four men by the jet, leaning against the steps, Faris was in a dark mood. In the Escalade on the way back here, he'd heard the two grunts bragging, running their mouths. Apparently, Henry had received a tip off that the DEA had surveillance in place at the airfield and had sent the two giants with the rifles to take care of it.

Faris was furious. *Why didn't he give it to me? I would have handled it properly.* He didn't like being passed over for that sort of responsibility, especially when any Americans were involved.

He was also wondering where Henry had sent Dominick; he had a million guesses and zero answers.

Slowly but surely he was getting cut out of the group.

And he knew what that meant.

In front of him, one of the big men holding the AR 15s made a cheap joke to his friend. Faris had learned that they'd cornered the two agents across the airfield, catching them completely unaware. Each grunt had given them thirty rounds from the machine guns.

Faris watched the two morons, glaring at their huge backs.

Karma was going to be a cruel, hard bitch.

Up ahead, the two cars arrived pulling onto the dark airfield, their headlight beams momentarily blinding the men by the jet as they swung round. They were vulnerable for a split second, but the lights continued to sweep past as the 4x4's came to a stop twenty feet away.

Six men stepped out, three from each car. The Albanians. Faris had set up the deal with their lieutenant, a man called Hicham, the second in command, Faris's equivalent. It was dark so Faris couldn't make out any of their features, but he could see their hands. Three of them were holding Uzi nine-millimetre automatic pistols, the other two clutching a Remington twelve-gauge shotgun each.

Only one of the men was unarmed. A gap in the clouds let the moonlight shine through, illuminating his face. It was Hicham.

Holding his hands in front of him in an open gesture, the man walked forward. He shook hands with Henry, who stepped forward to meet him.

'It's been a while. I wasn't expecting to see you here.'

Henry nodded. 'Let's do this. I'm cold.'

The other man nodded and motioned for him to follow.

He led him towards the back of one of their two cars. Behind them, the two separate groups of men stood in front of each other. No one moved. Both sides had enough firepower to stop a rhinoceros stampede.

By the rear of one of the cars, Hicham pulled the boot open. Faris could see from where he was standing that it was packed with stacks of tightly-bound US dollar bills.

Henry scanned them for a moment.

Then he nodded.

'Now the cargo,' Hicham asked.

Henry turned to the two enforcers. 'Get it out of the jet.'

The two guys didn't move for a split second. It seemed they were having a stare-down with two of the Albanians standing opposite them.

But they turned away and moved up the stairs to the aircraft, the AR 15s still cradled in their hands.

The whole trade took less than ten minutes. The cocaine was packed into the backs of the two 4x4s, the six million US dollars transferred into the jet.

As the last brick of powder was stowed, one of their men shut the door. Hicham turned to Henry.

'We should do this again,' he said. 'If the stuff is good, we'll be in touch.'

Henry didn't respond. The other man turned on his heel and walked over to one of the cars. His crew followed, climbing inside and firing each engine. The two vehicles turned, exiting the airfield and the Albanian cartel moved off into the distance and disappeared into the night.

Once they were gone, the pilot and the enforcers relaxed. They were happy. They'd just stacked six million dollars into the plane and naturally, assumed they were going to get paid handsomely for their assistance.

Across the tarmac Henry checked his watch then turned to the two giants.

'Go and stow your weapons then meet me back out here.'

The pair nodded obediently, turning to climb up the stairs of the jet, moving out of sight. A few moments later, they reappeared without the rifles and moved back down the stairs to the runway.

'Over there,' Henry said as he jabbed a finger, pointing across the tarmac.

The men looked at each other, confused. But obeying the order, they shuffled over to where he had directed and turned, wondering what was going on.

They were now standing away from the plane, their backs to the countryside, in the middle of the runway.

By the jet, Faris closed his eyes.

Henry approached the pilot and grabbed the shotgun from the guy's hands. The two enforcers didn't have time to react. Henry gave each of them four shells to the stomach. The weapon pounded explosion after explosion, the muzzle flashing as each shell erupted out of the shotgun as he worked the trigger. One or two shells would have been enough for anyone, but he wanted each of them to take four. Five hundred pounds of muscle were no match for the power of the weapon, and blood and shreds of flesh sprayed in the air as Henry relentlessly pulled the trigger.

Each man was dead before the third blast. They collapsed backwards on the runway, bits of them scattered around them like confetti. Henry walked forward and used the last two shells to shoot each man in the face, up close.

When the shotgun clicked dry he turned and tossed the empty smoking weapon back to the shocked pilot, who was trembling. He couldn't believe what he had just seen.

'Get in the cock-pit,' Henry ordered. 'We're leaving.'

The pilot nodded, struggling to tear his eyes from the two corpses, then scrambled up the steps, stumbling on two of them in his haste to do as he was told.

Henry turned to Faris, who was leaning against the steps, unmoved.

'Let's get out of here,' Henry said, stepping past him and clambering up the stairs.

Faris looked at the two corpses lying on the runway, looking like two giant starfishes beaten with a giant sledge-hammer.

Karma's a bitch.

THIRTY SIX

At 11 o'clock the next morning, a man ran as fast as he could down the street in Canary Wharf, south-east London.

He was dressed in a brown delivery uniform, the kind a guy who delivered packages and parcels for companies like DHL and UPS wore. However, he was carrying nothing in his hands.

His arms flashed back and forward like pistons as he raced down the street. Sprinting hard, he suddenly turned a sharp left, ducking into Canary Wharf Station, a stop on the London Underground system.

Dodging past bystanders and Underground employees, the man vaulted the ticket barrier, barely slowing. Around him, a few people shouted and remonstrated as they watched the man ignore the ticketing slots.

He hurtled forward, turning back to check behind him and suddenly collided into a woman walking the other way, smashing into her and knocking them both to the ground. Out of breath and winded, the man staggered to his feet, ignoring the stricken woman on the floor beside him and scrambled forward, running onto a long escalator that led all the way down to the platforms and descending the steps two at a time.

By the entrance, two police constables suddenly sprinted into the station. They too jumped the barriers, although this time to no complaint from the people standing there. They raced past the woman on the floor, who now had concerned people around her helping her back up on her feet.

The constables arrived at the escalator. Looking down, they saw the fleeing man near the bottom, pushing past people in his effort to escape.

'*Police! Stop that man!*' one of them shouted as they both started to run down the escalator, chasing after him.

As he reached the bottom, the guy took off to the left.
A train was waiting, the Jubilee line, bound for the city
centre. There was an extra security barrier, a series of
glass screens that ran along the platform. They were
sliding shut.

He threw his hand forward to try to and wedge a set
open so he could pull himself inside but they wouldn't
give. He started hitting and kicking the screen in a
frenzy. The train moved off and gathered speed, shocked
passengers watching from inside at the crazy man on the
platform so desperate to get on the train.

Cursing in frustration, the man saw a train on the other
platform was just arriving. He turned to run over the
tracks, but was smashed hard in a rugby tackle by one of
the policemen.

He didn't see the policeman coming and was taken off
his feet.

The other officer appeared just behind his colleague
and they pinned the delivery man to the floor as he tried
to fight his way free. Flipping him to his belly they held
him down, knees in his back, while one of the men
pulled a set of a handcuffs, locking them in place firmly.

Having finally restrained the suspect, the second
officer turned to his colleague, sucking in deep breaths.

'You sure it's him?' he panted.

The other man tilted his head to look at the delivery
man's face, his chest heaving as his lungs took in
oxygen.

The suspect was flat against the tiles, his cheek pressed
firmly on the ground.

The policeman looked at his profile, and nodded.

'Yeah. It's him.'

Across the city at the ARU HQ, it had been a long night.

290

The fallout from the shooting in Trafalgar Square had been severe. Once Archer had discovered the explosives hidden under the man's coat, the police had been forced to clear the area just as the fireworks were taking place which was no small task. Bomb disposal had arrived, the EOD team examining and confirming that the device was armed and ready to be detonated by trigger switch. They had set about dismantling and separating the explosives for what was the fourth bomb they had encountered that evening. This time, the weapon used was Semtex, a vicious plastic explosive as well as enough nails to renovate a mansion. There was enough of it strapped to the dead terrorist to, as a bomb disposal expert had put it, *turn the entire Square into a crater you could see from the moon.*

Back at the Unit's Headquarters, Nikki had checked the Met's emergency logs and had found a report from Hammersmith and Fulham Station. It was concerning a police constable named Eldridge who'd been absent for two days, having gone missing while on duty on Thursday. Two police detectives had reportedly found his body just before midnight, stripped naked. The terrorist had cut his throat and stolen his uniform.

Needless to say, Chalky was man-of-the-hour with the team. Any concerns Archer and Porter had regarding his condition prior to the shooting were immediately forgotten. He'd more than made up for his previous lapse. There was even a rumour circulating that the very grateful Prime Minister wanted to thank him personally. It had certainly been an eventful day's work for the young police officer.

It turned out he'd been chasing down the first suspect just behind Fox, Mac and Porter, but in that split-second he'd spotted something odd about a police constable nearby that had caught his attention. The officer was standing by himself, away from any other policemen

291

which in itself was odd and seemed to be talking to himself.

His eyes were half-open, not alert and scanning the crowd as they should have been.

Chalky could also see he was holding something.

But when he stopped and scanned the man, he caught a glimpse of something else.

A wire, running into the man's coat. Looking at the man's face under the helmet he'd realised in an instant who he was and the rest was history.

At around 3am, the task force had finally returned to the Unit and stowed their weapons. They'd been ordered to stay on call all night, so most of them found chairs in the Briefing Room and dozed off while they had the chance.

But two men who'd had zero sleep were Director Cobb and Special Agent Crawford. Neither of them had got so much as a wink. Crawford had pulled Cobb aside just after they'd figured out the situation at the Square. Apparently, the two DEA agents at the airfield weren't responding to his calls and Dominick Farha had been reported as separating from Henry's crew having been sent on an errand somewhere according to his sixth DEA agent. Crawford mentioned that he had another man in place but he was unable to pursue Farha at this current time.

Neither man could believe it. Right before their eyes, both of their cases were falling apart. Crawford didn't know if he'd got the deal with Henry on camera and Cobb was wondering how they'd let the leader of the terrorist cell slip away when they'd had him in the palm of their hand.

Needless to say, their working relationship was under severe strain.

But things were about to get a whole lot worse.

In the tech area, Nikki hung up on a telephone call and quickly removed her headset, walking swiftly over to Cobb's office.

The Director was standing by the coffee machine inside, pouring himself a drink and rubbing his eyes wearily. Nikki knocked on the door and moved into the office in the same instant.

Cobb turned as she entered, his eyes red-rimmed with fatigue and stress.

'Sir,' she said. 'I just spoke to Limehouse Police Station. They have Number Four in custody.'

Cobb looked at her, the information registering in his tired brain.

'Great. That's good news,' he said.

'Not quite, sir. There's a problem.'

'What kind of problem?'

'A big one,' she said.

Across the level in the Briefing Room, Archer stirred awake. He blinked, yawning, gathering his thoughts. He was slumped in a chair beside the noticeboards, his back stiff from the angle he'd been sleeping in.

He sat upright and stretched, yawning again, then saw Chalky sitting in the chair beside him. Archer noticed that in a complete contrast to yesterday, today his friend looked surprisingly fresh and rested. And not hungover.

'What are you so happy about?' Archer asked, rubbing his face.

'Got a good night's sleep. Crashed out in one of the holding cells,' Chalky responded, with a wink.

Archer rolled his eyes as his friend passed him a cup of tea.

'Thanks. What time is it?' he asked, yawning again.

'11:30,' said Fox, who was sat nearby. He was reading a newspaper.

Archer glanced at the Sports headline on the back of the broadsheet.

Chelsea-Manchester United fixture to go ahead, despite tragedy at Emirates.

'I thought the PM cancelled the game?' Archer asked, sipping the cup of tea and leaning back in his chair.

Fox shook his head. 'No. He gave a speech earlier demanding that the match continue in tribute to those killed. They're carrying out a ceremony before the game and holding a minute's silence.'

Archer nodded. 'What time's kick off?'

'1:30' he replied. 'All we need now is for Farha and the last terrorist to turn themselves in before lunch. Then I can watch the game.'

'Forget the game, I could sleep for a week,' mumbled Deakins' voice from nearby. He was lying back in his chair, his arms folded, his eyes closed.

Archer didn't reply. He was looking at Shapira across the room as she leaned against the wall, overhearing their conversation.

She was smiling.

'You a football fan?' he asked her.

She looked down at him. 'I am today.'

At that moment, Cobb entered the room, Mac striding in behind him, both of them moving quickly and purposefully. Most of the room was already up and awake and anyone who'd dozed off was given a quick prod or kick. Mac shut the door as Cobb got right down to it, wasting no time.

'Morning, lads,' he said. 'First of all, fantastic work last night. The whole operation was the perfect example of what we stand for as a Unit. You found the target and you took him down.'

He turned to Chalky.

'I spoke to Downing Street earlier. The Prime Minister wants to meet you after this is over and give you a commendation. Well done. You saved a lot of lives last night.'

There was a small cheer; someone wolf-whistled. But the room quietened immediately.

They could see from the look on his face that Cobb wasn't finished.

'I have some more news,' he continued. 'Two constables arrested Number Four about half an hour ago. They picked him up at Canary Wharf and he's over at Limehouse right now getting prepped for an interrogation.'

He paused.

'The officers who made the arrest saw the suspect coming out of a building. He was disguised as a delivery man, but they'd seen the news and recognised him. Good work on their part. The guard on the front desk said the man entered the building with a large brown package under his arm.'

'What was it?' Deakins asked.

'We don't know. He left without it.'

Silence.

'Which building, sir?' asked Porter, standing to the left by the noticeboards.

Cobb looked at him.

'One Canada Square.'

The moment he said it, Archer's blood froze.

Oh shit.

Oh shit shit shit.

THIRTY SEVEN

'Jesus Christ. That's the second biggest building in the UK,' said Deakins.

Cobb nodded.

'Yes, it is. And unfortunately for us, the business community doesn't care that it's a public holiday. We estimate there are just over eight thousand people inside, spread over all floors, and most of the shops on the lower levels are open too.'

He looked at Mac.

'The evacuation has already begun. CO19 and Bomb Disposal have been deployed over there. But I just spoke to the Prime Minister and he asked that you get down there too.'

There was a pause.

The room was silent as each man considered the sheer scale of the task ahead.

'How many floors in the building, sir?' asked Fox.

'Fifty,' said Mac. 'Each one is twenty-eight thousand square feet.

'Do they know what floor he got off?' Archer asked.

'Security is checking the CCTV as we speak. There aren't any cameras in the stairwell, so he might have stepped out of the lift and moved to a different level.'

There was an uneasy murmur in the room.

'We could search all week and not find this thing. It's like finding a needle in a haystack,' said Deakins.

'More like a needle in an entire hayfield,' added Chalky.

Cobb nodded. 'I know. I'm sorry. But we have to try. Now it could be nothing. Just a hoax. But judging by yesterday's events, I think we all know what it potentially could be.'

'If it's a bomb, the building could blow at any minute,' said Fox.

Silence.

The room was still. Any positivity had instantly vanished.

Cobb looked at his men.

'You need to get down there, lads,' he said, quietly. 'And make every second count.'

After his arrest on the platform inside the Underground station, Number Four had been taken back upstairs and hauled over to Limehouse Police Station, located nearby by the docks. Officers there had processed the suspect through to holding and he'd been dumped in an interrogation room, alone. Word had spread from a security guard at Canary Wharf that he'd left a package somewhere inside One Canada Square; they were now preparing to ask him what and where it was.

A CID detective stood outside the interrogation cell watching the arrested terrorist closely. His name was Davis. He'd been a Detective Inspector for twelve years and was also the father of a teenage son who'd been at the Emirates stadium the night before. The boy had been in the opposite stand to the explosion and had thus escaped unscathed, but Davis felt his knuckles whiten with fury as he stared through the window at the suspect.

The guy was slumped in his chair, navel-gazing. He was still dressed in the delivery uniform, his hands now cuffed in front of him, resting on his lap.

Davis watched him for a moment.

Time for a little payback.

Before he entered the room, the detective turned and moved through a side door and into the reception area.

A younger detective was behind the desk, manning the post.

'Did you make the call?' Davis asked.

The man nodded. 'Yes, sir. They've started evacuating the building. EOD and counter-terrorist teams are on their way over there.'

'Good.' Davis paused. 'Now let's go and see what our friend's been up to this morning.'

He turned and walked back into the station. He approached the door to the interrogation cell, taking a look inside as he reached for the keys to the door in his pocket.

But the terrorist wasn't in the chair anymore.

He was lying on the floor, blood pumping from his severed jugular. It was spilling out of him like a ruptured pipe leak.

Davis saw a small work-knife spilled to the floor, fallen from his hand.

The suspect was spasming and shivering on the floor as his blood pooled around him.

'Oh shit!' Davis fumbled into his pocket for the keys, staring at the terrorist bleeding to death inside the cell.

The detective next door had heard Davis shout and he ran in from the front desk, catching sight of the wounded man through the glass.

Davis eventually managed to get the key in the lock and twisting it open, the two men ran inside towards the terrorist.

He was jerking and gasping like a fish on dry land, lying in a vast pool of blood as his heart pumped it out relentlessly.

Without hesitation, Davis pulled off his suit jacket and clamped it to the man's neck, trying to staunch the bleeding. But it wasn't working; the blood just kept coming. Davis and the other detective were covered in it as they knelt beside the man.

Davis snapped his attention down to the small knife lying in the blood. The blade was only an inch long, but that's all the guy had needed.

'Where the hell did that thing come from!'

THIRTY EIGHT

Given the quiet Sunday morning streets, the three ARU police cars made it down to the Wharf in just under fifteen minutes. They pulled to a halt in the Canada Square plaza, the huge building looming above them like a giant monolith. Climbing out of the vehicles, each man slammed his door and shielded his eyes from the sunlight as he gazed up.

The building seemed to go on forever.

Archer stood side-by-side with Porter and Chalky, the three of them looking up in silence, seeing first-hand the enormity of their task.

When Cobb had told them it was this particular structure, Archer had felt his stomach turn. Standing over seven hundred and seventy feet tall, the building housed fifty floors and thousands upon thousands of people who moved in and out of the doors daily. It served as the central hub for London's hectic trading and financial district. In photographs, the place had always seemed big, its iconic pyramid roof now a familiar part of the London skyline.

Up close, it was enormous.

Deakins was right.

They could search inside for a week and not find anything.

Mac barked an order and the men brought their attention back to the plaza in front of them. Up ahead, scores of people were streaming out of the large entrance to the building. Various vehicles had been parked in the square, most of them street police, their lights flashing. To the right, Archer saw a black van with EOD printed on the side, a man standing beside it talking into a radio.

Bomb disposal were already here, which was good. Past the black van, he saw a cluster of other Ford 4x4s, which looked as if CO19, the city's other main counter-terrorist team, had also arrived.

As one, the ten task force officers made their way past the evacuees flooding the plaza as they headed towards the entrance and the lobby. Shapira and Rivers remained standing by the ARU cars, both staring up at the building. They'd both played a major and crucial part in events yesterday, but this was a job for the task force.

As the ten-man team moved into the lobby, Archer saw the other counter-terrorist unit standing to the left. Much like the ARU, CO19 were the London Metropolitan police's equivalent of an American SWAT team. The officers were dressed in much the same clothing as the ARU squad, save for the fact that each of them carried an AR15 Carbine assault rifle instead of the ARU MP5. As they arrived to stand side by side, both teams nodded to each other. Their sergeant stepped forward, a big, barrel chested guy with a sandy moustache. Approaching Mac, the two of them shook hands quickly and the other man updated him on the situation.

'We found him on the surveillance cameras,' the man said with a gruff voice. 'He got off on 30. But he could have used the stairs; we're not sure. Some genius didn't put any cameras in the stairwell.'

'Yeah, we heard.' Mac said.

'My lads can start on 30 and work our way down. Can your boys work up?'

Mac nodded. Not wasting a second, the burly CO19 sergeant turned back to his men.

'*Listen up!*' he called.

A silence had already fallen. The ARU guys were listening intently too.

'Here's the situation, lads. As we know, a terrorist suspect was seen leaving this building roughly an hour ago,' he said, checking his watch. 'The CCTV is telling us that he got off on the 30th floor, carrying a large brown package that he didn't bring back down with him. Unfortunately, he could have used the stairs so we're looking at a radius of probably ten floors each way. We're going to sweep them all, one by one. Be quick, but be thorough. You see something, call it in and let EOD take over.'

He jabbed his thumb across the lobby towards the main reception desk. Archer saw two members of the EOD, climbing into green blast suits. He recognised them as two of the guys from the shopping centre the night before. The burly CO19 leader continued.

'My team, we'll start on 30 and work our way down, floor by floor. Sergeant McGuire and the ARU squad are going to work their way up.'

'Any word from the suspect?' asked one of the CO19 officers.

The man with the moustache shook his head. 'He's dead.'

There was a moment's pause.

Everyone frowned, confused.

'He cut his own throat inside a cell at Limehouse,' the man explained. 'He must have had a knife or something that they missed when they frisked him. And that means we're going to have to do this ourselves, lads. Whatever this thing is, it could very well be a shitload of explosives, possibly on a timer. So all of you, move quickly, be thorough and just find the bloody thing. Let's move.'

He turned immediately, jogging across the marble floor towards the lifts. His men followed immediately behind. Mac turned to the ARU squad.

'First team, with me to 31,' he ordered. 'Deakins, take Second Squad to 32.'

'Yes, sir,' the task force said in unison, and together, the group of men headed for the lifts.

Across the city Dominick Farha was staring at the grass by his feet, wondering both what to do and also how the hell he'd ended up back in London.

He was in a small clearing, surrounded by pine-trees and leaning against the side of a small helicopter that had brought him here. He was thinking about the task ahead of him. No matter how many times and different ways he looked at it, the same undeniable fact kept on presenting itself.

I need a gun.

After meeting his uncle in the Parisian café and somehow managing to get out of there alive, Dominick had climbed into the back of the car that was waiting outside on the street. It had taken him through the streets of Paris on a journey that had left him completely clueless, no idea where the hell he was. He'd been tense the whole trip. Half of him suspected it was a trap and there would be an unpleasant final surprise waiting for him whenever or wherever they stopped.

They'd arrived in a small field, gated off from the public; the driver had pulled up alongside a small white helicopter parked in the field.

Once Dominick had stepped out, the car immediately turned around and sped off into the night. He saw a small, wiry man standing by the helicopter and the rear door to the vessel was open.

The guy saw Dominick standing there and without a word, turned his back, and starting climbing into the front seat.

Henry had mentioned these men were reliable and that they worked for an associate. They certainly moved like drug-runners. Neither the pilot nor the man who'd brought him here hung around for a second longer than necessary.

Dominick had glanced behind him cautiously and slowly approached the helicopter. He still wasn't sure if this was a trap. He didn't want to turn his back and suddenly get jabbed with an autojet syringe, a pistol-shaped injection weapon that Henry used to sedate his victims.

But no-one was lying in wait. He'd approached the helicopter and climbed in. The pilot wasn't wasting any time, the rotors were starting to spin, gathering speed, the engine whining as it warmed up. They'd been in the air in less than five minutes and heading back towards London.

The whole journey had taken around ninety minutes. Farha had watched in silence from the back seat as the inky waters of the Channel glinted dully below them in the moonlight, on his guard the entire time.

He didn't fancy having a gun pulled on him and being told to jump out.

But they'd made it to London around 1am UK time. Dominick was wondering if his man had succeeded at Trafalgar Square, but he had no way of finding out seeing as he'd ditched his mobile phone a few days ago after arranging his escape with Faris.

The helicopter had landed in an empty field under cover of darkness. The pilot had shown great skill. He'd navigated the vessel down in a small clearing, surrounded by a cluster of tall pine trees, the perfect place to lay low.

And if Dominick got a move on, they wouldn't be there for long.

This whole trip had left a bitter taste in Farha's mouth. He'd spent a year almost to the minute hatching a plan to get the hell out of this country, but he'd been away for less than an hour then immediately sent back. It was almost laughable. If it had been any other person on the planet telling him to do this Farha would have spat in his face. But his uncle was the one man who could make him do it; hell, he could make him do whatever he wanted.

After the helicopter had landed, Farha had debated whether to make a move there and then in the darkness, or wait until morning and hatch a plan. The nervous tension of the day had hit him like a freight train and he realised he was more tired than he thought. He'd nodded off in the back of the vessel and had woken up again after the sun had come up.

He hadn't gone anywhere yet though.

If this whole thing was going to work, he needed to plan his next few moves carefully.

He checked his watch. It was coming up to midday, UK time. The sun filtered in through the trees which was bad. The good weather meant there would be more people on the street, not indoors as there would be during inclement weather. He needed to lay low; his face was all over the news channels and papers and he was the most wanted man in Europe right now.

And Henry's proposition was a risky one. More than risky; potentially suicidal. It could either be incredibly hard or surprisingly easy. He had to be careful.

And he needed a weapon.

Some sort of gun would be perfect. Anything would do at this point. He cursed. If he had more time and access to weaponry, the job would be a cinch. He could do the deed from a distance and be out of the country before anyone realised what had happened. *But where can I get one?* He couldn't risk using a phone, or using one of his old contacts. He couldn't trust anyone.

A light bulb suddenly turned on in his head; he turned to the pilot.

'Does your boss have a safe-house here? Any weapons?'

By the front of the vessel, the pilot shook his head as he read a paper.

'Don't even bother. I'm not taking you anywhere else. My job was to get you here. If you don't get going soon, I'll go ahead and leave without you. I'm going to leave to refuel in ten minutes anyway. If you're not back by sundown, I'm off.'

Farha felt his temper start to rise.

But he couldn't react. This guy was the only way he was getting out of the country again.

He thought for a moment, searching for another solution.

'You got a toolkit?' he asked.

The guy nodded, not looking up from the paper. 'Under the front seat.'

Farha moved to the pilot's door, opening it, and checked under the pilot's seat. Sure enough, there was a red toolkit there, about the size of a large shoebox.

Pulling it out, Farha put it on the pilot's seat and opened the box. It was mostly full of stuff he couldn't use. A map, two flares, some small screwdrivers. But he did find something that could work.

He pulled it out, examining it in his hands.

It was a jack-knife.

He pushed the switch, and the blade slid out. He tested the edge with the tip of his finger. It was as sharp as a razorblade.

Suddenly, he felt a little bit better.

He really needed a gun.

But a knife would do.

THIRTY NINE

High up in One Canada Square, Archer glanced out of a window from the 31st floor. The winter sun was shining down across the city and the view was spectacular. From here, he could see all the landmarks; the London Eye. Big Ben. Westminster. Even Wembley in the distance. Tourists would have paid handsome money for a view like this but he snapped his attention back to the present.

He wasn't here to sight-see.

He was standing in a long conference room, ten chairs positioned each side of a lacquered, polished table. Across the room Porter was kneeling down, searching under the table and checking the drawers.

'Nothing,' he said, shaking his head and climbing back to his feet.

Archer nodded and looked around his end. No luck.

The package wasn't here.

Together, they left the room and moved swiftly out into the corridor. The 31st floor was a maze of hallways and different rooms. There were endless tables, drawers, cabinets, countless potential hiding places.

Archer looked around and cursed. The damn thing could be anywhere.

Up ahead, Mac appeared from a kitchen, Chalky alongside him. They both looked equally frustrated.

'Anything?' Mac asked.

Archer shook his head. Mac then pushed the pressel to his radio, as the three officers beside him continued to sweep the floor.

'Second Team, report, over.'

Deakins' voice came up in each man's earpiece. *'Nothing up here, Mac'.*

Fox's voice followed. *'Nothing here either.'*

Mac swore and pushed the switch. 'Keep looking.'

'Roger that.'

Mac turned to Archer, his face strained and wrought with concern. He knew the suspect had got off on 30, which was nearly the exact middle of the building. Demolition logic meant if the package contained explosives, which it probably had, and if he'd placed them well, they could detonate and the whole building would go down in seconds. The charge would rupture the building's support systems and the top half would collapse, crushing the lower portion like a crumpled accordion.

'Go with Chalk up to 33,' he ordered. 'Port and I'll finish here. This is all taking too long.'

Archer nodded; together, he and Chalky ran to the stairwell, pulling the door open. The two of them sprinted up towards 33, both increasingly uneasy.

Whatever and wherever the package was, they were running out of time.

Almost directly above them on 32, Deakins and Fox were clearing the floor together. They'd just entered an executive office belonging to someone who was clearly high up the trading food chain. The office contained nice furniture, ornaments and a television that probably cost more than either of them made in a year. A polished desk and chair were pushed against the far wall, taking pride of place.

Deakins whistled. 'Whatever this guy does, I-'

Fox suddenly cut him off.

'Shhhh!'

He jabbed a finger to his lips. Deakins immediately paused.

'Listen,' Fox added quietly, his brow furrowed.

Both of them stood motionless, looking at each other as they concentrated their hearing.

Fox was right.

There was a soft sound gently breaking the quiet.

It was so faint, you could barely hear it.

But there was no mistaking what it was.

Ticking.

It was coming from the desk.

Fox crept towards it. The table had three drawers on the left hand side, hidden from view from the door. Softly, Fox knelt beside it and put his ear against the wood.

His eyes widened.

· He looked back at Deakins and nodded.

They stayed silent, as if any noise might trigger whatever was hidden within the drawer. Fox took the handle in his hand; Deakins had moved to stand beside him. Fox took a deep breath and then eased the drawer open, as Deakins winced.

The ticking suddenly got louder as it filled the room. They both looked down.

It was just an alarm clock. It was resting on some papers inside the drawer, ticking away like a practical joke.

311

Sagging with spent tension, Fox reached in and grabbed it. He tossed it to Deakins, who cursed as he caught it.

Fox stood, and turned to his team-mate.

'Forget this, let's go to 34.'

Dominick was on his way out of the clearing. He'd walked through the trees and into a park. It was quiet, almost empty. He saw a group of kids away to his left kicking a football around. Behind him, he heard the helicopter take off which meant he needed to get moving.

He passed an old brick wall to his immediate left, part of some house that had been demolished long ago; someone had stacked a series of empty bottles and jars on a smaller brick level just ahead of it, forming a make-shift shooting gallery. He figured some kids had probably been taking pops at the glass with a .22.

God, I wish I had a gun, he thought.

The knife in his pocket had its advantages. It was silent and wouldn't jam, but also meant distance would be a problem. Luckily however, Farha was dressed in a suit. At the moment, he looked like a guy who'd woken up in an unfamiliar place after partying too hard the night before, or maybe a guy who'd got lucky and was on his way home, an extra kick to his step.

As he walked, Dominick started smoothing down the suit jacket and adjusting his tie. With a bit of smartening and fixing up, he'd pass for a businessman. He suddenly remembered he had the thick sunglasses in his pocket. He took them out and gave them a quick polish, sliding them up over his nose.

For the first time that day, he smiled. It would be hard for anyone to recognise him now.

He could walk straight up to his destination.

He exited the clearing and turned onto a residential street. The place was quiet, no one around, just the odd car moving slowly along the road. As he was wondering how long it was going to take him to walk, he remembered he had some spare English banknotes stuffed in his wallet. He saw a black taxi turn to move up the road ahead and raised his hand, sunglasses over his eyes, the knife hidden inside the inner pocket of the suit jacket.

The taxi moved forwards and slid to a halt on the kerb beside him. The driver had the window wound down and he looked over at him.

'Long night?' he asked with a smile, noticing Farha's suit and shades.

On the pavement, the most wanted man in the country nodded, smiling.

'You can say that again.'

33 was just as quiet as the other floors but the lay-out up here was slightly different. The centrepiece of the floor was one large square room that served as the nucleus for the rest of the level. There were scores of desks and chairs in cubicles, walled off from each other to separate each worker and provide privacy, a pretty typical office environment.

Looking around, Archer swallowed.

The place was giving him the creeps.

It was eerie as hell. Pens without their lids had been discarded on desks, resting on documents. Computer screens around the room hummed, cursors blinking expectantly. The evacuation had been so sudden that many of the screens hadn't yet had time to flip to a screen-saver.

Half-drunk cups of coffee and mid-morning snacks were scattered on various desks.

I thought today was a holiday, thought Archer as he scanned the room. He guessed it was true, the stocks never slept. Chalky suddenly appeared from a conference room across the office floor, looking agitated.

'Anything?' Archer asked him.

Chalky shook his head, kicking a swivel chair in frustration. 'Nothing. Not a damn thing. We could be in here all month and not find it, Arch.'

The blond man pressed the switch on his vest, as he walked back towards the lifts. 'Mac, this is Archer. I'm with Chalky on 33. I wouldn't bother coming up here. It looks clear.'

Mac's voice responded. '*Roger that. Get up to 35.*'

Chalky heard this through his own earpiece and was already moving towards the stairwell, pushing open the door.

Turning, he noticed that Archer had paused.

He was staring at something.

Chalky frowned and walked back to join him.

Archer's gaze was fixed on a small kitchen, fifteen feet to the right of the stairwell. It looked standard. A coffee machine. Mugs and cups stacked by the sink. A refrigerator. All of it perfectly normal.

Chalky turned to Archer. 'Arch, what-'

314

Archer cut him off. He pointed at something inside the kitchen.

Chalky looked.

His gaze landed on the cord to the fridge. It was unplugged. Someone had stuck a piece of paper with *Out of Use* written in black pen to the front of the unit.

On any other day, that wouldn't have been any cause for alarm.

But this wasn't one of those days.

It was slightly out of the ordinary and that was enough for Archer.

Not saying a word, he moved forward slowly, entering the kitchen.

He reached out, his hands touching the front of the white rectangular fridge.

'It's warm,' he said.

Without a word, Chalky had also entered the room. He stepped past Archer and leant forward over the counter, peering behind the back of the refrigerator. He searched for any mechanisms, trips or anything that shouldn't have been there.

'Looks clear,' he said.

They both looked at the handle.

Archer took it carefully in his hand. He turned to Chalky, who realised he was holding his breath.

'Ready?'

Chalky nodded.

'Do it.'

Archer pushed down the handle and gently eased the door open.

They both looked inside.

'Oh my God,' Chalky whispered.

In the same instant, Archer's hand flashed to the switch to his radio.

'Mac! Mac! You need to get up to 33 right now. We've found it!'

As Archer called it in, Chalky stared at the inside of the fridge.

The shelves were packed with Semtex plastic explosive.

Each brick was bright orange, almost ludicrously bright. There must have been close to twenty of them, probably more. Conjoining all of the explosives were an assortment of wires, which all led into a small rectangular box. The battery.

The detonator.

But that wasn't the worst part. There was a panel on the front of the bomb, an electronic clock-face.

There were a series of constantly-changing red numbers on the digital screen.

2:59

2:58

2:57

The bomb was on a timer.

And they had less than three minutes to go.

FORTY

EOD made it up there in just over ninety seconds. Mac had arrived with Porter moments after Archer called it in from the floor below. The frequency was shared with the CO19 team, so he'd already shouted that they had located the device, it was on a timer and that they had less than three minutes, ordering every person to get the hell out of the building.

Only Mac, Archer, Porter and Chalky were left. They stood watching the device, helpless, waiting for the two bomb disposal experts to arrive.

After what seemed an age, the lift finally dinged and two men rushed out, each struggling to run in their green blast suits. They hurried into the kitchen and examined the device before them.

The clock was ticking down.

1:20

1:19

1:18

They reacted instantaneously. One of them started frantically opening a tool box he had brought with him, while the other spun to the four police officers standing behind.

'Get the hell out of here right now!'

They didn't need to be told twice. Porter was already moving down the corridor. He jammed his hand in the lift doors, catching them just before they shut, and ducked inside as Archer and Chalky followed.

By the kitchen, Mac took a last look at the two men kneeling by the refrigerator. All his experience had taught him never to leave a man behind.

However, one of them sensed he was still there and whirled around.

'Go!'

Mac ran to the open lift. Porter was frantically pushing the button for the ground floor.

Eventually the doors closed and the lift started moving down.

In the kitchen, the two bomb experts were scanning for any trip-wires, collapsible circuits, anything that would prevent them from touching it.

The red numbers on the clock face ticked down mercilessly.

1:10

1:09

1:08.

The lift doors opened in the lobby. The moment the metal doors parted, the four officers rushed out and sprinted towards the front entrance. Ahead of them outside, police and CO19 officers were frantically trying to push the gathered crowd back from the plaza.

There were hundreds of people out there.

Archer glanced back as he ran, checking to make sure there was no one left behind. He didn't see four stairs that led to a lower level in front of him and he stumbled, landing on his ankle awkwardly and heavily.

There was a loud *crack*. He fell to the floor, shouting in pain, as his three team-mates ran through the exit and out into the sunny plaza.

Chalky, hearing the shout, turned and realised Archer was still inside, staggering to his feet from the floor and trying to get out of the building.

Without hesitation, he ran back for him.

He sprinted across the lobby and hooked his friend's arm around his shoulder.

'C'mon Arch, we've gotta go!'

Helping his friend, Chalky took Archer's weight as the two of them moved to the doors as fast as possible.

They made it outside and moved as quickly as they could across the plaza, Archer grimacing in pain.

Thirty-three floors up, the clock ticked to *0:30*.

Thirty seconds to go.

The two men worked fast. All their training and experience came down to this; if the bomb exploded, the two of them would become vapour in an instant.

The lead guy was called Harry Jameson. He was a Staff Sergeant and one of the best. The device in front of him was his hundred and ninety-fourth. He'd done two tours of Afghanistan with 11 EOD Regiment, the Explosive Ordnance Disposal, men and women responsible for defusing IEDs and bombs left by the Taliban and the rebels. Before that, he'd done five months in Iraq in 2003. There, he'd knelt before everything aside from a nuclear weapon.

But this batch of Semtex was the most powerful device he'd ever seen. He couldn't move it; he didn't have time to anyway and it would most definitely go off if

319

disturbed by motion. He couldn't cut into the Semtex and extract the explosive materials into an acid bath. He didn't have time. The bomber had fitted an anti-defusing device behind the panel, tucked away from view. It was an electronic fuse, an even charge running through it. If Jameson tried to cut one of the wires, it would sense the difference in current and react, triggering the explosives. That meant every wire was tripped. And the bomb in front of him wasn't like those from the movies, where the wires were all different colours.

Every wire on this device was red.

Distinguishing them was a nightmare.

'Shit!' his partner said, seeing the time running out.

Jameson was thinking, thinking.

Suddenly, he jerked round to the other man.

'Liquid nitrogen!'

The guy reacted instantly, and pulled a spray gun from a pocket on his thigh.

Jameson grabbed it and started spraying the battery and anti-defusing device. It wouldn't stop the device from detonating, all it would do was delay it.

When the countdown ended, a charge would kick through the battery into the blasting cap. Jameson could freeze the battery, buying them seconds.

Once it warmed to room temperature, the charge would go through.

The device would blow. He would have to cut the wire leading into the battery within the following few seconds.

If the battery wasn't frozen, the bomb would explode.

The red numbers on the digital clock ticked down.

320

0:05

0:04

0:03

'C'mon!' screamed Jameson, squeezing the gun as hard as he could, willing the battery to freeze.

'C'MON!'

Outside in the plaza, people were fleeing. The ARU officers took cover behind parked police cars, looking up.

Time was up.

It didn't blow.

The battery had frozen. But the charge was in there.

They had seconds.

Jameson grabbed a set of pliers and found the wire.

'Hurry, Joe, hurry!' his partner said.

And with one swift movement, Jameson clicked it in half.

And just like that, they were safe.

The cut wire had severed the current.

The bomb was defused.

Both men sagged with relief. They rocked back to sit against the wall, their chests heaving. They were both covered with sweat.

Jameson turned to his partner and shook his head.

'Jesus Christ. I need to get a new job.'

.

Outside, the crowd was confused.

'What happened?' shouted Mac to a third bomb disposal member, standing by the EOD truck.

The guy was listening to the radio, covering one ear with his free palm. He suddenly smiled and called out.

'We're good. We're good!' he repeated. 'It's defused! They did it!'

Everyone in the plaza sagged with relief, like hundreds of balloons deflating all at once. There was a small round of applause and some cheers.

Behind one of the ARU vehicles, Archer had taken cover next to Porter and Chalky. The three of them had their backs to the car, but Archer was grimacing in agony, his ankle feeling like it was broken.

'Good job,' Porter said happily. 'We did it, Arch.'

'Great,' the younger man muttered, his teeth clenched against the pain.

Right then in the north of the city, the taxi driver had just arrived at his passenger's requested destination. He was about to pull into the place, but Farha asked him to keep going down the road. The guy obliged, they came to a stop beside some office buildings in the heart of the city.

Farha paid the fare then got out, shutting the door. The cab drove off and he was left alone.

He turned and started walking slowly back down the way they'd just come. The street was relatively busy, but wasn't hectic. As he strolled, he came across a newsstand. *Terror strikes city* said one of the tabloid headlines. *London rocked by terrorism* said another.

He glanced at the headlines but didn't slow and continued to the end of the street. He stopped by the corner; leaning against the wall, he casually peered round at the address he'd been given.

It was an impressive building.

He looked hard, but couldn't see what he was after.

He briefly considered making a move, but decided against it.

He'd scope it out.

Wait for his target, who'd appear soon enough.

Then he'd move in and be out of here before anyone knew what had happened.

FORTY ONE

'So let's get this straight,' said Deakins, leaning against one of the Unit vehicles. 'We've spent the last twenty-four hours going to war with a nine man terrorist cell. Ten, if you include the girl at the airport. And the only injury we sustain is when Archer trips and breaks his own ankle.'

There was laughter, a welcome release from the tension of the last twenty four hours. The team had gathered around in a ragged circle. Archer was being helped by Chalky and Porter into the front seat of one of the cars.

He laughed with the other officers, but the jolting jarred pain into his foot, so the laughter changed to wincing.

'I'm never going to hear the end of this, am I,' he mumbled through gritted teeth, shaking his head. The men chuckled as Porter moved around the car to the driver's seat.

He climbed in and both men pulled their doors shut.

'C'mon Arch, I'll take you back to the Unit,' he said, inside the car. 'We'll get you patched up.'

Archer nodded as he grimaced in pain. 'Thanks.'

Porter fired the engine and the vehicle moved off back towards the Unit's HQ.

The men watched them go, still grinning. The remaining officers were standing in a circle in the plaza, enjoying a moment of much-needed relaxation.

Smiling, Mac looked around his men.

'Hey, where's Fox?'

'I forgot to tell you, Sarge,' said Deakins. 'He left with the woman, Agent Shapira, a few minutes ago.'

'Why? Where'd they go?'

'She said she'd received an urgent call from her agency. There was some kind of situation at Stamford Bridge.'

'The football ground? There's a game there today, isn't there?'

'No, it was cancelled, out of respect,' said one of the other officers, Mason.

Deakins shook his head. 'No, he's right, the game's still on. United-Chelsea. Kick-off's in twenty minutes,' he added, checking his watch.

Mac frowned, thinking.

'Why the hell wasn't it cancelled?' he asked.

'The Prime Minister demanded that it take place,' Chalky said. 'I think he's there, with his family. They're doing a big remembrance ceremony before the game.'

'Shapira didn't have a car so Fox offered to take her,' Deakins told Mac. 'You know he's a big United fan. He probably just wanted to be outside the ground before the game.'

Mac frowned again, his brow furrowed.

'But what the hell do Mossad want down there?'

He paused, thinking.

He didn't like it.

'And what situation is there that we don't know about?'

Just as the officers were discussing this in the plaza, back at the ARU's HQ Nikki had stolen her first moment of quiet in what seemed like forever.

She was sitting behind her desk in the Operations area. Cobb and Crawford had been standing beside her moments before; the computer system in front of her was hooked up the police radio so they'd heard all the drama unfold in One Canada Square. The building secure, the bomb disarmed and everyone safe, the two men had retreated to catch their breath and take stock of the situation.

Glancing over her shoulder, Nikki saw Cobb sat at his desk. Crawford had said he was going outside for a cigarette.

His presence here was making her curious. The DEA's arrival and involvement in the Unit's case had only been explained in passing to her and Cobb and the American had been working side-by-side the whole time, which was unusual for Cobb. Nikki knew he hated to be lumbered with unnecessary operational weight so she was surprised by his apparent willingness to work with Special Agents Crawford and Rivers.

Over the last twenty-four hours, she'd heard snapshots of conversations between them, especially during the times she'd entered Cobb's office. She hadn't heard explicit details, but she'd picked up that Crawford was trying to take down some Middle Eastern drug cartel. That was pretty much it.

But she'd also heard one name over and over again. It seemed to be involved in every conversation she caught.

Henry.

It seemed a curious and bizarre name for someone involved in a cartel. It sounded so quaint, and English. Unthreatening. With some time to kill and her curiosity piqued, she clicked onto the Unit's database and typed in the name *Henry*. The ARU shared a lot of files with MI5, MI6 and GCHQ, not to mention the Met's database and crime log, so thousands of results came up.

She narrowed the search, typing *Henry Drug*.

This time, hundreds of results. She tried one more time.

She typed *Henry Cartel*.

This time, just one file came up.

She clicked it open.

There was a moderate amount of information inside. They had a surveillance photograph of a large man, taken from what looked like the inside of a bar. He was vastly overweight, wearing a beige suit that was bulging at the seams from his excess body fat. He had small dark eyes, a bald head, and was looking in the photographer's direction, which was unnerving; he had a cold, hard, emotionless face.

Nikki examined him for a moment, then clicked off his photograph, reading on.

There was quite a bit of information about him. Not so much for his apparent involvement in drugs, but for his potential terrorist intentions. The log said that both his parents had been killed when a British missile had hit his house during the Gulf war. Cobb had mentioned yesterday that the attacks in London were designed for Dominick Farha to win back favour with some cartel. She could now see why he'd chosen the UK as a target.

Amongst the detailed commentaries, there was another file. It came from someone called McArthur. She clicked it open.

It contained a series of surveillance shots and a report from 2006. She examined it. It appeared that McArthur had been an undercover detective with MI5. He'd been positioned in a bar in the Upper West Side neighbourhood of New York City. His team were working to bring down a Real IRA cell recruiting and buying weapons. They'd been tipped off that in the bar that night the leader of the cell and a prominent East Coast gun runner would meet.

However, the meeting had never taken place but there had been another surprise. The operative, McArthur, couldn't believe his eyes when he saw who walked through the door. He emphasised in the report the freak coincidence. He knew of Henry who was a priority foreign target for the agency. The man was renowned for being extremely hard to both track down.

And here he was, inside this bar in New York.

Clicking on a photo, Nikki saw the initial surveillance shot of Henry. McArthur had taken it from his seat in the bar. She continued reading the report. The agent said that someone had entered the bar and met with the drug lord.

Suspected family member, McArthur had written on the report. *Treats her like such. Not a lover.*

Nikki saw that there were more photos in the file. She clicked them open. The person had their back turned in all of them.

But then in one shot they'd turned, her face looking down the bar past McArthur who'd taken a photograph.

Nikki gasped.

She couldn't believe what she was seeing.

The woman was Agent Shapira.

She was sitting with Henry in the bar.

FORTY TWO

The man known as Henry had a reputation for being impossible to scare or intimidate. He cared about nothing, nor anybody but himself. He murdered government agents and members of his own crew for fun; he'd even killed his own brother-in-law after he'd once drunkenly mocked him for his weight.

As the head of a cartel, it was impossible to gain leverage on him. Over the years many had tried; rivals, upstarts, young guys from the surrounding areas who, in a state of delusion, thought he could be stopped or dethroned. But each story ended the same way. They all ended up either shot in the face or at the bottom of the sea, seventy pounds of concrete moulded to their feet, screaming as they plummeted into the abyss.

But there was one thing no one knew about him. Not a soul.

Henry had a secret. Only one. But it was powerful enough that he would sacrifice his entire business for it in a heart-beat.

His daughter.

Mia.

Her mother was a maid who'd lived inside his compound. Henry had drunkenly mounted her one night when he was eighteen, still a lieutenant in the business and the next time he'd laid eyes on her, the bitch was three months pregnant. He considered drowning her but decided to wait, curious to see what effect a child would have on him. If it was a boy, he was even considering raising him as an heir, seeing as when the woman was seven months pregnant he'd ascended to his position at the top of the cartel.

But it had been a girl. The first moment he saw her, Henry experienced a feeling that he didn't like. Attachment. He realised he actually cared about the child much to his surprise.

But he hated it; it felt uncomfortable and unfamiliar.

It also meant one thing, and he knew without a doubt it would mean the same word to his enemies.

Leverage.

After the girl was born he'd kept the maid and baby in the compound, hidden away from the outside world and prying eyes. Only two other people, a pair of other maids, knew of the baby and who the father was so they were quickly disposed of. And one night, twenty five years ago, he'd put the maid and baby on his private jet and flown them to New York, far away from any potential danger. It was a fact of life that if word got out that there was someone he cared about, the child would one day either be held hostage or killed. It was inevitable, like the sun rose and set every day.

He had snuck meetings across the Atlantic to see the child. He couldn't afford to risk using JFK or Newark, so he used a private airfield in New Jersey and had then taken a limo into the city. He'd set the two of them up in a place in the Upper West Side, on 79th and Amsterdam, a safe neighbourhood. It had been dangerous going there alone. He couldn't take any security with him due to the secrecy and he had a lot of enemies stateside, both Federal and criminal. When the child had been old enough to attend private school, he'd enrolled her and strangled her mother. And with each passing year, Mia was proving to be an increasingly pleasant surprise. She was definitely her father's daughter.

He saw that she was not intimidated by pain or death. She didn't mourn her mother's passing. She was resilient, resourceful and also highly intelligent. Despite his passion for secrecy, Henry had shared more and more with her until eventually, she knew the ins and outs of his entire business. His passion for drowning his enemies. His associates. The obscene profits. Rather than be scared she had often provided surprisingly sound advice for him on ventures and people who needed to be eliminated. And all this while living in New York, anonymous in the city.

To her friends, she was Mia, the college grad.

To Henry she was his pride and joy, the only other person in the world he cared for.

She was also the only person in the world that he trusted implicitly. He'd called her from Riyadh a year ago on a private and secure line. She had never heard him so angry. He informed her of what Dominick had done at the Four Seasons and the new enemies they now had as a consequence. The other organisation had contacted Henry in a rage, demanding answers and blood. Henry had promised them retribution; but he needed Mia's help.

Unlike her father, there was no black mark against her name on any government databases. She had a fake passport and no one had any idea who she really was.

Henry asked her to fly to England, to track down her idiot cousin.

And to take him out.

The prospect of murder didn't intimidate her. Henry had helped her kill her first man when she was fifteen. The guy was an informant, so he deserved what he got. Henry had injected the man with an autojet sedative, knocking him out cold and he showed Mia how to cinderblock and cement a victim. He'd let her push the guy into the Hudson from a boat in the early morning, the man's mouth duct-taped, his eyes wide as saucers, Henry's proudest moment as a father.

For Mia, finding Dominick had been easy. The guy was a complete idiot. He'd rented a flat in a part of London called Knightsbridge using his real name on the lease, showing just how stupid he really was. As a result she tracked him down quickly, but before she made a move something told her to stay back and observe, just for a few days, to see what he was up to. Slowly but surely, as she tailed him wherever he went, she realised what he was doing. It looked as if he was recruiting some kind of cell. She'd even followed them on a train to a deserted plain in south Wales two months ago, and watched from far away with binoculars as the cell practiced demolitions out there on the moor.

But her interest was fading. She had a job to do. When she got back to London from the Welsh moor she'd called her father, telling him how she'd found Dominick and where. She offered to waste him the moment he got back.

But Henry had been intrigued. The boy had always been a disappointment, just like his father.

Could he finally be about to do something useful?

Mia had reluctantly held back. She was worried for her father. If the police got wise and took Dominick into custody, he knew far too much about Henry's business to be safe. She'd reminded him of this fact on the telephone three days ago. He'd come to his senses and finally gave the order for her to move in and take him out.

She'd broken into his apartment that night with a silenced pistol, ready to shoot him between the eyes as he slept.

But he wasn't there.

He'd packed his bags and was gone.

Pulling back from the apartment, Mia had wracked her brains, trying to figure out where he could be. She didn't have a clue and was angry with herself for letting him slip away. But yesterday morning, as she prowled the street trying to think, she'd caught a glimpse of a television in a shop window. It was giving breaking news of a raid on a house in North London. She'd raced over there as fast as she could, easily getting past the police cordon and breaking into a house opposite the street. From her vantage point, she'd seen police officers arresting two members of the cell that she recognised from the Welsh moor.

She'd contacted Henry, telling him of the situation. If the cops got hold of Farha before they did, he knew enough to bring down the entire cartel. Henry's response had surprised her. He told her to forget about him. He'd take care of it. But he wanted her to do something else.

For all Dominick's stupidity and clumsiness, he'd given Henry an idea.

She knew her father hated the UK. He'd been sent to school with his sister during the Gulf war only to return and find a crater where their house should have been. That had planted a seed of hate inside the boy that had grown over time. Aside from Mia, his mother was the only other person he'd ever truly cared about and the British had killed her. Although inept, Dominick's intentions had been on the money. Henry had never dabbled in terrorism.

But the boy had wet his beak.

He'd arranged for a package to be delivered from Riyadh and contacted a man in the UK who would send it where it needed to go. The guy wouldn't fail. He was part of Henry's team. Mia had listened to the plan; it was genius. If it worked, it would go down in history and no one would ever realise their involvement.

But then a major problem had arisen.

One of Dominick's morons had blown himself up at the Emirates.

Security would have been tough to infiltrate before, but now it would be like breaching Fort Knox. That was even if the game ever took place. Mia and Henry had been about to give up, thinking the whole plan was finished, but then they got a stroke of luck. The Prime Minister hadn't cancelled the other matches that weekend. Better still, he was going to be attending the Chelsea-Manchester game with his wife; it was as if fate had intervened for Henry and Mia.

Through her surveillance photographs from the raided house, she'd learned that the squad of policemen who made the bust were known as the Armed Response Unit, some new police detail set up by the English government. Judging by the way they took charge at the crime scene, Mia figured they had access everywhere. She'd followed one of their cars back to what she assumed was their headquarters.

When the bomb had gone off at the stadium, she'd tailed them there too. Across the car park, she'd seen four of them separate and run back to one of their vehicles, jumping in and speeding off. She'd followed them all the way to a shopping centre, but there was a logistical problem when she got there. The police had parked on Parkfield Street, but there was nowhere for her to go.

There was a gathering crowd outside and she didn't want to draw attention to herself, thus she'd been forced to drive around the block, ending up on the other side of the shopping mall, on Upper Street. And just as she was preparing to get out and move in to see what was happening, she couldn't believe her luck.

One of Farha's men was right there in front of her on the street.

He was standing beside an ambulance. She watched him attempt to detonate something and saw that it failed. He'd jumped into the ambulance and she followed him to the stadium. She figured out his plan the moment she saw him approach the Emirates, so she held back and took him out just before he could detonate the device. She had considered detonating it herself, but then the police officer had appeared. It was perfect. She pulled the fake badge Henry's guys had made her a few months previously. *Agent Shapira. Mossad*, she'd said. She'd watched the cop look at her badge, then at the unconscious terrorist.

She'd saved the day.

Infiltrating the police unit had been surprisingly easy. She knew enough about Dominick's cell to back up her Mossad story and she'd already earned their trust by busting up the ambulance bomber. Her plan was to lay low until Sunday when she'd need their help to get past security at the football stadium. But when she'd taken out the guy with the rocket launcher, they were practically throwing her a party.

But one thing had taken her by surprise. She was keeping to herself inside the Unit's headquarters but she couldn't help notice the presence of the two American agents. Crawford and Rivers. From the DEA. Through overheard conversations and snippets of trusted detail from Rivers, she pieced together that they'd been building a giant case against Henry. But not only him. The evidence they'd gathered incriminated other cartels. She knew of such a method of trial. They called it a RICO case.

Trial by association, in other words.

After she'd whacked the kid with the rocket launcher on the roof, Rivers was totally on her side. She'd used her increased standing to ask him for details about the DEA operation's situation, and he'd told her that they had two men tailing a drug buy at an airfield outside Paris. It was the culmination of their entire operation he told her. Henry was never seen present at a deal.

If they captured him tonight, it would be the closure they needed to bring down the cartel and all those around it.

Panic had kicked in then. She'd managed to sneak a phone call to Henry, warning him off, and he'd sent some of his men to fix the problem. Soon after, she'd received a phone call from a private number. A man she didn't know. He'd confirmed that Henry's package from Riyadh was in place.

The rest was up to her.

Where Dominick had screwed up was his rationale. He had figured the more bombers he had, the bigger the destruction. That wasn't true. What he should have done was pick his targets carefully. Like Mia. Stamford Bridge football ground was the home of Chelsea football club. It had a maximum capacity of 41,837. Over 41,000 souls in one place, every single one of them distracted, focused on events on the pitch.

And today the Prime Minister would be there.

So would his wife.

How ironic, she thought.

They all gather to mourn the dead, yet every single one of them will die before the end of the first half.

She smiled to herself at the thought.

She was sitting alongside one of the ARU officers in his car, making their way to the stadium. She'd given him some bullshit story about how Mossad needed her help at the ground. Some kind of situation, she'd said vaguely, but much to her pleasure the idiot had driven her down willingly.

She was planning to kill him, but wouldn't get rid of him yet.

She still needed him to get her inside.

Beside her, the cop pulled to the kerb on Fulham Broadway. Around the car, fans in blue and red shirts were pushing forward, heading to the entrance turnstiles of the large football stadium. This was as close as they could get to the stadium without walking.

'Here we are,' he said, applying the handbrake.

He turned, noticing a grin on Shapira's face.

'What are you smiling about?'

'Just looking forward to the game,' she replied. 'Let's go.'

FORTY THREE

The first thing Nikki did was rush straight to Director Cobb's office.

She barged in without knocking and immediately told him what she'd found. He'd listened closely, then jumped up from behind his desk and ran through to the ops room to Nikki's computer to see for himself.

Right now Nikki was frantically trying to pull any files on Shapira, but there was nothing. No one anywhere seemed to have any idea who she was.

At that moment, Cobb's mobile phone rang. Pulling it out of his pocket, he saw it was Mac.

'Mac, are you on speaker-phone?'

'No, sir.'

'I need you to apprehend Agent Shapira right now!'

There was a pause.

'She's not here, sir. She's gone.'

'What? Gone where?'

'She said her people had needed her at Stamford Bridge. The football stadium. Fox is driving her down there.'

Cobb swore.

'Get on the phone to Fox right now. Order him to make the arrest. Get over there as fast as you can.'

'What's this all about, sir?'

Nikki turned to Cobb, having realised the connection. 'Oh my God.'

He looked at her, the phone to his ear.

'She's Dominick Farha's cousin.'

At the stadium, it was ten minutes until kick off. Scores of wreaths and tributes had been laid outside the ground, including many Arsenal and Tottenham Hotspur shirts with messages and tributes written on the front. They were gathered by the gates like a sort of shrine.

Shapira ignored them as she moved with Fox towards the entrance. Armed security and police were everywhere. At the entrance, one of them stepped forward, seeing that the ARU officer was armed.

'Who are you?' he asked.

'Ryan Fox. I'm with the ARU,' he said, pulling a badge from a sleeve on his uniform. 'This is Agent Shapira. She's with Mossad.'

The man turned his attention to her. She'd already pulled her badge and ID and passed them over, cool and calm. The forgery was perfect. He examined them both for a moment, then passed them back, satisfied.

'OK, so what can I do for you?' he asked.

Fox turned to Shapira, letting her take over.

'Some of my team are already inside,' she said. 'We think there might be a security issue.'

'Not likely,' the guy said stubbornly. 'And whatever it may be, it's not your issue. Our team will handle it.'

'We can stand here wasting time, or you can listen to me and we can go fix the problem,' she said. Her phone rang in her pocket. She grabbed it and saw it was Henry's private line. Thinking on the spot, she showed them the ringing phone. 'See? They're calling me right now. You can come with me and see for yourself.'

The guard thought for a moment.

'OK. Fine,' he said. 'But both of you, weapons stay here. You can collect them on the way out.'

Fox nodded. He checked the safety on his MP5 and un-looped the strap from his shoulder. He passed it over, along with the Glock 17 pistol from its holster by his hip. The guard took the guns and put them in a security hut behind him. Shapira pulled her Sig Sauer pistol and passed it over. She didn't mind.

She had another weapon.

The guard nodded. 'OK. So let's go.'

Together, the three of them moved into the ground. There was still a large crowd outside the stadium itself as fans bought match-day programmes and drinks before taking their seats in the stands.

As they moved forward, Fox felt the phone on his tac vest vibrate as it rang. He pulled it out. It was probably Mac, calling him back to the Wharf.

He answered it. 'Mac?'

He heard murmuring at the other end but he could barely hear him over the crowd. He turned, putting his finger in his other ear.

'Speak up, Sarge. I can't hear you,' Fox shouted.

'Fox, take Shapira into custody!'

Fox frowned. 'What? Why?'

'She's Dominick Farha's cousin!'

Fox froze.

He felt the hackles on his neck rise.

'Don't let her out of your sight. We're on our way!'

Mac's voice disappeared. The next moment, Fox spun around.

But Shapira was gone.

He scanned the area around him, but she was nowhere to be seen.

She'd vanished into the crowd.

FORTY FOUR

The Sunday afternoon lack of traffic meant the ARU police car moved at break-neck speed through the streets. Stamford Bridge to Canary Wharf was approximately nine miles; behind the wheel, Deakins had an encyclopaedic knowledge of the city streets, and he was putting all that information to good use. The streets flashed past; they were almost there, making fast time.

When they'd received the call from Cobb outside One Canada Square the officers had hit a problem. They only had one car. Fox had taken one of them with Shapira, Porter the other to take Archer back to the Unit's HQ. They didn't have time to arrange other transportation, so only four of them could go.

Deakins was behind the wheel, Mac in the front seat beside him. Behind, Chalky was on the right, Rivers to his left. Mac realised that the American had spent a lot of time with the woman over the last twenty-four hours. He figured he might have some ideas as to where she could be.

He checked his watch again. *1:26pm.*

'Floor it, Deaks,' he ordered.

The officer behind the wheel nodded, and pushed his foot down, the vehicle speeding on towards the stadium.

Inside the stadium, Mia was now on a lower level.

She'd been waiting for the two policemen to turn their backs. All she needed was a split-second. They'd given her an opportunity and in a heartbeat, she'd taken her chance and gone. She knew they'd call in her sudden disappearance via radio and alert other members of the security upstairs.

She needed to get on the lower level before they did.

And she had. Upstairs, it sounded as if the players were now walking out onto the pitch.

There was thunderous noise above her as the fans cheered their arrival.

The place rumbled as if they were on a fault line and it was an earthquake.

The white corridor she was currently striding down was empty; all the security were watching the crowd or the players on the pitch.

Not down here.

But just at that moment, a guard appeared from around the corner ahead of her. He frowned when he saw Mia walking towards him and moved forward, confronting her.

'Who are you?' he asked.

She didn't respond, bearing down on him.

Then suddenly, she lunged her body forward.

Her hands were up, going for his throat. She grabbed his neck either side and with a violent wrench she broke it with terrifying speed, as if it was a dry twig, killing him in an instant.

Once he flopped to the floor, she grabbed his body by the ankles, and pulled it around the corner.

As she did so, she saw that she'd arrived where she needed to be. Ahead of her was a vending machine, Coca Cola printed on the front, white letters over a red background.

Dumping the guy's body beside it, she leaned back and double-checked both sides of the corridor again.

She was alone.

She pulled something from the rear waistband of her suit trousers, hidden by her jacket. It was a small electronic tool. A screwdriver.

She reached up and pushing the tool into a slot in the corner of the front panel of the vending machine, she pulled the small trigger.

The tool whined and it started spinning the first screw on the drinks machine, drawing it out.

Across the city, Porter pulled to a halt outside the Unit's headquarters. Archer was beside him, wincing in pain. On their way back, Mac had called Porter's phone, ordering him to get over to Stamford Bridge as quickly as he could. He hadn't been specific, he'd just said there was some situation with Shapira and for Porter to get down there as soon as possible.

Archer looked out of the window and saw that they were outside the ARU car park, twenty five yards from the building.

'I've got to get over there, Arch,' Porter said. 'Don't want to piss Mac off.'

Archer nodded, pushing open his door with a grimace.

'Thanks for the lift. I'll see you shortly,' he said through his teeth.

'Alright, mate. Take care. Get someone inside to take a look at that ankle.'

Archer nodded as he climbed out awkwardly and slammed the door behind him. He found he could put the slightest pressure on his foot, but not much.

He hopped and hobbled into the car park like an old man as he heard Porter speed off behind him.

Suddenly, he realised something and swore. He'd left his MP5 on the back seat of the car. The Unit had a strict policy on the care and protection of their weapons; he was going to be in deep shit with Mac when he found out.

Cursing his carelessness, Archer limped into the car park and started hobbling slowly towards the entrance twenty five yards away

The place was quiet save for a solitary figure standing to the left of the doors.

Looking closer, Archer saw it was the DEA agent, Crawford, smoking a cigarette.

Archer gritted his teeth and continued on towards him.

The police car containing the three ARU officers and Rivers screeched to a halt on Fulham Broadway. They saw the other Unit vehicle, parked there on the kerb.

Climbing out, the four men ran towards the entrance gates. Even from here they could hear a voice on a microphone inside the stadium, calling for a minute's silence to remember the lives lost at the Emirates last night. They saw Fox approaching them from inside the ground, a cluster of guards with him.

Mac and his three companions were let into the ground without delay, their weapons still in hand. He strode towards Fox who had arrived by a small boxed room by the gate.

The guard inside passed him over his weapons.

'Where is she?' Mac asked.

'She was out here, Sarge. I turned my back to talk to you and when I looked back, she was gone.'

Mac kept his voice low as a sudden silence had fallen inside the stadium. He turned to the men around him. Including the stadium security, there were nine of them.

'Find her!' he said urgently, in a hushed voice.

The men nodded.

The nine of them split up, and they ran into the bowels of the stadium.

Back in the car park at the ARU, Archer was struggling to make it to the doors.

His ankle was causing him agony. He could put hardly any pressure on it at all and he was severely pissed off. This would put him out of action for the next couple of months and it had all happened because of his carelessness. With him out of action, some other guy could come in and momentarily take his spot.

Gritting his teeth, he looked up and saw that by the doors, Crawford had noticed the young police officer's struggle to get across to the entrance.

Flicking away the cigarette, the American started walking forward to help him.

On the lower level of the stadium, Mia finished with the last screw on the front of the vending machine. Placing the electric screwdriver to one side, she grabbed the panel and pulled.

The front of the machine lifted away.

Inside the rectangular metal box, there were no cans of drinks.

There were two large canisters instead, each containing glowing amber liquid.

Black lettering was printed vertically down each cylinder.

VX Nerve Gas

It was the most lethal nerve agent ever synthesised, five hundred times more toxic than cyanide. Once inhaled, the gas shut down an enzyme in the body that controlled muscle and nerve function. A person would shudder and fit so hard they either bit off their own tongue or swallowed it. Their back would break from the muscle spasms.

And they'd die, their skin melting, blood pouring from every orifice.

She smiled and looked inside the transparent casing of each cylinder. The liquid was oily, golden in colour. Seemingly innocent enough. But these two canisters of liquid would kill every person in the stadium with ease once it was airborne. And scores more unlucky enough to be outside on the street would die from the fallout.

The weapon had been sitting in Henry's private aircraft hangar for almost a year, an unwanted gift from an associate who'd requested a large haul of meth and who couldn't front up the cash. Beside the canisters was tucked a silenced pistol, a Heckler and Koch USP. Mia smiled. Her father knew any weapon she had would be confiscated at the gate; he'd even thought to include a silencer.

She reached forward, taking the weapon and racking the slide, loading a round in the chamber and flicking off the safety catch.

With her bare hands, she was dangerous.

Now, she'd be close to unstoppable.

Returning her attention to the nerve gas, she set to work arming the device. She would detonate the gas via a remote trigger. The switch for the detonation was also tucked inside. She'd make her way out of the ground and push it from a safe distance.

Suddenly, she realised the stadium upstairs had gone quiet.

A minute's silence, she thought.

The whole place was as silent as a church in prayer.

But not for long, she thought, with a grin.

In the sunny car park across the city, Archer was glad to see the American approaching. Even only light hopping was jarring savage pain up into his body from the ankle. He'd need help before he got any further. The DEA agent was fifteen yards away and closing.

As he approached, something over the man's shoulder caught Archer's attention. Another figure had entered the car park. Archer didn't recognise him, but he was walking fast, approaching Crawford from behind.

The guy was dressed in a suit and sunglasses; there was something about him that seemed familiar.

And then, all of a sudden, the guy's face rang a bell, even behind the shades.

Archer froze.

He realised who it was.

For a split-second, he wondered if he was delirious from the pain.

But he blinked and realised what he was seeing was real.

Dominick Farha was walking straight towards Special Agent Crawford.

FORTY FIVE

At Stamford Bridge, the minute's silence had ended with the cheep of a whistle and a long round of applause from the crowd that built in volume until it seemed the earth shook. Down below, Mia was finishing arming the VX gas. Above, the crowd had started chanting.

It was making the lower level rumble as the noise swelled.

Suddenly, a guard rushed around the corner to her left. He was searching around, hastily, looking for something or someone. *Me,* she thought.

He paused as he saw her, then the contents of the vending machine and the dead body of the guard with the broken neck.

He froze for just a split second as his brain registered the situation.

'Hey!'

Mia already had the silenced pistol in her right hand and she shot him in the face. His head rocked back as he took the round and he collapsed to the floor in a heap. She moved forward, grabbing his ankles and pulled him out of the main corridor.

Blood and brains from the gunshot had been spattered all over the white corridor behind him, but it didn't matter.

She was ready to leave.

For a split-second, a million questions ran through Archer's mind, like access codes on a high-tech computer.

It can't be him?
It's him!
Why is he here?
What's that in his hand?

348

Special Agent Crawford was now just thirty feet away and Dominick Farha was closing down on him from behind. He was gaining fast on the DEA agent, who had no idea he was being approached.

Archer saw what the terrorist leader was holding.

It was a knife.

Chalky and Rivers were searching for Shapira together. They'd given up looking around the stadium floor and had gone down to the first sub-level. Chalky had his MP5 up tight in the aim, Rivers his pistol.

They pulled open a door and moved down the corridor, silently and swiftly. Chalky ducked his head into a changing room as Rivers pressed on. He saw something against the wall, and on the floor ahead of him.

He moved forward, looking closer.

It was blood.

And suddenly, someone rounded the corner, colliding with him.

Shapira.

She had a pistol in her hand. Rivers reacted instantly. He tried to wrestle the gun from her hand as he pulled his own weapon from its holster on his hip. She snapped her head forward, head-butting him hard, breaking his nose with the crown of her head. His eyes filled with water and he was momentarily stunned and blinded from the blow.

She shot him in the stomach, and he fell to the ground, hunched over and out of the game.

However, Chalky had gained some ground on her. He'd raised his MP5 to get a shot, but Rivers had been in the way so he'd moved closer. Too close. She knocked the gun out of the way. It wasn't strapped to his shoulder, and it clattered to the floor, out of reach.

She raised her own pistol, but he threw himself at her with a cry, knocking her own gun from her hand. They wrestled on the floor; Shapira was thrashing and fighting like a hellcat, trying to bite his face and gouge his eyes.

Beside them, Rivers writhed in agony as he bled out on the floor down the corridor.

He watched helplessly as the two of them fought on the ground, blood pumping from the wound to his gut.

Archer reacted fast.

Remembering that he didn't have his MP5, his hand flashed to his right thigh. He pulled his Glock 17, flicking off the safety catch in the same instant.

'HEY!' he screamed at Farha, raising the weapon.

In front of him, Crawford's eyes widened with confusion, but Farha reacted in a flash.

He lunged forward, behind Crawford, blocking Archer's line of sight and grabbed the DEA Special Agent by the collar, wrapping his arm around his neck like a vice. He pushed the knife to the helpless man's throat, nestling the blade beside his jugular.

The movement knocked off his sunglasses, and Archer saw his eyes for the first time.

They were red-rimmed, dark and filled with hate and fury.

'BACK UP!' he screamed at Archer, from behind Crawford's head. *'BACK UP!'*

The officer didn't move, but he didn't have a shot, as Farha was hidden behind Crawford.

Adrenaline pumped through Archer's veins, and he stood on his injured foot to steady his aim.

He didn't even remember it was broken.

In the lower level of the stadium, Chalky had the upper hand. Shapira was fighting like a wild-cat, biting and scratching, but he was physically stronger than she was and had wrestled his way on top.

350

But suddenly, she grabbed his arm and threw her legs up and around his neck, pulling them tight into a jiu-jitsu triangle choke.

Chalky tried to fight it, but she had the hold locked in tight.

He gasped, feeling the pressure around his neck tighten.

His face turned red. He was suffocating. He knew he was seconds from passing out. And Shapira knew it too.

As he desperately tried to free himself, she snarled at him from the floor.

'Drop the gun or he dies!' Farha screamed.

Archer was trying to get his cross-hairs on the guy, but he was clever. He'd pulled himself around Crawford, protecting himself, leaving only two inches of his head in Archer's sight. One of his eyes glared at the young policeman from beside the DEA agent's neck.

Behind them, Archer saw Cobb, Nikki and Frost running over from the entrance to the building. They must have seen or heard the commotion from inside. Farha sensed them coming, and twisted to look at them, keeping his head tight behind Agent Crawford's and out of Archer's firing line.

'Back off! Back off or I kill him!' he screamed.

Cobb, Nikki and the older detective stopped in their tracks, their hands up. Archer saw them all realise who he was, shocked.

Under the guy's arm, Crawford's eyes were wide with terror.

Farha turned his attention back to Archer, who still had his Glock aimed.

The terrorist pushed the razor-sharp blade harder, so a trickle of blood slid down Crawford's neck.

'Another ounce of pressure, he dies because of you,' he screamed. *'Drop the gun!'*

Chalky was seconds from unconsciousness.

He gathered all his strength in one last attempt and scooped the woman up off the floor. Her legs were wrapped around his neck and she rose in the air as he lifted her high, her face burning with hate.

And he slammed her down, as hard as he could.

It worked. She yelled in pain as her back smashed into the floor, her legs loosened, which released the choke hold. Gasping for breath, Chalky fell back. He saw his pistol on the floor by the wall in the corridor; clutching his throat and coughing, he dived for it. Behind him, Shapira had recovered fast. Chalky heard what sounded like a phone book slamming onto a table then felt a thud and a searing pain in his back.

Suddenly, his legs wouldn't work.

He collapsed, reaching forward desperately for his weapon.

It was just out of reach from his fingertips.

'Last chance!' Farha screamed.

Archer hadn't moved, but his damaged ankle was starting to send shooting pain through his entire body as he stood on it. It was affecting his aim. The sight on the Glock in his hands was moving from Farha to Crawford to the car park then back to Farha.

More people had rushed outside from the Unit HQ, stopping dead when they saw the stand-off.

Crawford was staring at Archer, his eyes wide, silently pleading for help.

Blood was trickling down his neck staining the blue collar of his shirt from the puncture wound.

Farha had the knife jammed by his artery.

An extra ounce of pressure, it would be cut and Crawford would bleed to death on the spot.

But Archer didn't look at Crawford.

He was staring into Farha's one furious eye, through the top-sight of his pistol.

In agony from the bullet wound, Chalky tried to crawl towards his weapon. There was another thump as another phonebook hit a desk and white plaster exploded from the wall as she fired deliberately close to his head. The white chalk mixed with the blood on the floor from the bullet wound in Chalky's back.

She had him and he knew it.

He turned, rolling onto his wounded back.

She was holding a silenced pistol in one hand.

In the other was a switch.

He could see behind her the two large canisters of nerve gas.

And now she had the weapon aimed at his head.

As Archer and Farha stared at each other, an image suddenly came into the police officer's mind.

Big brown eyes, the colour of hazelnut. They were beautiful. But scared.

And filled with tears.

The eyes he was staring at now were narrow, filled with hate and fury. Not a drop of compassion.

And he was the man who had left that girl to die.

'*OK, you piece of shit. The American dies!*' he screamed.

'You never came back for her,' Archer said quietly.

Suddenly, five gunshots thundered in the corridor.

Shapira was thrown back, five nine-millimetre bullets tearing into her torso, pieces of her chest and blood spraying in the air. Her pistol and detonator fell to floor as she skidded back down the corridor. She was dead before her body came to a halt.

Clutching the wound on his back, Chalky looked the other way.

Rivers was lying on the ground in a pool of blood, his weapon aimed where Shapira had been standing.

He lowered the gun, clutching his stomach with his other hand, grimacing and gasping in agony.

Chalky tried to call to him, but he found he couldn't speak. The room was starting to swim. He felt sleepy. He suddenly felt warm.

With no more pain.

As his eyes started closing, he saw the door down the left end of the corridor open. Mac, Deakins and Fox were running towards him, shouting something.

Upstairs, he could hear the roar of the crowd. He felt his eyes close, and a peaceful feeling swept over him. It felt good.

His back didn't hurt anymore.

And he drifted off to sleep.

Number Nine hesitated.

Archer didn't.

He shot him through the eye.

The policeman had maybe two inches to work with, but it was perfect. The bullet skimmed Crawford's neck. Farha wasn't expecting it, and the bullet thumped into his eye socket, throwing him back like the whiplash from a sudden car accident as it tore through his brain and exited the back of his head in a bloody spray.

The knife twirled from his hands like a baton from a juggler's grip and he fell back onto the hard concrete with a thud, his legs and arms splayed. Crawford stood motionless, like a statue, afraid if he moved the man might still be there.

Archer stayed just as still, his pistol aimed where Farha's head had been, the pair of them like two statues.

And suddenly, the adrenaline started to wear off.

The pain screamed through his body as if his ankle was on fire. He felt as if he was going to throw up.

He staggered, and fell back onto the ground. Cobb, Nikki and Frost ran over to help him as he sat on the tarmac, his pistol spilling from his hands.

He looked over at the dead terrorist, who was laid out across the car park thirty feet away.

'Found you,' he muttered.

FORTY SIX

It took everyone concerned a good few hours to fully understand everything that had just happened and put together the whole picture, piece by piece. The Manchester United- Chelsea match was mysteriously cancelled half-way through the first half. According to ground staff, apparently a gas pipe had ruptured under the stadium and they needed to clear the area immediately. A number of fans in the South Stand said that they heard five distant bangs, but apparently that was just the sound of the pipe rupturing.

The game was postponed until a later date, but everyone made it out OK.

In reality, the other ARU officers and the stadium security had arrived to find a bloodbath in the white corridor of the lower level. There were three dead bodies, two guards and Shapira, and two critically wounded men. Before anything else, Rivers and Chalky were rushed to hospital as quickly as possible.

Rivers especially was in a seriously bad way.

The EOD squad had arrived from Canada Square as soon as they could and quickly inspected the nerve gas. There was no timer, no trigger switch aside from the one dropped from the dead woman's hand. They disarmed it without any difficulty, then loaded the canisters up securely and removed them from the site to be destroyed.

However, there was more shocking news. Mac had received a call from Director Cobb as he and his men watched Chalky and Rivers being loaded into the ambulances outside the stadium. He couldn't believe what Cobb told him.

Apparently, Dominick Farha himself had appeared out of nowhere outside the Unit's HQ and tried to kill Special Agent Crawford.

However, he hadn't counted on the presence of the youngest member of the task force, hobbling his way through the parking lot after Porter dropped him off.

The phone to his ear, Mac smiled. After a standoff, apparently Archer had shot the terrorist leader in the head, no negotiation, no mercy. His ankle was a mess though, broken in two places, and he was taken to hospital immediately afterwards. After hearing all this, Mac informed his men and without a moment's hesitation, they all piled into the Unit's cars and headed for St Mary's Hospital. Mac was surprised to find a spare MP5 resting on the back seat of one of the vehicles. It had to be Archer's. However, considering what had just happened and what the young police officer had just done, he'd let him off the hook.

Just this once.

Once Agent Crawford was patched up and had recovered, he'd received some mixed news himself. French police had contacted the American embassy, informing them that four dead bodies had been found in an airfield outside Paris. Two of them had ID and were confirmed as Agents Adrian Flynn and Jack Brody, DEA. Both men had been murdered as they lay in a hide on the edge of the airfield, machine-gunned from behind. However, Henry had made a huge mistake. Crawford had another agent in place as back up, a man whom no-one aside from him knew was there. The man had witnessed the entire trade with the Albanians and called ahead to Riyadh. The moment Henry's jet landed, an entire division of Saudi Police and armed agents from the DEA appeared on the runway. He was done.

Back at the ARU, Cobb and Nikki pieced together Shapira's involvement. According to the log at Stamford Bridge, the vending machine containing the canisters of nerve gas had been delivered the day before. Henry and his daughter had planned the attack all along, but it seemed the bomber at the Emirates had complicated their plans. Security would have been tight before. After the incident at the Emirates, it would have been close to impossible to get inside Stamford Bridge and to the nerve gas without authorisation. Shapira had been forced to improvise and had infiltrated the Armed Response Unit.

Cobb was wracked with guilt at being deceived by her, but no one blamed him. She'd prevented the ambulance bomb outside the stadium and also shot the guy on the roof with the RPG, currying favour and allaying any suspicions. No one had ever considered the thought that she could be on the other team.

After talking with Crawford's sixth agent and looking at timings, it appeared that the woman had also been providing Henry with intelligence all along. The drug lord all of a sudden knew about the DEA's involvement and operation, hence how Brody and Flynn had been compromised. They realised he'd also ordered Dominick to put the hit on Crawford. Cobb guessed it was a way of buying the drug lord time to get back to Riyadh, while at the same time getting rid of Dominick and also exacting revenge on the DEA Special Agent.

Shaking his head at it all, Cobb took a deep breath.

He couldn't have scripted this day.

He was now alone on the upper level of the Armed Response Unit, inside the tech area. Once it became clear the operation was over, he'd told the tech team to take a few days leave, effective immediately. The task force, who'd also been given some well-deserved leave, were all down at the hospital, checking up on Archer, Chalky and Rivers. The Prime Minister had also called once he'd been evacuated from the stadium at Stamford Bridge, saying he wanted to meet each member of the detail and thank them all personally. Cobb looked around the empty level, smiling.

They'd earned it.

Leaning over a desk, he powered down the last computer as Agent Crawford appeared from the stairs behind him. He had a plaster stuck to the right side of his neck. They were the only two people left in the building.

Cobb turned as the man approached.

'Good news. I just spoke to the hospital. Rivers is going to make it.'

Crawford sighed with relief. 'That's great.'

A broad smile appeared on his sandy Southern features. *Like a young Robert Redford,* Cobb had thought when he first met him. That seemed like a lifetime ago.

Crawford's smile faded though.

'And your men?'

'They'll be fine. They got the bullet out of Chalky- I mean Officer White's- back. And Archer's getting a cast on his ankle. Broken in two places. But he'll be OK.'

Crawford smiled.

'That's good. I'm glad. The guy saved my life. That was some shooting.'

Cobb nodded.

There was a pause.

'I'm sorry about your two men. Three men, I mean.'

Crawford nodded. 'Me too. But we got what we needed. My last agent watched the whole thing first hand. Right now, he's got Henry in custody himself. We had an entire division waiting for him in Riyadh. Working with the Saudi police, we've already started raiding his compound and seizing his assets. It looks like we have enough evidence to take two other cartels down with him.'

'Congratulations. That's great news,' Cobb said. He meant it.

There was a brief silence.

Then Cobb pulled on his suit jacket. Crawford had travelled light; he was ready to go. The two men walked to the stairs, Cobb flicking off the light switch as he passed. Together they walked down the stairs and arrived in the reception area, pushing open the door and walked outside. It was surprisingly warm after the cold of the previous few days; a bright January afternoon. The sun was just starting to set in the distance.

Twenty five yards away, Cobb saw a black taxi waiting on the street outside the car park.

'Yours?' he asked.

Crawford nodded. 'I've got a plane to catch.'

'You headed home?'

Crawford shook his head, with a smile.

'No. Not yet. I've got one final pit-stop to make first.'

There was a moment's silence. Then Crawford offered his hand. Cobb shook it.

'Thank you. For everything you've done,' the American said. 'I couldn't have done this without your help.'

Cobb nodded. 'Same to you. You ever need my help again, don't hesitate to call.'

Crawford smiled. Turning, he walked across the car park towards the taxi, then stopped and turned back one last time.

'Did you know Agent Rivers was part of the team that took out Bin Laden?'

'I didn't.'

'He never made it into the house. His helicopter crashed before he got there. The first time I met him, he told me his biggest regret from that night was that he'd never have anything special to tell his grandchildren about what he did in his life.'

Cobb smiled. 'I guess he does now.'

Crawford stood still for a moment, smiled, then walked across the car park, climbed into the taxi and pulled the door shut.

The driver released the handbrake and the vehicle moved off and down the street until it disappeared out of sight.

Cobb turned back to the entrance to the building, set the sophisticated alarm system and locked the door with a set of keys pulled from his pocket. He climbed into the front seat of his car. Just as he went to slot the key into the ignition, his phone rang in his pocket.

He pulled it out and answered.

'Hello?'

'Hey Dad.'

Cobb smiled. 'Hey buddy.'

'Are you coming home today? We're all worried about you.'

'I'm just leaving now. I'll be home soon, OK.'

'OK.'

The called ended. Cobb pushed the key in the ignition and fired the engine. Reversing, he took one last look at the Unit.

What a day, he thought.

He moved out of the car park, and drove down the road towards his family and his home.

What a day.

*

Four thousand miles away, a man woke up from a deep, deep sleep.

As he opened his eyes, a dazzling glare from above momentarily blinded him. Throwing his arm up to shield his small, reptilian eyes, he tried to focus. Where the hell am I? He could feel a familiar rocking and swaying from the ground beneath his obese bulk. He realised the glare was coming from the sun.

Then he smiled. He was on a yacht. His yacht. He must have dozed off.

He went to climb to his feet.

But he couldn't.

Confused, he pushed his upper body upright, looking past his immense gut.

His socks and shoes were gone. Someone had looped his feet through a cinderblock. He looked through the gaps.

Three pairs of handcuffs had been fastened the other side.

And for the first time in over twenty five years, Henry was scared.

He started pushing himself forwards, trying to reach past his belly and frantically scrabbling at the metal.

'That won't do any good,' said a familiar voice, behind him. 'You of all people should know that.'

He twisted his head, sweating and in disbelief.

It was Faris. He was in a white shirt and khaki shorts, sipping on a drink, sunglasses over his eyes.

'Undo these cuffs,' the fat man ordered.

His lieutenant looked down at him and smiled.

'Faris, undo these cuffs.'

'My name's not Faris,' the man said. 'It's Special Agent Cruz. I work for the DEA.'

Henry blinked, his fatty torso soaking his suit with sweat. Faris's accent had changed. He now sounded like an American.

Cruz smiled as he saw the fat man register this. He continued.

'You never had a clue, did you? See, first of all, I knew you would try to kill me when we got back to Riyadh. I saw it in those puffy little eyes of yours. So I sedated you on the plane. You don't remember? I got out of my seat to use the bathroom and pulled the autojet from behind you. You're a big boy, so I gave you a double dose. You've been out for two days.'

Henry blinked.

He had a distant memory of sitting in his seat. A prick in his neck, like someone pinched him. The next thing he knew, he was waking up here.

'You piece of shit,' Henry screamed. 'Undo the cuffs.'

Cruz smiled, sipping the cocktail.

'See, I spoke with the British government. We realised how you'd known about our surveillance at the airfield. Your daughter had managed to infiltrate one of their counter-terrorist teams. She'd gotten talking with a guy from the DEA and you couldn't believe your luck, could you? You knew all about our surveillance at the airfield. You sent the two meathead assholes to take them out.'

Henry didn't reply.

'The two agents you had your goons murder at the airfield, they were friends of mine. And you thought you were in the clear. But I was standing right behind you. I watched everything. Little did your stupid little brain realise there was an American DEA agent standing right beside you.'

Cruz sipped his drink again and checked the watch on his wrist.

'Right about now your compound has almost been emptied. Every person who's ever been on your payroll is going into custody. See, I worked hard and gained your trust. You had to tell me about all your hides and stash houses so I could pay people off, didn't you? My agency is now seizing all of it. Every dime. We've done the math already. It looks like it's going to be close to half a billion dollars.'

He whistled.

'Oh, and I've forgotten to tell you. Seeing as I was a member of your crew for so long, our case was so complete that police are moving on the Albanians and the New Yorkers. It's probably a good thing you're out here on the water. There'll be eight or nine figures on your head after this.'

Henry was sweating.

363

'Bullshit,' he said, unconvincingly. 'You're full of shit.'

'Oh, and two more things. Your daughter failed at the stadium. A DEA agent shot and killed her before she could blow the nerve gas. Everyone there is safe, and she's dead. And Dominick failed too. You sent him to kill my boss, didn't you? That was part of the deal, him getting off and all, right? Your daughter told you all about Special Agent Crawford, and the strength of his case, so you sent Dominick to kill him and erase the problem. He was close. Real close. He had a knife to Agent Crawford's neck, apparently. But a British cop shot him in the head.'

Silence.

'Take me back then, asshole. You need me for trial,' Henry said

At that moment, a blond man appeared from inside the hull, dressed in a suit with a blue shirt and red tie. A band aid had been stuck to his neck.

'Let me introduce Special Agent Crawford,' Cruz said. 'He's the head of our team, the six men that have taken your whole business down. The man you sent Dominick to kill. I was going to take care of all this myself, but he insisted on joining me.'

'I don't give a shit. Take me back to land. You work for the government. You have to follow rules.'

Cruz smiled. Crawford didn't.

'Well that's the thing,' Cruz said. 'We have everything we need; we're seizing everything you've ever owned and arresting every guy who ever worked for you.'

Cruz sipped his drink.

'But we don't need you. It's down as a real tragedy in the report. We confronted you on your yacht, out at sea. We planned to take you in out here, away from the public. But you decided to try and shoot your way out, so we were forced to fire back. Unfortunately, one of the bullets knocked you into the sea so we couldn't recover your body. Shit, it's a hell of a long way down. We'd never find you if we searched all year.'

Henry blinked, and stayed still for a moment. Cold fear seeped into his belly.

Then he frantically started scrabbling at the cuffs by his ankles, trying to reach over his fat gut.

'It's useless. You're a big boy, so I used three sets.' Cruz pulled three things from his pocket. Henry saw they were steel keys. As he sipped his drink, he threw them overboard, one at a time.

He then drained the cocktail and placed the empty glass to one side, checking his watch.

'Right. I think it's time for you to go.'

Henry started bucking and thrashing, screaming, as Cruz approached him, trying to break the handcuffs from the cinderblock. It was no use. His feet jangled as his chubby ankles pulled the cuffs tight against the concrete, the metal solid. He then started trying to grab something, but it was useless.

He'd been placed in the middle of the space at the back of the yacht, nothing to grip but slippery white deck.

Cruz approached and stood near him, staring down.

'My friend Faber is down there. You drowned him two days ago. Diving teams haven't been able to find his body yet. Try to hold your breath. You owe him an apology.'

Behind Cruz, Henry saw Crawford walk forward, his face expressionless. The two of them moved past the drug lord, towards the edge of the water. Cruz looked down at him.

'Tell Faber we said *hi.*'

The two men each gripped the rail, to prevent Henry from pulling them down. They bent down.

And pushed the cinderblock into the sea.

The concrete hit the water with a splash and pulled the fat man down like whipcord. He slid off the deck, scrabbling for something to hold, but the polished deck didn't provide any grip.

He screamed like a stuck pig as it pulled him into the water, vanishing under the surface.

And all of a sudden, it was silent.

Peaceful and calm.

The only sound was the lapping of the water against the side of the yacht.

Cruz stood still for a moment, looking down at the clear blue water and the beige round shape becoming smaller and smaller as it disappeared into the depths.

It's over.

He's gone.

Thoughts and memories flashed into his mind, like someone flicking through a series of photographs. When the DEA had needed an agent to go undercover, the other four guys hadn't even considered it for a moment. So Cruz had swallowed his fear and stepped up. He knew they needed him. He'd been in for over a year. He'd been forced to do some terrible things, things that would stay with him the rest of his life.

But to protect the flock, you need to catch the wolf.

And the wolf was finally gone.

Cruz turned back to Crawford who was standing, watching him. He nodded and smiled at his agent, the man who'd been known as Faris for the last thirteen months.

'You OK?'

Cruz didn't respond. He just smiled.

'Ready to have your life back?'

Cruz nodded. 'I can't wait, sir.'

'Let's get back to the bay,' Crawford said. 'We'll be on the next flight to DC, First Class. I called ahead. Your wife and son will meet you at Dulles.'

Cruz felt a lump in his throat, and readjusted his sunglasses. Crawford smiled and moved back into the hull of the yacht. Twisting the key, he fired the engine.

He took the wheel in his hands gently, as the motor pushed the sleek vessel forward.

And the sun shimmered across the calm, still water as they headed back to the harbour.

THE END

About the author:

Born in Sydney, Australia and raised in England and Brunei, Tom Barber has always had a passion for writing and story-telling. It took him to Nottingham University, England, where he graduated in 2009 with a 2:1 BA Hons in English Studies. Post-graduation, Tom moved to New York City and completed the 2 Year Meisner Acting training programme at The William Esper Studio, furthering his love of acting and screen-writing.

Upon his return to the UK in late 2011, Tom set to work on his debut novel, *Nine Lives*, which has since become a five-star rated Amazon UK Kindle hit. The following books in the series, *The Getaway, Blackout, Silent Night, One Way* and *Return Fire* have been equally successful, garnering five-star reviews in the US and the UK.

Nine Lives is the first novel in the Sam Archer series.

Follow @TomBarberBooks.

Read an extract from

The Getaway

By

Tom Barber

The second Sam Archer thriller.

Now available at Amazon.

*****

ONE

They were in and out of the bank in three minutes.

It was late summer, a beautiful August morning in New York City, and the heat and humidity were at just the right level, pleasantly warm yet not stifling or uncomfortable. Above Manhattan, the sun beat down from the cloudless sky on the sea of tall buildings and skyscrapers scattered all over the island below. It had been a scorcher of a summer, the daily temperature consistently in the high 80s, but today was slightly cooler and brought much welcome relief for the eight million people living in the city area.

It was just past 9 am, Monday. As a consequence the streets were flooded with people making their way to work, sipping coffees, talking into phones or just striding on, head down, ready to get to the office and get started. The sidewalks and subway were crowded, but the slight drop on the thermostat meant that tempers were under control, making the journey into work a little more pleasant than it had been earlier in the summer.

One particular business opening its doors for service that Monday morning was a Chase Manhattan Bank. It was located on 2nd Avenue between 62nd and 63rd Streets, towards the southern tip of the Upper East Side, a neighbourhood running up the right side of Central Park that was renowned all over the world for its affluence and wealth. Chase had thirty banks in various locations all over Manhattan and this was one of the best placed of them all.

Across the United States, Chase as a financial institution enjoyed a staggering amount of daily custom and had amounts of cash in their reserves that could cure a third-world country's deficit. With a company ATM inside the hundreds of Duane Reade drug stores in the city and immaculately clean and professional branch headquarters set up in locations such as this, it came as no surprise that Chase was one of the founding pillars of *The Big Four*, the four banks that held 39 % of every customer deposit across the United States. As a business, Chase had earned all those dollars and custom with the convenience of their branch locations and their excellent quality of service. They were renowned as one of the most reliable and dependable banks out there and it was a reputation they had worked hard to earn.

On that summer day it was also the last Monday of the month, August, and that meant something else to this particular bank.

Delivery day.

To keep the branch fully supplied with dollar currency, two men and a thick white armoured truck arrived at 9 am sharp every second Monday, never early, never late. One of the two men would step outside, unload a considerable amount of money from a hatch on the side of the vehicle and then take it into the bank, headed straight to the vault. It was an awkward yet vital part of running a financial institution: no bank can operate without money inside. Most modern banks around the world were built like military bunkers, the kind of places to give bank robbers nightmares. But for those twenty minutes or so each month whenever cash was delivered the bank was momentarily vulnerable, their collective managers secretly on edge despite their pretending to the contrary.

On the other side of the deal, anyone who decided to take a job inside the armoured truck was made well aware of the risks that came with that line of work before they signed on the dotted line. With the second highest mortality rate amongst all security roles in the United States, anyone inside one of these vehicles knew three undeniable facts.

One.

There were people out there who had a great interest in killing you.

Two.

There were people out there who had a great interest in protecting you.

And three.

At some point every fortnight, someone inside the vehicle had to step outside holding the cash.

That morning, the clock had just ticked to 9:03 am. The reinforced white armoured truck had pulled up outside the Upper East Side Chase bank three minutes ago, right on time. The two guys inside were both middle-aged, efficient yet relaxed, accustomed to this routine. They were retired cops, like most guys in this profession, but figured the rate of pay and healthcare plan that came with the job was worth any potential risk. They'd been working together for over two years and had set up a rota where they would take it in turns to deliver the cash, sharing the risk, giving one of them a week off while his partner took responsibility for the dollars in the bags.

That morning, the man in the front passenger seat unlocked his door and stepped out, slamming it shut behind him and hitching his belt as he moved to the side cabin on the truck. Back inside, his partner grabbed a copy of the *New York Post* and leaned back, going straight to the Sports headlines on the rear pages. He was relaxed, and rightfully so. He was sheltered behind twenty seven tons of reinforced steel and bullet-proof glass, enough to stop a firing squad of machine guns on full automatic or even an RPG. He and his partner also had a fully-loaded Glock 17 pistol on each hip, seventeen rounds in the magazine and two more clipped to their belts as extra insurance, a hundred and two extra reasons to feel confident about their safety. Chase and the armoured truck business took great care of the men inside these vehicles. They were carrying their profits

372

and investments. If the two men got jacked, they weren't the only ones who would suffer.

Outside the truck, the guard unloaded the supply from a cabin in the side of the vehicle, glancing left and right down the sunny sidewalk. Once he had the bags containing the money on a cart, he shut the cabin door and headed towards the entrance of the bank. As he approached the doors he started to relax. *Another week down.* Taking another quick look each way down the street, he shook off his unease as he grabbed the door handle and pulled it open. He'd been doing this exact routine for two years with no problems. And besides, this was the Upper East Side, not the ghetto. Movie stars and politicians lived up here, not gang members. *No one in their right mind would ever try to rob this place*, the man figured as he strode inside and headed towards the manager by the vault.

He was wrong.

Across the street to the north, three men and a woman watched in silence as the guard entered the bank. They were sitting in a yellow NYC taxi cab pulled up on the street corner between 63rd and 64th, twenty five yards behind the armoured truck. Vehicles passed them on the left as they headed downtown but the cab stayed tight to the kerb, the engine running, the light on the roof switched off to dissuade anyone from trying to hail it. No one paid any attention to the vehicle; it was just another normal part of everyday New York life, as common as pizza slices and Knicks jerseys.

Which made it the perfect getaway car.

Inside the vehicle, all four passengers were dressed in pristine white paramedic uniforms, lifted straight from a hospital supply depot in Queens a day earlier. Before taking the clothing out of its plastic wrapping, each of them had pulled three sets of latex gloves over their hands, serving as triple insurance against any tears and guarding against fingerprints or DNA that could be left on any of the equipment or clothing they used. Over the medic uniforms, three of them were also wearing white doctors' overcoats, the kind a GP or a chemist would wear in a lab, also fresh from the packets. The driver wasn't wearing one of the coats. He was staying in the car and wouldn't need one.

The outfits were crisp and clean, covering every possible source of trace evidence, not a speck or stain on any part or any piece of the white fabric. If anyone studied them, the outfits would seem absurd; the three passengers were wearing a medic and a doctor's uniform combined, something that never happened at the hospital or in the O.R. But to a casual observer, the clothing wouldn't cast suspicion. There were much stranger and wackier outfits being worn across the city at that very moment, outfits far more peculiar than these.

Beside the driver, the guy in the front passenger seat checked his watch.

9:04 am.

He glanced up at the front door of the Chase branch.

No sign of the guard returning yet.

Inside the bank, the time lock on the vault would be off for another six minutes.

The world-wide back and forth battle between banks and thieves throughout history had seen modern vaults become close to impenetrable from the outside. The latest designs were cased with thick, steel-reinforced concrete, rendering the vaults themselves stronger than most nuclear bomb shelters. There was a famous story from the past of how four Japanese bank vaults in Hiroshima had survived the Atomic bomb of 1945. When survivors and rescue aid had eventually worked their way through the ruins of the city, they'd discovered the steel vaults fully intact. And when they got each one open, they also found that all the money inside was unharmed while everything else around each vault had been completely levelled by the devastating nuclear blast and subsequent fallout. The designs in those Teikoku banks that day were now over sixty years old. Bank vaults were amazingly resilient back then, able to withstand nuclear weapons, but now they were as close to impenetrable as was humanly possible to design.

The model in this particular Chase bank could definitely survive the same kind of destruction and punishment. It was a rock-solid piece. Two layers, an outer steel and concrete shell controlled by a spinlock code leading into a second vault, which was opened by simple lock-and-key and only by the bank manager himself. Once closed, it was pretty much impossible to open. Explosives would be useless. Anyone who tried to use them to open it would bring the building down before they made a scratch on the surface. And even if the correct combination was entered on the outer spinlock dial, the vault still wouldn't open outside this fortnightly ten-minute window.

But despite those factors and the seemingly insurmountable odds, the four thieves inside the taxi were cool, calm and confident.

Because they knew one unalterable fact.

No matter how strong any bank vault was, at some point it had to be opened.

The man in the front seat checked his watch again. 9:05 am.

He looked over at the bank, lit up in the morning sunlight. Still no sign of the tubby guard. He hadn't come back out yet.

Any major drop-off, deposit or withdrawal from the vault itself had to happen every fourteen days in those two ten-minute periods. The manager had to plan all those things far in advance and operate fast from the moment the big hand on the clock ticked to 9am, working through a spread-sheet of planned transactions and satisfying every business and customer on the sheet. Hundreds of thousands of dollars were delivered from the truck, topping up the branch's supply from the banking organisation itself, and equal amounts were often withdrawn. But outside that ten minute window every fortnight, the electronic lock would stay shut and the vault wouldn't open, even if the correct code was entered.

An extra security measure was also to have an alarm code. If under duress or with a gun to their head, a manager or teller could pretend to enter the code to the vault and instead enter a six-digit code that triggered a silent alarm. The thieves would be standing there, waiting for the steel vault to open and suddenly find an entire police ESU team bursting in through the front doors behind them. Banks and their security divisions were constantly having to come up with new ways to foil any attempted bank robbery, methods and tricks the thieves didn't yet know about; the silent alarm dial code was one of the latest and favourite measures at their disposal.

The man checked his watch again.

9:06 am.

Four minutes to go.

He didn't panic. He'd observed the last four drop-offs. The guards in the truck, despite both being out of shape and relatively slow, always worked to a clock and the fat guy inside would be out in the next minute, giving them three left to work with.

One hundred and eighty seconds. Plenty of time.

And just then, right on cue, the front door of the bank swung open. The guard reappeared, walking to the truck, and tapped the passenger door three times with his fist, waiting for his partner inside to put down his newspaper and unlock it.

'Mark,' said the man inside the taxi.

He watched the guard pull open the door and step inside the truck. At the same time, all four of the thieves in the taxi looked down and clicked a black digital Casio stopwatch wrapped around their wrists. The clock was ticking.

They had three minutes and counting.

The next instant, the guy behind the wheel took off the handbrake. Above them, the light flicked to green, perfect timing, and the driver moved the taxi forward, parking outside the bank like he was dropping off a customer. As the armoured truck drove off ahead of them and turned the corner, disappearing out of sight, the guy in the front passenger seat of the taxi grabbed the receiver to the vehicle radio off its handle. It had been retuned from the taxi dispatch depot to the NYPD frequency. He gripped it in his gloved hand and pushed down the buttons either side.

'*Officer down, I repeat, Officer down!*' he yelled into the handle. '*I'm on East 95th and 1st! I need back-up, goddammit!*'

As he spoke, the man and woman in the back seat lifted white surgical masks over the lower half of their faces, right up to their eyes, and pulled scrub hats over the top, concealing the upper half of their heads. All four of them were already wearing large aviator sunglasses, covering their eyes, the defining characteristic that would leave them identifiable to a witness and CCTV. Not wasting a second, the three thieves pushed open the doors and moved swiftly out of the car, the driver remaining behind the wheel, checking his watch.

From his seat he watched the rear-view mirror and saw a commotion in the traffic behind them, right on cue.

Police cars were streaming into the street from a building four blocks north, speeding east and north, their lights flashing, responding to the distress call. He smiled.

The NYPD's 19th precinct, New York City's finest.

Every car and officer heading the opposite way.

And at that same moment, the three thieves entered the bank.

The second they passed through the front doors, the trio moved fast. The first task was to subdue everyone inside, most importantly the two guards. That had to happen before anything else. The man and woman from the back seat each pulled out a weapon hanging from a black strap looped around their right shoulders, hidden under the doctor's coats. They were two Ithaca 37 12-gauge shotguns, police issue, the stocks sawn off so the weapons could be concealed under the coats. Clyde Barrow of *Bonnie and Clyde* fame had come up with the idea of removing the stock and hiding a shotgun under a coat when pulling a heist. The weapons possessed brutal power and with the stocks gone they were a cinch to conceal, unlike machine guns which were too bulky and wide to hide effectively. Clyde had called the sawn-off shotgun a *whippit*. The Sicilians, who were fond of the weapon themselves, called it a *lupara*. With seven shells locked and loaded inside the weapons, the three thieves robbing this bank called it instant crowd control.

They ran forward, each racking a shell by pulling the brown slide on the barrel of the weapon back and forth with their left hand, the weapons crunching as a shell was loaded into each chamber. Across the bank floor, customers turned and saw the sudden commotion. It took a split second for what they were seeing to fully register in their brains.

Then they reacted, some of them covering their mouths as others started to scream.

There were two guards in the bank, Walter Pick and Peter Willis, both retired NYPD, both sporting a paunch that middle age and the promise of an imminent pension brought. Both men also had a Glock 17 on their hip, like the two guys in the truck, but neither had a moment to reach for it as the three thieves ran forward, two of them brandishing the sawn-off shotguns, shoving them in people's faces.

'Down! Everybody down! Down!' they shouted.

Meanwhile, the big guy who'd been in the front passenger seat of the taxi had already vaulted the counter. He was the point man, the guy who would control the room, but his first job was to get to the tellers. He knew the button for the silent alarm and the direct line to the 19th precinct four blocks away was by the third teller's foot. Before the woman had time to react and push it with her toe, he was already too close, pulling his own shotgun from under his coat, racking a round and pointing the weapon an inch from her face.

'*Up! Get up!*' he shouted. '*UP!*'

He grabbed the woman by her hair and hauled her from her seat, dragging her around the counter and throwing her to the floor to join the others. He turned, the shotgun aimed at the other tellers, and they all rose and rushed out to the main bank floor quickly, joining everyone else face down on the polished marble, trembling. The point man grabbed a civilian who was cowering on the floor, pulling him to his feet. The guy was young, in his late twenties and dressed for the summer in t-shirt and shorts, sunglasses and a backwards cap on his head. The point man took his shotgun and put it against the man's jaw, who started shaking with fear in the man's grip as the barrel of the weapon nestled in under his chin.

'*If anyone makes a sound, tries to do something stupid, I blow this guy's head off!*' the man shouted. '*I want this place as quiet as a church! Clear?*'

No one replied. Everyone was face down on the marble, no one daring to speak or move.

'*Everybody, get your phones out,*' the point man shouted, quickly. '*Out! Slide them across the floor. If any of you don't and I find out, this guy's brains will be sprayed in the air like confetti!*'

The people on the floor all complied and the sound of scores of cell phones sliding across the floor echoed off the silent bank's walls. Across the room, the other two thieves finished plasti-cuffing the two guards, pushing them face-down to the marble floor, each guard landing with an *oomph* as the air was knocked out of them. The bank robbers reached over and pulled each guard's Glock pistol from their holsters and threw them over the teller counter, out of reach, the guns clattering against the wood and marble as they hit the floor. That done, the pair ran forward to their next tasks. The man vaulted the counter and slammed open the door to the security room, rushing inside. A series of monitors were in the room, the place humming, each small screen showing a different view inside the bank and on the street. He yanked out a small white bag from the inside pocket of his doctor's coat and started pulling out all the tapes from the monitors, dumping them in the bag one-by-one, checking the time on his wrist-watch as he did so.

Fifty seconds down.

2:10 to go.

Back inside the main floor, the woman spotted the manager cowering on the floor across the room. She moved towards him swiftly, the shotgun aimed at his head, her gloved hands around the sawn-off pistol grip.

'Up,' she ordered, standing over him.

He hesitated then rose, unsure.

He had good reason to be. In the same moment, she smashed the barrel of the shotgun into his face hard, breaking his nose. People started to scream, shocked at the violence.

'*Shut up! Shut the hell up*' the point man shouted, his shotgun against the hostage's neck. '*Or I'll kill this man and you can decide who takes his place!*'

That got them quiet. The manager had fallen to the floor, moaning and gasping with pain, blood pouring from his nose, leaking all over the clean white marble. The woman grabbed him and pulled him back to his feet with brutal strength for her size. She dragged him around the counter and towards the vault as he clutched his face, blood staining his hands and fingers and slammed him against the steel with a *thud*.

She put the shotgun against his groin, her finger on the trigger, her face hidden behind the surgical masks and sunglasses.

'Open it,' she ordered.

Two words. One shotgun.

All she needed.

Without a moment's hesitation, the man reached for the lock with his right hand, clutching his smashed nose with his left, blood pouring out and staining the sleeve of his white shirt. He twisted the dial, trying to keep his shaking hand steady, and paused three times on the combination then paused again. It clicked. He had a key looped on a chain attached to his top pocket. She grabbed it and yanked it off violently, then hit him in the face again with the Ithaca, dropping him like a stone. He fell to the ground, covering his nose, whimpering from the second blow. He wasn't going to be any trouble.

The woman grabbed the handle on the vault, twisted it, and pulled open the steel door. It led into a room holding a second vault, but this one had no spin-dial, just a normal lock. Rushing forward, she pushed the key inside the lock and twisted. It clicked, and she pulled the handle, opening the door to the second vault. Inside were a series of metallic shelves, like four large filing cabinets pushed against the walls. Each shelf was packed with stacks of hundred dollar bills, bricked and banded.

She moved inside quickly. Dropping the shotgun and letting it swing back under her coat on its strap, she unzipped the front of her medic's overalls and pulled out two large empty black bags. Back outside on the bank floor, the point man tilted his wrist so the shotgun nestled against the hostage's neck, and checked his watch.

'*Forty seconds*!' he called.

Inside the vault, the woman worked fast. She swept the bill stacks from the shelves straight into the bags. Once loaded, she zipped them both shut. The third man had just finished taking the tapes in the security room and rushed inside to join her, taking one of the bags and looping it over his shoulder, keeping his shotgun in his right hand and the white bag of security tapes in the other. She took the other bag and followed him, and they moved outside, pulling the vault doors shut behind them, twisting the handles, then heading towards the front door. They paused by the exit, tucking their shotguns away under the coats, then pushing their way through the doors, left the building.

The point man checked his watch and started backing away to the door, dragging the terrified hostage with him, his gun still jammed in the guy's neck.

'This guy is coming with us,' he shouted. 'If any of you move, or we see anyone on the street in the next two minutes, he dies. *DO NOT MOVE!*'

He turned his back and shouldered his way through the doors, taking the hostage with him.

And suddenly, the bank was eerily quiet.

They were gone.

In the silence, everyone stayed face down, too terrified to look up or even speak. The large hand on a large clock mounted on the wall ticked forward.

9:10 am.

And across the bank, the lock on the vault clicked shut.

Printed in Great Britain
by Amazon.co.uk, Ltd.,
Marston Gate.